YOUNG PHIL

Third in the sequence
'A Chronicle of Ancient Sunlight'

Also available in Zenith Books

'The Flax of Dream'

THE BEAUTIFUL YEARS

DANDELION DAYS

THE DREAM OF FAIR WOMEN

THE PATHWAY

'A Chronicle of Ancient Sunlight'

THE DARK LANTERN

DONKEY BOY

YOUNG PHILLIP MADDISON

Henry Williamson

'God made the country, and the Devil made the suburb.'
Traditional saying

'You are only young once; make the most of it, m'boy!'
Saying of Thomas Turney

ZENITH

A Zenith Book

Published by Arrow Books Limited
17–21 Conway Street, London W1P 6JD

An imprint of the Hutchinson Publishing Group

London Melbourne Sydney Auckland
Johannesburg and agencies throughout
the world

First published in Great Britain 1953
by Macdonald & Co. (Publishers) Ltd
This paperback edition 1985

Reproduced, printed and bound in Great Britain by
Hazell Watson & Viney Limited,
Aylesbury, Bucks

ISBN 0 09 939540 1

To
JOHN HEYGATE

Readers may like to note that there is now a

HENRY WILLIAMSON SOCIETY

If you would like to know more, please write to:

CONTENTS

Part One

AN EDWARDIAN BOYHOOD

Part Two

SOME SCOUTING FOR BOYS

CONTENTS

PART THREE

THE WIND'S WILL

PART FOUR

WONDERFUL TO BE ALIVE

Part One

AN EDWARDIAN BOYHOOD

Chapter 1

ST. VALENTINE'S EVE

WHEN Phillip reached the Socialist Oak he found the fog thinner on the Hill; it had been thick, almost yellow, down in Pit Vale. He had hurried on his way from school, avoiding even the much-admired Milton after they had passed the Obelisk together, in order to be alone to think. A daring and tremulous idea had obsessed him all day: to send a Valentine to Helena Rolls, in disguised writing, of course, lest her parents find out who had sent it, a thing too awful to be thought about. He had waited in his mind, while hurrying up from Pit Vale, until he reached the Socialist Oak; and then, upon the rustic seat erected around its trunk, he sat down. The tree would do his thinking for him; it would put ideas into his head. For it was very old and wise, Mr. Mundy the Vicar had told him. It was older than the elms on the ridge, though much smaller.

During the previous summer Mr. Mundy—a sort of harmless joke in the neighbourhood, a genial ecclesiastical figure who wore, throughout the year, a black straw hat speckled with yellow, and rode a bicycle on the pavements of the suburb, and on the gravel paths of the Hill, despite the law—had explained to Phillip that the oak had probably been dropped as an acorn by either a pigeon or a rook, and there had taken root. There must have been other seedlings, said Mr. Mundy; but sheep, which grazed close, would have cut them off with their teeth. In those days the Hill had been glebe land; and it was possible, said Mr. Mundy, that the oak had started to grow in Queen Elizabeth's reign, more than three hundred years before. It was of starveling growth, as Phillip could observe for himself: and could he explain why?

Thereupon Mr. Mundy had launched out, much as Gran'pa did, into his rather funny way of talking about antiquarianism. There was something about smoke drifting from the factories in the old marshland south of the river, and the acid dust in the atmosphere, which hung low with fog from the Thames and slowly poisoned the leaves of the oak. So it was stunted, fighting all the time for pure air, just like a human being. For a tree, Mr. Mundy told Phillip, breathed through its leaves. If the leaves were choked, a tree or plant would surely die—or remain stunted.

That fact had moved Phillip; and ever since he had seen the Socialist Oak as more than a tree, a living thing ever trying to escape its fate of having to breathe acid air coming from London.

One day a wonderful thing had happened while he was sitting with Mother under the tree. A bird with a red head and green wings had flown to the oak, hung to the bark a few moments, and then with a sort of laugh, had flown away again. It was a woodpecker, said Mother. She had often seen them when she was a girl, at Cross Aulton in Surrey.

Mother loved the sunshine, and told him about the herb fields around her old home in Surrey, and the wonderful smell of burning lavender roots in autumn. Mother was always talking about how, when Father retired, she would perhaps realise her dream, and live in a cottage in the country, and have all sorts of herbs in the garden, with a lavender-border to the path, from the gate to the front door.

From his earliest years Phillip remembered playing under the Socialist Oak, near which men spoke to the crowds on Sunday afternoons. He remembered when his sister was too young to walk, and he helped to push her up the Hill in the mail-cart. He remembered Mother telling him that the round brown things on the twigs were called oak-apples; and about the torn paper kite on the very top of the tree, which dangled there on its twisted string, grey with soot. Mother had told him a story about that kite. It was always hoping that the wind would set it free, so that it could find the little boy to whom it belonged. Perhaps he was a poor little boy, and the kite was his only toy, said Mother. Had the little boy cried, Phillip asked, tears in his eyes. When Mother said she expected so, Phillip had felt sad for the poor little boy who had cried, and sad for the poor kite, all alone on the top of the tree. But he had hidden his tears from Mavis, who always pointed at them, and laughed.

And there the kite had remained, year after year, until only a little bit of twisted black string was left, tied to a piece of wood that had been part of the frame. Since then, Phillip had grown up. He had won a scholarship and gone to a school on the Heath beyond Pit Vale; he had made and lost many newspaper-and-bamboo kites of his own in the eternally long summers in which it seemed that the sun was always shining; but the leaning black oak tree had remained his secret friend. Whenever he wanted to think nowadays—which meant when he was unhappy or worried, which was often—sometimes he sat on the rustic-work around its base, and there, remaining still, waited until something told him what to do.

No thoughts came into Phillip's head from the tree, as he sat there in the dripping fog; and gradually his fears and apprehensions began to take shape. Dare he send a Valentine to Helena Rolls? And how could he disguise his handwriting, if he did so? For Helena must never know that he had sent it. She might be offended. He knew himself to be in the Rolls' bad books. One of the reasons why they never asked him and his sisters to their parties was because he was a swearer, and rude. They were much richer than the Maddisons, too, though Mr. Rolls could not be more of a gentleman than Father, for the Maddisons, Phillip knew, had once been high-up people. Although grandfather Maddison had been run over when drunk in London, by a heavy dray, and had been rather a bad lot, yet he had been Captain Maddison, of a crack cavalry regiment. Still, that did not make up for the fact that Father was, as he had often said, a poor man; that he himself was a scholarship boy, and, apart from his swearing, must be looked down upon by the Rollses on that account. Mother said it did not matter what you were, so long as you behaved yourself in every circumstance: but that was the trouble, he knew that he behaved badly in nearly every circumstance. And however hard he tried to be better, he never could be.

Milton was a friend of the Rollses. If only he could be like Milton—who sang anthems in St. Simon's choir, who was always one of the top boys in his form at school, and good at all games. Milton had fair curly hair; not almost black, like his own. Milton had good muscles, not skinny ones. He could dive from the high board in the Randiswell Baths; whereas he, Phillip, always went a belly-flopper even from the side of the bath, and water got into his nose and throat, choking him. Milton was easy and smiling; he himself was usually afraid, and unsmiling. Milton had regular, fine teeth; his own were crowded in front, his dog-teeth having grown over the others.

In dejection, Phillip sat on the seat under the Socialist Oak, hearing slow drips of fog from the branches above, and trying to think, while all sorts of pictures would come into his mind and spoil his thinking. He thought best in summer, alone in the long grass of the Backfield, lying on his back with his face to the sky, and seeing the red of his blood through his eyelids. That was the best way of all, to lie in the sun and let ideas float into the head, and imagine all sorts of wonderful things, while Helena Rolls' blue eyes were part of the sky, and her hair was gold as the sun.

The Valentine! Quick, before beastly Ching, who always tried to hang on to him, whom after leaving Milton he had dodged in Pit Vale, found him by the tree, and spoiled it all. Quick!—think! Tom Ching always mucked things up.

Closing his eyes as he sat on the wet, soot-grimed seat, Phillip thought of Helena Rolls' face. Her eyes were blue as the bluebells under the trees of Reynard's Common, where he had gone by train with Mother and the girls for a picnic the year before. It was a Sunday, and Father had cycled out to join them. And thinking of bluebells, suddenly he remembered a poem which went

The rose is red,
The violet blue.
Both are sweet
And so are you.

Got it! Change violet to bluebell! In excitement he clenched his hands on the knees of his blue serge knickerbockers. He spoke the lines out loud, to the tree.

The rose is red,
The bluebell's blue.
Both are sweet
And so are you.
O maiden fair
To me be true.

That was it! That would do! Cousin Polly Pickering, staying with them, was a ripping painter, and if he swore her to secrecy, she would paint a bunch of bluebells for his Valentine, then write in the poem below, and nobody in the Rolls house would know who had sent it!

Getting up from the seat, Phillip said goodbye to the Socialist Oak; and tucking his arms into his sides, set off at a jog-trot along the gravel path. Next month was the inter-House Harriers Race at school, and it was time he got into training.

Mavis and Doris, his sisters, were of course curious to know why Phillip asked Polly to speak to him alone in the front room, after tea.

"What are you up to now, I wonder?" asked Mavis.

"'Curiosity killed the cat'" he quoted one of Father's remarks. "Come on, Polly."

He opened the sitting room door, and together they went along the passage to the front room. It was dark, for the gas-mantle in its rosy glass globe hanging from the hall ceiling was unlit. Usually this burned with a tiny light all day, the by-pass; and when you pulled the chain, the light popped and the mantle glowed. But when Mother had pulled the chain before opening the door for him, the by-pass had died out. He had offered to light it; but as usual, Mother had stopped him.

"No dear, perhaps we had better leave it until your Father comes home. You know how upset he will be, if the mantle breaks, as it did last time I tried to light it."

"Yes, but you're not me! You let too much gas get inside it, and the explosion bust it. The tap should be turned on only a little. I'll do it. Where are the matches?"

"No dear, I would rather you did not, if you don't mind. If the fog thickens, and Father's train is delayed, he will be tired, and I would not like him to be upset when he comes home. It's entirely my fault, I pulled the chain too quickly."

Remote muffled fog-signals on the Randiswell line during tea seemed to confirm the thickening of the fog. They were still thumping as Phillip went along the lightless passage, followed by Polly. He was glad it was foggy; it meant more time before Father returned. He closed the door.

"Well?" said Polly Pickering, standing still, and looking at him. Her face was faintly laced by the halo'd light of the street-lamp, two doors down, coming through the lace curtains. "Well? What do you think you're trying to do?" with a slight toss of her head.

Polly always spoke to him like that when he got her alone, a sort of challenging look. She had the same manner towards Uncle Jim, her father, especially when he flew into a temper with her, when she would not obey him. "That I won't!" she would say, tossing her head, and stamping her foot. "That I won't! So there!" with toss of curls, and chin held up. Uncle Jim could never make her do what she did not want to do. Nothing would make her, once Polly had set her mind on anything. Uncle Jim would glare at her; then growl like a dog, and go away, leaving Polly with her head held high.

Phillip said in a humble voice, to get Polly on his side, "You are my friend, aren't you?"

"You know I am, Phillip."

"Well, do you swear on your honour you won't give me away to anyone? And that includes Mavis. You know how she laughs at me."

"What is it you're up to this time?" asked Polly, with a little laugh.

"Well, I've got a friend, who I promised to paint a Valentine for. Will you do it for me? I'll pay you for it. I want a bunch of bluebells, and a poem underneath. And remember, you've given me your solemn promise not to tell."

Polly looked at him for a moment. "Who's it for?"

"I told you. A friend of mine. I promised I wouldn't tell his name to a soul."

"Then why is it so secret?"

"A solemn undertaking is a solemn undertaking. I promised him I wouldn't split. He wants to post it tonight. Will you do it? For a penny?"

"I might."

"Go on, be a sport, Polly. We're friends, aren't we?"

"Are we?"

"You know we are!"

"All right, I'll do it, for you, but not for your friend. If you like to give it to him you can, but I don't want any money from you for it, see?"

"That's jolly decent of you, Polly. I'll take you tomorrow afternoon to the Electric Palace, if it's raining. Otherwise I shall have to play footer, as it's a House match. Will you do it right away?"

"Perhaps I will. You won't mind if Mavis and Doris see me doing it? I'll have to do it on the kitchen table, while they're doing homework."

"No, it won't matter, so long as you don't say it's for me. Oh carramba, I'd forgotten! It's library night! I've got to take back that bloody book on birds! What a fool I was to write on the pages! And with a relief nib, too, too thick to rub out! My God, if Father sees it, he'll take me to the police station! You won't split, will you?"

"Of course not. Don't you know me better than that?"

Phillip did not heed Polly, now that he had got what he wanted. Then an idea came to him.

"I know! I'll put on my Etons! Then the library assistant won't think of looking in the book when I return it. She wouldn't suspect anyone in those clothes."

Polly laughed. "I think you're funny," she said, as Phillip dashed out of the room, and into the kitchen.

"Mum! Have you got my collars mended? I want one to put on, now, at once!"

"Say 'please' ", his sister Mavis called out from the scullery. "Mother, you spoil Phillip. Let him get his own collars, why not?"

"They're in my bedroom cupboard, dear. I'll fetch them for you." Hetty left the kitchen and went up the stairs, leaving the two cousins at the bottom.

"Why do you want to put on your Etons, I should like to know?", called Mavis from where she was washing up.

"Because they want airing, before I have my photo taken on Saturday, if you must know." To Polly he said, "We can go on the way to the Electric Palace!"

"What about football?"

"Oh, damn football! I can say I had a bilious attack. The last time I played I got a hefty hack on my shin, and a moment later, where did you think the ball hit me?" He glanced up the stairs. His mother was in her bedroom, judging by the light, and the sound of a drawer being opened. He whispered, his face close to Polly's, so that her curls tickled his face, "I'll give you one clue. If it had hit you there, Polly, it would not have hurt you at all."

"How do you know, I should like to know?"

"Would you like me to prove it?"

Mavis came out of the kitchen, and looked round the edge of the door of the broom-cupboard. "What are you two up to, standing there in the dark, and whispering?"

"We're discussing football, if you must know," said Phillip. "Anyway, get on with the washing up, and mind you don't splash any filthy greasy spots on Timmy Rat's box! Or on him, the soda gives him eczema of the tail."

"It isn't that at all, it's his dirty box! I wonder Father doesn't forbid you to keep him in the scullery. You don't renew his sawdust twice a week, as you promised Father you would."

"Rot! Timmy's cleaner than you are. Anyway, shog off, I'm talking to Polly."

"Ha, I know, you're up to something."

"And you get down to the sink. Shog off!"

"Phillip—Phillip!" came Hetty's voice, from the landing above. "Your language, my son!"

"It's in Shakespeare, Henrietta."

"Ha, you only read the rude bits!" cried Mavis.

"Mavis dear, I'll come and dry up for you in a moment."

"I will, Aunty Hetty," said Polly, her eyes gleaming as she looked at Phillip. That boy, after a swift turn of the head to make sure that his sister had gone, put his hand on the black serge material of Polly's waist, and slid it down below her patent-leather belt, in order to experience the thrilling sensation that he had felt when, together with Mavis and Percy, Polly's brother, the foursome of small children at the Pickering's country home, some years before, had played a game, innocently enough, called *Mothers and Fathers*.

"What do you think you're trying to do?" whispered Polly.

"You know!" he whispered back. "Shall we do it together, one day?"

Polly tossed her head. "Wouldn't you like to?" she breathed.

"Yes, wouldn't you? Ss-sh!"

Phillip moved away from her. He had heard his mother's footfalls come out of the bedroom. Lightly, two at a time, without sound, he pulled himself up the stairs by the banister rail. "Hullo mother, got 'em?" he asked. "I was just coming up to you. Blime, you need to be a glow-worm to get about in this house."

"Phillip, I've told you before, you should not use that expression, it is not nice. Here are your collars, dear, I had them from Aunt Dorrie. Don't forget to thank her, when you see her."

"What, for these old hand-me-downs! Still, if they were Bertie's and Gerry's, I don't mind having them."

Remotely more muffled bangs of fog-signals came through the darkness.

"You'd better wash now, Phillip. Come into the bath-room, before your Father comes home. Here's some matches, if you will kindly light the gas."

"No, I will unkindly light it for a change."

The burner flared up. Phillip looked critically at the starched linen collars. They were indeed hand-me-downs, the front tags much-broken-and-stitched at the stud-holes.

"The mends won't be visible, dear, your tie will cover them. Now wash your face, and don't forget your neck and ears. And promise you won't read? It's bad for you, Phillip."

The bathroom was often used by Phillip as a library, as he sat comfortably on the mahogany seat, behind the locked door, with a book.

"Not me! I've got work to do. Beastly Latin tonight, then foul Euclid, and stinking Algebra."

"Really Phillip, your language! Well, don't be long, dear. I'll lay out your Etons for you, in your bedroom."

"No, I'll be short, like Mrs. Bigge next door."

"Really Phillip!" laughed Hetty, as he followed her into the bedroom. "Sometimes I wonder where you get it all from."

"From the beastly Turneys," replied Phillip.

"Well, you certainly don't get it from Father," said Hetty, indulgently. "Oh, I heard from Aunt Dora today. I sent her your essay on Timmy Rat, you know, and Aunt thought it very good. She says you have a gift for writing."

Phillip thought of what he had written in the library book. He quivered within.

"Shall I put on a clean dickie? Or will the fog muck it up? Quick Mummy, quick! It's library night!"

"I think I sent your old one to the laundry, Phillip. Can't you do without one just for tonight? You must look your best for your photograph tomorrow, you know. I want to send one to your Aunt Victoria, and another to Uncle Hilary. I thought it would be considerate of you, as they always remember your birthday."

"I don't like either of 'em."

"Hush Phillip! They are your Father's sister and brother, and they have both been very kind to you."

"I won't hush! Aunt Viccy always looks at me as though I were some sort of freak. When I went to stay with her after Christmas she said 'Even when you were a little baby of nine months, Phillip, your big wondering eyes were filled with fear. Why, why, why?' As though anyone can help what they looked like! But you know, I did sort of think of a reply the other day.

Shall I tell you? It was this. 'Well Aunt, it must have been caused by what I was looking at!'"

"Phillip—Phillip! You naughty boy!" Hetty went out of the room, trying not to laugh. She had never felt easy with that particular sister-in-law. She felt that Victoria always *tried* to like her, but it was against her real nature to do so.

Left alone, Phillip set about undressing. Then he examined his face. His eyes stared anxiously back at him from the mirror upon the tall mahogany chest of drawers. They looked dark and gloomy in the light of the yellow-fringed gas-flame issuing from the gilded burner. Were his eyes filled with fear? He felt sad. Then thinking of Helena Rolls, he sighed. He had a very ugly face. The Valentine! Quick, before Father came home! It would be awful if he were to see it.

A hasty tip-toeing to the bathroom; face held down in cold water to give his cheeks a healthy look; a rapid soaping and blowing of water through hands; an equally quick drying, then back again to his room, and a flurried donning of clean flannel shirt smelling slightly of Mrs. Feeney—soapy rinsing water. While he dressed, a wild thought came to him: dare he ask Helena Rolls if she would like a photograph of him? After all, faint heart never won fair lady.

Phillip thought with some excitement of Mr. Woods' studio in the High Road, of the ordeal of facing the big mahogany camera on the wooden tripod, while the black cloth was over both box and photographer's head during focusing. He *must* remember not to grin, for that would show his crowded front teeth; his dog's-teeth, as Mavis called them. Nor must he look too serious, or Father might say again that he looked weepy, as though he had been out in the garden to eat worms. The hypo-marks on one of his last photos had looked just like tears, Father had said. He was always crying at the least excuse, said Father; he was not a manly boy; even Aunt Viccy had told him that, when he had pretended to cry after she had threatened to tell Father he had taught cousin Adele a bad word. "And why tell lies?" she had asked, when he said that the word he had used was *tart*: he had told Adele that too many tarts caused indigestion, or vice versa. He had pretended to look very contrite while Aunt Viccy had solemnly lectured him for using "grubby little words".

His Aunt Victoria's pale face was associated in Phillip's mind with the word *Why?* Why was it necessary to tell fibs? Why did he use such bad words, such grubby little words? Was it nice, to repay hospitality in that manner? Why was he not more manly? Why did he cry at the least thing? Why could he not look her straight in the eyes, instead of having such a shifty gaze? Why could he not be like other boys, decent boys, from decent homes? Why did he worry his Father so much, with his constant prevarications? Why could he not go straight?

"Look at me, Phillip! Look into my face! Now tell me, why are you such a young rascal? Where do you get it all from?"

He had stared straight into her face. "I don't know, Aunt Victoria".

Aunt Viccy had smiled. He puzzled her, she said. He had always puzzled her.

"Why, even when you were nine months old, your baby face was filled with fear! You stared just as you are staring at me now. Your eyes were always filled with fear, you started at the least sound, you had, even at that age, a guilty look in those large eyes of yours! Why, why, why?"

"I don't know, Aunt Victoria".

"Well, buck up, old chap, that's my advice to you. Keep a tight rein on yourself. Don't do things which annoy your Father. He has a lot to put up with in his life, you know! No man wants a son who is always telling fibs, who is never to be trusted, who is always peeping and prying into other people's affairs! I had you here to stay as I hoped you would be able to benefit from different surroundings, but I cannot and will not have Adele taught ways and expressions of a street boy. And you must learn not to cry at the least reproof, it isn't at all manly, you know. Will you promise me, if I let the matter go no further, that you will never again use that expression?"

"Yes, Aunt Victoria."

"Very well, then, we'll say no more about it, this time. But if it occurs again, I shall have to send you home. Now go to your cousin Adele, and beg her pardon."

Phillip had gone out of the morning room, and said to Adele that he was sorry. Then he had tip-toed upstairs to his bedroom, packed his bag, tip-toed down again, and so away from the house, to run most of the way to Epsom station and, with his return ticket, back to London, and home. That was during the

Christmas holidays; and after a "wigging" from his father, and an enforced letter of apology to Aunt Victoria, the matter had ended.

Looking at himself somewhat anxiously in the glass, Phillip tried to arrange his small face so that it would look larger, and so resemble one belonging to a manly figure, with out-jutting chin, and stiff upper lip. This was rather difficult to do: for his jaw could only be made to stick out by putting his lower teeth over the upper, and then his lips almost disappeared, and the upper lip was not only too stiff, but flat. If only he were good-looking, like Milton, who was a friend of the Rolls'!

Ah well, it was no good hoping that he could alter his face; but he could alter his habits. That was the only way to get into the good books of Mr. and Mrs. Rolls. In future, he swore to himself, he would always behave like a little gentleman. He would turn over a new leaf. He would learn the Collect on Sundays without being badgered to do it by Mother. He would reform himself from swearing, and become a choir boy. Visions of the benefits of reformation filled his mind. He might even be chosen, in time, to sing the anthem on Sunday evenings at St. Simon's Church, where Mother sometimes took him on Sunday evening to listen to the Rev. Mr. Mundy. Milton was the head choir-boy there; perhaps his own voice, if he trained it properly, would soar up to the roof, like Milton's did. *O, for the Wings, for the Wings of a Dove!* Hearing the new voice, perhaps when Milton was taken suddenly ill, Helena Rolls, in her rented pew, would sit entranced. Afterwards Mrs. Rolls would say "Was that really Phillip stepping into the breach, with that beautiful clear voice? Oh, we must ask him to tea, Gerard,"——

At this point Phillip began to feel hot all over with a kind of fear.

For in Phillip's eyes Mr. Gerard Rolls was a figure as grand as he was aloof. He was extremely handsome, tall and straight, always very well dressed, always affable, a very distinguished person indeed. He always was the same—never angry, or cross, or anything but very well bred. To sit in the same room as such a tall, blue-eyed, twisted-moustached man was—unthinkable. Phillip's fingers trembled at the stitched stud-holes. Careful!

Having brushed his wet hair flat, he put on his Eton jacket, the one cousin Gerry Cakebread had outgrown. To complete the picture of rectitude and reformation, he then drew on a pair of brown dog-skin gloves; and after smiling at himself for awhile in the looking-glass to fix the right expression on his face, he turned the gas out, and feeling unnatural, tip-toed along the passage and down the stairs.

Passing the kitchen door, he saw the light underneath it and heard the girls' murmured voices. Opening the door cautiously, he peered round. Mavis and Doris were crocheting beside the table, while against the wall, paint-box open before her, dabbling her brush in an old potted-meat glass, sat Polly.

"Oh, just look what's come out of the fog!" cried Mavis, as she pointed out the glistening head poked round the door. She leant back in her chair, laughing. "Oh dear, look—look at his hair! It's collapsed with sheer fright! He looks just like Timmy Rat after a bath!"

"At least I don't lick myself all over with a flannel when I wash."

One of Richard's criticisms, made half as a joke, of his favourite daughter Mavis was that she washed herself like a cat, in sections, in the bathroom of a morning. It was likewise a criticism, half-serious, that none of the children cared for a cold tub in the morning. He himself, of course, took one the whole year through.

"No, for you don't wash at all, do you?"

Polly laughed, and seeing her bright eyes, "How do you do," said Phillip, very politely, acting the role of an imagined little gentleman. He held out a gloved hand to be shaken. "Busy with brush and palette, I see. What is this for, the dear vicar's bazaar?"

Then noticing the top of the window opened, his tone changed. "Who opened that window? It's bath night, and you know very well if the window's open the cold air comes in there, and chills the pipes." He pushed up the window, and opened the lower sash frame. "There, if you must be fresh air fiends! I say, Polly, will you be long? I promised to take Peter Wallace his picture by six o'clock."

"Go on, Phillip! We know you too well, old boy! We know who that Valentine is for!"

"I bet you don't!"

"Oh yes, I do. I bet it's for Helena Rolls!"

"You liar!"

"Ha ha, we know! That's why you've got your gloves on, to create an impression! You are going to call on Mr. Rolls, and ask him for his daughter's hand, ha ha ha! Do you remember what happened last time you wore your gloves, when you called on the Todds? Muriel's dog bit you, ha ha! Yes, Tiny nipped you in the leg."

"It mistook me for someone else on that occasion," said Phillip, glad of the chance to lead the talk away from Helena Rolls. "Yes, the little over-ripe banana-skin mongrel called Tiny, who lives at Number Six, Polly, was on that occasion entirely working by instinct," exclaimed Phillip, with an animated glance at Polly's friendly face. "Tiny smelled my gloves, as belonging to the skin of an erstwhile rival." He held up his hands. "They are made of dogskin, these gloves, you see. And the Todds' blinking mongrel, scared to death of my gloves when they were part of his old enemy, crept up behind me and snapped at the first thing it saw, which happened to be my leg. Look, I'll show you the scar," and rolling up his trouser, he showed upon the calf of his right leg two slight depressions almost joined together. "Caustic silver stopped any ill-effects. Do you learn chemistry at school?" he asked Polly. "It comes in useful for making bombs or pills. Well goodnight, girls, if I don't see you again," and bowing ironically to them, he withdrew, closing the door quietly behind him. For a moment he listened, to hear what might be said about himself; but a more urgent matter had come into his mind—the stomach-turning thought that soon he must return the library book which he had hidden under the windsor side-board in the front room, and what would happen if the librarian spotted what he had written about various birds, including the Raven, the Gull, and worst of all, the Shag.

Father had said at breakfast that he might be home early; so there was no time to lose. He went into the front room, got down on hands and knees, and pulled the heavy book from under the cupboard. For safety, he took it upstairs, and hid it under his bed.

However hard Phillip had tried to erase the words he had written in *Birds of the British Isles*, he had not succeeded; the broad thick strokes of the relief nib, made with such hilarity, had remained. The idea of tearing out the offending pages had not occurred to him; he thought only that he must either rub out what he had written, or return the book without his crime being discovered.

Having hidden the book, he returned to the kitchen, to do his homework. The girls left, to be with Mother in the sitting-room. Phillip seated himself at the table, and poured out the contents of his leather satchel. Homework, ugh! The written subjects had to be done, but the Shakespeare could be learned by heart tomorrow while walking to school. He knew he could not learn anything tonight, what with the Valentine to be delivered, and the ordeal of the library book. Golly, if he got out of it this time, he would never do it again.

While he was working at his Algebra, the door was slightly kicked, and Mavis' voice said, "Open the door, please". Since it was Mavis speaking he let her wait a little, before getting up; and as she came in, carrying a sewing machine, he exclaimed testily, "How can I be expected to do my work, if you don't leave me alone?"

"I bet you're reading instead!" She put down the machine, and darted to his satchel. In it was concealed a copy of *Boy's Life*. "There, I knew it! You just put it in there! It's warm! You thought it was Father, I bet!"

"Look, the ink's wet on this equation! Now apologise!"

"I won't, grumpy. Anyway, you know Father does not like you to read trash!"

"You spy! You want me to muck up my work, and get me expelled! Stop grinning at me, ugly mug! And take that awful sewing machine away."

"Father doesn't like the noise in the sitting room, and I must get this done tonight, for someone's birthday tomorrow."

"I know, it's for your beloved Miss Wendover! You're soppy about her."

"Not half so soppy as you are about stuck-up Helena Rolls!"

Phillip's feelings burst into irritable rage. He threw his satchel at his sister, who fled from the room, crying, "Ah, you can be very brave, with girls to fight, but you can't fight your own battles with boys, can you? That's why you have to get Peter Wallace to fight for you!"

"Now children, children, you mustn't quarrel," said Hetty, coming into the room.

"Why can't Mavis leave me alone? I've got my homework to do, and it's Latin tonight," complained Phillip. "And French irregular verbs, which I can't understand. You know how I feel, Mother, don't you?"

"Yes, dear, of course your homework must come first. Only your Father may be home any minute now, and he will want to be quiet, dear. It's a very quiet machine really, and Mavis is keen to get her work done tonight, before bedtime, Phillip. Oh, before I forget, have you changed the sawdust in Timmy Rat's box?"

"Not yet. Oh, I can't do Algebra!"

Phillip's head was now held in his hands, elbows on table, fingers plugged in ears. The Latin primer was open before him. Quietly his mother lit the gas jet in the scullery, filled a kettle at the tap, and returned with it to the kitchen, to set it on the range.

"Oh, curse this muck," he muttered. "What's the use of the ablative absolute? What does it mean, anyway?"

"I expect it will have a use in after-life, dear."

"Which one do you mean?"

"When you are grown up, of course, dear."

"Oh, I thought you meant when I was dead."

"Hush, Phillip!"

Hetty tried not to laugh, though she thought it was rather funny, the serious way he said it. He was, in many ways, like her brother Hugh. Poor Hughie! she sighed. What a wasted life, what a tragedy! Pray God that Phillip would never make the same terrible mistake that Hughie had made. It was rather a terrible thought, but often it seemed that it was the gay, the bright ones of this world who were destined to come to a sad end. Hugh had never found happiness; nor, for that matter, had Dora, whom Hughie had loved so dearly. Ah well, troubles in this world were sent to try us.

"Mother," Mavis was saying, a strained expression on her face. "Please make Phillip let me have the Singer in here. I must finish my sewing tonight."

"And I must finish my homework, Mum!"

"Yes, dear, I know. Mavis, can you wait just a little while? Then when Phillip has gone to the library, you girls can have the place again to yourselves."

"You favour Phillip, it isn't fair!" cried Mavis. She was near to tears. "I shan't have time to finish it now! The others have got their presents for Miss Wendover already made!"

"Fancy being so potty on a games mistress!"

"Fancy you being potty on Helena Rolls!"

"I'm not!"

"You know you are! 'The bluebell's blue, The rose is red, I love you true, I'm soft in the head! Ha ha!" Mavis laughed, with a quaver in her voice.

"You beastly little swine! You fool!"

Hardly had the insults been shouted, when there came a jingle of keys from the porch without, and the slight creak of paint parting from rubber beading as the front door was opened. Both children were immediately silent.

Chapter 2

IDYLL IN FOG

As he sat with Latin primer open before him on the kitchen table, Phillip heard the returning click of the Yale lock, then the soft sounds of Father's boots being wiped on the cocoanut mat. He knew the noises with all his being. They were always the same. After the wiping of boots, the sides of each, followed by one toe, then a heel, then another toe and heel, there were the steps forward on the oil-cloth, followed by the little knock of Father's umbrella handle striking its peg of the mahogany clothes rack; the slight *blonk* of the bowler hat following; the ruffle of his raincoat being withdrawn from his arms, the careful hanging of it by its black chain on another peg. Then the extra sounds tonight: rattle of match box, striking of match, little soft pop of the gas: Father pausing while he turned it down, to save gas.

Phillip waited in dread for what he knew was coming next. Father's voice saying, "Phillip, did I hear you call your sister a fool just now?"

"Yes, Father."

"Why, may I ask?"

"I beg your pardon, Father."

"That's all very well, but apologies for continual rudeness tend to lose their validity, you know. Do not let me hear you speaking like that to your sister again."

"No, Father."

"You will apologise to your sister, if you please."

Well, I don't please, muttered Phillip to himself; but aloud he said, "I beg your pardon, Mavis."

The kitchen door opened wide.

"Anyone would think you two children were deadly enemies, to hear you speak to one another. Why," exclaimed Richard Maddison, moving to shut the bottom of the kitchen window, "when I was a boy, neither I nor any of my brothers would have dreamt of talking to one of our sisters the way you do, Phillip. Nor would your Aunts ever have thought of retaliation, in the unlikely event of one or another of the brothers being rude to them. Where you, Phillip, get it from beats me! Not from my side of the family certainly, nor do you get it from your Mother. In future let there be a great improvement in the matter—please! Do you hear me?"

"Yes, Father."

Hetty came cheerfully into the kitchen. "Well Dickie, I'll soon have your meal ready. I do hope the fog did not delay you."

"Oh, it is hardly more than a mist. Well, I was about to remark to Phillip that I saw a big dark bird flying over the Hill just now, but perhaps he is too deep in study to take it in."

Phillip pretended to be studying gerundives, pluperfects, and past participles.

"Phillip dear, your Father——"

"Oh, don't disturb the student——"

Phillip looked up. "Oh, I hope it was a tawny owl, Father!"

Both father and son tried to pretend to themselves that their surroundings were still part of the country.

"I fancy it was larger than a tawny owl. They live in the big trees in Twistleton Road, I have heard them ever since the time when I played tennis there, years ago. No, this bird was a big fellow—possibly an Eagle Owl, or a Snowy Owl. Are there plates of any owls in that book you got from the library last week?"

"I don't know, Father," Phillip replied, in a weak voice. He pretended to be studying the primer; but sat brittle and thudding.

"Has it gone back yet?"

Richard sat down to remove his boots. Phillip did not know what to answer.

"I don't know, Father."

"You don't know?"

"I mean—I mean——"

"He's trying to learn his Latin, Dickie," said Hetty.

"Oh, I see! Your best boy has turned over a new leaf, evidently! Well, I'll disturb him no more."

Phillip sat easier as Father, having changed his boots for carpet slippers, went upstairs to wash. When he came down again, he wore his smoking jacket, which he put on when he was in a good mood. It was of dark blue velvet, an old one which Uncle John had sent him. Phillip felt that Father wasn't so bad when he put on the "smoker", as he called it. The frogs across the front made Richard think of Sherlock Holmes, of a world quite different from the one he was living.

When Father's tray had been taken down by Mavis, and all was quiet down in the sitting room, Phillip said, to his Mother making some coffee, "I think I'll go to the Library now, Mum."

"Very well, dear. Don't be late, will you?"

"No, Mum."

Outside in the hall Polly beckoned to him. She held out the card. The sitting room door was shut. Phillip pulled the mantle chain, to get more light by which to examine the precious Valentine. There it was, on thick white album paper; a bunch of bluebells, and the poem underneath, in neat black writing. Polly had an envelope, too, addressed to Miss Helena Rolls. Was it all right? Yes, said Phillip, it was wonderful.

"Now I'll slip up and put it in the letter box. I hope their bulldog doesn't bark! Wish me luck, Polly. You know how I feel, don't you?"

"I think so. She is pretty, isn't she?" said dark little Polly.

"She's wonderful! Of course, I've no chance. Still, one day, perhaps. I hope it's foggy, then no one will see me. So long!"

He put on his coat. He was shivering. "I'll be back in half a mo. Then I must hop along to the library, and get rid of that awful book. My lord, if I escape this time, I swear I'll never do it again."

"Why did you, Phillip?"

"For fun, you know. Of course it's the Shag that's dangerous. I could be sent away to the reformatory for that. Oh dear. What shall I do?"

"Well, deliver the Valentine first, and I'll wait in the front room, and let you in when you come back. Then get the book, and change it, but look ordinary when you do so, then they won't think anything's the matter."

"All right. See you later."

If you open a letter box in a door on a cold foggy night, and you feel a warm air on your brow above your eyes and you hear charming voices and see a well-lighted hall and a dining room door open, and smell a roasting chicken—a house where they have dinner at night, and not just cold mutton for supper—it is like seeing into an enchanted palace until with a growl and a pattering of slipping claws on oil-cloth a bulldog rushes at your eyes behind the open letter-box and you turn tail and run away in alarm into the fog, knowing that if you are not quick the thick fat spring on the gate will send it back with a clash and catch the back of your heel.

A dark figure loomed; the boy's arm, Valentine in hand, was caught and held.

"What were you doing there?"

"Nothing, sir."

It was Mr. Pye, who lived next door to the Rolls. The houses were attached; and Mr. Pye's, the lower, had steps up to his front door. The steps were always well hearth-stoned.

"Who is it, Phillip?"

"Yes, Mr. Pye."

Mr. Pye's voice spoke quietly. "Why were you spying through the letter-box? It's not exactly the thing to do, is it? It is not a pleasant role, that of a peeping Tom, Phillip, to add to that of a boy who has his battles fought for him by someone else, I have noticed, let me tell you!"

Phillip could not speak.

The worst happened. The door opened. Mr. Rolls stood there, the light behind him.

"Hullo!" his rich and easy voice said. "Oh, it's you, Pye. I wondered what was happening, with Mike skidding about all over the place."

"Oh, we just happened to meet," replied Mr. Pye, in the same easy voice, but more level, not so rich as Mr. Rolls'. "Our young friend and I happened to meet outside your gate, in fact we bumped into each other. It's Phillip Maddison."

"Oh, Phillip, how are you," said Mr. Rolls. "Not hurt, I hope? It certainly is a dark night. Well, I must not keep you. Goodnight, Pye! Good night, Phillip."

Mr. Pye raised his big grey felt hat—a cigar hat Phillip had thought of it ever since he had seen a poster of a brown-faced jovial man on an ocean liner by the rails in such a hat, a globe-trotter smoking a cigar, the wind on his cloak. Mr. Pye sometimes wore such a cloak on the Hill when walking with his wife, who was deaf, and his children. The tweed cloak had an extra cape over the shoulders to shoot off the rain.

Phillip raised a cap that was not there. The door of Turret House closed.

"Well, young man," said Mr. Pye, shortly, in a low voice, "I will bid you goodnight. And take my advice, don't go spying on other people in their houses again. The next time you may not escape so easily."

"No, sir."

When Phillip got back, almost breathless with joy because the great Mr. Rolls had spoken so nicely to him, Polly was there to open the door for him. He told her the amazing adventure. The Valentine was still in his jacket pocket.

"You know, Polly," he concluded his whispered story in the dim secrecy of the front room, "the funny thing is, I swear Old Pye had an envelope in his hand, and had come to put it in the letter-box! Only he didn't! Now, if he had come to deliver a note, why didn't he give it to Mr. Rolls? That's what puzzles me. It's a mystery, isn't it? Oh, I never liked Old Pye. He's so fat, almost oily." Phillip thought a moment, then burst out, "Do you think he was going to slip in a Valentine, too? Do old men send them?"

"I think some do, Phil. To their old sweethearts. Perhaps it was to Mrs. Rolls, she is very pretty, isn't she?"

"Him!" exclaimed Phillip, with disgust. "What—to Mrs. Rolls! Why, Pye's a fat old slug! Not likely!"

"What are you going to do with yours?" asked Polly. "Go back later?"

"No jolly fear! I've had one narrow escape! Oh damn, now I've got the book to take back. Oh Lord, if I get out of this, I'll never have another book out, I swear it!"

"Shall I come, Phil? Aunty might let me, if you ask her."

"No, thanks. I must tackle this alone. The book's under my bed. If I'm discovered, I shall have to run away to sea. What shall we do with the Valentine? I know, let's give it to Mother! After all, she deserves a little consideration. Will you write out another envelope, and drop it in the hall, as though it's come through the letter-box? It will be a nice surprise for her, won't it? So long, Polly, you are a good sport, you know."

He crept upstairs; and a minute later was on his way to the Free Library. He did not want Polly with him, as he had a secret meeting at the Library every Friday night with Cranmer, with whom Father had forbidden him, on pain of a caning, to associate.

Cranmer was a poor, ragged boy, living in slum-like dwellings in Skerritt's Road, near the Library.

Chapter 3

NEW LEAF

WITHIN the past few years the Free Library had been built along the High Road, where now the wayside elms were but a memory to Phillip. Electric trams droned up and down the smooth and regularised way, to the Crystal Palace and beyond. Usually on Friday nights Phillip entered the swing doors between seven and half past, passing the scarcely-noticed bronze plaque of Andrew Carnegie upon the wall, and with the subdued air of a diffident small boy when grown-ups were about, approached the desk where books were returned.

He was one of several hundred boys in the neighbourhood who came, more or less regularly, to the Free Library. The subdued expression on his face was characteristic of many children of the district in the first decade of the twentieth century: a remote look in the eyes, as though the living scene were generally being evaded; a pallor upon cheek and brow, due to long hours of sunlessness in school, and to existence in a smoky, often foggy atmosphere during half the year; and on a diet the main food of which was bread whose composition lacked the beneficial germ, or "sharp", of the wheat berry, being made of the interior filling whose whiteness had been enhanced by chemical bleaching.

Some of Phillip's secondary or final teeth were already decayed in several places, though visits to the dentist had, supposedly, arrested the decay; while frequent exhortations by his Father, that he clean his teeth without fail before going to bed, and again when in the bathroom of an early morning, were generally ignored by the boy, who had come to regard all monitive and didactic utterances of grown-up people—except those whom he liked—to be avoided in so far as this could be done without punishment. The avoidance of all matters of what was insisted upon as his duty was not—except with his mother—accompanied by defiance; on the contrary, he was both timid and fearful, with only the least resistance to pain, or its threat, whether mental or physical. He cried as easily and as frequently as he was disobedient; truth in his life was subordinate to fear. Indeed, lying was, as his father Richard Maddison had often declared, second nature to him. That second-nature—to use the term of the period—was accompanied by occasional boasting and bullying, and an enhanced idealism centred upon an eleven-year-old girl, daughter of a near neighbour in Hillside Road.

While not, perhaps, a typical product of a lesser London suburb of the Edwardian age, Phillip Maddison bore certain characteristics of those who were being brought up in a district where the living soil had been partly suppressed by an industrial civilisation. His chaotic inner living, direct reflection from his environment, was apparent upon his features, in the melancholy cast of the countenance in repose, particularly in the drooping corners of the wide mouth, and the sad expression of the eyes.

At the moment of approaching the assistant librarian's desk, to await his turn with the fair-haired young woman wearing *pince-nez* eye-glasses which added to the lifeless expression of her prim face, a more immediate fear was in Phillip's eyes. His feelings were verging upon panic, arising out of guilty terror. He was quivering inwardly, struck with fear that the assistant librarian would open the book he was about to return, discover what he had written upon some of the pages, and report him for having a "depraved appetite". That would mean only one thing—the police. He had recently looked up the meaning of the word *depraved* in the dictionary at home. "A state of corruption; viciousness, profligacy; perversion, degeneracy"—the words were familiar enough, from Father's condemnations.

The Birds of the British Isles was a weighty, quarto volume illustrated with coloured plates. Phillip, having it with him in the kitchen while supposed to be doing his homework during the preceding days of the week, had read beyond his interest limited to those birds with which he was familiar; and out of boredom, and a sense of fun, had composed extra verbal descriptions of those larger birds which had seemed to him to be sinister or grotesque as he regarded their portraits in colour upon the various plates.

Using a broad relief nib in his wooden pen-holder, he had added various alliterative epithets to the formal descriptions; and to disguise his writing, had penned them in large capital letters. Thus a big black bird had become the RAPSCALLION RAVEN; a thin, tall stilted wader, the HUNGRY HERON; a sea-diver with beak of several colours the PAINTPOT PUFFIN; a common grey and white sea-bird, the GOLLOPING GULL. Thereafter his fancy had taken a cloacal turn, inspired by the portrait of what to him was a rather foolish-looking fish-eating bird squatting above the sea upon a black rock almost completely whitened by its own droppings.

The bird had a narrow beak and head, with a little tuft of feathers on its crown, looking like untidy hair. Its black wings, iridescent with sheens of purple and green, were extended in an effort to gulp down into its crop various fishes, including an eel, whose tails stuck out of its open beak. Phillip had read that the upper mandible of the SHAG'S beak was hooked, the better to pierce and hold its prey seized in submarine hunting. With sudden daring, and a suppressed chuckle, the boy, seated at the scrubbed deal table with his undone homework scattered before him, had boldly limned the appropriate alliterative adjective of six letters; and several heavy blots shot off his nib around the coloured plate had followed, to show his scorn of the greedy, dirty bird, which was described by the author of the book as an enemy of fishermen.

If it had seemed frightfully funny at the time, it seemed now frightfully bad, as, trying to control his feelings, Phillip stood by the librarian's desk, uttering a voiceless, wordless prayer to Saint Anthony, the saint most frequently evoked by his mother when she was trying to find something she had lost.

The book was taken; the date stamp examined at the front of the volume; a card swiftly sought in the index and slipped into the envelope at the back. His library ticket was returned, to his silent-shouted relief.

"Thank you," he managed to say, raising his school cap, with its badge sewn on the front, as he bowed slightly to the young woman. She looked up a moment in surprise, wondering if he meant to be sarcastic, then decided to take no notice, in case he was. Like most people, not of the looked-down-upon working class, in the district, she bore herself usually with reserve, enclosing a feeling of superiority to most other people living in the neighbourhood. Behind the reserve was a defensive touchiness, at times showing itself in hauteur.

Tremulous with relief, Phillip turned away. He hesitated before going into the Reading Room.

A tram-bell clanged loudly outside in the street as the main swing-doors opened to admit an old man entering with a cold gust of air, its effect heightened by the livid colour of his face revealed above the black breathing-pad held across his mouth by black tapes fastened at the back of his hair. Phillip had often seen him, a figure inspiring mild fear. Laboriously with a stick the apparition tapped towards the reading-room doors; but before they had swung-to behind his entry, as he was making for the only unoccupied seat, Phillip darted past him, and snatching a copy of the *Automotor Journal* from a table, seated himself in the vacant place. Safely there, he looked at the library ticket concealed in his hand, while exulting that now there was no proof that he had made the blots and written the awful word about the shag. Now he really would be better! His prayer had been answered! He swore he would turn over a new leaf!

Taking out his note-book, he began to write the name of a motorcar upon a page which already held a list of several makes, with their numbers and descriptions. The collection of motorcar numbers was one of the local boys' current hobbies; but unlike most other boys, Phillip did not confine himself to numbers. He had ridden in a motorcar but once; his interest was, by that experience, more technical. There was a common saying among boys that one day a big prize would be given for the biggest list of registration numbers, though who was to give the prize, and where it was to be got, was never stated.

In Phillip's book were recorded, in his laboriously neat hand —with its immature resemblance to his father's—the following details.

Motorcars seen on the road leading to Reynard's Common by Phillip Maddison, Esq., of Lindenheim, Wakenham, Kent.

1. 15 h.p. Panhard et Lavassor, 4 seater, my Uncle Hilary's motor. I was one of the first passengers.
2. 5½ h.p. Peugeot, a voiturette. Tall and tiny, with curving radiator. Seen by Cutler's Pond.
3. 4.9 h.p. Pick, tiny 2 seater. In Wetherley's coach works.
4. Hurtu, an old broken down crock. Pulled by horse near Obelisk.
5. Lutzmann, with 4 carriage wheels. No radiator, but cooling tanks, and spoon and ribbon brakes. Seen in blacksmith's yard in High Street. No good.
6. Lanchester. Seen by cousin Gerry.
7. Oldsmobile, an American. Seen by Father who passed it (while boiling) up Brumley hill on his 3-speed Sunbeam. (The motor was boiling, not Father).
8. Locomobile steam-car. Outside Green Man, Cutler's Pond.
9. White's Steam car. Seen by Harris, in my form at school.
10. Arrol-Johnstone dog-cart, old-fashioned veritable old-iron, slow and panting. Seen by Cutler's Pond.
11. Mercedes, very sporty and fast, brass snake-like exhaust pipes on one side. Seen in Wetherley's coach works. Not for sale, he told me.
12. Mors. Spidery. Mors is Latin for death. It looked like it, said Father. Seen on Sunday, two men pushing it.
13. Darracq, French make. Seen in *Daily Trident* photo, so can be half claimed as seen by me.
14. James and Brown, London built. Think I saw one, but am not certain (must not cheat too much).
15. Siddeley-Deasey. Stopped on way up hill to Heath. Man said make-and-break spring was broken.
16. Fafnir motor-bike, German. Father told me Fafnir means dragon. Yellow and black, more like wasp. Seen on Brumley road, Sunday.
17. Star. It passed fast through Fordesmill, and very likely fell into police trap along Brumley road to Cutler's Pond, Father said.
18. Royal Enfield, "made like a gun". It certainly made bangs in silencer box. On Sunday walk to Cutler's Pond with Father.
19. de Launy-Belville. Going down Stumps Hill. Seen by Father, who reported it to me.

Phillip was writing the latest entry, 20. *Wolseley, seen in* Automotor Journal *in Free Library*, when the old man stopped by his chair, and staring down at him with red-rimmed eyes that held a fixed expression of misery, pushed up the black pad and said, wheezily, "That is my cheer yar sittin' in. I seed it fust, d'n I tho."

The chair was next to a hot-water radiator. The old man had come in to get warm. His own house, in Skerritt Road nearby, was fireless.

"Well, I got here first," said Phillip in a whisper. He pointed at the SILENCE notice on the wall. "But I won't be half a mo."

He pretended to be looking at the periodical; but the old man's presence took away all thought, all life from him. He stayed an uneasy minute longer, then remembering Cranmer, got up and, pulling back the chair, offered it to the old man, with a mock bow, and a sweep of his hand. Then catching a whiff of the strong, acrid smell emanating from the dark, creased clothes of the old man, Phillip's nose wrinkled up, and he stared at the ceiling.

"You cheeky young limb," growled the old man, fixing Phillip with his ruined eyes.

" 'A year ago I used Pears' Soap, since when I have used no other'," murmured Phillip, half to himself. The words were from a well-known advertisement, originally a drawing in *Punch*. It showed an unkempt, bearded man, short clay pipe in mouth, writing a testimonial for the soap. Phillip and his mother had a private joke about the picture; they pretended that it was Father.

The old man lowered himself slowly into the chair, while Phillip waited to be thanked. After all, it was *his* seat, and he had unselfishly given it up. When the old man uttered no word, Phillip said sarcastically, " What do you say? ", but meeting only the same miserable stare from the eyes, turned away to examine a newspaper, one of many flat on the sloping stands around the walls. Its turning edges were frayed and dirtied by many wetted fingers and thumbs. Glancing back at the seated figure of the old man, Phillip saw that he was holding a page of the *Automotor Journal*, while staring at a picture, and rolling the edge of the page between his finger and thumb, preparatory to turning it over.

"H'm," muttered Phillip, in contempt. "One of the dog's ear brigade."

Recently the boy had been checked by his father for doing the same thing. A book or magazine, said Richard, should be respected. Its pages should be turned lightly, not held as though they were a dog's ear, to be rubbed.

There was no interest in the newspaper—nothing about Birds or Motorcars—and remembering that he was due to meet Cranmer at seven, with a glance at the clock Phillip walked between the rows of drab-dressed people sitting silent except for frequent coughing and throat-clearing; and passing through the swing-door, went to the shelves of books in the lending department. Here, before volumes ranged in alphabetical order of their classified contents, he stood hesitant, facing the word ANTIQUITY.

Phillip knew that Antiquity was rather like History, which was utterly dull and uninteresting. Antiquarianism was about things like tombstones in old churchyards, dark old buildings, churches and cottages with moss and lichen on their roofs—all very interesting to Mother, who often talked with Mr. Mundy on the Hill. Perhaps Mother would like a book on it? For he must leave NATURAL HISTORY alone for a bit. If he took home an antiquarian book, it might put the librarian off the scent; also, it would help to put Father in a favourable mood.

Phillip took a volume from the section, and opening a page, saw a photograph of the High Road before the elms had been cut down. There was Pennison the barber, standing outside his sweetstuff-shop near the corner of Comfort Road. Across the road was Sprunt's pawn shop, with the three golden balls hanging over it. Sprunt's where once he had bought a horse-pistol, and fired it off too, with black powder—a wonderful weapon!

"I would like to take out this one, please. Antiquarianism is so very interesting, I think," he said, in unconscious imitation of his mother's manner.

The young woman gave the small boy with the soft, distinct voice an upward glance. She recognised him as the one who had raised his cap to her ten minutes earlier. Seeing his deep blue eyes and gentle smile, she was sorry for having taken no notice of him before. He had such black hair, and such a gentlemanly voice. Her face took on a gentle look, her lips lost their hard line, and lifted with a smile as she withdrew the card from the book, and having stamped it and the front page, took his ticket and said,

"You're one of the brainy ones, I can see. Well, don't let your brains kill you, dear."

"Oh no, I won't do that!"

She smiled openly with the stir of warmth that arose in her as she absorbed the look on his face, which seemed to shine from within.

Responsive to her feeling, Phillip felt clear and happy. He had turned over a new leaf! He stood smiling at the assistant, thinking that her mouth and chin and cheeks and brow were lovely in shape. His gaze dropped.

"Thank you," he said softly, and taking the book, raised his cap, while giving her a fleeting smile, and a little bow, in imitation of his Father.

At that moment the swing doors of the Library were edged open, and the well-known parsonic figure of Mr. Mundy in black straw yard and long knitted muffler flowing from several turns around his neck—he never wore an overcoat—came through on a bicycle. He had a large wicker fishing creel, which held books, slung over one shoulder.

Leaping off the bike, Mr. Mundy greeted everyone boisterously, like old friends. He saw Phillip.

"Hullo, the very man I wanted to see! I think there is a specimen of either Nyctea Scandiaca or Bubo Bubo Bubo on the Hill! Snowy Owl, or Eagle Owl! I must write to *The Times*. I've just seen Sprunt the pawn-broker, who is a great bird-man, and described it to him—my gardener saw it in the row of elms—and I've come to identify it. Bubo Bubo Bubo sounds terrifying, doesn't it, m'dear?", turning to the assistant. "It's the classification of Linnaeus, as of course you know."

Everyone was now looking at the vicar; heads in the reading room, seen through glass-panelled doors, were turning.

"Well, m'dear," he went on, "I wonder if you have any books of reference—Gould's *British Birds* is what I want." He stood his bicycle against a wall. "Now, Phillip—hullo—where's he gone, I wonder?"

"My God, Cranmer, quick! They're after me! Down to the cemetery!"

Cranmer ran beside Phillip, away from the Free Library. Soon the fog hid the lights behind. They stopped outside the sweet-shop opposite the Boys' Entrance of Wakenham Road School. Then Phillip told Cranmer what had happened.

Cranmer was Phillip's companion of many a secret walk around the fields of Joy Farm, and the allotments by the Workhouse in Randiswell. Cranmer was a faithful friend, with whom Phillip had kept up the friendship of pre-scholarship days, when they had gone to Wakenham school. Both boys would soon be fourteen. Then Cranmer, who had remained at Wakenham Road School, would start work.

Meanwhile, the light in his life was his friendship with Phillip. Cranmer had a father who spent most of his wages, when in work, in a pub called The Jack. Because Cranmer came from Skerritt Road, that place of supposed evil, most of its children in broken boots and ragged clothes, Phillip had been forbidden to see him. Hetty was never afraid of her son's contamination. The boys therefore were chums in secret, meeting every Friday night outside the Library.

"I can't stop tonight, I've got to hurry, Horace. Can you walk with me s'far's the Cemetery gates?"

"Yus. I ain't doin' nothin' t'night. Carry yer book, Phil?"

"Thanks."

Cranmer took the volume gratefully. Phillip was pleased that Cranmer always wanted to do things for him.

As they walked upon the smooth square slabs of the new pavement, beside the iron railings of the cemetery, he told Cranmer about his fears.

"If Mr. Mundy reports me, I'm a goner, Horace. I'll have to run away from home."

"I'm wiv yer, Phil. Anyfink you do, I do."

"What about your father, Horace?"

Cranmer spat. "Pah, my ole man don't care what I do! Only what about your'n?"

"Oh, he doesn't care either."

Cranmer considered this.

"I don't want to git yer in no trouble, Phil, but my bruvver knows a bloke dahn Green'ich what's got a barge, ole piper 'e takes, bundles 'n bundles er ole piper all pressed tergevver, an' tugs take 'm dahn ter'r piper mills in the Medway somewhere—cor, it ain't 'arf some sport on'r Thames barge, Phil!"

Cranmer spoke through his clenched teeth, his lips parted slightly, in the approved manner of the streets where everyone was against you, and if you didn't look after yourself, no one else would. Everyone was out after a poor boy—Cranmer had known that from the time he could walk, and learned to hurry away from kicks, back-handers, and beltings. As he spoke he drew his lips back against his gums (half his front teeth were decayed) and his words came without facial movement—as though a slop, otherwise copper, bluebottle, or policeman, were eternally waiting to catch him.

"I ken 'alf-inch s'm tins'r stuff from ole 'Ern, an' we kin live off'r'm an' 'ide up among'r piper bales, Phil. No one won't see us."

Phillip was silent. Pinching from a shop was not right. It was all right to scrump apples, or pull carrots from the allotments near the workhouse, but taking things from a shop was stealing. Besides, Hern the grocer was a nice man, a friend who told him of his adventures in Canada. Phillip often visited him in the little room behind his shop, where Hern did his accounts at a stand-up desk. Cranmer was an errand-boy for Hern on Saturdays.

"How much do you get at Hern's, Horace?"

"'Ern gimme tuppence, Phil, only I hev to give it to me Mum."

Cranmer worked from 9 a.m. until 8 p.m. for that sum; but he received, in addition, odd ends of reasty bacon, a bag of broken biscuits, various chunks of stale cheese-ends, as well as other scraps, all of which he took home in an old perambulator.

"I don't think we ought to half-inch from Hern, you know, Horace."

"P'raps you're right, Phil. I was on'y sort-er finkin' of you, reely."

"Perhaps I ought to go and see Mr. Mundy now, and confess. He's a decent old fellow, you know."

"I know!" cried Cranmer, "You kin say you come ter join ver Siety fer properation er gospital! Ven you can tell 'im your sin and 'e'll forgive yer!"

"Yes, I might join the S.P.G.," said Phillip, eager with this hope.

They became silent as the place of parting came nearer. There was a stone hidden on the wall of the cemetery; usually the boys played football on the pavement with it, quiet little dribbles, Cranmer being Woolwich Arsenal and Phillip being Aston Villa—but tonight Phillip did not feel like playing. At the cemetery gates he said, "Well, I must say so long now. See you next Friday? Same place? By the way, there is a terrific owl about now—probably flown down from the North Pole—no one knows exactly what it is, but it may be an Eagle Owl. If so, I think many a small dog may be missing in the future near! So keep your eyes skinned. I'd like any observations to go into my notebook."

"Blime," said Cranmer. "Does it tike kids's well's dorgs?"

"I shouldn't be surprised! Well, goodbye for now."

Stopping at the corner of Charlotte Road, Phillip looked back. The fog was clearing, before a wind. From up the road came a long hoarse whistle, Cranmer's speciality. Cranmer had thrust three fingers into his mouth and emptied his lungs fervently and rapidly through the finger-spaces. The result was a sort of miniature railway-engine screech. Phillip thought it was rather a common noise; he must remember to tell Cranmer not to do it in future. Also, Father might hear it; it needlessly advertised their whereabouts when together.

A lighted tram rushed past, its steel wheels seeming to whoop in the rails as the brakes were put on before the stop by the Unitarian Church on the far curve. Under a clearer, star-seen sky the driver was expressing his relief. His brown and yellow vehicle had groaned all day slowly, with clanging bell, through the traffic; while a bitter dew had lain upon his lashes, stinging the lids of his eyes, vulnerable to detritus falling from one or another of a hundred thousand chimneys of South London.

Chapter 4

" HISTORY OF THE BOROUGH "

HAPPY in his thoughts of a new beginning, Phillip hurried along Charlotte Road. When he came to St. Cyprian's church, the sight of lighted windows for the usual Friday night choir-practice gave him an idea. He would go in and join the S.P.G. right away. He hesitated. Perhaps it would be safer to join the St. Simon's branch, and throw himself on the mercy of Mr. Mundy after all, as Cranmer had suggested. St. Simon's reminded him inevitably of Helena Rolls; it was as though a lead plummet dropped in his breast. He would go over the grass of the Hill, and down through the thorns above the gully, in order to see the lighted windows of Helena Rolls' house at the top of the road.

It was thrilling to walk over the grass at night, to climb silently over the hurdle fence; and avoiding thorn twigs with slow care, to creep, in the shadow lines of the street-lamp, to cover by the park gates. While he stood there, he saw Mr. Pye's front door open, and the figure of Mr. Pye descending the steps. Phillip pressed himself against the iron post of the park gate, and kept rigidly still. He saw Mr. Pye tip-toeing up by the Rolls' hedge, pause to open their gate, pass through, close it very carefully, and go to the front door. Phillip watched him put something through the letter box, and then Mr. Pye tip-toed back to the gate. He opened and closed it very quietly, and then tiptoed back to his own house again, and up the steps to the front door he had left a little bit open.

What had Mr. Pye put through their letter-box? A Valentine? Phillip was thrilled with the mystery. Could it be, as Polly had said, that he was sweet on Mrs. Rolls? Surely not, for they were both quite old.

After a safe interval, Phillip crept down the asphalt pavement on the opposite side of the road. He walked down until he was beyond range of the lamp-post light outside Mr. Groat's in No. 9; and then, darting over the flinty road, he walked up rapidly to his own house, keeping close to the garden fences, then rushing through the gate and so to his front door as though he were being pursued.

He gave a small ring on the bell, thinking it best not to use the knocker, since Father was at home. Mother, making cocoa in the kitchen, came to the door. Observing that the sitting room door was half-open, Phillip wiped his boots carefully on the mat, hoping Father would hear; then he gave his mother the library book, saying in a voice loud enough to be heard in the sitting room, "It's most interesting, all about when you first met Father, Mum. I thought you and Father would like to look at it, as it's Antiquarianism."

"Thank you, dear, what a very kind thought."

In the kitchen, Hetty glanced at the book, and whispered, "Show it to your Father first, dear! I am sure he would appreciate your doing so."

"Ah, I wonder what you are up to now!" said Mavis.

"Shut up!" hissed Phillip. "Must you glue your optics on me for ever?"

He led his mother into the scullery.

"Mum," he whispered. "I think I will join the Society for the Propagation of the Gospel!"

Hetty looked surprised. What had he been up to now?

"Yes dear, of course, if you feel you should. Is anything the matter?"

"Of course not! I only thought I would join, that's all."

"Very well, Sonny. Now have your cocoa, dear, and then take the book down to your Father."

He delayed over drinking his cocoa, to put off the moment of being in Father's presence. The girls were in giggling mood: they annoyed him, taking glances at him, as though they had some secret. At last they prepared to go upstairs to have their baths, excited by the thought of all three getting into what Father always called "the tub", together.

Phillip, calling Polly into the front room, told her what he had seen outside Turret House. Then, struck by a sudden fear, he said goodnight, and taking the book, went down to the sitting-room. Would Mr. Mundy call to see Father that night, now that the fog was gone? Or would the police be told first? Any moment there might be a knock on the front door, a loud urgent ring of the electric bell.

Father was sitting in his green leather armchair, reading *The Daily Trident.*

"Good evening, Father."

"Hullo, old chap. How's the fog?"

"It's cleared off, Father."

"That is good news."

Phillip seated himself quietly, in his usual place at the table, behind Father's chair. Father usually read the paper all through, then he had a game of chess with Mother. Phillip put the library book on the plush cloth of the table, quietly by Father's side.

Not long afterwards Hetty came down, and took up her basket of darning beside her chair. Phillip blinked at her, and indicated the book with his nose.

After a few moments, when Father did not move, he said, with another glance at her, "I think I would like to learn to play chess, you know, Mum."

Richard put down the paper, and got on his feet, to stretch himself. Standing with back to the crackling coke fire, he looked at Phillip quizzically, and said, "Who is this I see before me?

What does this sudden glory foretell? Bless my soul, you are scarcely recognisable, Phillip."

"I thought it a good thing to let him air his best clothes, Dickie. Tomorrow he is going to have his photograph taken."

"For heaven's sake let the boy speak for himself, Hetty! And there is no need for you to speak in that apologetical tone of voice. After all, I merely asked a question."

"Yes dear, of course, naturally."

This familiar remark of Hetty's seemed to irritate Richard.

"What do you mean by that expression? I must have heard it a thousand times in my married life, and each time I have wondered what exactly you meant by it. 'Of course' means a matter of course, or habit. But your habit is always to try and come between me and Phillip. 'Naturally' presumably means what is natural. Is it natural for a mother always to be shielding her son?"

Hetty smiled. There was sadness and resignation, together with an unquenchable sense of fun, in her eyes. Suddenly the fun departed; acute sadness remained, a sense of tragedy, of the perpetual, unchangeable sameness of Dickie always taking the simplest thing she said, in the wrong way. "I hardly dare ever say anything," she once confessed, in a tearful moment, to Phillip. "Father always takes it the wrong way."

"Well, Phillip," said Richard, turning to his son, who was sitting unnaturally still. "This is indeed a surprise. Are you intending to call on your best girl, it being St. Valentine's Eve?"

Richard spoke in the chaffing tones that always disconcerted Phillip, used as he was to a tension of resistance against his father. Richard however, was also sensitive, though in different degree; and his sense of decorum would never permit him knowingly to embarrass his son. He knew nothing of the Valentine painted by Polly Pickering; his remark came from an article he had been reading in *The Daily Trident* on the origins of St. Valentine, and old country beliefs about birds pairing off on that date. Phillip thought Father was chipping him. He made no reply. Then to his relief, Father said, "Well, so you want to learn to play chess, do you?"

"Yes, I would, please, Father."

"I wonder what put that idea into your head?"

"I don't know, Father."

"Come, old chap," said Richard, in kindly mood, regarding the prim, wide-eyed boy. "Share the secret with me!"

Before Phillip could think, there was a ring of the front door bell. He started.

"Hullo, what have you been up to now?" said Richard, jokingly, seeing the start. "What's in the wind this time?"

Hetty saw the boy's pale face.

"Is there anything the matter, dear?" she said. "Tell Father if there is," as she opened the sitting room door.

"Oh, be quiet!" exclaimed Richard, in mild exasperation. "Let the boy speak for himself."

Hetty went up the stairs to the front door. With beating heart, Phillip listened.

"There's nothing to tell, Father."

"Oh, I see."

Richard picked up his newspaper, seated himself in his armchair, and looked again at what he had already read—the words of a big-moustached man whose photograph appeared in the middle of the article designed to rouse an apathetic nation against the danger of the projected Kiel Canal from Baltic to North Sea. *They mean war, these people, who rejoice under the heel of militarism*, wrote the prophet, Robert Blatchford. Richard wondered why he wrote in *The Daily Trident*, since this ex-sergeant of the army was supposed to be a Socialist. However, there was some sense in what Robert Blatchford now wrote.

Richard had never forgotten what his mother, of a Bavarian family destroyed in Bismarck's war of federation, had always said about the Prussians. Sitting in the chair, his thoughts reverted to what his sister Theodora had recently written to him in a letter containing what he considered to be a farrago of nonsense about the wrongness of England generally, and in particular in the Englishman's attitude to the subject races of the Empire. And this was the very same Dora who was making a nuisance of herself in the agitation for the franchise to women. Dora, more of a crank than ever! A woman without a true vocation. She had never grown up.

But Theodora Maddison had not written to her brother what she had written to her sister-in-law. Dora had written to Hetty, among other things, these words:

I do not think that I have ever known such an unhappy little boy as

Phillip used to be. It is so strange, Hetty, that history in our family, as among the nations, seems to be repeating itself. "There is nothing new under the sun"—yes, I know what the old biblical poet says—but surely signs are not wanting of a revival of ancient Truth, of a spiritual awareness in the world, which shall bring Light anew into our struggling humanity, and fulfil the dreams of the artists and poets of the ancient world.

Be gentle with my brother, dear Hetty. He is a lonely man, very proud, and has suffered much from the previous generation, more perhaps than we shall ever know. Cause and effect, effect and cause: only God can, with His infinite mercy, see beyond the dark forces which beset us all, the misunderstandings which isolate all of us, each in their different perplexities. Be patient, dear friend; and never cease to believe in the ultimate goodness of mankind.

When Richard looked up from his paper again, a few moments later, and turned in his chair to look at Phillip, an incredulous expression came over his face. The boy's neck was bent, his face hidden; a slight choking noise came from him. Tears were dropping upon the plush table-cloth!

"Good heavens, what's the matter now? Why are the water-works turned on?"

Phillip hid his face the more.

"Well, I'm blowed!" said Richard. "You are a most extraordinary cuss!"

"What's the matter, Sonny, don't you feel well?" asked Hetty, returning to the room, an envelope in her hand. "What has happened, Dickie?"

"I'm blest if I can understand any of you!" cried Richard, seeing tears in his wife's eyes. "You are a weepy lot, all of you! Come on, Phillip, chuck it! Be a man! You really must learn to cease taking refuge in tears if anything goes wrong! What you will do when you grow up, and go out into the world, I hardly dare think! Come on now, old chap, tell us all about it!"

Sensible of Father's rough sympathy, Phillip felt more hopeless. He was ashamed, too. And what was the letter in Mother's hand? Was it a summons, already?

"Tell your parents, dear, if anything is wrong," said Hetty.

Ah, it was a summons. He would kill himself. It was the end of his life. He gulped, and said the first thing that came into his head—one, indeed, of many worries. "I can't learn my Latin, Father."

"Why ever did you not say so at first?" said Richard, indulgently. "If that is all that is troubling you, I can assure you that it is the normal worry of every small boy when first he goes to school. Why, do you know, I could not make much headway with my Latin, when I was a boy at a private school. Just do your best, and stick it out, that's my advice to you. Things will come easier later on."

"Yes," said Hetty, smiling. "Everything is difficult at first. 'If at first you don't succeed, try try again'."

Phillip tried to look suitably grateful for this advice.

Encouraged by the look on his son's face, Richard went on, in some relief that at last the boy seemed to want to listen to him.

"Everything has to be learnt, you know, old chap. Just like riding a bicycle, or a horse. Suddenly you acquire balance, and then you wonder how you could ever have found it difficult." He pulled out his watch. "Now Hetty, do you feel like a game of chess, old girl?"

Hetty laughed, remembering when he had objected to her asking him, once, if he felt like a boiled egg for his tea. Dickie feeling like a boiled egg! She laughed and laughed. The tears in her eyes had been of tenderness—how kind of the little girls to send Phillip a Valentine!

"What is tickling you now?" asked Richard. "'Pon my soul, you are a pair, you two! First the waterworks, then nothing can stop you laughing. Come on, tell a fellow the joke."

The envelope lay on the cloth. Phillip got up and looked at it. He recognised the hand-writing.

"Why, it's for me!"

He opened it. He saw at once it was a joke—the girls, of course. Mavis' doing, obviously. There was a Cupid, in an Eton suit, looking over the shoulder of a fat man in a large black hat and black cloak, obviously Mr. Pye, who was kneeling to slip an envelope through a letter-box. Then he read the verse underneath.

I stand and sigh
The bluebell's blue
I've got my eye
On who knows who?

Was this meant to be Polly's hint to him, just because once, long ago, they had been childish sweethearts? Obviously Mavis had written the poem. He put it in his pocket.

Mother and Father were staring at the chess-board. Phillip opened *History of the Borough*, which was by an Old Boy of his school, Mr. Graham, and turned the pages to find something of interest. He found an old-fashioned picture of the High Street, trees beside the muddy high road, a wooden Roe Buck Inn set back behind a long wooden horse-trough, and a coach standing in front, a man holding the horse's head. The date was 1810. There was another picture on the opposite page, of the Old Roebuck in 1830, and Plough Green in front of it, and the brook on the other side of the road. There was a chestnut tree near the inn, and the book said it had, according to local tradition, been planted in 1683, and was the parent tree of those in Bushey Park.

> The stream which ran through the village, passed the "Roebuck", and joined the Randisbourne at the bridge, which at this spot yielded many a good fish to the angler.

Why that was just near where the Obelisk was now! He passed over the bridge twice every day, going to and coming from school, but he had never seen any fish, except stickle-backs. Sometimes he had seen boys with glass jars paddling among the old pails, rags and thrown-away things on the stony bottom, hunting for them.

Phillip yawned.

Hetty saw the yawn, and said, "Why not go to bed dear? I expect the girls are out of the bathroom by now."

"Have I got to have their water?"

"No dear, of course not. Only don't take too much."

"And not too hot—it's enervating, Phillip," said Richard.

He got up. "Goodnight, Father, goodnight, Mother."

About five minutes later, when Richard called "Check mate", Hetty got up, saying, "I'll just go and see if Phillip is all right, Dickie."

"Ah, you do not like leaving your best boy for long, do you?"

"Well, he doesn't look very well just now, Dickie. I won't be long."

The door closed behind her; and with a sigh of relief, Richard settled himself at his ease for the first time that evening. Picking up the book on the tablecloth at his elbow, he opened the title page. *The History of the Borough, with an Itinerary* looked interesting; and for the next hour and a half, while Hetty went next door to see her parents, and Richard sipped his cup of hot-water—to flush the system, as recommended by a regular medical correspondent in *The Daily Trident*—he was absorbed in the pages, while thinking of what he might have missed by not continuing in the local Antiquarian Society, its field-days organised and led by the vicar of St. Simon, Mr. Mundy, accompanied by that siren, Miranda MacIntosh, for whom, in his secret thoughts, Richard still felt at times a sort of sentimental affinity, mingled with thoughts of dislike and derision for that Amazonian beauty: thus to dismiss from his mind the half-shameful erotic feelings which he had felt to be unworthy of himself, apart from the fact of his being a married man, and a father.

To his further secret guilt, Richard was now aware that some of these thoughts had been transferred to his daughter Mavis. He must take himself in hand!

Against the sky outside, seen through the uncurtained french windows looking on the garden, was a greenish flash. He got up to look, and saw by the clear haze of light in the lower sky that the fog had cleared. The glow came over the rooftops from the distant High Street, where electric trams ran in a blaze of light from shops and tall light standards—a street remembered by Richard for its darkness at night, relieved at long intervals by lamp-posts with single gas-jets when first he had come to the district; when horse-drawn waggons, loaded with corn and vegetables, had moved on their way through the borough to the Old Kent Road, and the markets of London.

There was quietness then—and peace.

Chapter 5

SWEET VIOLETS

THE Backfield, an area behind the garden fences of Hillside Road of about eight acres, was considered by Phillip to be his particular property. It was steep, grassy land, the upper slopes of which opened in wide cracks in summer, being yellow clay. In the highlands of this wilderness, among bird-sown thorn bushes, Phillip had his camp. He was the leader of a band of boys by virtue of ideas rather than of strength. Here they baked potatoes in the embers of a camp-fire, and conducted war with any rival bands that came that way, which was seldom.

Phillip had been forbidden by his father to climb the garden fence into the Backfield. He had been forbidden, too, to climb over the spiked railings, five feet high, which enclosed the L.C.C. park, called the Hill, to the north. The main reason, said Richard, was that it was bad manners to trespass on other people's land. In vain had Phillip, once, feebly suggested that the Backfield had no legal owner. It had been enclosed, he said, by Antill the builder, who hoped that after twenty years the land would become his, by a squatter's title.

"I don't know where you get that idea from, my boy. I know only that it is not my land, and therefore you will not go upon it."

Phillip forebore to say that he had heard about it from Gran'pa Turney. Gran'pa had declared that, as title could not be proved by Antill, no action for trespass could be sustained in court.

"Then it can belong to anyone who squats for twenty years, Gran'pa?"

"Certainly, m'boy. Why, are you going to enclose a bit of it?"

"Yes, Gran'pa, I have already, the bit above the red ballast heap. That's where our camp is, you know. We defend it from all comers."

"He-he-he," laughed Gran'pa. "You mean your prize-fighter friend does, don't you?"

Phillip did not like this reference to the boy who did his fighting for him. Peter Wallace, Phillip's right-hand man as he called him, was Scots. He was one of a family of brothers and sisters living in Charlotte Road. Peter Wallace was a sturdy, round-headed boy with close-clipped hair. He wore steel-framed glasses, being very near-sighted. He had an effective, indeed an invincible way of dealing with any opponent in a fight. Quietly Peter would remove his glasses, while his opponent stood on guard, waiting for the usual procedure of doing first dags, then cowardies—challenge and acceptance—before the real blows of combat. Quietly Peter would fold his spectacles, and put them in their case, while appearing to ignore the other boy facing him. Without glasses Peter could not see; his eyes and face were therefore expressionless; but suddenly he leapt upon his dim-seen opponent, flung his weight upon him, enwrapped him with his muscular arms, got the helpless boy's head under his left arm, while with the fist of his right hand he jabbed again and again at the downheld face until no fight was left in his adversary.

Phillip had no idea that Peter Wallace was such a terrible fighter until one morning, during the past Christmas holidays, he had come to his help upon the Hill. On that occasion Phillip had been set-upon by four rough boys from the Borough, who had recognised him as the " posh boy " who had asked them to stop tormenting a local destitute character called Jack o' Rags, who slept in an old swan's nest in the Randiswell Recreation Ground at night, and hung around the market stalls and carmen's coffee houses by day, for odd scraps of food. Jack 'o Rags was a bearded and dirty short man, with a hoarse voice, about whom there were many rumours, connected with wealth he had rejected; it was always the poor boys of the neighbourhood who sauced him, pelting him with horse-dung and other garbage.

"It's 'im, come on, mob 'im, boys!" cried the leader, recognising Phillip on the Hill during the Christmas holidays. Phillip stood his ground, too proud to run away. "Jack o' Rags is a poor old man, really," he said, white in the face.

Thereupon, seeing him afraid, the scowling bigger boy promptly rushed at him, with swinging fists, together with his three companions. Soon the four roughs were on top of Phillip, who between his sobs cried for help. Peter Wallace had run up; lugged off one boy and sent him spinning with a thump on the ear; butted a second in the stomach; bitten a third on the thumb; hauled off the leader, and then in the words of Phillip's Uncle Hugh, who had watched it all, "the bra' bracht moonlacht laddie proceeded to get the poor wretched devil's head into the position of a cask on stools, in order to tap his claret."

With such a brave friend beside him, Phillip thenceforth had felt confident to address boys bigger and stronger than himself, should they be doing things of which he disapproved—such as twisting the arms of other boys, throwing stones at stray dogs, or otherwise being guilty of what he deemed to be hooliganism. With Peter beside him he found that he could interfere in such cases with impunity, and redress what he fancied were wrongs. When Phillip was challenged to fight, Peter by his side stepped forward and said, "You want to fight me, do you?"

The dialogue on such occasions usually went on familiar lines.

"Yuss mate! An' I don't trouble what sawney tool-greaser I takes on—sparrer-knees or yerself—Four Eyes, cor, laugh at 'im! Four Eyes!"

Peter removed his glasses at this. He was so quiet that the other became threatening.

"Right, mate, you arst for it! Here's your dags. There's yer cowardies! Now 'it 'im! Come on, 'it 'im!", as he stood back on guard, scowling, fists clenched.

Fascinated, Phillip watched Peter Wallace during the folding and pocketing of spectacles; he waited with shortening breath for what was coming—the sudden leap, the clinch, the pummel, rapid and sustained, of right fist upon downheld face, blow after rapid blow until the falling away, the stagger, the doubling-up of the victim, his nose streaming with blood. Phillip felt tremulous pity for the beaten boy, coupled with the flaring feeling of terror-excitement he had when he saw flames spreading in the dry yellow grasses after he had deliberately set fire to them in the Backfield, on a scorching summer day.

One morning during the Easter holidays Phillip, Peter Wallace and his brother David, and another boy were baking potatoes in the embers of their fire, in a fold of the ground above the Red Ballast Heap. This was a conical mass of several hundred tons of burnt clay, left by Mr. Antill the builder some years before, after the completion of a row of houses to the south of the Backfield. Without any warning a shower of hard red lumps fell upon the camp, where the four boys were sitting. In the first volley Phillip received a hit on the nose which knocked him backwards; but Peter and David Wallace immediately gave chase. While the intruders fled from Peter's wrath over the spiked iron railings which marked the boundary of the Hill above, Phillip sat on the ground and cried with pain. His nose seemed very big, the skin was broken, and smarted when he touched it.

He thought he would go home; but changing his mind, he climbed over the railings and went to find out what had happened to the others. Peter had caught a boy near the tennis courts; and was sitting astride him, waiting for Phillip. When he arrived, Phillip saw that the prostrate boy was Alfred Hawkins, son of the barber in Randiswell, who had the cheek to be sweet on his sister Mavis.

Peter Wallace let Alfred Hawkins get up, but held his arm in a grip which, if forced, was supposed to break it at the elbow: a policeman's grip.

"Who threw the bit of ballast that hit Phillip? You did!"

"I never!"

"Then why did you run away?"

Alfred Hawkins was silent.

"Who were the others?"

"I've told you, I don't know. I never sin them before."

Phillip, fixing Alfred Hawkins with accusing eyes, said, "If you weren't with that band, then what were you doing in the Backfield?"

Alfred Hawkins looked on the ground.

"Ah, you daren't answer! Well, I know why! You came after my sister, didn't you!"

Alfred kept his gaze lowered.

Several people were watching the little group. Among them was Mr. Pye, who was with his two children throwing up their diabolos into the air, and catching them on the string again. Phillip felt uneasy as he came towards them.

"What's the trouble, Phillip?"

"Nothing, Mr. Pye."

"Well, you boys don't want to fight on a fine morning like this! It's almost sacrilege! Why not shake hands and make it up?"

None of the boys moved. Mr. Pye, after a pause to look at the white clouds passing in the sky, hummed a little tune to himself, and moved away to his children who were still spinning their new red diabolos.

"Come on, Peter," said Phillip. "Let's go. I know damn well what you were after, Alfred Hawkins, skulking round by my fence. If you trespass on my preserves again, you'll be sorry!"

Phillip's scorn of the blushing, smiling boy with the downcast glance left sitting by the tennis court was derived, unconsciously, from Richard's various remarks about lovers lying on the Hill at night. Phillip had developed a feeling of revulsion and scorn for "lovers", or any idea approaching the figment. They were *filthy* people. As for Richard's attitude, it too was an unconscious reflexion of ideas generally held among incomplete men towards sex: a suburban horror of irregularities, based on the fear of venereal disease, and its effects on the innocent.

This jangle of half-living had made Alfred Hawkins, in Phillip's eyes, a figure that had no relation to the truth of Alfred Hawkins. He was a dreamy, high-minded boy, whose mother had died when he was young. His father was half-paralysed, a barber owning a little shop in Randiswell, where poor people had their hair cut; and this by itself was almost enough, in Phillip's eyes, to show that Alfred Hawkins was not fit to have anything to do with his sister. Alfred Hawkins had gone into the Backfield to look at the house, from a distance, where the object of his dreams lived. He had stood there for an hour, elevated by the illusion of love, beauty, and service. He had been on his way back from his vigil when, fancying himself pursued by Peter Wallace, he had panic'd and taken to his heels.

Alfred Hawkins wrote little notes to Mavis with poems copied out in them, and Mavis replied similarly. Shyly, almost dreading to meet one another, they exchanged these tokens of the spirit in a crack of one of the posts of the fence.

"And what's more, Alfred Hawkins, you steer clear of my sister, or I'll know the reason why!" And with this warning Phillip went away, all unconscious that he was a pattern of his Father's moral indignation.

For twenty-five years Richard had been going to and from the City, and in that time, as he had estimated one recent evening while compiling his diary, he had crossed upon the flag-stones of London Bridge, in the roar of iron wheel-bands and horses' hoofs on granite, approximately on fourteen thousand five hundred occasions. He might have added, had he been a man used to observing himself objectively, that on the last ten thousand or so occasions he had done so almost entirely out of a sense of duty towards wife and family. Duty and decorum were the ruling abstracts of his life. However, in moments of unhappiness he did allow himself to reflect that, if he had not married Hetty—if he had gone away after Mr. Turney had forbidden him to see his daughter—if he had not weakly given in to the illusion of love—he would by now be an entirely different man, living an open air life of action in Australia, where his younger brother Hilary had farming and other interests.

City life, nevertheless, had its compensations. During the spring and summer months he could cycle into Kent and Surrey, and enjoy his own life of green fields, trees, water, the sight of sheep and cattle, the song of birds, sunlit flickering of butterflies. Now once again it was almost time to take to the wheel, to wipe vaseline off plated handlebar and pedal crank, and polish the enamel of the frame of his faithful iron steed. How well was that machine named—his all-black, all-weather *Sunbeam with the Little Oil Bath*, built in Wolverhampton, made to last a lifetime by British craftsmanship, the finest in the world!

Proud of his thoroughbred possession, its black frame lined with gold after twelve stove-enamellings, its bright parts solidly plated with nickel-silver, Richard, during the seasons of light and life, kept the Sunbeam polished, lubricated, and adjusted; while the Dunlop tyres were always pumped to the recommended resilience against those enemies of the pneumatic tube—the innumerable pale flints of the white and dusty roads of Kent.

At breakfast Richard announced his intention of cycling that Saturday afternoon to the Salt Box on the North Downs, for a tea of boiled eggs and brown bread and butter, should the weather keep fine. Would anyone (meaning Phillip) care to accompany him? No one apparently would.

"Well, don't all speak at once," said Richard, after a silence.

"How about you, Phillip?" said Hetty, with forced cheerfulness.

"I may have to play football for the House this afternoon."

"Well, if your name is not on the list, I am sure you will want to accompany your Father, won't you dear?"

Before Phillip could think what to say, Richard said, "Oh, please do not force the boy to do anything he does not want to do! My Father always used to say, 'One volunteer is worth ten press-men'."

"Do tell us about when you were a boy, Dads," said Mavis. "I simply love hearing about what you did."

"Humph," said Richard, not displeased. He was very fond of his elder daughter. He looked at his watch. "Another time, perhaps, my gipsy—— Hetty, I hope to be home at a quarter to two o'clock this afternoon."

A pleasant scene greeted Richard on his return from the City. The sun was shining brilliantly after a doubtful morning; the warm bright rays of April filled the south window of the sitting room, where the table was laid for lunch. The place had been cleaned, the floors polished by Mrs. Feeney, the charwoman. Everything looked fresh, almost new—a pleasing condition for Richard, so meticulous in his sense of neatness and order, both within and without a house. No smells of cooking, or over-cooking, greeted him from the kitchen; nothing was burning, or had burned, after boiling over; instead, the scent of—could it be?—wild sweet violets had greeted his nostrils as he entered the front door.

There they were, his favourite flowers, opposite his place at table, in a cut-glass jar with a silver rim—three dozen or so wild English violets, their stalks in clear water; and among them, in the centre of the deep purple petals, a solitary wood anemone, a wind-flower, fragile and white. Richard smiled with delight. Through the faint scent, instantly he perceived himself as a boy in the West Country, among happy brothers and sisters, bringing back from the woods the first violets of the year for Mother's boudoir. For a moment he saw her face, as she stood at the window, in the room above and back from the porch, with its iron-studded oaken door.

Memory, through the sense of smell, induces the most piercing of all emotions of the past, since that sense originally was old in man when sight and hearing were new. It is startling, it is stilling, it is sad when old scenes thus return, as in resurrection, from the past. Momentarily overcome, Richard stood still, by the french windows. Mother, Mother!

"Hullo, Dads!"

Mavis, in blue-serge gym uniform, had come silently into the room on plimsoled feet. She flung her arms round his middle, jingling his watch-chain.

"Hullo, my gipsy! Got a kiss for your old Dads?"

Stretching up, she kissed him on the lips, the only place on his face—apart from nose, brow, cheekbones, and eyes—which was not rough and tickly. Richard had never shaved.

"Do you like the violets, Dads?"

"Yes indeed. I got their scent as soon as I opened the front door."

"Would you like to have them, Dads?"

"How very kind of you, Mavis. But perhaps Mother would care for them."

"She knows I got them for you, Dads."

"Well, we'll all enjoy them, shall we?"

He moved the glass eighteen inches or so away from his place at table, putting it in the centre of the tablecloth. Unaware of the child's disappointment, he went on, "Where did you get them, Mavis, not round here, I'll be bound!"

"Not very far away, Dads! You see, we were playing lacrosse in the Rec.—I mean the Recreation Ground—this morning, and I heard two of the girls talking about some flowers they had got for Miss Wendover, you know Dads, our games mistress. I smelt them, and they were lovely. They got them from the garden of that big old empty house that goes down to the river, you know, the one you told us might be haunted when we passed on the walk one Sunday, where nobody lives, and the carriages stand in the coach-house, all wet from the slates fallen off the roof. So my friend and I went and got some, and we found the white one under some trees in the wood—what is it, Dads? Mum says it may be a kind of Flower of Parnassus."

"Oh no! That's an ordinary windflower. The proper name is wood-anemone. We had lots of them growing in the woods at home when I was a boy. This one's somewhat early, I fancy, for flowers are earlier in the west than here, owing to the Gulf Stream. Usually the anemones were out in force when the birds had laid, towards the end of April. We boys used to go through the woods with the under-keeper, looking for nests. It was safer, you see, to put them under broody hens. A wonderful sight it was, too, to look at twilight down the ride of one covert where the coops were, and see a row of lighted lanterns hung on sticks stuck in the ground. Can you tell me why the lanterns were there, now?"

"For people to see to ride by, Dads?"

"Oh no, my gipsy!" Richard laughed. "You see, a ride in a wood is a long clearing among the trees—though no-one would ride there in the rearing season, of course—but anyway, this particular ride was kept for the coops. And the lanterns were lit for—well now, try and guess!"

"Oh, I can't, Dads! Do tell me!"

"Try and think, young woman."

"Oh, I simply can't. Unless it was for the hens to see by."

"What, at night, when they were snug in their coops? Now what would they possibly want to see for?"

"Well, *what* for, Dads?"

"Ah, you must guess!"

"Oh, I simply can't. The lights must be for someone or other to see by."

"Ah, getting warmer!"

"The keeper?"

"A little warmer. He would not need to *see* the lights, I'll give you that hint."

The bright light suddenly ceased in the sitting or garden room. A rain-cloud covered the sun. A bird was singing in the top of the elm in the garden.

"He's got a nest somewhere, I'll be bound," remarked Richard, going to the french windows. "Can you tell me what bird that is?"

"A thrush, Dads! I was named after a thrush, wasn't I?"

"Yes, and it may well be after that very bird out there!"

Richard watched the slate roofs of houses beyond the waste ground shining again, as the cloud moved away.

"I bet he's got a nest somewhere near. Do you know how a mother thrush builds her nest?"

"Yes Dads, you told us on the walk last Sunday, don't you remember?"

"Ah, but do you know the difference between the *masoning* methods of thrush and blackbird, when they build their nests?"

"Yes Dad, I remember. The thrush uses cow-droppings and bits of tinder wood to line its nest, but the blackbird puts all the mud in the bottom of his, before lining with little grasses. Oh!"

"Why, what's the matter?" said Richard, his back to the room, as he drew pleasure from the new green of the elm at the bottom of the garden.

Mavis hesitated. She had, a moment before, caught sight of her brother under the table. Phillip's face had looked out, making a frantic grimace, an anguished request not to be betrayed. He had slipped under when he had heard Father's footfalls on the top step of three leading down from the hall to the passage below; and now was in an agony lest he be discovered, and be made to feel a fool, or worse, be rated for eavesdropping. He had hidden on sudden impulse, as a sort of joke; optimistic despite the fact that most of his jokes went wrong.

The last one had involved the spreading of jam. Father, during tea, had gone out of the room for a moment, and while he was out, he had put some apricot jam on Father's bread and butter. Mother had been having tea next door at Gran'pa's. He had thought Father would regard the jam as a mystery; instead, Father had been cross.

"I wonder if Master Phillip has oiled his cycle and cleaned the chain, in preparation for our spin this afternoon."

Phillip, under the table, waved a frantic hand at his sister to tell her not to look at him. Fortunately at the moment Mother called her to fetch the tray from the kitchen, and Father said, "Go and help your Mother, dear, like a good girl," and then followed her out of the room, to wash his hands.

"Phew!" exclaimed Phillip, as he crept from under the table. Hearing Father's footfalls going upstairs, he nipped into the kitchen, and washed his hands at the scullery sink. There was Timmy Rat, his pet, looking at him with pink eyes and twitching nose, behind the wire-netting of his box on the lid of the copper.

Timmy Rat was waiting to be scratched. Timmy Rat bolted out of its sleeping corner through a fret-work hole whenever it heard Phillip approaching, its tail knocking on the wood. Then standing up, its whiskered pink nose to the wire, it waited for Phillip's finger, closing its eyes for pleasure as the tip gently touched the basic pink skin of its ear. Phillip was supposed to wash his hands after handling Timmy Rat, but he did so only when Father was about.

The white rat was in its third year of life. It had been a present from Richard to his son, when Phillip had won his scholarship. That he had allowed Phillip, from the first, to keep it indoors, was a great concession to his son, though no one in the house suspected it. Richard had bought the rat on an impulse of some emotion, recalled from the scene of the boy in bed, nearly in a delirium, from fear of failure, on the eve of the examination.

A concession, yes: for to Richard, cleanliness certainly was next to godliness. He had no belief in a future life, as preached in the churches, chapels, and missions of Mother Country and Empire, as he had no idea of the meaning of the epigram, God is Love. Standing alone, Richard's whole living was devoted to doing his very best on all occasions. In money matters he was scrupulous to a farthing; his word was his bond; and whatever he did, in his own limited scope, he worked to the full extension of his powers. He lived austerely; he was a man of great loneliness, because he could not compromise with the views, or worlds, of others.

In vain this uncompromising man had tried to make his son see that the greatest care, the strictest attention to detail, combined with punctuality, cleanliness, a proper appearance, and (ironically) due regard for other people's wishes, were the only real basis of a happy and useful life. Canings, solitary confinement in bed with bread and water the only permitted nourishment, exhortations, pleadings—none of the ordinary ways of correcting an errant child in its early years appeared to have been of any use.

Yet on one occasion at least, the slow petrifaction of self had dissolved. On the eve of the scholarship exam, when he had visited his son in bed at eleven o'clock at night and found him with a temperature and on the verge of delirium, Richard had been astonished, bewildered, and touched by the despair, and anxiety to do the right thing, revealed by the cries of the little boy. He had related the moment to his own childhood; suddenly he had seen himself in his son, so that tears had come into his eyes—which of course he had concealed—as he perceived himself to be Father, a being with almost total power of happiness, or unhappiness, over the little mother and her three small children under his roof. He was his own Father over again!

The moment of revelation had passed; to be shut-in, and forgotten in the press of material, or superficial, life. Even so, Richard had kept a white rat when he was a boy: that had been in the country, far from sewers and the diseases of a city: nevertheless, on the day following the news that his son had won a scholarship, he had visited a pets shop in Leadenhall market, under whose glass roof he had often wandered during his luncheon hour in the City. For a shilling a young albino buck rat was his, to be carried in a wooden cage and kept on the floor of the Messengers' Box until he left the Moon Fire Office at six o'clock that evening.

Phillip had been greatly excited by the present. He had promised fervently to keep the box clean, the floor sprinkled with fresh sawdust half an inch thick, to be changed twice a week, regularly. Richard had explained about the risk of disease, with reference to the Black Plague and the cleansing Fire of London, both occasions being due to the Black Rat, he declared; for if people in the wooden City of those days had not been so insanitary and careless, neither plague nor fire would have resulted.

"And then—who knows—perhaps I should not be one of the men in the Moon! For it was only after the Great Fire that the idea of insurance was born!"

Timmy Rat, to give the rodent its baptismal (under the scullery tap) name, had lived in its box on the lid of the scullery copper for almost two years now. It was graniverous and herbivorous. It kept itself clean by frequent washing. Even so, Phillip observed that fleas managed to exist among its hairs. Timmy Rat hooked an occasional one, after rapid scratching, in one of the claws of a hindleg. The little brown tormentor was promptly cracked between Timmy's teeth: a slight but pleasurable shrimp-eating noise, while Timmy closed his eyes with satisfaction.

While he scratched Timmy's ear, Phillip was trying to puzzle out why those lighted lanterns had been hung on sticks along the woodland ride in Father's boyhood. Returning to the kitchen, he said to Mavis, "Be a sport, my gipsy, and say you just gave me a précis of what Father said to you in the sitting room. Else he'll suspect I was under the table. On my honour, I only went there for a lark, not to eavesdrop, so I wasn't doing anything wrong, was I, Mum?"

"That's what you say!" retorted Mavis. "When you say 'on my honour', I always know you are fibbing!"

"Mavis, Mavis!" exclaimed Hetty. To Phillip, "It is best never to hide when grown-ups are in the room, Sonny. They may want to talk about other matters, beyond children's understanding, you see."

"But Mavis isn't a grown-up."

"No, but you weren't to know that your Father might very well have sent her out of the room, and called me down for something, were you?"

"About me, you mean?" he asked quickly, his nostrils opening wider. "What have I done now?"

"Nothing dear, there's no need to feel alarmed, I am sure."

"Did you oil your old bike, Father wanted to know," said Mavis.

"I heard him, dolt!"

"Then you were eavesdropping. Wasn't he, Mum?"

"Only accidentally, Mavis. Not deliberately, I am sure."

"Not like you did when those girls at your school had the violets out of the haunted garden!" retorted Phillip, antagonism in his tone. "I bet I know why you went, like the copy-cat you are, to get some! To give to your beloved Miss Wendover, whom you're sweet on! I bet she was gone when you got back, so you decided to give the violets to Richard Edward Maddison, instead! Second-hand flowers!"

"Poof, a lot you know how other people think."

"And a fat lot you know, too, Brother Smut!"

"Hush Sonny, hush, your Father may hear you! And I won't have you use that common expression! I've told you before."

"Phillip is common himself," declared his sister.

"I bet I'm right about them stinking violets, anyway."

"Phillip, how dare you! I shall tell your Father if you are not a good boy."

"Father would laugh at you, in that case, Henrietta Turney. 'Them stinking violets' is what Jorrocks said, if you want to know. It's in that old red book in the bookcase."

"Well, even if it is, it isn't a very nice thing to say just now, dear, after the kind way Mavis brought them home." Hetty peered at the frying pan. "I do so hope these chops are done to your Father's liking."

She put down the pan, and opening the gas-oven door, felt to see if the plates inside were hot. A blast of torrid air struck her face, already flushed from cooking and the slight anxiety she always felt whenever her husband returned home, lest things should go wrong, and disappoint him.

"Oh dear, I'm afraid they are too hot! And last week they were not warm enough to please your Father! Now where did I put that cloth? Mavis—Phillip—oh dear, Doris has woken up."

The youngest child was in bed with a bilious attack. Her cry for "Mummie" came down the stairs. "Go and see what she wants dear, there's a good girl, Mavis. The pot's under her bed, if she wants to be sick again. Tell her I won't be long. I mustn't keep Father waiting for his lunch. Oh dear, no peace for the wicked!" she smiled at Phillip, as there came a knock on the front door. "Who can that be now?"

"I know, by the knock! It's Peter Wallace!"

Phillip went to the door. It was Peter, wanting to know if he would be coming out that afternoon.

"I can't today, Peter," whispered Phillip. "I've got to go on a bike-ride with my Father." He heard the unlocking of the bathroom door above. "Goodbye. I'll see you sometime," and closing the door, he darted back into the kitchen, in dread of being seen from the stairs above.

He heard his father's footfalls down the stairs, and with relief heard him going on down into the sitting room.

"Mother," called down Mavis, urgently from over the banisters above, "Doris' sick has turned green! Please come at once."

"Well, dear, it's probably only bile. Can't you look after her?" cried Hetty, with a rueful little laugh at Phillip, "It would happen just as I am dishing up, wouldn't it?", as she wiped her hands. "I've turned out the gas in the oven, the plates are nice and hot, I won't be a moment. Phillip, mash these potatoes, will you, like a good boy?"

Phillip heard Mavis saying upstairs, "I did try to comfort her, Mummy, but she wouldn't have me—she kept crying for you."

"Mavis, mash the spuds, will you?" he said, when his sister returned. "I want to look at my bike. Mustn't keep Father waiting after dinner."

Bilious attacks were not uncommon in the house, for some reason. Too many cheap and nasty sweets, declared Richard, referring to the children's bouts. He had never had a bilious attack; indeed, his wife had never known him to be ill. Over-eating, he said, or bad food, was the sole cause of stomach derangement; and people who did not bother to look after themselves deserved to be ill. Hetty often wondered if her husband really believed that her frequent nervous headaches, and the awful bilious attacks which she had about twice a year, prostrating her for as much as two days at a time, while she took only *nux vomica* in water, were due to her bad house-keeping? For Richard declared that the remedy lay in her own hands: in the avoidance of "tainted food". Tinned food was absolutely forbidden. It was one of the evils of Free Trade.

Grace having been said—"For what we are about to receive, the Lord make us truly thankful"—the meal went off without any unhappy incident. The chops were cooked to a turn, declared Richard; while Hetty, smiling with relief, said that she was so very, very glad. The spirit of the sunny April day, the prospect of a fine week-end, as shown in the mood of the master of the house, prevailed. After the mince pies, and Grace at the end, with heads bent as before—"For what we have received, the Lord make us truly thankful"—they were folding their table-napkins, and putting them into their silver rings, when Phillip said, "Please Father, may I ask a question?"

"You may, Phillip, but I shall not promise to answer it. It depends wholly on the question."

After this not unexpected reply, Phillip hesitated.

Richard, unaware of the effect of his words, waited. "Come on, out with it."

"It's about the lanterns on sticks in the wood at night, when you were a boy, Father. Mavis said——"

"Ha, ha! So you want to know why, do you? Well, curiosity killedthe cat, remember!" said Richard, prepared to enjoy the fun.

"Oh Dads, *please* be serious!"

"I am serious, Mavie. Curiosity killed many a stoat and weasel in the same place, too. There now, there's a clue, plain as a pikestaff!"

Phillip, nervously sitting on his hands, said, "Father! Would hollowed-out turnips, like those you and Uncle John and Uncle Hilary hung up in the trees, you remember you once told us, well, if they had candles inside, and slits for eyes and mouth and nose, would they do as well as lanterns?"

"You mean would they have done as well as lanterns on sticks, in the ride, near the keeper's cottage, as substitutes in the particular purpose for which the lanterns were used?"

"Yes, Father."

"Well then, why did you not say so? But if you mean, is there any connexion between the hollow turnips of Hallowe'en, and the lights by the coops, then the answer is no. Does that help you?"

Phillip had forgotten what his question was. He frowned at the bread platter, as though to find answer there.

"What you really want to get at is, *why* were the lanterns lit at night, isn't that so?"

Phillip hesitated.

"Answer your Father, dear," Hetty encouraged him.

"Now Hetty!" warned Richard, "Let the boy speak for himself."

The boy was silent.

"Come on, speak up, like a man! Don't spoil it all by sulking, old chap." Richard made an effort to subdue his impatience.

"I'll give you three guesses, as I gave Mavis before lunch."

"To scare poachers," Phillip guessed at random, hoping Father would not laugh.

"Well, you are warm, I'll say that much! Two more guesses. Mavis, you try too, come on, everybody join in! But if you know the answer, Hetty, please do not say."

"Of course not, dear." Hetty tried not to laugh. Only someone who did not know the answer must give it!

"Do you know, then?"

"No Dickie, I haven't the slightest idea."

"Oh, I thought that your merriment indicated that you did. Very well, I'll give you three guesses. Your turn now! Phillip has had one."

"To keep the hens warm, I say, then!"

"Oh pouff! One lantern every hundred yards, in a damp spring night, in the open, to keep hens in coops warm! Very cold, I am afraid! Mavis, your turn."

"For the hens to see if their eggs are hatching!"

"Quite cold. Phillip."

Phillip began to giggle, imagining a hen with a tea-cosy on her head, to keep her warm at night. Trying to put away the ridiculous vision, he frowned, screwing up his eyes as he stared about the room, trying to force the answer out of the ceiling. He clenched his hands, and made small grunting noises as his gaze moved about, straining for the answer to come to him. Lanterns, lanterns, lanterns in the dark mysterious wood, on sticks, in a row—signals to someone, but to who? He thought of Jack-o'-Lantern, the hero in the *Boy's Life* serial who rescued aristocrats from the guillotine: always being pursued by the drunken chief-of-police, Gaspard, who, in a most mysterious manner had been shot in one instalment and buried in the forest; then two instalments later he was chased on horseback through the same forest, caught, hanged to a tree, and found there the morning after, cold and stiff; yet in the fifth instalment in *Boy's Life*, which for some reason had been much bigger than the others before it, nearly as long and wide as *The Daily Trident*, Gaspard was alive again, this time in a punt, which later had upset, and drowned him in the River Seine. Much puzzled, Phillip had waited for the mystery to be solved, but *Boy's Life*, to his great disappointment, had not come out any more: and so he would never know the answer to the mystery.

Now, sitting at table, he imagined Jack-o'-Lantern thundering on a horse down the ride after tipsy Gaspard. What *could* he say to Father? Why did hens need lamp-posts at night? He giggled again, seeing them going out of their coops to cock their legs against them, like dogs. Suddenly the answer came.

"For the keeper to see they don't get out in the darkness!"

"You're getting warmer. Now it's Mavis' turn."

"To see that they are all right, Dads."

"A little warmer! Hetty. Come, you ought to know! What is it about chickens at night, that the hen-wife concerns herself with? I will give you a hint. What smells like a brewery?"

"I can't imagine, Dickie, unless it is thieves who've been drinking, poachers I mean."

Gaspard in the serial had once been described as smelling like a brewery, thought Phillip. Had Father read his copies of *Boy's Life?* He had not forbidden them, as they had come from the same people who did *The Daily Trident.*

"Well yes, poachers of a sort, perhaps. Now I'll give one more hint, my very last one. They have a very strong scent, and violets in early spring can get in the way of it."

Them stinking violets! Jorrocks!

"Foxes!" cried Phillip. "To scare the foxes!"

"Phillip wins the prize!" said Father. "A bar of Callard and Bowser's cherry toffee."

"Tell us some more, Dads, you know, what you did as a boy!" said Mavis.

Richard was sitting with his back to the fireplace, wherein coals, sticks, and paper had been laid that morning by Mrs. Feeney, ready for a match should the east wind return. He was warm about the face and chest, with the last of the sun shining through the southern window—for soon the gable end of the house below would cut off the direct April light and warmth. The sun expanded his spirit, as the wings of a hibernating butterfly draw life and hope after the dark seclusions of winter, renew colour, and power of flight, from the celestial orb. The children were always eager to hear about Father when he was a boy. Father as a boy could not be realized as such; Father in the stories as a boy was faceless, bodyless, without frown, fear, or shadow. He was something in the sun, unseen and formless; a feeling of enchantment.

"Oh do, please Father, tell us about when you were a boy!"

Phillip's face now had light in it; so had the face of Hetty, auroral almost with the pristine happiness, thoughtless and irresponsible, of childhood.

"Tell us about the tame partridges, Father, you know, when your Father's boots were the chicks' foster parents, after their mother's head was cut off in the hay field!"

"Ah, that was a wonderful sight, to be sure! Hearing my Father's voice on the lawn below his sanctum, where they had been left asleep on a rug, suddenly a dozen little partridges, no bigger than sparrows, would all fly together through the open window, and settle around his feet. Well, that was a very long time ago now. Let me see, it was—yes, all of thirty-four years ago, when I was a boy then, younger than Phillip is now."

"How old are you now, Dads?"

"Ah, my gipsy, that's a secret—but I will give you one hint—I am as old as my tongue, and a little older than my teeth! How old does that make me, do you think?"

"I know, forty-two, Father."

"How the dickens did you know that, my boy?"

"I saw it written inside that prize you won at school, Father, 'The Life and Explorations of Captain Cook'."

"Did you, b'jabers! You know too much, for a small boy!"

"You lent it to me, Father."

"Oh, I see. Well now, we must not waste this sunshine, Phillip. Is your bicycle in order—oiled, tyres pumped, chain lubricated, as I told you?"

"Yes, Father."

"Waterproof cape rolled under the pillion, tied to the forks?"

"Yes, Father."

"Well, I hope to show you some of my especial places in the north-west corner of the county of Kent, where you were born, my boy, though whether that makes you a Man of Kent I'm blest if I know! I fancy there is a line somewhere, one side of which one is a Kentishman, the other side, a Man of Kent. There are rapid changes taking place now in the world everywhere today, and by the time you are a man, probably all where we are going will be built over, and unrecognisable; and I, for one, think that will be a pity."

"Yes, it will," agreed Phillip, thinking of old Antill and the Backfield.

Chapter 6

BICYCLES AND BLUEBELLS

"TRAFFIC on the roads today is quite different from what it used to be," said Richard, as, watched by mother and the two girls, they stood outside the house, ready to set off on their cycle ride together. "Now pay attention, please. You must be most careful to keep in close to the left of the road. Follow me, do as I do, and you will be all right. And do not forget to hold out your hand before you turn a corner, to give any following cyclist, or driver of any vehicle behind you, ample warning of your intentions. This is a courtesy to other travellers, as well as a precaution for your own safety. One slip, and you may very easily find yourself a cripple for life, if nothing worse!"

"I know, Father."

"Oh you do, do you? And how do you know, may I enquire?"

"You told me before, Father."

"Well then, now I tell you again, my boy!"

"Yes, Father."

"I am sure Phillip will be very careful, dear," remarked Hetty.

Phillip thought Father's face was rather like that of a thin lion in the Zoo as he looked at Mother, and said, "Why are you interfering between me and the boy, may I ask? Please do not interfere. It confuses the boy."

"Yes dear, of course, naturally."

Hetty smiled—almost a hopeless smile—as she thought with a little inward tremor, what a pity it was that so seldom did Dickie approve of what she said, to try and help——. Then she saw the face of Mrs. Bigge next door, gazing with nods and smiles between her lace curtains. Hetty waved. Mrs. Bigge waved back.

Richard turned, and raised his cap. Thereupon Mrs. Bigge disappeared; she was hurrying to her front door. Mrs. Bigge was always ready to pop out and give a smile and a kindly word to her neighbours.

"You are always coming between the boy and me," sighed Richard, his tone between exasperation and complaint.

The truth was that he never meant to be irritable or carping with his wife. In his opinion it was her nervous attitude which was invariably the cause of upset between them. It had been so before the boy arrived; it was so now that he was growing up. Hetty, he considered, was a bit of a noodle at the best of times, and a negative influence as far as any real progress with the boy was concerned. In what had her solicitous over-care for the boy, during the thirteen years of his life so far, resulted? He was cowardly, untruthful, and a bit of a namby-pamby—all because he had been his mother's darling. And how did he repay her, for her constant attention to his precious little person? By being a little bully, as he had good reason to know, as soon as his own back was turned. He had his friend Peter Wallace to do his fighting for him: ah, he knew, he knew! Phillip bullied his sisters as well, lording it over all three of them when he, Richard, was out of the house. That was what happened with a doting mother who pandered to her precious little pet's every whim and pleasure.

"Well, it's time to be off now, if we are to get anywhere at all," announced Richard, as the door of "Montrose" opened, and Mrs. Bigge trotted past the little border of lobelia, daisy, and primula, edged with white marmoreal stones, to her gate.

"Have a happy time, Mr. Maddison! Give my love to the country! Enjoy yourself, Phillip!" she called out, as, with caps raised again, father and son set off down the road, wheeling their cycles.

Hillside Road was considered by Richard to be unsuitable for riding upon, chiefly owing to its flints. When alone, Phillip always rode down, to swoop round the corner; but now he followed Father sedately.

At the corner of Charlotte Road Richard prepared to mount his Sunbeam. "Follow me, Phillip. Keep both brakes on, old chap, down the hill. And don't forget to keep well into the left, as I told you, and do as I do."

"Yes, Father."

Thereupon Richard put one brown, single-strapped leather cycling shoe on the step projecting from the hub of his rear wheel; grasped the grips of his handle-bars firmly; pushed off with the right foot, and then, rising almost horizontally along the length of his Norfolk jacketed and knickerbockered body, adjusted himself to saddle and rubber pedal: a familiar sight to many who lived in the flats. It was almost a ceremony when Mr. Maddison mounted his all-black Sunbeam with the Little Oil Bath.

Phillip's bike was a second-hand Murrage's Boy's Imperial Model, costing two pounds nineteen and six when new. He had not had it long. Richard had chosen and approved it from a second-hand shop near Wakenham station, priced thirty shillings. Phillip had paid for it out of his scholarship grant of eight pounds a year. It had a fairly small gear, 68, which meant much pedalling to keep up with Father when the Sunbeam was in top gear with a following wind; the brakes, of the long lever type, shuddered as he put them both on; the front mudguard rattled, the bell was dented, making it cluck when you tried to ring it; still it was a bike, and would do until he bought a new one, with a 3-speed Sturmey-Archer gear, like Father's.

It took Phillip several false starts before finally he dared to throw his leg over the saddle. And to his relief, the vault into the saddle came off, without him squashing his nackers, as he had dreaded doing. In some exhilaration, he thought he would try riding with his hands off; but a sudden swoop towards the red pillar-box outside Peter Wallace's house made him clutch the handlebars, in time to avert a crash. Phew! that was a near one. Father was already round the corner.

Richard alighted on the humped bridge over both the railway station and the Randisbourne brook beyond, and looked back, waiting for sight of Phillip. He waited until the boy was riding up the slope, and then mounted again, to free-wheel down past the laundry on the lower side of the bridge, past the Randiswell Baths, the Police Station, the Fire Station with its red doors and new motor engine gleaming with paint and brass, at the corner of the High Street. Holding out his right arm, almost with the rigidity of a wooden railway signal, to indicate to following traffic—in other words Phillip, who must be given a good example in such matters—Richard turned to the right, and crossing over the tram-lines, rode parallel to the kerb-stone, about a yard from it, which he considered to be a proper distance.

The new chocolate-and-yellow electric trams of the London

County Council now ran through the High Street of the Borough as far as Fordesmill. Many familiar trees had vanished during the laying of the steel rails; Caroline and Georgian inns, weather-boarded cottages and houses, long part of the scene of Richard's life as he cycled out into the country, were in process of being pulled down, to be replaced by ugly, modern buildings. Ah well!

However, the surface of the road was a decided improvement. Smooth wooden blocks, saturated in creosote, were far superior to the old grey stone metalling, the laying of which had been so laborious—first the digging up of the old surface, then the spreading of cartloads of granite stones, followed by crushing with steam-roller, watering with cart, more crushing and more watering, while the unemployed, temporarily in work, dilatorily brushed, with long-handled brooms, the grey liquid upon the flattened surface. Did the grey mud thus created bind the surface together? Richard doubted it. The result had looked very nice immediately afterwards, no doubt—level, grey, and shining—but the mud so created worked up through the stones when it rained, making the surface slippery and treacherous. Waggon-wheels in winter increased the mud; and then in summer up it all went in dust, behind beastly motorcars driven by road-hogs who had no consideration whatsoever for others upon the road. The trap beyond Fordesmill, where hidden police waited with stop-watches, had caught a good many exceeding twenty miles an hour, and jolly well serve them right, too!

At this point in his thinking, Richard decided to dismount, and give Phillip the benefit of his advice. He held up his arm—a rigid signal—several seconds before reversing the former process of mounting. Phillip stopped by lifting his leg over the saddle, and gliding up, his weight on one pedal, the brakes of the Imperial Model shuddering on rusty rims.

"In this coming age of the motorcar there is a further danger I must warn you of, Phillip," said Richard, "and that is the danger of skidding in the tramlines. This applies also to the condition of the new wood blocks after rain. Both are treacherous. You must always cross tramlines boldly, at a wide angle, to avoid catching your front wheel in them, and taking a toss; but always make sure, before you do so, that the road is clear behind."

"Yes, Father."

"We must expect April showers at this season of the year."

"I've got my cycling cape, Father. I don't mind a bit of wet."

"Still, we must look after you, you know, old chap. Can't have you getting rheumatism at your age."

Phillip had had a touch of rheumatic fever as a child. This was supposed to be the cause of his comparative lack of growth.

They remounted. Soon father, followed by son, had passed the Bull at Fordesmill, the tram-terminus, and were upon the main road, of pot-holed metalling and drying grey mud. In front, round the curve, was the police trap for motorcars. Phillip looked for policemen hiding behind garden fences with stop-watches, but he saw nothing. Then they were past the houses, in country with cornfields on one side, and meadows on the other, beyond tall elms lining both sides of the road.

Behind Phillip, thundering along, was one of the new white steam-omnibuses. He kept well in to the left, hoping that Father would go faster, for it was possible to race a steamer, at least to keep them behind; but Father went on steadily as before. Phillip trembled as the hissing monster, bright fire blazing under its bonnet, roared past, its solid tyres bumping into the pot-holes and splaying out streaks of liquid mud. He tried to keep up with it as it drew away, but with Father in front, it was hopeless. People were riding inside, and on the open top, straw hats on heads.

Father said, when they stopped later on at Cutler's Pond, that when the bus had passed it was probably exceeding the speed limit of twelve miles an hour.

"Beastly things, I wish they had never been invented."

"Hear hear," agreed Phillip.

Cutler's Pond was a familiar scene, with its moorhens, little island with willows, and a cherry tree now in blossom upon it; and mud-bubbles rising up where eels moved unseen. Phillip and his sisters had walked there with Father on many a Sunday morning, never tired of the story of how Father had once seen, with Mother, a monster trout under the road bridge, on the day before he, Phillip, was born. They had always looked over, hoping to see a trout; and Phillip did so today; but there was nothing, as usual, beyond sticklebacks.

"Now I will take you to one of my special places, Phillip."

They turned back the way they had come, and repassing a big house beside the road, with a high wall round its courtyard, cycled up the lane beyond.

At a bend in the lane, with some woods in front, Richard dismounted.

"This," he said, "is Whitefoot Lane. It has been for me a veritable oasis. You would think you were in the real country higher up, with the arable and the strips of woodland on either side. I will show you, farther on, the keeper's cottage where your Mother and I spent our honeymoon—let me see, it was in eighteen ninety-three, you were born in 'ninety-five—how old are you, just turned of thirteen, yes"—said Richard, working backwards—"it will be fifteen years ago, this coming November, that we were married. It was a hole and corner business, but there were reasons for it, I am sorry to say."

Richard consulted his watch.

"H'm, perhaps we had better give it a miss today. We want to make the most of the afternoon, don't we? Very well then, we'll turn back now, and make for Reynard's Common without further ado. We'll visit the Fish Ponds, and then perhaps we might go on to Green Street Green, and the Salt Box beyond, for tea. That is another favourite spot of mine. The old woman serves the most delicious boiled eggs with brown bread and honey in her parlour. I think perhaps that will be enough for your first day, but bit by bit I'll show you my particular spots, then when you are older you will be able to visit them by yourself, won't you, old chap?"

Richard hoped that his son would reply that he would like always to go with him; but Phillip dutifully replied, "Yes, Father."

It was a weary boy who pedalled past Cutler's Pond some hours later, in the mellow rays of a westering sun gleaming on the water, still following well in to the left of the road. Father and son returned as sedately as they had gone; but now they were being passed by hundreds of other cyclists, in droves and couples, or singly, all hurrying, staring ahead as with tinkling bells, backs bent, faces set as though they were in for a race, they crouched over handlebars, while enormous bunches of bluebells, white clustered ends of long stalks dropping, were tied behind their saddles. Phillip thought that the cyclists' faces were nearly as white as the stalks where they had been pulled out of the bulbs in the leaf-mould. A few motorbikes went by, drivers with caps the wrong way round, held there by goggles; but for every motorbike or motorcar, there were fifty cyclists and a dozen traps and dog-carts, also seeming to be in a hurry to get back to the streets, alleys, and lodgings of South London, from which they had come.

Some traps stood outside the Bull by the tram-stop. The ponies' heads were held by ragged boys and men; but the cyclists went on, bells tinkling, swiftly among the gleaming tramlines. Here and there on the wood-paving bluebells lay, scattered amidst bits of paper and orange peel, banana skins and squashed horse dung. Hawkers, barrow boys, men beside wooden stands displaying fruit and vegetables, clothes, fish—the Salvation Army Band playing, shrill voices of women singing to the beat of tambourines—it was the familiar Saturday evening scene. To Phillip, it felt rather dull to be going home again; but he had Ballantyne's *Coral Island* out of the Free Library to read, and that wonderful story would last all through Sunday, thank the Lord.

Richard, relaxed in his armchair in the sitting room, read *The Daily Trident*. Once again his eye glanced over the paragraph of the Cannon Row Police Station; wherein his sister's name was mentioned with other Suffragettes who had been creating a nuisance. What a mess Dora had made of her life! Why was it? He paused, the paper held unseeing before him. He sighed. Well, it was no good thinking about the past. Nor was it much good thinking about the present. The old days were gone, never to return.

"Phillip."

"Yes, Father."

"I hope you will never go into woods belonging to other people, regarding it as a right. Look at the way those hordes of cyclists behave—they go out in their hundreds, nay, thousands, nowadays, and pull up and destroy everything they can lay their hands on. Nothing is sacred to them."

"Yes, Father."

"In a few years, at the rate things are going now, there won't be a bluebell left, or a wood unravaged, for miles around London. I think it is a great pity."

"So do I, Father."

"It is all very well for people like this Lloyd George person to talk of equality, and the wickedness of landlords, but if he and men like him have their way, what would be left of the beauty of the countryside?"

"Yes, Father."

"Are you listening to what I say?"

"Yes, Father."

"Then please have the courtesy to remove your eyes off your book when I am speaking. What is the book?"

"*Coral Island*, Father."

"Ah, that's a good book. A spiffing yarn, isn't that what you would call it? A capital story, as my Father would have said."

"Yes, Father, it's frightfully exciting!"

"Well," said Richard, picking up *The Daily Trident* once more. "I won't disturb you further."

After a few moments he put down his paper and said, "There is something on my mind I must say to you, Phillip. I am sorry if I appear unpleasant, but I have my duty to do. You are old enough now to begin to think of fighting your own battles. Do you know what I mean, my boy?"

Phillip swallowed, before saying, huskily, "Yes, Father."

He was relieved when Mavis came into the room. She sat on Father's lap, while Phillip sneered inwardly as Father put his arm round her, and kissed her. Sucking up to Father, he thought—she would!

Richard touched her brow with his lips, and then, feeling a flow of life in him, her mouth.

"Now Mavis," he said immediately afterwards, in a sharp voice, "I think it is time you went to your Mother, to enquire if you can be of any help to her."

Feeling that this was a good time to get away, Phillip went to sit by himself in the front room, to enjoy the coming of the pirates to Coral Island.

Chapter 7

BULLY BOY

ON the following Saturday something occurred which so upset Richard that, hearing his brother Hilary was home from his travels, and staying with Victoria at Epsom, he determined to cycle over on the Sunday and confide his distracted thoughts in his brother and sister. He took Phillip with him: a very subdued and silent Phillip, who obediently pedalled behind his father all the way to the Crystal Palace, across Thornton Heath, through the areas of the herb fields around Cross Aulton (now being built upon) and so to the North Downs and the polite pleasances of villadom, where among lime-trees, and far from Sunday noise of pony-cart and motorcar, lived his brother-in-law George Lemon. Never once during the journey did Richard speak to his son: the boy was in disgrace.

They arrived at The Lindens at noon. It was a sunny day; the blossom of cherry, plum, and pear gave the garden a virginal appearance. The visit was unexpected; and though the visitors were made welcome, Richard would accept no hospitality beyond a glass of water. Phillip, anxious to conform to everything his father required, said, when asked if he would like some ginger pop, that he would like a glass of water also.

Pressed to stay to luncheon, Richard thanked his sister, but said that he must be getting back shortly. The feeling of constriction was so obvious, despite the superficial geniality in the garden, that Victoria asked her brother if all was well at home.

"Yes," replied Richard, but in such a way that his sister knew something was troubling him. After some conversation on general topics, she invited him to see the conservatory, and Hilary accompanying them, Phillip was left alone with his uncle George Lemon, and Aunt Beatrice, the beautiful person he remembered as a child.

Soon, under the influence of the sympathetic Cornish brother and sister, Phillip's misery broke, and his tears fell.

"My pet," said Beatrice, looking with her big blue eyes into his face, and taking his hand. "Confession is good for the soul. Poor Phil," she smiled at her brother. "He was always in the wars!"

"Let's come up the garden, to your old hiding place among the apple-trees," said George Lemon. "Then you can tell us all about it."

Meanwhile, inside the house, Richard was unburdening himself to his brother and sister.

While he had been crossing the Hill from Wakenham station a week previously, enjoying the south wind of the equinox on his face—walking with his long swinging stride, rolled umbrella on one arm, bowler hat in hand—Richard had been accosted by a neighbour, known to him only by name, who had stopped him to make a complaint about Phillip's behaviour.

Richard did not particularly care about the appearance of Mr. Pye, who was fat; while he himself was lean. However, he listened to what he had to say with some appearance of courtesy. He was wanting his lunch; and Mr. Pye's manner and attitude were, although correct, in some way antagonising. Having raised his grey homburg hat, which matched his grey, heavy, clean-shaven face, Mr. Pye had begun, in punctilious tones that were, in Richard's ears, verging on oilyness.

"I trust that you will forgive me for what I am about to say. Believe me, my dear Sir, I speak only after some considerable hesitation, fully aware that I am liable to be accused of undue interference. Be that as it may, I consider it my duty, as a neighbour, to inform you of what I have seen this morning, and upon other occasions. If it were, indeed, an isolated incident, I should not be undertaking what is, as I see it, my duty, however unpleasant. But I will come to the point. Your boy," went on Mr. Pye, while with the ferrule of his polished malacca stick he disturbed a pebble on the gravel path, "is in the habit of provoking quarrels with other boys, here on the Hill, for no other reason that I can see except to get his friend—Peter Wallace I think is his name—to thrash them for him. I cannot call it fighting, for Peter Wallace's practice is to get his opponent's head under his arm, and then to pummel his face so violently that I wonder serious injury is not done to the victim's sight. More than once I have seen Phillip and the Wallace boy walk away, leaving the victim with his head hidden in his arms, sobbing upon the grass. It is, in my opinion, the most disgraceful behaviour, and I think you will agree with me, as Phillip's parent, that it should be stopped."

Mr. Pye was trembling as he finished his prepared speech.

"You are aware that you are making the most serious charges against my son, sir?" said Richard, as he strove to control his feelings. "I have my witnesses," said Mr. Pye, his face now a yellowish-green.

"Well, I shall have to talk seriously to my boy. Good-day to you," and with a stiff small bow, Richard walked on towards his home, feeling that the entire spring day was now spoiled. There was, in his mind, no doubt of what his neighbour had said. Mentally Richard addressed several remarks to the image of his wife, on a familiar theme of the inferior nature of her son, and its obvious derivation from her family. Of one thing he could be sure: Phillip did not get it from him, or from any of the Maddisons!

At the same time, was he not taking too much on trust? There were some fearful little ruffians on the Hill; and after all, the antagonisms of small boys were natural. And on this slightly easing thought, Richard entered his house.

The subject of Phillip, as a bully—safe behind his friend—recurred again that evening as he showed Hetty the latest news of his blessed sister, the crack-pot Dora. There it was, for all to see and to read in *The Daily Trident*.

"Theodora, with many others of her sort, was detained yesterday for an hour and more by the police, after a march along the streets with banners, to protest, if you please, to Campbell-Bannerman in Downing Street, against some of their unruly, window-breaking friends being sent to prison for hooliganism! There is her name, in the list of viragoes taken to Cannon Row Police Station. Blest if I know where she gets it from!"

With Dora in mind, offset as it were by Mr. Pye's complaint, Richard said nothing just then to Hetty about Phillip.

On the following Saturday morning, coming home from school, Phillip thought he saw members of a rival band upon the lower slopes of the Backfield; and swarming over the spiked railings, he and Peter Wallace crept down to the camp in the hollow beside the thorn bushes. From here it was possible to move, without being seen, almost to the back-garden fence of the Rolls' house at the top.

When the two friends got there, they stood up, and seeing no one, Phillip told Peter to hide in the grass, while he would do some exploring.

"Perhaps if they think I'm alone, they'll come for me," he said. "If I give a yell, come to my rescue. Only don't be long —you know I can't fight."

No-one was in the elm thicket behind his own garden fence, which had grown up when the trees had been felled some years previously. Phillip lay down, to be able to see along the various dog-tunnels in the black thickness of the twigs. No one was there.

About to climb over the fence to his garden, to get his bamboo stick for throwing clay bullets, he was surprised to hear Mavis crying on the other side. Mother was speaking. He listened.

"But Mother dear, we weren't doing anything! We were only talking."

"I know, dear, but other people may think otherwise, if they see you over there from their back-windows. It would not be nice, Mavis, so you must promise me never to do it again. You don't know life as I do, dear."

"But Mummy, he is ever so nice really! And we were only talking!"

"I know nothing about the boy, except that he is not the kind you ought to consort with, Mavis. Your Father would be very angry, if he were to hear of it. So don't let me hear of such a thing again!"

Then they went indoors. Phillip climbed over the fence. In the sitting room sat his younger sister Doris, playing with her dolls'-house.

"What's up, Doris? Tell me, quick!"

"Mavis was lying in the grass."

"Who with?"

"Alfred Hawkins."

At this, Phillip became hotly indignant. He ran into the kitchen and demanded to know why Mavis had been in the field again with Alfred Hawkins. *And lying in the grass with him*—his sister!

"You ought to be ashamed of yourself!"

Hetty was surprised, and a little saddened, to notice how Phillip was beginning to adopt his father's intolerant manner in some things. It might be Dickie talking! It was really comical, her little boy so indignant, so angry: at any rate, it showed that he had some care for Mavis after all!

Phillip rejoined Peter, who had found a robin's nest. After feeding the young with bread-pills on a twig, they went back to their camp, and dug for mica in a crack in the clay. Phillip had an idea that where there was mica, there might be diamonds. Anyway, it was fun pretending.

Father was not due home yet, so there was plenty of time. Then Phillip began to feel hungry, and suggested they depart. Peter, he said, could come over his fence, and through his house to Hillside Road, a short cut to his own home.

They went down to the Red Ballast Heap, and along the alley fence behind the row of houses built by Antill several years ago; and crossed over the dried-out marn-pits, now grass-grown, below a clay cliff at the top of which, a dozen yards back, were the familiar fences—Rollses', Pye's, Gran'pa's, his own, Bigge's, Groat's, "Sailor" Jenkin's, Todd's, the "Higher" Low's, (who were Catholics, and called "Higher" Lows by Hetty to distinguish them from the "Lower" Lows who lived near the cemetery) and downwards, among the not-knowns, to No. 1. Phillip knew all about their gardens, by the rubbish they tipped over their fences—this one had a decent lawn, that one threw over a lot of weeds in spring, another always had straw, with old strawberry plants. The only clean ones were his own, as Father composted everything; and Mr. Rolls'.

Scrambling up the grass-grown clay cliff, where he had once found a hedgehog's nest, Phillip saw a figure standing by his garden fence, half-hidden behind the leaves of an elm sucker.

"So you sneaked back again, did you?"

Alfred Hawkins smiled feebly at Phillip. He had on a new jacket, and a butterfly tie. His hair was neatly brushed.

"Hullo," he said, going red in the face.

"You horrible cad, Hawkins!" said Phillip, disliking his tie almost violently. "I warned you once before not to come to our fence!"

The upshot was that the quiet boy, a sad drooping smile as though fixed upon his face, was seized by Peter Wallace; and a minute or so later he left, crying silently, his new bow-tie and jacket front splashed with blood.

"I bet he won't have the nerve to come after my sister again," said Phillip, who was quivering within. He now felt sorry for Hawkins. Also, he felt as though part of himself was gone, or broken within.

Another feeling arose in him a couple of hours afterwards, when Mr. Hawkins the barber, hauled up Charlotte Road in a bath-chair by his two sons and an assistant from the shop, called to see Peter's father. Phillip was in Peter's garden when he arrived. He swarmed immediately over Peter's back fence, and dropping into Randiswell Lane below, ran up to the cemetery gate, round Ivy Lane, up the footpath by St. Cyprian's Church, and over the grass to the gully; and so home, in a state of alarm.

Meanwhile Peter Wallace was confronted by three severe faces a foot and more above his own. After the interview Peter was lugged upstairs, and his trousers forcibly removed, preparatory to being thrashed by his father, who was a sergeant in the Volunteers, the London Highlanders. In the bedroom a struggle ensued, by no means a one-sided affair, for after the first slash of the cane Peter sprang at his father, clung to him, and bit him across the back of the hand, making his teeth meet through the skin.

Later, as Phillip was pretending to learn Latin in the kitchen, there was a knock on the front door. Phillip recognised the knock, and ran to open the door. There in his best suit stood Peter Wallace. Without preamble Peter Wallace said,

"My father says you are a nasty little coward, and that I am to tell you that you can fight your own battles in future," whereupon he turned away and departed, leaving Phillip with a pale face.

He had always known he was a coward, and been ashamed of not being able to fight for himself; now he was branded a coward in Peter's, and everyone else's, eyes. Should he take poison? There was some, in the little red boxes of his *Magician's Chemical Set* upstairs.

He closed the door quietly, and went into the front room, to sit down and think about it all. With a shock he saw Father there already. He was oiling the motor of the Polyphone. Why had he not swallowed the poison straight away? Father looked at him sternly.

"Well," he said. "Your chickens appear to have come home to roost."

Phillip looked at the carpet.

"I have heard about your practices, my boy, from a neighbour, but I have not said anything so far, as I thought I would give you the benefit of the doubt."

Phillip looked at Father's face; then quickly his glance fell again to the carpet, while the word *terra-cotta* kept recurring to his mind, as this was the colour Father said was reddish-brown in the carpet pattern.

Wagging his finger, Father said,

"You are, as your friend has just said, and as I have had on more than one occasion to remark, an unpleasant little bully. I have already received, as I have told you, a complaint about your conduct from Mr. Pye, which substantially bears out that you have made a regular practice of assaulting others with the aid of your bully. Now let me tell you this!" cried Father, his voice going higher, as he shook his finger more towards him. "A few minutes ago, as I was coming up the road, I had a further complaint from the invalid father of the boy you caused to be injured!"

At this point Hetty opened the door, and seeing them there, stopped.

"Oh, I didn't know anyone was in here! I'll come back later, dear, if you two are talking."

"No, remain if you please!" cried Richard. "You may as well hear the latest about this precious boy of yours!"

"Oh dear, what is it now, what have you been doing to annoy your Father, Phillip?"

Phillip, hanging his head, began to weep.

"There you are, you see! Found out, he blubbers, like all bullies!"

Richard then recounted to his wife what had happened.

Turning to Phillip, Hetty cried, "Why did you do it, Sonny? It isn't like you at all! I just can't understand it, Dickie! The other boys on the Hill call him 'Grandma', you know, because he is usually so concerned when smaller boys are hurt. He really does try and stop them from getting bullied, you know. Oh dear, I don't know what things are coming to!" She sat down, sighing deeply, and held the arm of the chair. "I don't understand, Dickie! Why, when it rained once, Phillip lent his overcoat to a little boy who had not got one, and took him home to Randiswell, because he was crying, leading him by the hand! Hern the grocer told me. He thinks the world of Phillip, you know."

Renewed sobbing from Phillip followed this unexpected tribute. He thought he would swallow the brown crystals in the red box in his *Magician's Chemical Set*, labelled *poison*—the potassium cyanide crystals.

"All the same, his present conduct has been most unmanly, to say the least of it! So much so, indeed, that this fellow Hawkins went to the Police about the assault on his boy. And only a few moments ago, I heard what Phillip's friend had to say to him. He called him, in these very words, 'a nasty little coward'. Is that not so, Phillip? Answer me, sir!"

"Yes, Father."

"I think it was something to do with the boy in question wanting to see Mavis, Dickie," said Hetty; and immediately she regretted her words for Richard said:

"Oh, and what about, may I ask? This is the first I have heard of it."

Thereupon, in reply to Father's questions, Phillip stammered out part of the story of Alfred Hawkins waiting for Mavis over the fence, and going with her into the long grass.

Richard remained silent after this information. His face was thin-looking. He breathed deeply. Then, controlling his emotion, he said, his voice much higher than usual, "This puts quite a different complexion on the matter."

He left the room; but returned almost at once, to enquire where Mavis was. Hetty said she was on the Hill with her little friends, playing tennis. Putting on his straw-yard, and taking his walking stick, Richard went to find her, his face set.

"You bad, bad boy, Phillip!" complained Hetty, in distress, when Richard's footfalls had gone up the road. "Now your Father has put an entirely wrong construction on Mavis' action! There was no harm in it at all, in the first place! But now Father has got an idea into his head, goodness knows where it will end."

It ended, for the meantime, in Richard returning with a weeping Mavis. Hetty watched anxiously through the window as Richard closed the gate behind him. Then she went to open the door. Richard said, "Now up to bed you go, my girl!"

"Oh, Dickie, I beg you! There is some mistake, I am sure!"

"Dr. Cave-Browne will be able to decide that, I consider! Then I shall be able to determine whether or not you are a proper person to have a young girl in your charge! I think your injuries, years ago, must have affected your brain!"

This was a reference to the time when Thomas Turney, having learned that his daughter Hetty was secretly married to Richard, while still living at home, had knocked her down; and she had remained in a fit for several hours. Hetty had been pregnant, with Phillip, at the time.

Hetty began to weep. Phillip did not know what his father had meant; but the sight of his mother crying made him exclaim,

"Don't, Mum, don't! It is all my fault! I will atone for it."

Outside he heard Father saying, "No, I will never forgive you, my girl! I do not love you any more," and Mavis' sobbing as she went up to bed.

"There, you see what you have done, my son?" whispered Mother, her face all twisted with crying. "Your Father——" Her mouth worked, but could not pronounce words. Phillip went into the scullery, to cry to Timmy Rat.

When darkness came, Mavis got up from her bed, unknown to anyone, dressed herself, and creeping downstairs, opened the front door and hastened up the Hill, still weeping, with a wild smothered idea of running away and never returning. She believed that her father had ceased to love her. At the top of the gully she wandered about aimlessly in the darkness, finally going down into the grassy area known as the Warm Kitchen; and lying down, hoped she would catch a chill and die.

It was nearly midnight when Richard, now alarmed, found her near the Bandstand, cold and shivering, and took her home to the house in Hillside Road wherein two other children lay in bed, Doris at one end of the house and Phillip at the other, awake and frightened in the darkness. Mavis was given some hot milk with brandy in it, then put to bed with a stone hot-water bottle, after kneeling with her mother and saying her prayers, asking God to protect her and all her family, and to make her a better girl in future.

On the return from Epsom, Richard never referred to the incident again; but no longer did he and Mavis share their former affection. The shock to the delicate, fanciful girl, believing herself no longer loved by the father she adored, was greater than Richard ever knew; it lasted throughout her life, long after he had forgotten the night when she had run away.

Phillip went down to apologise to Peter Wallace, and to Alfred Hawkins. Peter would not shake hands, but Alfred would. This made Phillip cry. After apologising, he felt relief that now there would not be any more horrible fighting to be done by Peter Wallace. He promised his mother that he would reform all his wicked ways; and with this in mind, he avoided interference with other boys, big and small. Occasionally, however, the taunt of "Grandma" was borne to him across the grassy spaces, where in the evenings of longer light boys played their versions of cricket, football, hares and hounds, and other pastimes.

Then hope came to him one spring day, as he was walking down from the Heath, after school. It came in the form of a penny weekly magazine, of a kind he had not seen before.

Chapter 8

ENIGMA VARIATIONS

WITH an expression of thoughtful care upon his face, Phillip walked sedately down the hill from school, satchel slung on shoulder. At the bottom of the hill, where the trams passed, he saw a man standing and giving away something white. The man had a white bundle under one arm, there was another pile at his feet, resting on a sack. Boys were walking away with copies.

Phillip took one. Eagerly he read the title on the front page, *The Scout*, *Volume* 1, *No.* 1. He walked on under the railway bridge, absorbed in the pages, and continued along the pavement beside the brook which he could just remember being made to flow in a concrete bed behind iron railings, after old black willow trees on its bank had been pulled out by horses. Leaning on the railings, he waited for Milton, but when he did not appear, he crossed over to the Obelisk, where the electric trams stopped; and walking on, came to Mill Lane. Under another railway bridge beside a wood-yard; and so to a row of small early Victorian cottages facing the Randisbourne, and a tall and dingy brick mill, which was worked by a water-wheel.

Mill Lane, or Botany Bay as some called it, was a poverty-stricken place, noisy with ragged bare-foot children, slinking dogs, and women with tousled hair. Some, in winter, had mud on their clothes; Ching said it came from being whores, a word he pronounced hoo-ers. Phillip was frightened by them.

Still reading, Phillip went along the path of trodden cinders towards the other end of the lane, past the row of tiny dingy cottages, and through two posts sunken there to stop the entry of carts. Under another railway bridge, and up the road rising to the tree-grown outline of the Hill. All these objects and places were insubstantial to Phillip. He was reading *The Boys of the Otter Patrol.* Up and over the Hill he went, past the Socialist Oak, and so down the gully.

Leaving the gully behind, he was passing the park gates, when he saw on the asphalt pavement opposite Gran'pa's house a small boy throwing stones at one of the sheep on the other side of the railings. There was a bigger girl with the small boy. Phillip crossed over, and had said no more to the boy than, "I say, please don't do that, for the ewe has got a lamb!" when the girl, who was thin and had very black hair, turned on him and smacked his face hard, several times. Phillip shut his eyes. The pain and humiliation made him cry. He turned away without a word, and was crossing the road when Mr. Pye came out of his gate and pointing at him cried,

"I saw what happened! Let me tell you this, you thoroughly deserved all you got!"

Deeply mortified, Phillip walked on down the road, hoping that Mr. Pye had not recognised him as Mr. Maddison's son, and would think that he lived down Charlotte Road somewhere. Turning the corner, he hung about for some moments, while wiping away the signs of tears with his handkerchief; then noticing that a woman in one of the flats opposite was looking at him, he hurried up Hillside Road, and slipped through his own gate.

At tea, eating hot beef-dripping toast with his mother and sisters, Phillip did not speak. *The Scout* took all his attention. Hetty was glad to observe his absorption in the new magazine, which he had shown to her on coming downstairs after washing his face and hands and brushing his hair, determined more than ever to turn over a new leaf.

Hetty was happy because the meal proceeded without any of the usual bickering between Sonny and Mavis; the two were antagonistic, they were different from one another in the first place; and, she feared, Dickie's marked preference for Mavis, as soon as she was born, had very early in life put Phillip's nose out of joint. She had tried to show equal affection and love to the children, always; but Dickie had been the one they looked to, until—but beyond that point Hetty flinched away in thought.

"It seems a very nice paper, dear. What is it about?"

"Boy Scouts, Mum. Look, it tells you how to track wild animals, and recognise birds by their footmarks in snow."

He turned over a page. "This tells you how to build a boat,

and whoa back, look at this, how to tie all sorts of knots! Then you can make a bivouac of branches, this way, see, look at the picture! No no, don't keep it, I want to read it before Father comes home, in case he confiscates it."

"Oh, I don't suppose he will do that, Sonny. It's only those other papers he considers to have a bad effect, dear."

"I know. Here it tells you how to build a camp fire. Look, this page is about signalling by semaphore. And there are dozens of hints and wrinkles, how to keep boots dry, et cetera. Oh, and you can buy tea pellets, too, and drop one in a cup of boiling water, without needing a teapot, see here's the advertisement! I do hope Father will let me be a Boy Scout! I bet he won't. Do you think he'll give his permission, Mum?"

"I should think so, dear. But you must ask him yourself."

"To form a patrol," went on Phillip, "you only want six boys in all. Then you can go camping, and find your way about by the stars at night, and cook on a camp fire, and have a singsong. A wide-awake hat costs four and sixpence. Look at these wonderful tents, from the Boer War! Coo, they're expensive, seven and six! Perhaps I can save up for a wide-awake, and do without a tent to sleep in! Stop grinning at me across the table, Mavis! Mum, tell her to stop grinning."

"Phil is funny," said Mavis, amiably. "First he says he must have a hat to keep him wide awake, then he wants a tent to go to sleep in. Ha ha! How like him, to want to go to sleep and remain wide-awake at the same time!"

"I *never* said I wanted to sleep in a wide-awake! Of course I shan't sleep in my hat! Do you think I'm an old crone, snoring in bed in a nightcap? Anyway, who wears thick woollen socks in bed? Mum, could I have a Scout's hat, for an extra birthday present, do you think?"

"Ah, I knew that was coming!" exclaimed Mavis in triumph, pointing across the table. "You were just trying to get round Mother, to buy you something! I know what's behind all your ideas, every one of them! I can read you like a book!"

Mistaking his sister's sense of fun—he rebuffed all attempts at affection from his mother and sisters—Phillip sought for something sarcastic to say, which would shut her up. Unable to think, he made an ugly face at her.

"Sonny, if you could only see yourself," said his mother.

"Well then, stop Mavis getting at me, Mum. More tea,

please." With head held down reading, slowly he held out his cup. "What's the jam? Gooseberry? I don't like it very much. Can I have marmalade?"

"Say 'Please' to Mother," said Mavis. She was a pretty, delicate girl, with dark brown hair, regular features, and the large brown eyes of her mother. These eyes nowadays often held a far-away look.

Behind the china teapot, and its thick woollen cosy, Hetty presided over the children's tea. She was always hoping that Phillip and Mavis would be friends, she was always trying to reconcile them to each other; for their habitual bickering distressed her. Hetty was generally optimistic, her natural gaiety never far away, but she felt it a strain so often having to play the part of peacemaker; and under her cheerful exterior she grieved that her efforts seemed unavailing.

She sometimes wondered if she had made a mistake in never having had Phillip, after the first few months of his life, to sleep with her. She had been afraid of him becoming too dependent on her; for Richard had seemed to feel that he was no longer wanted. Once he had said that she cared more for her "best boy", as he called him, than for himself.

So Hetty had denied her natural instinct, the common instinct of animals, to share a common warmth; and Phillip had grown up alone, with no feeling of shared warmth; and no spontaneous feeling of sharing with another—until he had made friends with Cranmer, who was in large part animal.

Regarding Mavis, Hetty had rejoiced that Dickie had cared tenderly for his little daughter from the first; but now it looked as though a deep reserve had come between Dickie and Mavis. For Doris, the youngest, Dickie seemed to have no fatherly feeling at all: she had taken, he once declared, his place in his wife's affections. It was quite untrue. She had no favourites. All were equally dear to her. He was a strange man, she often sighed to herself.

"Be friends, children!" said Hetty. "Life is too short, to be always bickering."

"Can I have some marmalade, please, Mum?"

"I am afraid I forgot to get some more Golden Shred, dear."

"I like the Oxford marmalade," said Phillip. "It has bits you can chew on. Can I have some, Mum? Just a little?"

"But Phillip, you know it belongs to your Father."

Richard still received from his brother John a case of Cooper's Oxford marmalade every Christmas. The case was hidden under the floor of the lavatory, next to the 'cello. This comestible was particularly understood to be his own; he ate of it sparingly, and the same amount every day. One china pot stood on the higher larder shelf, to be taken out and put on the table, with its heavy lid and his own particular christening spoon, only when he was at home. It was a ritual, a link with his old life; it had been so in his Father's time, when neither he nor any of his brothers or sisters would have dared even to think of expecting a spoonful, unless invited to have some. But the old punctilio, the old idea of what constituted good manners, had gone by the board, Richard had long decided. Nothing was sacred to Master Phillip. So the case was hidden; and a new pot brought forth at night, when the old one had been scraped clean.

Often when he took off the lid, he saw that someone had been at the contents, and although the identity of the culprit was obvious (for there was only one person in the house who habitually ignored the law of *meum et tuum*) Hetty, of course, must try and suggest some excuse or other, such as, "Are you sure, dear, it isn't as you left it?" or, "It may have dried a little, during the recent hot weather, dear"—anything but the plain truth that it had been pilfered!

Richard had once loved his son, in those earliest years of commingled warmth. Then, he had been delighted that "the little chap" had imitated all his ways, wanting to do things as he did them, to copy him in every respect. This flow between them had been broken by Richard trying to break imitative habits in his son which previously he had encouraged, with delight, as a natural thing—as indeed it was. But by trying to break this natural habit of imitation, by use of the veto, and later by punishment, he had, without knowing the effects of his actions, tried to put the little machine in reverse; never realising that a child can truly go only forward, not backward. So the child mind, or its impulse, had gone in other directions—apparently. In reality, it was a variant of the parental model or direction: but round the barriers. So Phillip became a disobedient boy.

In Cranmer's case, the child-will had been broken in its own home; he had become a wild street-boy; and finding kindness from Phillip, had grown to him as an ideal.

The wooden case of white marmalade pots stood in darkness, under the lavatory floor, hidden away. So these thoughts were hidden away in darkness, from those who lived in the rooms above, in those Edwardian years.

Richard, product of Victorian respectability, of rigid Mosaic commandment, was unaware of any irony in his attitude to his son. Let the boy's schoolmasters, he complained, try and reform him; let Hetty ruin him with her indulgence; let the boy go his own way, and find out for himself, when he was a man, the errors of his ways! He, the boy's Father, had washed his hands of him!

Thus Richard in his wearier moods, after a long and confining day in the City, underfed, indeed permanently undernourished, an exile from the countryside where he had been born and bred —on plenty of butter, eggs, milk, poultry, occasional game and venison, brown wheaten bread, mutton, beef, and bacon.

What the stomach feels in the morning, the head thinks in the afternoon, as Hugh Turney, his despised brother-in-law, once said.

"It isn't fair to take Dad's own marmalade," said Mavis. "He always knows, and blames Mother for letting you take it."

"It isn't often that I take some, anyway! Only just now I feel it would go with the dripping, Mum, to stop indigestion."

"Mavis is quite right, Phillip. Your Father trusts you, you know. After all, it *is* his marmalade. I'll get some Golden Shred tomorrow, dear."

"It's too sweet! Oh well, I'll do without any, and get indigestion! Then *how* can I learn my Latin, Algebra, and Euclid? Mum, can't I have half-lunch at school? It was apple tart today. I am sick of free lunch, of cold mutton sandwiches, also you always put on too much salt."

"Don't listen to him grumbling, Mum."

"I'm not grumbling! I'm telling the truth, which fools can't see, ever! I always feel better after oranges or marmalade, so I know what I'm talking about! Very well, you people, as I'm not wanted here, and always shouted down by Father, or chipped by Mavis, I'll leave the house as soon as I can! No one's really friendly to me in this house!"

"Hush, Sonny! You ought not to speak like that, even in fun."

"I won't hush! And please don't call me Sonny!"

In the retort, Hetty heard her husband's tones.

Phillip sighed, picked up *The Scout*, and pushed back his chair. At this, Doris, whose round face and serious little eyes had been turning from one speaker to another, as though wondering what the words were about, said with her gaze upon her big brother's face,

"Don't go, Phillip. I'm friendly."

Unheeding this unexpected tribute, Phillip left the room, quietly closing the door behind him. He went into the scullery, to talk to Timmy Rat. The usual thud of Timmy's tail striking the wood of the hole as it dashed out, greeted him.

"Hullo Timmy, you old devil," he whispered, regarding pink eyes and twitching whiskers in the light entering by a small window facing the back yard outside. Then an idea came to him. Turning the wooden button on the lid, he opened the flap and withdrew the soft, warm animal and held it against his neck, to feel its comforting warmth for a few moments before putting it inside his coat. At once it crawled up until it lay distended and relaxed in the warm space between collar-bone and shoulder. Unlocking and unbolting the back-door, Phillip went down the concrete steps to the gate in the fence leading to the next house, and so to grandfather's back door. This, in contrast to his own, was usually unlocked.

Phillip thought it was just like Father to have so many locks on his doors. There were two on the front door, besides the chain, and bolts both top and bottom; while the back door had a key to turn, two bolts, and a chain.

He went into Gran'pa's kitchen, where the cook was making bread-sauce. A cockerel, trussed and headless, lay on a plate. There was a dish of macaroni and cheese, and mince-pies on a tray, ready to be baked. Cook told him that the Chairman of the Firm, Mr. Mallard, with his wife and son, were coming. Also Mr. Newman, from Randiswell.

Anyone connected with the Firm was uninteresting to Phillip. Once when he had been taken to see the works in Sparhawk Street, Holborn, old Mr. Mallard had patted his head, and said childish things to him which he had not known how to answer. Most grown-ups were like that; they made you feel small and silly; but not Mr. Newman. Mr. Newman was nice to call on, in his little cottage in Randiswell below the humped bridge over the river. There he sat in a little parlour filled with his curios of travel, and whenever he went there Phillip was offered half a glass of port to drink, with biscuits. Mr. Newman always bowed to him when he arrived, in his grey frock coat and high collar and cravat with a pearl pin stuck in it, and again when he left.

"Is Mr. Newman here yet?"

"Not yet, Master Phillip. But your Gran'pa and Grannie are in the dining room."

Phillip found them, sitting in their chairs before the fire. As usual Gran'pa had Sammy the cat on his knee. Sammy stared at him, though without much interest, for it was only in the gardens and Backfield, where the cat went to hunt mice and birds, that Phillip chased Sammy, and flipped pebbles at him from his catapult. Sammy was a big animal, a neuter who had been seen-to. Sammy hunted other cats and howled at them, sometimes biting them. Once in the Backfield Phillip had stalked Sammy as Sammy was stalking cat-lovers in the long grass, and to his delight he saw them turn on Sammy, and chase him away. Mrs. Rolls' cat, a mother one, hated Sammy, and hissed at him whenever she met him. Phillip was always tenderly protective towards Mrs. Rolls' cat, which had a small head and one blue and one brown eye, since it was nice in itself, but chiefly because it belonged to Helena Rolls.

"Well, m'boy," said Thomas Turney. "How did you get on at school today?"

"Very well, thank you, Gran'pa."

"What did you learn?"

"Nothing."

"Oh," said Gran'pa, with a short laugh. "Then what did they try and teach you?"

"Latin, Geography, History, and Mathematics, Gran'pa. And some mouldy French."

"Are they going to teach you Spanish at your school, m'boy?"

Gran'pa always asked him this question, so Phillip thought he would give a different answer this time, more interesting to Gran'pa.

"I think so. I heard two masters discussing it after lunch today. But it might have been something else they were saying," he added, remembering the new leaf he had turned over.

"Spanish is the language of the future, m'boy. South America will be the coming focus of world trade. Their natural resources are hardly known, let alone developed."

"I know some Spanish already," said Phillip, thinking of the Spanish pirate, on the hulk in the Sargasso Sea, in that wonderful serial, the end of which he would never know, as *Boy's Life* was now no more.

"Oh," said Gran'pa. "Let's hear you, then."

"'Quando tiempo' is all I know, and 'Carramba'."

Thomas Turney chuckled.

"Do you know what that means, eh?"

"What time is it, and A curse on you, Gran'pa."

"Well, both are useful expressions, sometimes, m'boy, he-he-he! Take my advice, and learn some more. Be prepared for the future, Phillip."

"Yes, Gran'pa. I would like to speak Spanish in the Boy Scouts. I want to be a Scout, and have a patrol. The motto of the Scouts is 'Be prepared'. It's all in *Scouting for Boys.* I am going to save up to buy a copy."

"You can get thirty-three and a third per centum trade discount if you get it through the Firm," said Gran'pa.

Phillip disregarded these figures. He had no money, what he wanted was Grannie to say she would buy the book for him.

"Yes, Gran'pa, but you see I'm saving up for a new bike. My old one isn't safe."

Gran'pa laughed again. The apparent *non sequitur* had enabled him to read his grandson's thoughts.

"Ah, you can't spend the same money on two things at once, m'boy."

"It's a wonderful book, all the same."

"Well, you save your pennies, and then you'll be able to own it. There's no satisfaction in life like that of the reward of hard work, or thrift."

"Do not tease Phillip," said Mrs. Turney, softly, as she peered at the boy's shoulders. Were they uneven, had he a hump? Surely not, she would have known of it from Hetty, long ago. But one shoulder did look slightly thicker than the other.

"I'm giving Phillip a simple lesson in money, Sarah. You must save up, m'boy, if you want to acquire anything. Get it with your own efforts, that way brings the only satisfaction."

Thomas Turney got up, holding the cat in his arms, and put it carefully, not to disturb its peace, in the chair behind him. "I'm going to get some claret, to warm it on the chimney piece.

Never drink claret cold, Phillip, it's indigestible unless brought to an equable temperature, besides being rough on the palate."

"I like stone ginger beer best, Gran'pa."

As soon as the door was shut behind his grandfather, Phillip's manner changed. Grannie might buy him a wide-awake hat, as well as the book, and with luck, a wooden water-bottle, of the kind advertised, from the Boer War. In the past Grannie had bought all his fret-work articles, but since losing interest in that hobby, he had had nothing to sell her.

"Tell me about the Boy Scouts," said Grannie. He needed no further encouragement. He deemed it wise to recount the Scout's virtues.

"Sir Robert Baden-Powell, the Chief Scout, says that the Boy Scout mustn't swear or smoke, Grannie, or have bad thoughts. He must do at least one Good Turn every day. Boy Scouts are in patrols, with names of birds and animals. They have to learn to imitate the cries, and they wear shoulder ribbons, with the colour of the bird or animal of their patrol. Which would you like to be, Grannie, if, say, you were going to be a Boy Scout? Wait a mo', before you choose, I'll tell you what there is to choose from. There's the Lion Patrol, the Bear Patrol, the Otter Patrol, the Wolf Patrol, and the Bloodhound Patrol! Which would you like, Grannie? Look, I'll give you the cries first, then you can choose which you'll be. But first I must tell you what birds there are. There's the Woodpigeon, with grey shoulder ribbons, with its cry of Book-boor-ro; the Owl, boo-hoo, boo-hoo; the Kestrel, with kek-kek-kek, just like they do over the Backfield sometimes. You must have heard them, haven't you, Grannie?"

"Why yes, of course, dear. And well I recall hearing them over the fields and spinneys at home, and especially round the corn stacks, when I was a girl. The mouse-hawk we called it, and sometimes the windhover. Why yes, my father shot one once. It was taking mother's chicks. He shot a cuckoo too, the same day, and had both set up in a glass case."

"I wish I had a gun, Gran, then I'd have a lot of stuffed birds."

"Perhaps you will, when you are a man, dear."

"I know, Gran, but I would so like one now. I wouldn't break any windows with it, as I did with Father's air-rifle, when I was inexperienced. There are some spiffing walking-stick guns in Murrage's catalogue, only seven and sixpence, Belgian-made. If I had one I would be ever so careful."

Sarah Turney was concerned for her grandson's happiness, for she had suffered, with her daughter, when in the past the little fellow had been caned so often for his naughtiness. She wondered how she might get the idea of a dangerous walking-stick gun out of his head.

"Do you remember the wild animals and birds in the Duke's park, when you went to stay with your cousins Percy and Polly at Beau Brickhill, dear?"

"Yes, Gran. I saw emus and gnus, bison, antelopes and several other kinds of deer, as well as a lot of silver and gold pheasants. It simply swarmed with all sorts, Grannie. And there were so many flies along the drive, buzzing out from the trees."

"They have a sanctuary there, Phillip, no one ever shoots them. The Duchess goes out in a green costume and watches them, also taking photographs. That is much nicer than shooting them, I think."

"But how can you shoot flies?" cried Phillip; and at the very idea Sarah began to laugh. He pretended to be holding a tiny gun between his finger-tips.

"*Ping*, got that blue-bottle, *ping*, down comes a gnat, *twip-twip*, two daddy-long-legs!"

Sarah laughed until she ached, while he displayed before her. At last, getting herself together, she said that what she meant was that the animals in the Park were not shot.

"But they do shoot them, Gran! Uncle Jim Pickering told me so! They have platforms in the trees, and stand up there, and shoot the driven deer, to keep down their numbers! Uncle Jim says he sometimes gets a haunch of venison from the Head Verderer!"

"Yes dear, you are quite right. I was thinking of the other animals. The deer must be kept down, of course. But I know her Grace does not like shooting them," said Sarah, gently. She thought awhile. "Now I must not forget to tell you what I would like to be, if I were a Boy Scout, what bird or animal, I mean, must I? I expect you will want to be getting back to your homework soon."

"Oh no, Gran. I say, d'you remember the Hound of the Baskervilles? Well then, what do you think of the Bloodhound Patrol, with a baying cry, rather terrifying, boo-hoo, boo-boo!

The patrol leader has an orange head of a blood-hound on his pennant, and orange shoulder ribbons, to distinguish it from other patrols. I like orange. I shall call my patrol the Blood-hounds! Doesn't it sound wonderful, Gran?"

"Yes dear, but you must not let it interfere with your lessons, will you?"

"No. Scouting makes a boy work all the better. He has to keep fit, to be a good Scout, you know. Well, I must go now, I think. Good night, Grannie," he said, hurriedly kissing her. "Sorry I can't stay any longer. Oh, would you like to see Timmy Rat?" and he pulled the animal from under the shoulder of his jacket.

"Well, do you know, dear, all this time I have been wondering why you had a hump there! Isn't he clean and white? Well, good night, dear. Thank you for coming in to see us, and for letting me see your pet. It is so nice when the young folk remember the old."

"Well, I always *like* seeing you, you see, Gran. Goodnight."

Outside the door, he listened a moment to Gran'pa talking in angry tones to Uncle Hugh down in the garden room. They were always having rows; and unconcerned with them, Phillip slipped through the kitchen and so back into his own house, bolting the door behind him and putting Timmy Rat back into its box. He lingered a moment to scratch its ears, then went into the hall, to see, by the presence of bowler hat, overcoat, and umbrella on the coat rack, that Father had come home.

Subdued, he returned to the kitchen, lit the gas-mantle, and opening his satchel, settled at the table to do his homework. He spread around him various printed school books. The lid of the inkwell was lifted open, a pen stuck in it. Thus prepared, he placed the empty satchel beside him on the table, ready to slip *The Scout* into it at the first warning.

While he was reading, there came a loud thump on the front door, followed by a ring of the bell. Running to the door, he opened it to see the peaked cap and face of Carter Paterson's man, standing there with his leather apron and jacket with brass buttons. He had a large something beside him, covered with brown paper and tied with string. His boy, who always stood at the back of the covered van, holding to a rope from the roof, when it was going, now stood beside him.

"Package from the Stores."

"I'll tell my mother, just a jiffy."

Mother came to the door. The leather-aproned driver touched the peak of his cap. The peak had a little metal band on its edge. Phillip wondered if it was there to prevent the peak wearing out; for Carter Paterson's man made calls at people's houses all the time, and each time he probably touched the peak when they came to the door.

"Whatever is it, driver?"

"Looks like furniture to me, mum."

Hetty looked at the label. Yes, it was addressed to Dickie, and came from the Stores.

"Better tell your Father, dear," she said to Phillip.

But Richard was already on his way to the door, unhurrying, with an air of complacent mystery. He turned up the gas, so that the Veritas mantle glowed white; then he lit the mantle in the front room, a thing which in itself showed that something very out of the ordinary was about to happen. Having done this, he helped the carter and his boy to lift the package into the doorway of the front room. The carter remained on the mat, cap in hand, having sent his boy back to stand by the horse; not that it was likely to move, as it used such pauses for sleep; but the carter wanted any tip for himself.

Meanwhile, Richard was examining the delivery sheet carefully. Then he took out his stylo pen from his pocket. Writing the word *unexamined* in the space for his signature, he signed. Then he felt in pocket for twopence, the price of a pint of beer, and gave it to the man. Touching his forelock, plastered down on his brow, the man in the leather apron departed.

"Now," said Richard, pulling the chain of the gas, to keep it on the by-pass, "I will get on with my tea."

Phillip was almost screwed up inside with curiosity, but he knew it might be almost fatal if he asked Father. So he waited until he was in the kitchen with his mother.

"I've no idea, dear. I expect your Father has his reasons for not saying anything at the moment. Perhaps it is a surprise, dear. Let us wait, shall we, until he has had his meal. He is tired, you know, when he gets home from the office, and likes to rest awhile after his meal."

Phillip knew from the gas being left on the by-pass that something was coming. What a day of wonderful events! First *The*

Scout, now this mystery. The object had four legs; it looked like a small cupboard of sorts.

He waited as patiently as he could, meanwhile making some attempt to do his homework.

At last footfalls in the passage told that the great moment had come. He was required to help in carrying the object down into the sitting room. And when Richard unpacked the "surprise" in the presence of the three children and their mother, he did so far too slowly for Phillip: he folded the sheets of brown paper carefully, as he removed them, after unpicking every knot, and making little loops of the string for use another time: but at last it was done, and there stood, not a musical box like the polyphone in the front room, but a shining cabinet gramophone: and when Richard put on a record, letting it spin while winding the spring in case it should break, such music filled the room that Phillip had never imagined to be possible in the world.

Richard had warned them that they must not speak, or make a sound, while the gramophone was playing; but there was no need for this warning coming from what was a shy and often excruciating sensibility centred upon itself. Phillip sat entranced, in another world. The only other music he had heard had been in school or church, from Italian barrel-organ, Salvation Army band in the High Street, pantomimes at Christmas, Mother playing the piano in the front room, Uncle Hugh his violin, Mr Bigge his harp; and, of course, the thin steel discs of the polyphone that crinkled as they turned, and made a sort of music that did not last as music very long, it was too mechanical.

Hetty and Richard watched the children's faces. Phillip sat staring, his dark blue eyes open wide, his lips parted. Mavis was pensive, her eyes dreaming; Doris sat with her finger pointing at the open doors. Phillip looked at Mother, and seeing the gentle smile on her face, suddenly tears came in his eyes. He turned away quickly, before Father could see. He was imagining white angels, everything shining and beautiful high up in the sky, beyond the stars. There, too, was Minnie, his nurse of long ago, who had held him close and warm and safe when he was frightened of the dark, and of the dark loud noise of Father's voice to Mummy.

Richard stopped the motor, and changed the record; then he stood back to gaze from face to face, with anticipation in his eyes, as though beaming upon them the unique joy and beauty of the composition he had heard that midday for the first time. He had spent his luncheon break of three quarters of an hour in the Stores in Queen Victoria Street, listening to the same records, foregoing his light midday meal in a dream of chivalry, tenderness, and aspiration in the pictured English country of his birth and breeding. There and then he had made a decision: to buy the case of records, and the cabinet gramophone, and go hang to the expense!

There had been only one thing to mar, but slightly, his pleasant talk with the shop assistant, an amateur musician like himself. The shop assistant had mentioned with half-concealed enthusiasm that Mr. Elgar, the composer, was a great friend of George Bernard Shaw; and then, seeing the customer's face, he had said no more, lest the customer make a complaint to the management, and he be dismissed.

Richard had no use for G. B. Shaw. *The Daily Trident* had long exposed him as a charlatan who found nothing good in the country which had given him hospitality, and a certain competence—why didn't he go back to Ireland, if he found in England so much to complain of and sneer about? Richard did not like the Irish; was not Mr. Turney, his father-in-law, half Irish, through his mother, according to Hetty? For himself, Richard half-believed—a belief fully held by his sister Victoria—that the old man was entirely bogus, a Jew who had adopted an English name, who had lacked the courage to be loyal to his own origins. As proof of this contention, was the dark appearance of that bounder Hugh, who—it went without saying!—was an admirer of G. B. Shaw, another impostor, who wrote his plays with his tongue in his cheek! A cross between Jew and Irish—what a mixture! No wonder Phillip was such a cross-grained little funk!

Richard, however, had not got all his ideas about the renegade Irishman from *The Daily Trident.* In his youth, as a special constable on duty in Trafalgar Square on Bloody Sunday, when Cunninghame Graham and John Burns had incited the mob to violence, he had heard it said that the red-bearded anarchist was present with the insurrectionists. Later, he had learned that the anarchist had not even had the courage of his opinions; he had kept well clear, looking after his own precious skin, after egging-on others to do his mischief for him. How Elgar could be "a great friend" of such a character, Richard could not understand; however, it was Elgar's music that mattered; and obeying his desire, he had spent nearly five pounds that midday—one-eighth of a half-quarter's salary, but never matter! He would debit his savings with the expenditure, then it could not be thought that he had made his purchase at the expense of wife and family, out of income.

Thus, honourably with his conscience, *The Enigma Variations* had been purchased, together with the gramophone.

The magic lasted until half-way through the *Nimrod* passage, when Doris, who had been sitting unnaturally still, suddenly wrinkled up her face and cried "My dolly! My dolly!" She remembered she had left that talisman of safety in the kitchen, to look after her ball of yellow wool and knitting needles, with which she was making it a camisole. Hetty told her to hush. Doris said in distress, "My dolly, Mummy, my dolly!"

Immediately Richard, his inner harmony diminished, stopped the motor.

Firm against Hetty's pleas and apologies, he put the records back into their case, closed the veneered doors of the sound chamber, and locked the lid with a key on his ring. A special lock had been put upon the lid that afternoon, for he was not going to have Phillip's fingers, he told himself, ruining his latest possession. There was little in the house that the boy had not, somehow or other, got to know about, with his inquisitive, mischievous ways.

"Now up to bed, all of you, please."

"Say thank you to your Father, children, for the wonderful treat he has given you tonight."

"Thank you, Father."

"Thanks, Father."

"Thank you, Father."

"Now don't any one of you let the occasion be an excuse to forget to brush your teeth."

"No, Father."

Phillip went out of the room first, followed by Mavis, and Hetty leading a subdued Doris by the hand upstairs to the front bedroom, where she slept with her mother.

Richard occupied his dressing-room almost permanently: the

feeling of resentment towards his youngest child, which the music had temporarily displaced, was part of the crust of his existence.

Chapter 9

THE BIG PARADE

"O, THE beautiful, beautiful sun!" breathed Hetty to herself, as she stood at one window of what at first had been called the drawing room, but now, in the children's language, had become the front room. She yielded herself to the sun standing high over St. Cyprian's church, above the green shining of the grass across the road, the gleaming leaves and white trunks of the silver birches, the warm gentle breeze only just moving through the open window, stirring the leaves of her very own fern, the aspidistra given her by the rag-and-bone man in the little house in Comfort Road, long ago.

Sometimes when she saw the big, barn-like red brick building of St. Cyprian's church across the grass she recalled, with a smile, the phrase that the Parish magazine repeated every month, as it had for years on its pale blue cover, under an etching of the church with a tall tower—*Note. The tower is not yet built.* That was almost as funny as Dickie's remark, made when he first saw the magazine, "H'm, I see the ecclesiastical authorities have bitten off more than they can chew, in that tower!"

The front room was Hetty's room. Its yellow-gold wall-paper and cream-painted window-frames and woodwork glowed with light as she stood by the middle one of the four windows, all open wide in the warm May afternoon. She had come to take a peep at her son standing in the road outside. As she leaned forward, her cheek was touched by the leaves of the aspidistra fern in the brass bowl on the tall stand; she smiled, and made the gesture of a kiss towards it—dear little fern, it had been her friend for so many years, and had shared so many of her thoughts and hopes. She felt a positive love for the fern beside her, as her nature expanded in the glowing beams of the sun, her natural joy and gaiety welling up with the light.

Thinking, as usual, of others before herself, Hetty's present happiness was increased by the thought that her husband would have a lovely afternoon for his ride into the country. It was the only thing, beside music, which appeared to give the poor man any happiness.

Phillip had cycled home from school with all speed, and hurried through his dinner, because, he said, parade was ordered for two o'clock, and the patrol-leader must not be late. He had changed into his uniform, and was out in the road by five minutes before the hour. It was now ten minutes after the hour; he was still waiting for his "men" to appear. He had particularly asked her not to show herself during the parade; and "warned" Mavis not to make remarks. Knowing how seriously he regarded this first full-dress parade, Hetty had promised that no one would look. But she could not forbear to tip-toe into the front room, just to see how things were going on.

During the past week Hetty had been active with her sewing machine, in preparation for this parade. She had made six haversacks, cutting them out from an old print curtain, the pattern of flowers turned inside, of course. After running-up the flat little bags, each with its sling, Phillip had dyed them in tea. Thus the haversacks, which he had taken round to give his men, had something of the desired khaki hue. The result was not exactly khaki, rather a yellowish-brown; but it was sufficient, in Phillip's eyes, to give concealment in stalking, tracking, and general manœuvres. Phillip's white cricketing hat had likewise been immersed in the brew; afterwards, it had been starched and ironed, to stiffen the brim. A cricket shirt, blue shorts, black stockings and boots, and a tuppenny broomstick from Hern's, to which was tacked a white pennant with the silhouette of a bloodhound's head in yellow, and two yellow shoulder-ribbons, completed the uniform.

In Phillip's eyes, this was wonderful. He was a Boy Scout! In addition, but more wonderful, was the wooden water-bottle from the Boer War which hung on one side of his belt, and a French sword-bayonet of the type manufactured for the Franco-Prussian war, from the other.

Bottle and sword had been acquired during a visit to London with Hetty and Dorrie, the previous Wednesday afternoon. The two sisters had taken Phillip to High Holborn to see his cousin Ralph, who was apprenticed to Murrage's. This was a general outfitter's and miscellaneous shop of many rooms, with a large export trade. Thomas Turney had some shares in it. The three visitors had seen where Ralph slept, after climbing many brass-and-wood stairs to the long dormitory under the rafters. Two rows of iron bedsteads were lined up against the walls. Coming down again, they had been shown over the rest of the building, walking through the departments on the various floors, full of suits, shirts, saddles, furniture, and other things uninteresting to Phillip . . . until they came to guns, stuffed birds, fishing rods on the first floor; and equally exciting, on the ground floor, several motorbikes standing round a great big motorcar which had actually won races on the Continent, a Napier-Panhard which had touched over a hundred miles an hour! "Wait for us, wait for us!" Out came Phillip's notebook, and in a hurried hand the details were recorded and underlined, with several exclamation marks.

He was tremendously excited. There was more to come. The best display of all had been kept to the last. This was a real patrol of Boy Scouts actually camping out on the floor, behind a long plate-glass window facing the street outside. Two scouts were putting up a bivouac tent when Phillip first saw them, while a third was handling semaphore flags.

At the entrance stood a scout, on guard. He was obviously the patrol leader. From his pole hung the pennant of the Woodpeckers. Phillip gave him the scout's salute; but the patrol leader did not so much as give him a glance. He continued to stand to attention, staring straight ahead. His pole-holding arm was covered by a khaki sleeve, with a long row of proficiency badges. No wonder he did not speak to him, thought Phillip, as he went on into the room, entranced by the tent and artificial trees; the birch-bark canoe; the camp-fire made red by hidden electric light bulbs; the billy-cans, cooking pots, and all the impedimenta of outdoor life, just as he had imagined for his own patrol.

In some excitement Phillip returned to the patrol-leader by the door, and said to him, "Hullo! I'm the patrol leader of the Bloodhounds!"

As the patrol-leader of the Woodpeckers still did not answer, Phillip looked more closely at his face and saw that he was a dummy, staring with eyes of glass, face of wax, eye-lashes of cow-hair, and wig made of tow. A pink waxen hand held the pole, a clasp-knife hung from the dummy's belt. An awful temptation came to Phillip: dare he try and pinch that knife? Would he be seen?

Glancing around, he spotted cousin Ralph standing, hands behind him, beside a heap of white wooden Boer-war water-bottles, of the kind advertised in *The Scout* for 4½d. Ralph was staring at him, a faint grin as of being found out on his face. Just then Mother and Aunt Dorrie came through the door, and they all went to talk to Ralph, who, speaking out of the corner of his mouth, and with a furtive expression, said that he was in charge of the bottles and swords.

"You look very tired, dear boy," said Aunt Dorrie. Ralph told them the shop had opened at 8 a.m. as usual, it was now 3.30 p.m. but so far no one had bought anything. He shifted on his feet as he spoke, then complained that the hard floor made them swell, so that his boots hurt him.

Phillip knew that cousin Ralph had been expelled from the West Kent Grammar School, that was why he had entered a business career rather early. He did not know what Ralph had done to be expelled. All Mother had said about it was that it was a warning to others not to give way to wrong impulses, and to avoid bad companions.

"Coo lor, look at those swords!" exclaimed Phillip. Ralph told them that they were French bayonets, in gun-metal scabbards, from the Franco-Prussian War of 1870. A notice said *Souvenirs of the Entente Cordiale, useful as pokers, 1/6 each only.*

"We'll leave you two together for half an hour or so," said Mother. "Now don't get into mischief, Phillip. And don't interrupt Ralph too much, in the course of his duty."

At this Ralph winked at Phillip. When they had gone, he said, behind his hand, "What anyone can see in this bloody hole beats me. Waste of money to buy one of those old things for a poker, in my opinion. As for this Boy Sprout business, who could it appeal to but a lot of milksops? I had to help dress up that silly sodding dummy over by the door, that you spoke to when you came in. Sucked you in properly, didn't I, my lad?"

From these remarks an onlooker older and less passionately involved than Phillip might have deduced that Ralph Cakebread's salesmanship was hardly of the enthusiastic or persuasive kind; for Ralph, neither the customer nor the goods were ever the right ones. Even so, Phillip was his first purchaser of the day; one so persistent, indeed, that in the end Hetty, counting her small copper and silver, and against her better judgment, bought a sword-bayonet in addition to the water-bottle. In high feather Phillip carried them home, wrapped in brown paper, after tea in an A.B.C. Oh, hurry up Saturday's big parade!

Safe in the privacy of his bedroom, he unwrapped the parcel, noticing every crease in the covering paper, its smell recalling the wonderful shop in High Holborn. First he examined the bottle, thrilling at the whiteness of the straps, the roughness of the whitened leather, the grain of the wood, even the rust of the iron bands top and bottom.

It had a black airless smell when the leaden tap, tied to a string, was unscrewed. There was a broad arrow burnt into the wood at the bottom. He saw again Uncle Hugh and Uncle Sidney Cakebread, with turned-up brims to their wide-awake hats, in khaki uniforms with leggings and spurs, bandoliers and sabres, each with a wooden water-bottle, on the night of the farewell party—he saw the sparks from the back wheels of the cab on skids taking them down Hillside Road in the night. He heard again errand boys in the street whistling *Goodbye Dolly I must leave you*—and now one of those wooden bottles was his! Phillip sniffed again the dark, brackish smell inside the wood, an old and faraway smell, like the times the bottle had known. He ran to the bathroom, to fill it with water and to shake it vigorously, to clean it. Always the old dark smell remained.

Returning to his bedroom, he drew the long pointed blade of the bayonet from its scabbard. The original grease was still thick and brown upon the bright unused steel. He cleaned this off with newspaper, then polished the blade with metal polish. There being some time before Father was due home, he went down to the garden, and flashed the weapon upon the lawn. Striking at the ivy on the garden fence, and stabbing the bark of the elm, where cats had scratched its fibres, he enjoyed himself hugely until a window in Mrs. Bigge's squeaked up, and Mrs. Bigge looked out, to warn him that he might injure himself if he was not careful. Phillip said he would be; and to show her his power over the weapon, he ran at the dividing fence, and transfixed a plank. It required some tugging to pull the point out, and he fell over backwards; meanwhile Mrs. Bigge's voice had drawn the attention of Mrs. Groat in her garden farther down, and the two women began discussing the danger, accompanied by shakings of Mrs. Groat's head.

Phillip thought it time to go inside his own house; and pushing the blade into its scabbard with a click, he walked away, pretending not to have heard Mrs. Groat's voice asking where he had got it from, and did his Father know about it. And all because long ago he had broken her window pane with a shot from the horse-pistol he had once owned!

"Boss-eyed fool," he muttered to himself.

Hetty went away to see about Dickie's lunch. Phillip, who had seen her peeping at him, but pretended that she was not there, was swearing to himself. He felt lonely and dispirited. It being now half past two, near Father's time to return, he removed the sword-bayonet, and poked it into the hedge.

He was thinking of going to look for his men on the Hill when the click of a gate up the road startled him. After a glance to see if his trouser and shirt buttons were done up, and his stockings neat, he drew himself up to his full height of four feet ten and a half inches, while his heart began to beat rapidly. Could he get the sword and hang the guard on his belt in time? He was hesitating in near-panic when she came out of her gate. As she walked down the road and came near, he looked up with an assumed start of surprise, and gave her the scout's salute.

"Good afternoon, Phillip."

"I am just waiting for my men, we're having a field day this afternoon, Helena."

"Oh, are you. It's a lovely day, isn't it?"

"Yes, if it doesn't rain."

Phillip felt he had made some progress recently with the Rolls family. True, he had not yet been invited into their house, but he had been next door, when Mr. Pye had invited him and his sisters one evening to see his Magic Lantern display. Helena and her small sister had been invited, too; and Gilbert and Flossie Todd from number six, and some cousins of the Todds.

Anyone from "lower down the road" was felt to be not quite good enough to know; but the Todds were all right, they gave splendid parties at Christmas, with a lighted Christmas tree, and a present for everyone. "Up the road" was occupied by the highest local society, in Phillip's eyes; although Mr. Pye was, well, Mr. Pye. Still, he spoke like a gentleman.

Phillip was quite surprised when Mrs. Pye invited him and Mavis and Doris to see Mr. Pye's Magic Lantern slides. And when, in their best party clothes, Phillip wearing patent-leather dancing pumps with his Etons, they arrived, and he saw the Rolls sisters there, he trembled with mixed fear, joy, and self-suppression. He was getting on!

He was still afraid of Mr. Pye, and half-hid behind his sisters when they entered the house at half past six. However, Mr. Pye spoke kindly to him, so it was not so bad as he had imagined. The Magic Lantern stood on a tall wooden tripod like a photographer's. Chairs were ranged across the room, like a small hall. There were others there Phillip had never seen before. Mrs. Pye, who was rather deaf, sat in front with her children, and Helena's sister, Viola; then came some strangers; the third row was occupied by the Todds and their cousins; the last row was for the Maddisons. Helena stood at the back, by the lantern.

"My little assistant," said Mr. Pye, with a wide smile, before he turned out the gas.

There was a white sheet over the window, and a round yellow circle showed where the slides would appear. It was lovely in the dark, Phillip thought, with yellow marks on the walls and ceiling, from the chinks in the lantern. It smelled of colza oil, too, which reminded him of Beau Brickhill, when Percy had held Father's dark lantern to look for sparrows in the ivy of the stables wall at night, and he had shot at them with the saloon gun.

Once, just after a fresh coloured slide had been put in, Phillip looked sideways at Mr. Pye, and saw he was standing behind Helena. His arms were round her, and his hands were kneading her bosoms, which had grown full lately, Phillip had noticed, owing to puberty. Phillip thought of a cat working its paws on a rug before a fire, and wondered whatever Mr. Pye could be doing. He thought no more about it, and did not look again, in case Mr. Pye's eye should fall on him, and think he was not interested in the pictures, but in Helena. Phillip still suffered from what Mr. Pye had said, when the girl had boxed his ears after he had asked her brother not to stone a sheep.

Helena Rolls walked on down the road, while the smile remained on the face of the patrol-leader of the Bloodhounds long after she had turned the corner. Forgotten were sword, bottle, Father, his men, as he recalled the frank blue eyes and dark lashes, the curve of cheek, the thick clusters of golden curls under her white tam o'shanter. She had spoken so nicely to him. Was there shyness behind her smile, which would mean, as he knew from magazine stories, that she——. Trying to recall the exact amount of smile and interest in her greeting, he came to the deflating conclusion that she had remained cool and friendly only. She had looked straight at him, a level glance, which surely denoted absence of shyness or nervousness, which surely meant that she was fancy-free.

He saw his mother's face reappear beside the old fern. She waved her hand, and smiled.

"No one turned up yet, Sonny? Never mind, dear."

"Please don't call me Sonny any more!" he whispered urgently, coming to the gate.

"Very well, dear, just as you like. I'll try to remember to call you Phillip in future."

He went into the garden, and stood under the window.

"Mother, did you see her go by? She didn't say much, or turn back to look, at the corner. Is that, as a sign, good or bad, do you think?"

Phillip had often discussed his chances with Helena with his mother, advancing various observations to prove, and then to disprove, whether or not she was as keen on him as he was on her.

"Oh, I wish my men had turned up when she passed, Mum! Then I could have drawn my sword. I felt such a fool standing there alone, all by myself."

"I expect they will turn up soon, dear."

"They're always late! There's a rule of a ha'penny fine for being late, but no one will ever pay it."

The figure of Gran'pa appeared on the balcony, out of his bedroom door.

"Ah, you have responsibilities now, Phillip, and must learn to be patient, m'boy!" said Gran'pa's voice. Phillip ignored it, as he had ignored Gran'pa's appearance. "What are you going to do today, chase spies, Phillip, he-he-he?"

Why did Gran'pa always laugh at his own jokes, and such silly ones, too?

Phillip answered shortly, "Oh Gran'pa! What do you think we are? We're Scouts!"

"Oh, I see. He-he-he," chuckled Thomas Turney. "Are you there, Hetty?"

"Yes, Papa." She leaned out, looking upwards.

"I was just coming in to see you, to tell you about Hughie."

"Oh Papa, what has happened?"

"He's losing his sense of balance. Newman came to tell me that he saw 'im fall over, on the Hill this morning. Bolton dropped in just now, and suggested I get a man for him. What d'ye think, Hetty?"

"Oh, poor Hughie! Did he hurt himself badly, Papa?"

"No, Hetty, no cause for alarm. I just wanted to talk things over with you. Is Dickie home?"

"I'm expecting him any moment now, Papa. I'll come in and see you later in the afternoon, when I shall be alone."

"Very well, Hetty. I want to discuss my new will with you, too. I heard from Grandison, the broker, this morning. He says there's nothing to be done about those Canadian Pacifics. I ought to have sold my block when he advised, months ago. They're not likely to recover now the company has gone into liquidation. Well, even Homer nods, he-he-he."

"Oh Papa, perhaps they will recover! Even so, it is a terrible thing, I must admit."

"They went up, you see, on a rumour that the Company was going to make an offer, and I hung on for a rise. The first loss should be the last loss. Never forget that maxim, Phillip! Then you won't go through life blaming others for your own faults, m'boy, eh Hetty? He-he-he! Worry makes a man hesitant. There's your Uncle Charley, silly fellow, chucking up his steady job with the mining people, and buying an import business—Charley, who knows nothing about business!"

Thomas Turney opened his snuff-box, took a pinch, sniffed it up first one hairy nostril, then another. He sneezed appreciatively, blew his nose rigorously on a red silk handkerchief taken from the breast-pocket of his blue serge jacket, and went on with his remarks. "You know, Hetty, children remain children to their parents all their lives. Anxiety never leaves a parent, anxiety absorbs thought, and thought is energy." He looked down upon his grandson with a beam of benevolence. "Now you look out that you don't get caught when you grow up, Phillip, by a pretty face. Never marry for excitement, m'boy, he-he-he, like your Uncle Charley did."

"Oh shut up," muttered Phillip to himself, with a glance of distaste at his mother. He was used to Gran'pa's advice; he never listened. He was beginning to side with Father against Gran'pa Turney. Gran'pa was always discussing the making of a new will with Mother; always coming in to see Mother about it. Before the old man could say any more, Phillip slipped away into the road, to look and see if any of his men were in sight.

The talk from the balcony continued. Oh why *must* they talk about him, and so near to the Pye's house? And the Rolls' too.

"This scout idea will keep him out of mischief, Hetty. Who is his Scout-master?"

"I don't think they have one yet, Papa. Phillip is in charge," she said proudly. "He's taking his patrol for a field day this afternoon."

"He's too thin, Hetty. Don't let him walk too far, at his age, or go too long without food. Once you let a bull calf shrink, it never makes up for it. It's the same with human beings. We're all mammals, y'know."

You might be, but I'm not, thought Phillip. He was a little reassured by Mother saying, "Oh, Phillip is stronger than he looks, Papa. He's got a pound of sausages in his mess tin, to cook round the camp fire."

"Beef or pork?"

"Beef, Papa. Pork are rather expensive, at sixpence a pound."

"Well, there's staying power in beef, certainly, though not so much, I fancy, in this imported frozen stuff. I was going to ask ye, Hetty, what about that water-bottle Phillip has? A lot of fellows died of enteric in the war, you know, like poor Sidney. Has it been well disinfected?"

"Yes, Papa, I did it myself, with boiling soda water, then permanganate, as Dickie advised. Dickie is always very careful, you know."

Thomas Turney did not think much of his son-in-law, a cross-grained fellow whose complaining voice was far too often audible in the adjoining house. Nowadays, however, he kept his opinion on the fellow to himself; and a little praise, where it was due, was always gladly given.

"Yes, Dick's very thorough, I know that. You can't be too careful. Well, a boy is only young once, Hetty. Let him make the most of it. Come in and play me a game of bezique tonight, will ye? Come to supper, do. There's a macaroni pie, and some scallops, both easily digestible."

Phillip, who by now had given up all idea of putting on his sword, started to walk down the road in a mood of aimlessness. Then he saw, to his delight, cousin Gerry turn the corner. He waved his pole, and uttered the patrol call, *Boo-hoo!* Gerry was accompanied by a small boy, whom Phillip had seen about, but never spoken to. The boy lived in one of the flats in Charlotte Road, built at the same time as St. Cyprian's Church, in the space between the Wakenham and Randiswell stretches.

Phillip had wondered if Gerry would join the Bloodhounds and be the patrol-leader, he himself being corporal, but Gerry was too big; besides, he was in the cadet corps of St. Anselm's College at Fordesmill, where Gran'pa had paid for him to go after he had failed to win a scholarship. Phillip loved being with Gerry, he was his favourite cousin, he always seemed amused at what he did. Gerry had a girl, and was not afraid of policemen or keepers on the Hill. Gerry was never afraid to fight if there was trouble; Though Gerry was not quarrelsome, nor did he behave like a hooligan. He always liked to shake hands after a fight if he could, which was being British, he said.

"Hullo, you bloodhound," said Gerry. "Do you want a pup?"

"Father wouldn't let me have one, Gerry. He dislikes London dogs."

"I mean a recruit, you dough-nut," said Gerry, pointing to the modest figure of the small boy beside him.

"Oh, I see, a tenderfoot. Yes, we do want another Scout."

"Well," said Gerry, "you can have the blisters, but I prefer two penn'orth of dark at the flicks. Think of me in the dark with a belle, being an ordinary sort of dog myself. So long, hounds!"

"So long," replied Phillip, proud that the new man had seen what a fine cousin he had.

"I say, have you been to the Electric Theatre?" he said to the newcomer when they were alone.

The boy shook his head. "Mother is afraid of my weak chest. I might get the germs of scarlet fever, whooping cough, or diphtheria, so I am not allowed to go."

"Nor am I, not from germs, though. I went with Gerry one Saturday, soon after it opened, and stayed from two o'clock until it ended at ten, so my Father was crusty, and put the kibosh on me going again. It was a very funny film. There was a man on a motorbike who rode everywhere—through houses and rooms, bumping into carts and upsetting them, and into men carrying huge cans on their shoulders, lettered 'Alcool', which is French for 'Alcohol'. Coo, there was some sport!" said Phillip, reminiscently.

The newcomer looked at Phillip with awe. Phillip examined him, as he stood before him. He wore a grey flannel suit, and carried an overcoat, neatly folded, over one arm. His grey worsted stockings showed his brown bony knees. Rather nervously, the boy said, "Please, Phillip, Mother says, may I join your patrol."

"Yes, of course you can, we need a sixth man, only"—doubtfully—"you'll have to get a uniform, you know, and pay a penny a week subscription."

"Yes, Mother says I may do that."

"We're going scouting this afternoon, you can come with us if you like. What's your name? How old are you?"

"I'm nine, and my name is Desmond Worsley Whickham Neville."

Phillip thought that was a rather grand name.

"All right. I hereby pass you into the Bloodhounds." Phillip lifted his pole, and touched him on the shoulder with the pennant. "Got your penny on you? It's for the Tent Fund. In case you've heard any remarks from the Wallace brothers, I do NOT spend it on suckers for myself. If I have borrowed a bit now and then, it is all down in this book. And what's more, the money is covered by my grant, in the Post Office Savings Bank. Figures cannot lie."

Phillip showed the new recruit the notebook.

"Now, you're a witness that I have entered up your name, Desmond, and penny. Hullo! The other men are coming, after all!" and funnelling his hands around his mouth, Phillip cried, *Boo-hoo! Boo-hoo!*

The noise was answered by two boys standing at the bottom of the road.

"That's the bay of a bloodhound on the trail, Desmond. It sounds a bit eerie, I admit, but that's how we recognise one another in the woods, when we're tracking, without wanting to let it be known that we are human. Those two who just bayed are Peter and David Wallace. Freddy Payne ought to be coming along soon. He's got a bugle, so I let him join. He's only a little tich, he can't play for toffee, so I do it for him. Of course I can't play it properly, Father won't let me practise when he's home. Even when I went into the coal-cellar, with a candle, he stopped me. Well, if Mahomet won't come to the mountain, the mountain must go to Mahomet. We'll parade by the church, our usual place."

"Will it be all right if I come on parade with my coat?" asked Desmond, diffidently.

"Oh yes, for the first afternoon. As a tenderfoot, of course, you'll have to walk behind when we march off. Can't you leave your coat somewhere? It won't rain."

Desmond looked unhappy. "Mother said I must carry it. I've had bronchitis, and have a weak chest."

"Oh, in that case it might be safer to carry it. We are going to buy capes when we get some tin, and carry them rolled under our haversacks. At Murrages you can buy dark grey capes, made of old uniforms, one-and-six each. They shoot off the rain from your shoulders."

"Have you read Sherlock Holmes in 'The Hound of the Baskervilles'?" went on Phillip. "It's an eerie story. I want to get some luminous paste, for use on my face during night-work. It'll put the fear of God into anyone after us, should we be hard-pressed at any time! *Boo-hoo! Boo-hoo!*"

Phillip walked down the road, the new tenderfoot beside him, following the two other scouts towards the church.

They stopped by the right-of-way which led down to the lane behind the cemetery wall. The patrol usually marched that way, to meet Cranmer, who awaited them by the stonemason's yard opposite the main gates.

"You men are awfully late, you know. We'll never get to Whitefoot Lane woods this way."

"We had our dinners late," replied Peter Wallace.

"Oh, I see. Anyway, why don't you salute when you see me coming on parade? You should, you know. I told you that last time. This is our new man, Desmond Neville. Carramba! Do you see what I see? Freddy Payne's got a real wide-awake!"

A very small boy, approaching on the grass beside the West Kent Grammar School, stopped and raised his bugle. After a few preliminary squeals and toots a thin, discordant noise floated down; a mere strangulation of wind.

"Why doesn't that little tich wait until he comes on parade, if he *must* blow it himself," exclaimed Phillip. "That's what comes of having a kid in the patrol who wears his sister's boots!"

"It's his bugle, so he has a right to do what he wants to with it," said Peter Wallace.

"But it's my patrol, all the same. Those squeaky notes sound simply awful, especially when you think we are supposed to be Bloodhounds."

Phillip's description of Freddy Payne as a little tich was not intended to be unkind. He did not know that Little Tich was a malformed and diminutive music-hall turn; or realise that Freddy Payne was a product of pre-natal malnutrition. Freddy Payne was in his tenth year, yet only about half the height of his broomstick. His thin, rickety legs ended in high brown boots, for his ankles were weak.

As the patrol-leader had remarked, they were girl's boots; but Freddy's mother, at her son's earnest request, had had the soles and heels studded with blakeys to give them at least some likeness to boy's boots. The iron "protectors" clattered and clinked as Freddy crossed the road, the little pewter bugle suspended across his shoulder on an old crimson curtain cord a-swing with two big tassels. Phillip stared enviously at his new hat, the chin-strap worn under the owner's lower lip, to increase his martial appearance.

"Why are you late again, Freddy?"

"I had to wait to get my Father's permission before I could come."

"Oh, very well. Come on now, fall in, men. Corporal Wallace on the right."

They shuffled into line. Phillip produced his notebook.

"Subscriptions first."

The Wallace brothers glanced at one another. Phillip began with the bugler. "Got your penny, Freddy?"

Freddy Payne blushed again. He shuffled his boots, avoiding the patrol leader's gaze.

"Father asked me to say, Phillip, what's the subscription for, and who keeps the money we give you every week?"

Phillip frowned.

"As I told you before, the patrol is saving up for a bivouac tent, for when we go camping! It costs seven and sixpence! When we've got it, it will belong to the patrol, not to me! There's no need to be alarmed—I shan't pinch your blooming oof."

"Also, Father asked me to ask," went on Freddy, shifting on

another foot. "Supposing a scout leaves the patrol, what happens to his share of the tent?"

Phillip frowned more intensely.

"Well, we haven't got the tent yet, so your Father's hypothesis does not apply! Q.E.D. as Euclid would say. Anyway, we all agreed to pay a penny a week. Haven't you brought yours?"

"I've only got my one for broken biscuits."

"Well, bring it next week, don't forget. I'll put your penny down now, so now you owe it to me personally. How about yours, Peter?"

"What about your own?" replied Peter Wallace, unmoving.

His manner startled Phillip. A pulse of fear went through him. "Well," he said hurriedly, "I am keeping mine in my Post Office book, for the tent."

"That's what *you* say," retorted Peter Wallace. "I'll trouble you for our subscriptions back."

Phillip said faintly, "What have I done?" He was utterly bewildered by the sudden change in Peter's attitude.

"Where is the money?"

Peter's eyes glinted. Would he take off his spectacles, next thing?

Staring helplessly at Peter, Phillip managed to say that the money was quite all right.

"Then I'll call for it on Monday night. And don't forget it, accidentally on purpose, will you? We've had enough of your ways. Come on, Davie."

Phillip wondered wildly what he would do if everyone left like that. Oh, it was not true to say he had pinched the Tent Fund money. He had spent most of the subscriptions, but the amount was covered by his Post Office Savings account. Had Peter put Freddy up to refusing to pay? Thank goodness it had not happened in Hillside Road, perhaps with Mr. and Mrs. Rolls, and Mr. Pye, hearing what Peter had said.

A further shock was to come. When he was a dozen yards away, Peter Wallace put his hand in his pocket and drew forth a pennant. It had a dog's head on it, as Phillip saw while Peter was tying it to his pole.

"You might like to know that I have formed my own patrol, the Greyhounds," said Peter. "And our preserves are the woods in Whitefoot Lane, so keep clear of them, or you know what you'll get!"

"But Whitefoot Lane is my preserve," said Phillip, incredulously. "I took you there first, you know I did! They are my woods, and were my Father's before me! Say it's all a joke, Peter," he said, with a tremulous smile.

"The joke is that we've found you out. Come on, Davie."

"Half a mo', Peter. I did go to Whitefoot Lane Woods first, and my Father can prove it. He took me up Whitefoot Lane on my bike! I swear on my scout's honour it's true."

"Well, the Whitefoot Lane woods, and the Seven Fields, are from now on the territory of the Greyhounds! And you're a liar, and a swanker, pretending as though the woods belonged to your father! In case you don't know, I'll tell you that I looked in a reference book in the library, and discovered that the woods and all the land belong to Mr. Forster, who is a Member of Parliament! What's more, I wrote to him for permission for the Greyhounds to go in his woods, and he says we can after the end of the month, when the pheasants have hatched, if we don't interfere with them in any way. They are private woods, so you keep out of them, or you know what to expect!" The brothers walked away.

To complete his mortification, Phillip saw Uncle Hugh approaching up the passage way from Ivy Lane. He had recently begun to feel anxiety lest such a shambling figure be connected with him. Uncle Hugh was hobbling along on two sticks, which had rubber ferrules on the bottoms instead of the usual iron ones. He had an old yellow straw-yard on his head, while his jacket and trousers flapped loose on his thin frame. Uncle Hugh was a wreck, Phillip knew that; Gran'pa had said something about him having fallen down that morning. Uncle's thin hawk-nose was bruised, and his forehead was cut, and dabbed with yellow disinfectant.

"Ha ha!" he cried. "Now we shan't need a Navy any more!"

Waving a stick at his nephew, Hugh Turney stopped by the iron cannon embedded in the asphalt of the footpath. This greeting threw him off his balance, and to prevent himself from falling he clutched the mouth of the cannon, which, being filled with mortar, gave a grip for clawed fingers. Having maintained himself upright, Hugh stared jauntily at the boys, while giving the hongroised ends of his moustache a twist between finger and thumb. Then putting on a droll face, he stared gravely at

Freddy Payne, whose wide-awake was now upon his ears, and turning to Phillip, said,

"Who is this figure of martial grandeur and indomitable aspect? How old is this modern Napoleon? Is it a case of, 'Lost in London; found under the hat'?"

"He's only a tenderfoot, Uncle Hugh. He's nine, you see. We're just about to march off."

"Only nine! Ah, to be 'only nine' again! Why, you must have been born during the war, young feller. Don't tell me your name—I can guess it!"

Whereupon Hugh Turney, resting his sticks against the churchyard railings, raised his straw-yard with one hand, and clutching the mortar in the mouth of the cannon with the other, sang in an imitation music-hall voice,

'The baby's name is Kitchener Carrington
Methuen Kerkewich White
Cronje Kruger Powell Majuba
Gatacre Warren Colenso Boojer
Capetown Mafeking French
Ladysmith Thorneycroft Bobs
Fighting Mac—Union Jack
Lyddite Pretoria—Blobbs!'

Am I right?"

"No, it's Freddy Payne," replied Phillip, wishing Uncle would go away.

"Can he sound a tucket on his trumpet, enough to rouse the dead?"

"It's a bugle, not a trumpet, Uncle. Anyway, he's only learning still."

"Well, let's hear him sound the charge! We need men like Freddy Payne to wake up this district of soot and puritanism, which would, by God, be the same thing as waking the dead! Come on, Napoleon, let's see you blow out those front teeth!"

"I told you, he's only learning, Uncle Hugh!"

"Come on, let me have a go, then! Let an old trumpeter of the C.I.V.s show what he can do! The old war-horse smells powder!"

Phillip shook his nose at Freddy. Uncle Hugh had a bad illness, as Father had warned him many times. It was highly catching.

"We must go now, Uncle, we're late already. Goodbye. Fall

in men. You go the right, Desmond, you're tallest. Freddy, will you lend me your bugle, please? Then I'll give you a sausage at the camp-fire. I promise."

The instrument was handed over, and slung on Phillip's shoulder.

"What about your old pal Peter the Painter?" said Hugh Turney.

"He's formed his own patrol."

"Ah! The old, old story! Tadpoles become frogs, grubs become beetles, bloodhounds become greyhounds, our old shirts become fine quality of laid paper; while Napoleon"—he pointed at Freddy Payne—"is reincarnated! Phillip, old war-horse, take heart! Recruits are like women, there's always one to be picked up on every street corner."

Before Uncle Hugh could say any more awful things, Phillip gave the order to trail poles, left-turn, and quick march. Raising the half-size pewter bugle, he blew what he hoped would be notes as resounding as those of the full-size copper bugles of the Boys Brigade when they marched to church on Sundays.

"H'm, your notes are of the lost, stolen, and strayed variety, I see," said Uncle Hugh, as the three small boys marched off. "Eyes right!" he called out, as he drew his frame approximately upright, and raised a hand to the salute.

As the Bloodhound patrol disappeared round the corner into what was known among certain individuals as Love Lane, the bell in the cemetery chapel beyond the high brick wall began to toll. Bravura left the stilted figure balancing itself by the cannon. Hugh Turney's face became haggard.

"Christ!" he hissed through teeth loose in their puffy gums. "Christ, I can't bear it any more! I can't! O, Christ! I can't! Et tu, Brute!"

He knew that Phillip was ashamed of him.

Breathing heavily, he clung to the iron cannon, overcome with loneliness, with the anguish of ruined hopes. He shut his eyes against the horror of the forty brick-walled acres, filled with serried lines of white marble tombstones, amidst ever-new mounds of yellow clay covered with wilted flowers of gaudy hues; and among them, perpetually, women in black, heavily veiled, weeping, with red eyes and noses; while the bell tolled through almost every period of the day.

"I was once young!" cried Hugh, lifting his eyes to the sky.

"The years like great black oxen tread the world, and I am broken underneath their feet."

He sighed deeply. Then he heard a cuckoo calling. Thank God, in that marmoreal desolation! With a shrug of thin shoulders he turned to retrieve his sticks. "I hope to God that when my turn comes a wisp, or a covey, or a veritable gaggle of cuckoos will *shout* over my grave as they lower what is left of me into the pit, and the clay thuds on m'coffin! 'Criste did not spare to visite poore men, in the colde greve'," he quoted. Dear Jesus, He understood. He was the friend of all, however rotten the tenant in the house of flesh.

Hugh Turney consoled himself with various other thoughts, among them that many a better man than he had gone the same way before him: Beethoven, Chatterton, Nietzsche, Keats. With a feeling of being in some sense companioned, he set his straw-yard, with the colours of Trinity round the brim, more securely on his head, and hobbled away up the Hill.

A victim of locomotor ataxia, he could move forward only by throwing out his feet before him, so that to a beholder it looked as though his boots were loosely attached to the bones of his legs, like weights. As he progressed, he fancied himself as an old soldier, veteran of the financiers' swindle of the South African War; at least he was alive, and not dead from enteric or Boer bullet!

"Sidney, old friend, why didn't I get that blasted enteric, and accompany you into death's dateless night?"

Resting half way up the slope, he recited to an imaginary audience,

With a wench of wanton beauties
I came unto this ailing!
Her breast was strewn, like the path of the moon
With a cloud of gliding veiling.
In her snow-beds to couch me,
I had so white a yearning,
Her pale breast 'gan, like a naked man
To set my wits a-turning.
Save may you been, from Venus queen,
And the dead that die unrightly!

Two urchins, after passing him, turned to jeer. "Yah! Laugh at 'im! Scatty! Scatty! Laugh at 'im!"

"How I agree with you, gentlemen," said Hugh Turney, gravely, to the shouts behind his back.

He sneered as he recalled the fat, corset'd, malodorous female, with painted face and lampblack'd lashes, whom he had, confounded fool, with two bottles of claret inside him, allowed to steer him out of the Empire Promenade on that September night nearly fifteen years before. Why had he been such an Elsinorian idiot as to go against his own grain, just because he had set mind and heart on an unattainable refuge—ideal—idol—Theodora Maddison. All men killed the thing they loved, as Oscar Wilde had written in Reading gaol—knowing full well that the thing a man loved was his own soul! That had to be killed, usually in childhood by a tyrant father, before a man could become, by chance circumstance, what in the eyes of the world was known as a murderer. O, if he could but have peace and quiet, if only he could have known in youth what he knew now, what novels would he not have written! He would make George Moore appear the poseur he was! Now all was lost.

"I am dying, Egypt, dying——" he groaned to the air. "I have immortal longings for thee!"

The bell from the cemetery chapel tolled as he stood, a man partly paralysed from the pelvis downwards, upon the gravel path leading to the Hill dominated by the old red brick building of the West Kent Grammar School. As though desirous of getting away from the sound of the tolling bell, Hugh Turney threw his legs out before him, one after the other, while into his mind came a desperate hope, in which he did not really believe, but which he must adhere to: that if he exercised his body hard, he might sweat-out some of the poisonous toxin from his blood, and at least *arrest* the paralysis of his nerves. After all, the doctors had declared that *spirella spirocheta* was no longer active in his blood, and that the mercury rubbed into his skin, during the secondary stage of his illness, had probably gone from his system. Human will might yet triumph over the flesh! Up, up, get into a good lather, left leg, right leg, left leg, right leg! Keep it going Hughie, my boy, get into a lather! Sweat the vice out of the vehicle of worms and epitaphs!

From below, as he rested again, came a thin and puny note—the Bloodhounds' bugle. Phillip had seen Cranmer.

Chapter 10

BLOODHOUNDS ON THE TRAIL

WHAT a relief it was to see dear old Cranmer, a grin on his "physog", waiting for them! Cranmer wore the cricketing hat Mother had found, and starched, especially for him. Cranmer's shorts were rather big for him, obviously made out of a pair of old man's trousers cut off below the knees. Phillip blew another salute on the bugle: half the notes were of the "lost, stolen, or strayed variety", as Hugh Turney had remarked.

Cranmer replied with his four-finger-in-mouth whistle, a veritable screecher.

Hardly had the patrol, or what was left of it, halted when an elderly man with a face of salt looked out of an upper window of one of the small houses of the lane, and cried out irritably,

"Be quiet, you boys! Can't you see what is coming?"

Phillip saw it was Mr. "Lower" Low, father of Lennie Low, known to him only because he sometimes came to the house to fetch Mrs. Low, who sewed for Mother and Grannie.

The reason of Mr. "Lower" Low's warning was an approaching funeral procession. Phillip stared at the black high-stepping horses with top-knots like sweep's brooms on their heads, at the top-hatted mutes standing behind the crystal and nickel-plated sides of the coach, at the polished coffin, covered with white lilies, within. When all had gone through the iron gates, the patrol fell in again, and marched down the road to Randiswell. They hurried, for it was already late. At the High Street they decided to go by tram. It was a ha'penny fare each to Fordesmill.

When they arrived there Phillip, to show off his prowess and pride as patrol leader, decided to jump off before the tram stopped at the terminus. He was standing, when he jumped, with his face towards the rear of the tram, just as it was rattling over the points to take position for the return journey. He landed, not as expected, upon his feet, but on his back, with feet in air. His broomstick bounced into the gutter, upsetting an urchin who was carrying a ha'penny pail of horse-dung hopefully for sale to some local gardener. Phillip lay in the remains of the scraping, an agonised pain at the end of his spine. Then, remembering the bugle, he twisted over, to see with relief that it was not damaged. Slowly he got to his feet, and was picking up the "pole" when he saw Father on the Sunbeam crossing the road towards him.

"Why didn't you wait until the tram stopped, you silly boy? Why, you might have been run over, if a cart or motorcar had been following! This isn't the horse-tram any longer, you know. Well, it will be a useful lesson for the future. Do you feel all right?"

"Yes—thank—you, Father," Phillip managed to say. His back hurt, but his concern was lest Father should forbid him to go scouting any more. And supposing Father saw Cranmer? He dared not look to see if Cranmer was waiting with Freddy and Desmond by the tram-stop, in case he should give a clue to his thoughts.

Cranmer, having recognised the bearded figure on the bicycle, had skedaddled, to hide among the Saturday afternoon fruit, china, and lace-curtain stalls on the other side of the Green. From behind a barrow piled with mussels and cockles he watched anxiously, wanting to go to his great friend's aid, while realising that Phillip's Ol'man might give Phil a 'iding later on for 'aving 'im in the Blood'arnds. Waiting there, Cranmer forgot the kind of hat he was wearing: a hat which served the opposite purpose of that for which it had been imagined.

Richard recognised the face under the hat before the head bobbed from view. He said nothing, then or later; but reflected, as he cycled away from the litter of paper, banana skins, and cabbage leaves around the stalls, that if his son's so-called friend had had any decent feeling in him, he would surely have gone to that friend in trouble, instead of skulking until any possible trouble had blown over.

By the time he got to the bottom of Brumley Hill, a pleasant sweat had relieved Richard of this and similar grievous thoughts; and after cycling to the top of that tree-shaded slope, he was free to enter a private world of pleasure in the lanes winding through the orchards of north-west Kent. There had been no rain for a week and more; the white dust was thick and loose, glinting with particles of flint; various birds, including partridges and turtle doves, dusted themselves in front of him as he pedalled along to the haven of the Salt Box, for an ideal tea.

About half a dozen miles London-wards from the North Downs, Phillip and his shrunken patrol sat round their camp fire in Whitefoot Lane woods. They had seen no sign of Peter Wallace; and after a period of anxious deliberation, had made their fire, cooked their sausages and sliced potatoes, and made tea of the compressed pellets. Phillip imagined, as he gazed proudly at his pennant on the pole stuck in the ground, that they were a band of hunters, in the depths of Africa. Now was the time to teach his men the Zulu's chant, from *Scouting for Boys*.

Leader (in a shrill kind of whine):
"Een gonyama."
Chorus (in astonishment):
"Gonyama?"
(with emphasis, and rising energy and enthusiasm):
"Invooboo!"
"Ya bo, ya bo. Invooboo!"

"Now when Cranmer whines 'Een gonyama', you, Freddy"—Phillip chose Freddy to make him feel important—"will translate, and say, 'He is a Lion'. Then you all say together, in chorus, in sort of surprise, 'Only a lion?' Then you give a sort of triumphant shout, all together, 'Invooboo!" Then you, Freddy, translate this again, into English, only louder, 'No, he is greater than that, he is a Hippopotamus'. Hippo-pot-amus, Freddy. You can say just 'Hippo' if you like, it's a bit of a tongue-twister, I admit. It means 'River Horse'. Anyhow, you say it Freddy. Then everyone cries 'Ya Bo!' and then Freddy, you say the English 'Yes sir, yes sir!', and after that 'Invooboo!' once more. Then you all shout, 'He is a Hippopotamus!' Is that quite clear to everyone?"

Nobody replied.

"All right, you begin, Corporal Cranmer."

Cranmer gave a faint grin, and remained silent. Suddenly he slapped his knee. "Blime, these mosskeeters 'v' got beaks like bleedun parrits!"

"No swearing! Don't muck about, men. Come on, 'Een gonyama'. Then Freddy follows with 'He is a Lion'. Look, look! Coo, what a sod! Let's watch it!"

A mosquito stood on the back of his hand, gripping with its thin legs, slightly bent.

"Christmas, look at its blinkin' proboscis boring for my blood!

Keep your physog away, don't breath on it, Freddy! It may fly away. Aough! It's got through! Coo, look how it guzzles! Don't snuffle so much, Freddy, keep your snout out of it. I want to see how much a mosquito can drink. Look, it's filling out behind, like a little red airship."

"Blime, it's a soddin' Invooboo wiv' wings on," said Cranmer, admiringly.

The skin of the insect was visibly swelling.

"Just like a hippopotamus, isn't it?" said Phillip. "I hope the bloody thing busts! Don't you worry, I won't let it get away! Just let's see if it can fly when it's full. Then let's torture it!"

The body was now thrice its original size.

"It's got the best part of a whole drop inside it. Look, it's pulled out its beastly snout! Here goes!" Phillip squashed it, then rubbed off the smear of blood on a leaf.

"I votes we move on, there's more of the beastly things humming about, men. We must leave no sign of our fire, we don't want Peter to know we've been here."

The fire was stamped out. Mess tins were cleaned with roots of grass, and fixed to belts again.

"I votes we go down to Cutler's Pond! Fall in, men!"

Phillip was thinking of the tasty broken biscuits which could be bought in the little wooden shop standing below the empty, broken, ivy-grown mill house where once, Father had told them, knives were ground, and scissors sharpened.

A wizened dame, small in keeping with her shop, which was scarcely more than nine feet square, sat behind the counter. She sold farthing's worth of broken biscuits, sweets, and licorice root, besides whipping tops, marbles, and in season, red chinese crackers. There was ginger pop, too, but this cost a ha'penny a glass; and the tram-ride had seriously depleted funds earlier that afternoon. However, Phillip had a penny left; with this he bought four paper cones of broken biscuits for himself and his men, each holding a quarter of a pound.

"We ought to hurry home now, men. My father said if I was late, he'd forbid me coming out again. Napoleon, would you like to play the bugle, going back?"

Phillip was anxious about Freddy Payne leaving the patrol. He might easily decide to join the Greyhounds, then there would be no bugle.

"Fall in! Quick march! Play, Napoleon! It doesn't matter if the notes squeak a bit. You're much better'n I am, anyway."

Thus flattered, Napoleon did his best.

After Fordesmill, the pewter bugle swung cold and unblown against its owner's blue serge hip; there was hardly a puff left in Napoleon's body. Blisters on the balls of his feet corresponded roughly to the blakeys under them. The new tenderfoot Desmond also marched desperately, with blistered heels, carrying the coat which now weighed so heavily upon his arm.

At the Green, amidst the lights of trams, shops, stalls, and carts, Phillip decided to be a hero. He would carry Freddy Payne, who was now grizzling, over his shoulder, as in the illustration in *Scouting for Boys*. So Napoleon was hoisted up, and the Bloodhounds traipsed onwards, with frequent halts for rest. Phillip, too, had blisters. Only Cranmer, whose feet had been hardened by early bootless years, seemed fresh. Soon Napoleon was riding pick-a-back on the poor boy's back. It seemed an age before they left the High Street, and turned off through St. Mary's Churchyard.

Hardly had they done so, when Richard went by on the Sunbeam.

His afternoon had been serene, in a lonely sort of way—the loneliness of a man who felt he was growing old, and had never found love.

There was a steep narrow lane beside a wood near the Salt Box, descending to a wide open valley. This was one of his especial haunts, sunlit and quiet, where seldom another person was to be seen. Here he had found his peace. Strolling among mossy flints under the beeches, he had sat down to watch a family of green woodpeckers about their nest, chipped high up in a grey snake-like bole of a tree. The westering sun gilded its bark, and illuminated the paint-pot colours of the birds. Afterwards, returning to the small cottage of red brick and tiles built in the shape of an old wooden salt box, he said goodbye to the woman who had given him tea, and mounting his cycle, pedalled back the way he had come, between hedges in bud with wild rose, bryony, and plowman's spikenard.

He passed a quarry where chalk was burned for lime, and stopped to watch a young cuckoo on the gate-post beside the lane leading down to the quarry; and thence onwards again, to the Fish Ponds of Reynard's Common. Here under the pines on the banks of the cool and silent sheet of water he undressed and put on his bathing combinations, a woollen garment patterned with blue and white rings which buttoned up the front from waist to neck, and concealed all his body between neck, elbows, and knee-caps. Then a dive into the deep water, shattering the images of trees; and a slow, delightful circuit of the lake, with feelings that he was a boy again, back in a world of enchantment.

Refreshed after his swim, he dressed in luxurious aloneness, listening to the cooing of doves and the haunting cadences of a woodlark; and after a walk around the upper lake, green with floating lily-leaves, he departed with a wave of his hand, as to an old friend; and then back across the common, redolent of gorse in bloom scenting the air.

The sun was down in the west as he reached Randiswell, to pedal slowly through that village now almost entirely urbanised, yet peaceful under the windless, cloudless summer evening that gave a feeling of ease to most men out in the open air. He sighed, thinking of the home he was returning to.

He walked the Sunbeam, with consideration for its tyres, but really because he was tired, up Hillside Road.

"Is Phillip back yet, Hetty?"

"Not yet, Dickie, but I am expecting him any minute now."

Richard pulled out his watch, then exclaimed somewhat testily, "His time is seven o'clock, and it is now getting on for nine! Why is he not home? He knows his proper time! I shall have to forbid this so-called scouting, unless——"

When Phillip had not appeared by five minutes after the hour, Richard lit the Lucas silver-plated oil-lamp of the Sunbeam, and went out to look for him. Confound the boy, why could he not play the game? He was incapable of doing the decent thing. without the need for constant reprimand.

Having rested on the wide grey stone steps of St. Mary's church, the Bloodhound patrol went on again, Napoleon once more pick-a-back on Cranmer. Phillip had the bugle now, ready to show Randiswell, as soon as they got over the top of the bridge, what sort of a patrol they were.

His effort met with no sympathy. The little procession was greeted by the jeers of small boys, waiting for their parents outside the Railway pub, with its steamy lighted windows and shouted songs and cries within.

"Yah! Stone 'em! Boo! Boo!"

"'Ere come the Boy Sprouts, laff at 'em!"

"Don't take any notice, don't heed them, I say," said Phillip.

As he passed the clock in Hawkins the barber's window he saw it was nearly a quarter past nine. Crikey!

The bugling expired.

Opposite the area of waste-land beyond Hern's shop, where new hoardings for advertisements were being erected, Phillip suddenly cried out, "Cave! My Father! I must go!" and hastily unslinging the bugle, gave it to the new man, before diving under the wooden framework.

Richard, passing on the Sunbeam with its colza-flame showing red and green in the diamond-shaped side-windows of the silver lamp on his front forks, caught a glimpse of a pale cloth hat and pennant vanishing under the wooden framework of the hoarding; but when he entered the porch of "Lindenheim" six minutes later and unlocked the door, he heard the last patter of bare feet up the stairs as Phillip disappeared towards his bedroom.

He had his own idea how the boy had managed to arrive home before him; but for the moment he said nothing. If the boy were caught by the police crossing gardens, after climbing the fences of passage-ways behind them, and summoned for trespass, he would have to declare that he was out of his parent's control. If the boy's mother encouraged him to be deceitful, then she alone must bear the consequences. He felt that the beneficial effect of his entire afternoon had been spoiled by deceit and subterfuge—and he forbore to ask any questions to avoid being told any lies.

Phillip, unmoving in bed, was wondering dejectedly if Father would forbid him to be a scout in future. He waited in suspense for some time; and as full darkness came over the slate roof and red ridge-tiles of Gran'pa's house, he hid his head under the bedclothes, and closed his eyes tight, the better to make real once more all the happenings of the afternoon.

His reverie was interrupted by Hetty coming upstairs with some bread and butter and a glass of milk.

He hid the food hurriedly when he heard Father coming.

"Until you learn to obey, my boy, you are not fit to command others. Therefore I forbid you to go scouting until such time as you show yourself to have some idea of obedience. Is that clear?"

"Yes, Father."

Phillip cried himself to sleep that night; but the next day, after giving "his solemn word and promise" not to be late again, he was told that Father would think over the matter of withdrawing his veto.

"I don't always want to be bully-ragging you, Phillip, but you must learn to be punctual."

"Yes, Father, thank you very much indeed!"

"You'll thank me later on, you know, even if you don't now, my boy," replied Richard.

Chapter 11

TINY SEED OF LOVE

By the end of July the Patrol Tent Fund had risen to nearly five shillings; this sum, however, was on paper only, and belonged, with the tent, to the future.

Meanwhile summer holidays by the seaside occupied most of Phillip's thoughts. The Maddison family, less Richard, was going to Hayling Island for the first fortnight in August. When Richard asked Phillip what he intended to do about Timmy Rat, Phillip replied that a boy had promised to look after it for him, while hoping that Father would not ask who the boy was, since it was Cranmer.

Richard had revised his opinion of this boy, after he had seen him carrying a smaller boy on his back. But why did not Phillip confide in him? Why must he always be underhand in his ways?

Early on the morning of departure Phillip met Cranmer at the cemetery gates, and handed over the box. Timmy Rat, he knew, would be safe in his hands.

Hetty had promised the children a bell-tent by the sea-shore, where they could undress for bathing, and also shelter from the rain. Their new apartments were in the middle of the island, some distance from the beach.

The morning after their arrival, upon calling at the only shop where tents were to be hired, Hetty was told that all were in use.

"Oh dear, what a pity," she said to the woman in the shop.

"I ought to have written and bespoken one, I suppose, how very foolish of me not to have done so. And I had promised my little boy, too, that he should have a tent this year. I should have written to you, of course."

"We cannot reserve any tents by post, ma'm," replied the woman. "We only let on demand, by the week. You see, visitors are always asking for them, like yourself, ma'm, and we could let them many times over."

"Yes, of course. Well, it cannot be helped now, I suppose," and thanking the woman, Hetty left the shop. "You'll have to undress under your cycling cape, that is all, Sonny, as you did last year."

"But can't we *buy* a tent, Mother? There's a very nice one in the other shop near the hotel, for seven and sixpence."

"That's a lot of money, dear. I am afraid we cannot afford it just yet."

"But the bell-tent would cost half-a-crown a week, Mum, and if we buy this one, we can use it again and again, for nothing."

"It's the outlay, dear. We could only just have afforded the five shillings for the two weeks."

"But I shan't want any new plimsolls or bathing costume this year, Mother. Can't we have the tent, as part of my Christmas present? I mean, the other two-and-sixpenny worth. I can give you back my share as soon as I get it at Christmas, then you'll have not only nothing to pay for that part of my present, but have my part of the tent for yourself into the bargain."

Hetty laughed at this idea; and taking advantage of her good humour, Phillip pressed her the more.

"I'll tell you what, Mum, if you buy a tent now the patrol will hire it from you for our camp in Whitefoot Lane woods. A shilling a week, or sixpence for three days. I am sure my men will agree. If they don't, I'll take it out of the fund."

"Well dear, I don't like to say No, since I did promise you should have a tent; but really, Sonny, I cannot afford to buy one. Next year perhaps."

"Well then, will you lend me half-a-crown, Mum, until we get home? I can draw it out of my Post Office Savings Bank."

"Certainly not, dear, I've never heard of such a thing! The money in your bank is part of your grant. You know very well that your Father has forbidden me to draw out any money for anything except your clothes and school bills. Besides, if you were ill, it might be needed for the doctor's bill. No, I won't hear of it!"

"I might get ill undressing in the cold, sitting on that icy bare shingle. It's very chilly on it, sometimes."

Hetty could not forbear to smile at the ingenious way her little boy tried to get her to buy the tent. She suspected that the main reason he wanted it was for his scout camp, but she could not bring herself to tell him that Dickie would never permit him to go camping by himself: at least, not if he wanted to sleep out at night. It was not as though there were a proper scoutmaster to look after them. If she bought the tent, Phillip would certainly be the more disappointed later on, when he learned that he would not be allowed to go camping.

"Mother, my lungs aren't very strong, are they? Seriously, I often feel shivery when I undress on the shingle. I mean at first, not when I come out of the sea, with the brine to protect the pores of my skin."

"That reminds me, you must promise me not to stay in so long this year, dear. Your lungs are all right, of course. Doctor Cave-Browne found nothing wrong with them, but you were extremely delicate as a baby; and both Father and I naturally want you to grow up into a big strong man."

"Mum, if you buy the tent, I promise you I won't stay in more than ten minutes this year. I swear it on my Scout's honour! Now here's the shop. Look, isn't it a spiffing tent? Seven and sixpence, brand new, not like those old grey Boer War things. This one is water-proof when it's raining, if you don't touch it with your finger."

The tent stood open, under the verandah before the shop. It was a flimsy affair, of thin white cotton, with an umbrella top edged with red, just large enough for one adult at a time; if that adult was prepared to stand crookedly within and, awkwardly avoiding the central pole, undress—in fine weather. But to Phillip it was a tent, the most desirable possession next to a wide-awake hat—a tent for the Bloodhound Patrol.

"I must think about it, Sonny, I cannot decide at a moment's notice, dear. You see, I have had to save up for this holiday ever since Christmas——" but Phillip was not listening; all he wanted to hear was his mother saying yes.

Which Hetty did that afternoon, after Phillip, having undressed behind the life-boat house, limped over the shingle with blood on one foot, a cut from a broken bottle used as a cock-shy by some other boys.

Fortunately the weather remained fine during the fortnight's holiday, although for three days the wind blew in from the sea, and twice the tent was blown over. Phillip set about making it secure. He sought some heavy weights to lay around the red-lined skirt, finally lugging up from the beach two old rusty anchors, which he buried in the shingle, tying the guide ropes of the pole to their shanks. The tent held against the fiercer wind of the third day which tore spray off the tops of rearing waves and carried foam inland across the common, where a new wooden stage for a concert party was being built.

The holiday seemed to go much more quickly that year upon the island which Phillip had come to regard almost as his own. The life-saving cable, with its ride of hardly more than half a minute, holding to the handles of a pulley-block, was an old story now—it was a swizz to charge tuppence a go on that little thing! Phillip kept his pennies for ice-creams, sherbet-bags, licorice bootlaces, bottles of ginger pop, and of course *The Scout*. Every minute of the long days was filled with interest; always there was something to see—Dreadnoughts and other battleships off Spithead, sometimes showing their searchlights at night—fishermen hauling their nets upon the brown shingle ridge at high tide, turning out thousands of mackerel threshing upon the wet stones as the seine was drawn in with a wave; or maybe it was a shoal of garfish—long, thin, and green—with mouths like narrow beaks. Their bones were green when you cooked them.

Phillip decided that his special friend was a stonechat. Upon the bramble flats behind the ridge the little bird everlastingly watched him as it flitted from one salt-dead bramble stalk to another, uttering its cry like two pebbles lightly struck together. But the stonechat would not make friends.

The blackberries there were red and hard, unripe; good only for using as ammunition, to be lobbed sideways through open windows as you passed by quickly, looking the other way; and also to throw at cats and dogs, just before hiding yourself, and, keeping still, watch how they looked about them to try and find where they came from. It was your wits against theirs.

Once Phillip rattled an extra special handful against Miss Barber's windows in Seaview Terrace, just to show the old hag what he thought of her for saying that she would never again have him in her house—just because he had sometimes been a few seconds late for meals when they had stayed there on the first visit to Hayling Island!

Miss Barber was too quick for him. The casement shook open, and her brown bewigged head, on which sat a lace cap, poked out.

"I shall report you to your father, when I see him next!"

"And I shall report you to *your* father, when I see *him* next," replied Phillip, as he raised his cap, and walked away. He knew he was safe, because Father was cycling on Exmoor in Somerset for his holiday, after calling on Aunt Theodora at her cottage in Lynmouth.

Soon Miss Barber, and most other things, were forgotten in the coming of the Merry Minstrels: for with them was a beautiful fair girl, sight of whom made him forget Helena Rolls. Upon the wooden platform of the open-air theatre Phillip listened to every note and word as the concert party sang their songs, made their jokes with the funny man who wore a red wig, and sometimes played scenes from *East Lynne.* Little Willie in the play who died so sadly was really the girl, with her hair hidden under the lace collar of the velvet jacket. It was the same girl who wore the pink frock and the large pink hat with the pink ribbons hanging from it, as with long hair brushed to her waist she sang, taking little steps on the bare wooden platform and making slight movements with her hands.

If I should plant a tiny seed of Love
In the garden of your heart
Would it grow to be a great big flower one day,
Or would it die and fade away?

With this vision Phillip was enthralled. Every time the canvas curtain was pulled across the platform, revealing the Merry Minstrels on their seats, ready to begin, and the pianist at the cottage piano, he was standing with other boys in silence at the back, behind the last row of twopenny chairs—they were a shilling in the front row, only for very rich people.

At each show the chief Merry Minstrel, who also acted in the play on the stage, came round among the people standing beside and behind the rows of chairs, saying "Thank you, thank you, dear people", and rattling a wooden collecting box. As he came nearer the back rows, Phillip felt awe mingled with uneasiness, for not only had he spent all his holiday money, but he had not been able to borrow anything further from his mother. The great man approached, his heavy mulberry-coloured face losing its smile and looking cross as the other boys who had been watching began to move away towards the gorse and brambles beyond the area of thin, sun-dried grasses, leaving Phillip standing there alone—too ashamed to move after them now that he had left it too late.

On the final evening of the holiday, a Friday, there were to be two performances, the second ending after dark. The stage was to be lit by Chinese lanterns! Phillip was supposed to take down the tent and bring it back to his mother in their apartments after the first evening performance, which ended at seven; and also to buy a pound of digestive biscuits, and a pound of tomatoes, for the journey next day, to be eaten with cheese. For this, Hetty had given him sixpence. He intended to return without the tent, in order to have an excuse for going back for it after his supper—and so see the Merry Minstrels' second performance.

Just before the start of the play, which was to end the first show, the actor with the thick grey hair and raddled face approached the group of boys, rattling his box; this time the girl in pink was with him, Phillip saw with thudding heart. He was unable to move away; he stood there while the actor came right up to him, and shaking the box with a double shake said loudly, for all to hear, "You see the show often enough, why don't you give something sometimes, eh?" and again he rattled the box. Feeling hot and ashamed, Phillip felt for the sixpence, and put it in the box. An unutterable feeling came over him as he did so, that he was giving away part of his mother; and with the feeling was a dark desire that he would never go back, but wander off and never see her again.

The actor smiled, showing brown teeth with a big brown whiff of whisky close to his face. "You like the show, eh?" he said, nudging him with his elbow, and winking as with a jerk of his head he indicated the girl in pink with the straight fair hair. When she lifted her lashes, and smiled at him, Phillip felt such a surge of happiness that he had to clench his hands to prevent himself from giving a shout. He would eat bread and butter with cheese instead of digestive biscuits, and *not* be sick in the train tomorrow! Then Mother would not mind that he had given the money to the Merry Minstrels.

When the first show was over, he did not return for supper,

feeling no need for food. After packing the tent, he sat on the shingle, watching the little wavelets, sparkling with phosphorescence, almost tinkling on the shore as they formed and broke at the edge of the smooth grey sea. He felt a sad happiness as the sun went down over the gorse and bramble flats, beyond which was the golf course, and the floating iron tanks which supported the West Ferry, whereon he had caught a codling, a pollack, and several small eels. Farewell West Pier, lifting with the tide! Then in the clear, still air he heard voices, and standing up, saw the lighted Chinese lanterns glowing inside the wooden stage. For a moment he found it hard to breathe, with the wonder of it all.

So Phillip, heedless of anything save his own feelings which must be obeyed, once again forgot his life and circumstance as he stared at the girl in the pink frock and large pink hat under the row of round paper lanterns.

Would you care for it, and tend it every day
Till the time when all must part,
If I should plant a tiny seed of Love
In the garden of your heart?

The sun was nearly gone beyond the gorse and bramble flats, where the stonechat was silent, sleeping in his thick brambleberry bush. Perhaps he would never hear that same bird again, with its black and white and browny feathers. Father said the life of a small bird was very short. Goodbye, little stonechat!

The moon seemed to be moving up very fast over the dark treetops in the village, as though to see what the row of Chinese lanterns were doing on the common. Ah, this was his last night at the sea-side: what did it matter that he was over two hours late for supper, when soon the canvas would be drawn across the stage of the Merry Minstrels, and then, O sad thought, the lanterns be blown out? Tears ran down his cheeks as the little boy on the stage died, it was like what he had written in the scholarship composition over two years ago, a time which now was far away in the remote past.

Very bright and lonely seemed the moon when the lanterns went out, and all the people had gone, and the chairs were occupied only by their own shadows in the moonlight.

Lingering behind, Phillip followed the Merry Minstrels at a distance as they walked to their room in the public house where they had their meals and drank whisky, though not of course the girl in the pink frock. It seemed very strange that such a wonderful girl could be the daughter of the funny man in the red wig—who was not really awfully funny.

As they sat in the room, with the door open, Phillip dared to take a last glance upon wide soft shimmering hair covering the back of a pink frock as she took a big bite at a ham sandwich—how strange to think she could be hungry like any ordinary person—and then, after a pause in the lane beyond, while with shut eyes he faced a sudden terrifying thought that the scenes of his life could never never never come back again, Phillip set off down the blank white road, tent bundle under arm. He did not stop until he came in sight of the row of cottages in the middle of the island, wondering if he would be locked out finally this time.

Perhaps if everyone was in bed, Mother would come down to open the door for him if he threw up a small amount of gravel, with the bigger stones picked out, of course, in case the glass were broken. But the lamp was alight in the downstairs room. Mother was playing Patience with herself as she waited up. She was not angry. All was well.

Soon after the return home on the Saturday afternoon the dream faded, and life became ordinary once more. His first concern was for Timmy Rat, so he went down to Hern's to find Cranmer. Timmy Rat was all right, looking very much bigger, having been fed largely on oat-meal and cheese by a considerate Cranmer, who had brought the box to the yard behind the shop first thing that morning. Phillip told Cranmer about the tent he had got, which would do for their camp; but what they needed, he said, was a baggage waggon to carry their kit in. What about some old pram-wheels? He had some wood for the frame, and a box, but wheels were the problem.

Cranmer said at once that Phillip could have the "wills" off his family perambulator. They could be put back later on. With these promised, Phillip planned to make the baggage waggon on the Monday morning.

Sunday had to be got through first. This meant church in the morning at St. Cyprian's with his two sisters, and church again in the evening with Mother at St. Simon's. To make the visit to St. Cyprian's more interesting, Phillip arranged to call for his cousin Gerry. Ralph was there, home for the week-end from

Murrage's shop in High Holborn. Ralph's feet were so tired from standing all day that he was spending Sunday in bed until the time to return after supper.

Dressed in their Eton suits, Phillip in a straw-yard and Gerry in a small bowler hat, they walked before the three girls, who in white cotton frocks and black stockings with high-laced black boots, cotton gloves and large straw hats ornamented with artificial flowers, joined the many family parties walking sedately up Charlotte Road to the toll of the single bell in the roof of the red-brick barn-like church.

St. Cyprian's had been built at the same time as the new row of flats in Charlotte Road; but, as indicated on the blue cover of every monthly parish magazine, without the tower. Many of the inhabitants in what was a new suburb had no interest in any church, old or new, so the money estimated to come in from pew-rents had not materialised. For this reason there had been added upon the ridge of the roof, in lieu of the planned tower with peal of Loughborough bells, a little erection like a louvred ventilator on a stables, housing a single bell. *Dong-dong-dong* it tolled on Sundays from a quarter to eleven to within a few minutes of the hour of Morning Service—a dismal sound to Phillip, yet part of the feeling he always had, behind his life, somehow.

There being no graveyard to the new church, the land within its spiked railings had been left in the original state of twitch-grass growing wild on the yellow clay; so the church never looked like a church to Phillip, either inside or out. Once he and Gerry had wandered inside when it was empty during the week, and it had not seemed at all wicked to speak in ordinary voices when they saw a row of paint-pots and some ladders there. A sparrow had got itself trapped inside the church, hopping about between rows of new rush-chairs—the chairs alone showed it wasn't a proper church. The bird fluttered with open beak, too weak to fly. Gerry caught it, and gave it a drink out of the bowl on the altar, which had some flowers in it, while telling Phillip that some people would say he was committing sacrilege. Gerry let drops fall from his fingers into the sparrow's mouth. Afterwards the bird began to chirp in a queer, thin little way. They took it outside and let it go among the long grasses, where, said Gerry, it would have to take its chance of being caught by the numerous moggies that howled about the place, love-making.

Everything on earth, said Gerry, had its origin in what the yowling moggies were after. Then, while Phillip grinned shyly, Gerry repeated the words of a verse that Marie Lloyd, a hot piece on the halls, was said to have sung at the New Cross Empire one Saturday night during the second house while the audience was singing the ordinary words of the chorus

It's only human nature after all
To get a pretty girl against a wall
And give your humanation
To her abomination—
It's only human nature after all!

Phillip was not quite sure what the words meant; mentally he shied away from something rather nasty, yet fascinating. Fancy Gerry daring to say that inside a church! Phillip recalled the verse as he sat at the back, next to Gerry, trying hard not to giggle at the yam-yam voice of the parson.

He sought relief, as on previous occasions, in trying to force himself to read things in the Revised Prayer Book. His eye lit on a familiar sentence.

A woman may not marry her grandfather.

At last they were shuffling in the slow throng moving down the aisles past the rows and rows of emptying rush-chairs, towards the open doors through which passed about two thousand men, women, and children in their best clothes, to the thundering of the organ. Almost the entire congregation was bound for the top of the Hill, where every fine Sunday relaxation was sought from the subduement of self in the up-and-down walk upon the crest, for half an hour or so before descending to where, from chimney and open window, smells of roast beef, roast mutton, roast potatoes, Yorkshire pudding, onion sauce, and various kinds of cabbage would then be issuing, via gas-stoves under the surveillance of thousands of more or less anxious mothers and housekeepers.

Outside in Charlotte Road, in the free air and sunlight, Phillip said he had to meet someone on the Hill, to discuss the forthcoming camp.

"Ha, I *bet* it's not about your old patrol!" said Mavis. "We all know very well who you hope to see up there! Anyway, you needn't be so anxious, we don't want to come with you."

These remarks made Phillip angry, because Mavis had seen

through his real intention, which was to go on the Hill in the hope of seeing Mr. and Mrs. Rolls and Helena.

The girl in pink was far away, like a dream that was gone; the battle of the brain, the torment of his life in Wakenham, was once more centred upon the unattainable Helena. She was harmony, she was bliss, she was free air and sunlight, she was Love.

Phillip thought of the awful state of his mind, which sometimes overcame him in bed, as the battle of the brain; so violently did his thoughts make him hot, sleepless, and despairful in the darkness while they lasted. Hetty shared his secrets; all she could do was to sympathise, and to suggest that he must work steadily and so lay the foundation of a successful career, when he might win the one he loved. She was, at times, alarmed by the intensity of his feelings; she could not but take her little boy seriously. He was so passionate, so intense, so—distracted. Ah, if only she had been able to give him the warmth of her love when he had been little, perhaps this strange craving in him for a face—for that was all it was—would not now be so intense!

"Shut up, Mavis, you don't understand."

Phillip plucked Gerry's sleeve and, taking him apart from the girls, whispered, "Do you mind if I go on the Hill alone? I want to see someone there, you know who, but don't split, will you? See you later and tell you all about it."

"Good hunting," replied Gerry, with a squeeze of his hand for which Phillip was most grateful.

He hurried up the gravel path alone, drawing on his gloves. There was a photograph of himself in his pocket, which he had dared to think of putting into Helena's hand, when her parents were not looking. The thought made him feel slightly sick with apprehension.

Streams of people were moving up to the crest by all the paths. When Phillip got to the main path on the crest, which lay east and west, he entered the crowd of people moving both ways, passing and repassing one another. Parasols bobbed over all the heads to the far distance. The path was about ten feet wide. A dry and extensive crunching noise filled the air all along the ridge, made up of thousands of boots and shoes pressing upon the yellow gravel surface. It was the Sunday parade of Wakenham's upper classes. Accompanying the parasols was a black bobbing of top-hats. There were all shapes and sizes of faces, some smooth, a few bearded; there were big moustaches, some curling upwards, others drooping at the ends, as though with resignation to middle-aged respectability; there were black frock coats and newer morning coats, one or two pairs of lavender kid gloves, a great many brown gloves. Phillip knew by the clothes, shape of starched linen collars, gloves, sticks, and the way they walked which part of Wakenham they came from—from the big houses in Twistleton Road to the new little red-brick ones on the other side of the Hill.

Hundreds of walking stick ferrules tapped on the path. People passed almost in rows four and five abreast, meeting similar rows, weaving and interweaving. All had come out of the churches, Established and Unitarian, Catholic and Episcopalian, High and Low—six or seven thousand people passing and repassing one another upon six to seven hundred yards of gravel which ancient floods and seas had deposited with the underlying yellow clay of the Woolwich beds.

"Ah, our Rabelaisian naturalist! How do you do, Phillip!"

"Goo' morning, sir!"

Black straw of the Rev. Mundy, vicar of St. Simon, was courteously raised; Phillip's old boater was lifted in respectful return. The boy walked on with sudden confidence.

Beside the main concourse on the grassy areas beside the gravel path, other people were strolling, or stopping to chat in groups around the bandstand. Some had with them children on their best behaviour, conscious of everyone else being in their Sunday best.

On the other side of the bandstand, on the slopes above the Warm Kitchen, were the lesser lights of Wakenham, the people who did not go to church, most of them bowler-hatted or with strawyards slightly tilted, and wearing blue serge suits. Some of them wore yellow or brown shoes with tweed jackets, celluloid collars, and ready-made bow-ties. They strolled and loitered in the sunshine, content in the knowledge that they too had their place in the English Sunday, the Day of Rest, envying no man, for they could pay their way, and therefore could consider themselves respectable people.

Away in the distance, under much-climbed thorn trees, played the hatless children, the urchins, the partly cared-for and the partly-uncaring: human sparrows of the congested lower streets nearer Thames. They were completely at ease, they had shrill voices and no cares.

Phillip saw Cranmer near the bandstand. He waved. That was enough for Cranmer. He had come up for no more than that: recognition from his friend and hero. Cranmer strolled away, warmly happy within. He did not dare to, or indeed want to go among the toffs on the path, the splendid people so far above him, who wore shiners.

Phillip's life was without inward glow, without contentment. He was transfixed by his anxious quest, aware that his straw-hat was old and second-hand, slightly too big for him despite paper behind the leather band, that his Eton collar was much-mended at the stud-holes, that his hands hidden by gloves were unwashed, his boots not properly blacked, that he swore and was ill-mannered, that he was a scholarship boy because his father did not have enough money to pay for him at school, that he did not really belong to such nice people: by which he meant the Rolls family, whom he dreaded to meet, whom he hoped to see. And suddenly in an alarming instant there were four faces smiling, four heads inclining together, four people saying, "Good morning, Phillip." Milton was walking beside *her!* Then all four were gone past—and he had not had time to raise his hat!

Shame, confusion, black grief that he had disgraced himself for ever overcame him. Oh, thank God that he had not been so foolish as to offer his photograph. They were gone, the beautiful faces, hidden now by hundreds of other faces laughing and talking, faces, faces which had passed while he walked on unseeing, life darkening with shame that he had not raised his hat. He must get away from everybody, hide behind the bushes, hurry, but do not run, do not let them see you running over the empty tennis courts. Climb the forbidden hurdles and through the may bushes to the broad gravel before the Grammar school! Vault the tarred railing and into the empty sheep-fold, over more wooden hurdles and down through the steep clay slopes, cracked by summer heat, hat and face and coat scraped with thorns all the way down to the railings of the gully. Hurry down the gravel, past her house, past Mr. Pye's, past Gran'pa's —"Hey, Phillip, how are ye? I say, m'boy—why'r'ye in such a hurry—hullo, he's gone as though the devil himself were after him, he-he-he——"

Knock knock knock on the door. Ring the bell. "Quick quick, open the door!"

"Why, Phillip, whatever is the matter?"

"Is Gerry here?"

"He's in the garden, dear, on the grass with Timmy Rat."

"Thank God, oh thank God."

"Why, dear, is anything the matter?"

Hetty followed him into the front room, where he had flung himself down.

"When's Father coming home from his tour?"

"He is due back tonight, dear; why do you ask?"

"It doesn't matter. Everything is ended."

She waited a little anxiously, lest he have something to tell her—oh, pray he was not in trouble again!

She felt his hot brow. He pushed her hand away. Tragic eyes looked into her face.

"Mother, what have I done with my life?"

"Done, dear? Why, in particular, do you ask, Sonny?"

"I'm no good, am I? If you told the truth, you would say I was no good. You know what Father thinks of me. I'm a throw-back! That's why no one really wants to know me!"

"Sonny dear——"

"I've asked you particularly not to call me Sonny any longer! I am ashamed of the soppy name."

"Very well, dear, we won't use the name any more, if you don't like it. Only, you know, I still think of you as my little son."

"Then please don't do so any more."

To her dismay, she saw that he was crying. She sat beside him. "Go away," his muffled voice said, his face in a cushion. "I don't want you any more."

"Oh dear, I think the joint wants basting, I must leave you, Phillip," and she left the room.

He lay still awhile; then the sound of a gay, confident voice, heard through the four open windows, made him spring up, and tensely on tip-toe, but cautiously, he approached the most northerly space. Past Gran'pa's privet hedge and faded laburnum; past the flowerless honeysuckle on the fence beyond; past Mr. Pye's privet hedge and red hawthorn from which the blossom had long dropped; by the Rolls' privet hedge and horse chestnut tree was a movement, a flash of happy faces, happy voices laughing together, happy like the faces seen inside the private room of the public house on the edge of the common by the Merry Minstrels theatre. There was never any laughter like that in his own house.

If I should plant a tiny seed of Love.

Father was coming home that evening; the best part of the holidays was over; he had succeeded in nothing in his life, nothing, nothing, nothing.

Chapter 12

IN THE WOODS

THE next morning, the agony of dream having subsided after a sound sleep, Phillip set about making the baggage waggon. He had his own small oak chest of tools which Hetty had given him for a Christmas present two years previously. She had explained to Phillip that Father had not said anything about the tools he had taken without permission and damaged, when Father had found out.

"He does not want to appear always to be complaining, you see, Sonny, or punishing his only son; but now that you have your own tools, you must leave Father's things alone in future."

The gift of the tool chest, but not Hetty's exhortation, had brought about the desired effect.

Cranmer had brought up the two pairs of wheels the previous night, and hidden them by arrangement in the Backfield; so as soon as Father had gone over the Hill to the station—a very brown-faced, soft-voiced Father, who had returned the night before on a very dusty-white Sunbeam, having come that day from Salisbury—Phillip hopped over the fence and got the wheels.

He had two planks hidden in the Backfield as well, taken originally from the abandoned building dump there some time ago. These, held by nails to the axles, made a chassis for the box-body, which was to hold the food, the tent, and the blankets. The front axle was secured by one nail only, bent over underneath, to act as a swivel for steering. A loop of rope, tied to the ends of the front axle, was to haul the waggon. It was soon made, though left unplaned, as his plane was blunt and dug into the grain of the wood, and he had no oil-stone on which to sharpen it. The concrete steps as a substitute only seemed to make the blade blunter.

Phillip had yet to obtain permission from Father to camp out. He arranged that Father should see him with the waggon in the back-garden when he came home that evening. Father was sure to ask what it was for, and on being told, might answer favourably. The critical moment arrived.

"Hullo, old chap, making one of your favourite motor cars? At least it won't leave a trail of dust behind it, as the other beastly things do."

"It's a waggon, Father, to put the patrol kit in."

"H'm, what kit? I thought you scouts carried your own."

Phillip boggled. "Oh, just our stuff, Father." Try as he might, he could not bring himself to say the word *camping*.

"Well, I am off for a cycle ride to Reynard's Common, and a dip in the Fish Ponds. It's a lovely evening for a spin. How is your machine behaving nowadays?"

It was a hint to Phillip. He hoped Phillip would ask him if he might come along.

"It goes very well, thank you, Father, especially when I oil it, as you said." He changed the subject, since the oil used was from Father's can. "A boy at school has a bike with a gear of a hundred and eight. I can't scorch very fast with mine only sixty-eight, however fast my legs turn."

"Ah, the thing to get is a three-speed Sturmey-Archer, Phillip. How are your savings for your new machine?"

"They're all right, thank you, Father." A new 3-speed Swift, like the one in Wetherly's window, was £4 19s. 6d. With easy payments it could be spread over twelve months.

Phillip was studiously examining his pair of pincers.

"Father. Oh Father—I mean—I wonder—that is, would you mind—I—I——"

"Come on, out with it, old chap! What do you want to say?"

Phillip took a deep breath, felt himself go pale and cold, heard himself saying, "Please, may I go camping with my patrol next week?"

"You mean, sleeping out?"

"Yes, Father."

"Who will be in charge, pray?"

"Me, Father. Mother promised to let us have her tent."

"Oh, did she? It looks as though it would scarcely keep out the dew, let alone a storm. And where, may I enquire, do you propose to camp?"

"In Whitefoot Lane woods, Father. By the Seven Fields."

"Have you got permission to go on the land there?"

Phillip stared at the pincers.

"Now listen to me, my boy, and try and learn a little sense. You ask me if I will allow you to go camping. You have, on your own admission, no proper tent, no permission to use another's land, and—it is my duty to add—shown no signs of responsibility. In addition, you are a minor. Therefore, you cannot accept liability for the well-being, safety, and indeed the lives of six boys including yourself."

Why did Father *always* talk as though always the worst would happen?

"I wonder whether or not you have duly considered what would be the outcome if a boy should die of pneumonia, due to culpable neglect, which it certainly would be without a proper groundsheet, or a proper tent? Shall I tell you who would be legally responsible in any action to recover damages? I would, as your parent! No, my boy, I cannot but withhold my permission for you to sleep out. And if your Mother is wise, she will withdraw her promise—here and now, to avoid further disappointment—to lend you that—well, I can scarcely call it a tent—that little cotton canopy she brought back from Hayling. What induced her to buy such a useless fal-lal, I cannot imagine! Now go upstairs like a sensible fellow and wash your hands before tea. And please regard what I have just said as being entirely for your own good."

Which talk proved to Phillip, yet once again, that to ask Father for permission to do anything was to have it, as Father would say, knocked on the head. He soused his face in the bathroom basin, to remove traces of tears, before going down to tea.

Nevertheless, or *tamen*, the baggage or *impedimenta*—two words which the patrol leader had borrowed from Caesar's *de Bello Gallico*—managed to leave Hillside Road a few days later, for the summer camp of the Bloodhounds in Whitefoot Lane woods. Phillip intended to cycle home each evening, and return the next morning in time for breakfast round the camp fire.

No pewter bugle sounded the fall-in for this great occasion.

Napoleon, the owner of the instrument, had left the patrol after his first field day, when he had arrived home, feet blistered and knickers torn.

Others had come along. The Saturday afternoon parades had not passed unnoticed in the district; they had been watched by various small boys who lived there. One was a boy who, like Desmond Neville, lived alone with his mother. One afternoon this boy had waited in the porch for Phillip's return from school; and to pass the time, as well as to make his mark, had taken out his penknife and carved his initials on the thick layer of several coats of cream paint on the stone sill of the stained-glass window beside the door. Two large letters

B J

and a quantity of paint chippings on the tiles below were seen by Phillip when he returned, satchel slung over shoulder.

The boy had meanwhile gone home, leaving a message with Hetty that his Mother would be very pleased if Phillip could come and have tea with him.

Phillip received this invitation with mixed feelings, having regard to the deep cuts on Father's paint. He decided to hide B J under a mixture of candle-grease and flour, rubbed with coal dust, then the sap of a dock-leaf. What cheek, to cut his initials like that! However, any new man was not to be sneezed at.

To make a good impression, he changed into his Eton suit, and carrying gloves, went along Charlotte Road, and knocked at Mrs. Jones' door. He bowed as he shook her hand; he sat down upstairs only when asked to; and at the tea-table he continued to wear the good-boy smile on his face he had assumed while turning the corner of Hillside Road, after practice at home before his looking-glass. Mrs. Jones was a thin and rather frail person, he decided, with a rather sad smile something like Mother's, but with a more whispery voice.

When Mrs. Jones showed anxiety about the initials her son Basil had cut, Phillip said, "Oh, Father and I do not mind little things like that, you know," and changed the subject to his uncle Hilary's motorcar. Further to make the impression on Mrs. Jones of a respectable character, he showed her the photograph of himself leaning lightly with one gloved hand on the photographer's little table with a fern on it in a pot, and smiling amiably with lips over his teeth. "A Scout must smile and whistle under all difficulties," he quoted from the Scout Law.

Mrs. Jones had a big bump on her, which he pretended not to notice as she was arranging herself, saying she was a little tired, on the sofa after tea. Quickly Mrs. Jones covered this bump with the large flowered pinafore she wore from shoulders to feet, while Phillip, his back turned, showed his new friend the silhouetted heads of birds and animals in *Scouting for Boys*. He knew, of course, the reason for the bump. Mrs. Jones was going to have a baby.

So Basil joined the patrol. He brought a friend with him after the first outing, also from the red-bricked flats, each group bearing on their common front wall a large yellow stone plaque with a sunflower emblem.

Three mothers were watching the parade from their upstairs-flat windows beside the stone sunflowers. In Hillside Road Thomas and Sarah Turney, beside their daughter Hetty, looked down from the balcony above, as the boys gave their patrol leader the special salute he had taught them.

Een gonyama!
Slight banging of poles.
Gonyama?
Wagging sideways of poles.
Invooboo! Ya bo, Invooboo!
Greater banging of poles.
Invooboo? Ya bo! Canis sanguineus maximus est!

Cheers and waggling of starched cricketing hats on poles, while the Maximum Bloody Dog gave them the scout's salute.

Phillip had his bicycle with him, he explained to his men, for fast advance scouting. The rival Greyhound Patrol, under Peter Wallace, might be about, and it was as well to find out their whereabouts beforehand. The Bloodhounds would not be caught napping. There must be a sentry outside the tent at night. Subscriptions for the Tent Fund having been collected, he gave the order to come to attention. By the right, dress! Left turn! No mucking about! Bloodhound Patrol, advance!

On either side of the waggon, to restrain it, the boys went down the road and so to the corner, where Phillip gave a final wave to the spectators in the balcony.

"I'll free-wheel down, past Peter Wallace's house, and see if the coast is clear. You others follow, but take care with the waggon. I leave Corporal Cranmer in charge."

Mistaking the order, the remaining boys arranged themselves on box, running boards, and front axle. Corporal Cranmer held the loop of clothes-line, by which to steer. He sat in front, his feet on the axle which was held to the body by the single nail.

As motion increased, the combined weights of four boys (although one was but nine, and another ten) upon the chassis of two deal boards one-inch thick laid side-by-side, together with the weight of the box filled with loaves, sugar, jars of jam, potatoes, sausages, eggs, tea, bacon, and a long yellow bar of Sunlight soap, was greater than the tensile strength of the boards, which were, moreover, heavily knotted.

They sagged; they creaked; the waggon had no brakes. "Billo mate!" shouted Cranmer to a kitten standing staring in the road. The waggon just missed it, as spokes began to thrust themselves through the rim of the off-fore wheel, already, like its fellows, partly shattered by several years' vibration under the weight of babies, coal, potatoes, firewood, and miscellaneous Cranmer cargoes. The surface of the road was stony and uneven; while the law of gravity remained immutable. The vehicle, twanging and scraping and shedding its crew en route, ran away, Cranmer alone remaining upon it in a wild hope of bringing it safely around the double corner beyond which lay the hamlet of Randiswell.

When Phillip, who had waited in vain on Randiswell Bridge for sight of his patrol, returned to find out the reason for delay, he saw the remains of the baggage waggon scattered around one of the chestnut trees of Charlotte Road. The body had left the chassis. Upon the pavement lay the broken jampot. The bacon had skidded beyond it. The sugar was scattered with the tea. One loaf was soggy with milk, a string of bedraggled sausages lay in the gutter.

Cranmer's face showed the marks of tears. One boy had a bruised knee, bound by a handkerchief. Desmond limped, his face was greyer than usual.

"We're awfully sorry, Phillip."

"Is the tent all right, that's the main thing?" The tent was Mother's.

Tent and blankets were all right. So was the bar of Sunlight soap. "Hur, that's the only thing that didn't matter."

Phillip turned to Cranmer. "Why ever did you try and ride on the waggon? You've no sense of responsibility, you know. Just look what you've done now!"

At these accusing words Cranmer began to cry. There was a bluish lump on his forehead. His hands were bleeding, where they had scraped on the kerb. But he was used to physical pain; it was Phillip's reproach that broke him.

"It's all our faults, Phillip," said Desmond. "We didn't know."

"How about my Red Cross tin, is that mucked up too?"

Phillip's mother had given him the tin, containing bandages and ointment and black "new skin" plaster for cuts. He was not concerned with first aid, only with Mother's gift.

"Look, 'ere it is, safe and sound!" cried Cranmer, relief on his face.

Phillip felt happier. "Lucky there are no beastly Randiswell kids about to come around like flies."

"Vat's right," said Cranmer. "Vere's the Mission treat today, vey'r all gone to Elmer's End by train vis morning. I seed'm go off."

They stood together, looking at the wreckage. Then Phillip went round their scratches with the Zam-Buk ointment. But what about the waggon?

"What shall us do, can't us mend it?" asked Cranmer at last.

"H'm," replied Phillip. "It's had too bad a biff on the boko, if you ask me."

Cranmer began to collect the scattered things. Examination of the waggon revealed that both planks had broken at knot-holes. One front wheel was hopelessly buckled; the others, though loose of spoke, were all right.

"Some ole rope tied rahnd the rims'll hold 'em together, Phil."

"We might get some from Hern," said Phillip, hopefully. "Come on, all hands to the pump."

They managed to get the waggon as far as Hern's yard, while Cranmer went inside to see his master about rope.

Hern came out, apron'd and shirt sleeves rolled up, and looked at the damage. He advised blind cord, to be whipped tightly round the rims. The planks might be braced, he declared, with broomsticks.

"But here's a better idea, Phillip. Why not take that old milkman's push-cart standing doing nothing in my yard? You're welcome to a lend of it. And while you're deciding, what do you say to a tin of lemonade powder? Horace knows where the tap is. I'd like to help you lads if I can. And how about a packet of cube sugar? And a tin of cocoa instead of the tea you've lost? You don't want to touch that sugar of yours, it may have splinters of glass in it."

Hern gave them a pot of jam; and when all the *impedimenta*, as Phillip called it without any thought, or knowledge, of irony, had been transferred to the milk-cart, Phillip said, "On behalf of the Bloodhound Patrol, Mr. Hern, I would like to thank you for your great kindness. Invooboo!"

"Ya boo, Invooboo!" cried the others, while Cranmer threw up his hat and uttered an extra yodelling cry of joy. It was the first holiday of his life, to which he had been looking forward with an almost excruciating happiness; but above and beyond his own feelings was his desire to please Phillip. Then standing by the wall, Cranmer decided to give a show of his skill. Bending backwards until his palms were on the ground, he transferred the weight of his body from his feet to his hands, then walked up the wall with his feet until he was balancing upside down entirely on his hands. In this posture he walked slowly sideways along the length of the wall. Still upside down, he imitated the yelping of a cur-dog struck by a stone and fleeing down the street—familiar sight and sound in Skerritt Road.

Phillip wished that Cranmer would not behave like that, especially in uniform, and was glad when it was over. Another trick of Cranmer was to swarm up a lamp-post, and swing on the ladder-rest until his momentum flung him over backwards; and he would go over and over like a wheel for nearly half a minute.

After two mugs each of Hern's lemonade, they set off once again, feeling that now their troubles were over. As an encouragement to his men, Phillip stopped at the main grocers in Randiswell, where Hetty also dealt, and bought a pound of Alphabet and Animal biscuits, asking that it be put down to Mrs. Maddison's account.

Munching these crisp little objects, one only to be put in the mouth at a time, to make them last longer, ordered Phillip, the patrol entered the High Street, and proceeded south. When after

Fordesmill the biscuits were all gone, they began to whistle, pretending they were a drum and fife band. Cranmer was also the drum, beating time with a stick on the side of the baggage cart.

Soon the heat of noon made them silent. They walked on more slowly. Their faces were red when at last they turned up Whitefoot Lane, to rest in the cooler shade of the hedge, before going onwards and upwards, and to enter the northern strip of woodland from the edge of which could be seen, across the potato fields, beyond the red misty lines of new houses, far away in the summer haze the City of London from which arose, very small and blue, the dome of St. Paul's Cathedral.

The blunt little chopper, in the shape of an axe, struck branches of trees at right-angles, merely banging them and leaving dints, so the idea of a leafy shelter to screen the white tent and the yellow milk-cart was abandoned. There were plenty of dry sticks for a fire, from which the aromatic smoke of hazel and oak wandered. No one disturbed them; only the wood pigeon's wings smacked as he flew out, the jay screamed in the distance; a robin came near, to share crumbs with its new friends. The sun was brilliant in the treetops; then more golden as it moved away and down past the trunks; red-gold as the beams, concentrated in a fiery silken cocoon, sank down upon the horizon.

It was time for Phillip to return. He put off departure as long as possible.

"Well so long, men. I'll be out early tomorrow. Don't forget to clean your teeth with sticks beaten out on stones, like in the book."

"So long, Phillip."

The way home lay between those familiar elms whose lower leaves in summer were grey from the road-dust which arose in long billowing clouds behind nearly every motorcar. Phillip noticed that motorists crept very slowly through the police trap, having been warned by A.A. men who held up white plates. Having got through the trap, the more sporty motorists moved down the levers of their throttles on the steering columns until their carburettors were hissing with the intake, as Phillip had often heard. Now, imagining himself driving a Napier, a Grand Prix Napier, three tons in weight, its bright driving chains crashing, a mile-long funnel of dust behind him swirling up to the topmost leaves of the wayside elms, he pressed on homewards, pedalling his fastest, his thoughts away from reality; to be jerked back to reality as he came near the outer limit of the trap when he saw the figure of Father on the Sunbeam cycling towards him, well into the left of the road as usual. Father was unmistakable in the distance; no one else on a bike wore a brown Norfolk jacket and knickerbockers with brown stockings that had an adder-pattern around the tops. No one cycled so upright, in such a straight line, so near to the left of the road, as Father. As the figure came nearer, Phillip began to feel himself becoming all bits and pieces from what he had been in the woods, and he made up his mind to pretend not to see Father, not to salute him or to stop. He pedalled his very fastest, bending head and back over the handlebars, pretending to be racing home in the greatest hurry as he stared at the blurred grey of the front tyre, and heard the cyclometer below going *tick-tick-tick-tick* rapidly.

When he got home, his supper was on a tray ready for him—a slice of cold mutton, slices of buttered bread, and a jar of sweet chutney. Mother was next door, playing her nightly game of bezique with Gran'pa. Cocoa in the pot, already mixed with milk, stood on the gas-stove. A message on paper by his plate said, in pencil, *Back soon, don't forget to keep flame low under cocoa and turn out all taps, Mother.*

Phillip chewed his mutton in solitary enjoyment; it was nice to be alone in the house. He was eating his cold prunes and custard when Mother came in through the scullery and asked him how he had got on.

"Oh, all right, Mum."

"Did you find a good dry site for the tent, dear?"

"Oh yes."

"Good boy, you've turned out the gas at the main, as well as in front."

"Just to prevent the prophesied paternal explosion."

"Hush, Sonny!" laughed Hetty. "You must not laugh at your Father like that."

"*I'm* not laughing; you are. Where is he? Kite-flying?"

"Oh, didn't you see him, dear? He cycled out to look at your camp, to see if you were all right. He has slung the hammock under the tree in the garden, and says you can sleep out in it, if you like."

"Oh lor', I hope he won't find our camp, and see Cranmer."

"Well, perhaps he will then see what a nice boy he really is."

"Huh. I think it's beastly of Father to make me come back every night like this, when I am the patrol-leader."

"Father is only thinking of your own good, dear, as you will realise when you are older."

"How old, Henrietta?"

"Phillip, how dare you! Don't you let your Father hear you calling me that," laughed Hetty.

"I quite understand," replied Phillip, as he went down the garden to look at the hammock.

He was lying in it, undressed and between a sheet and blankets, when his father returned. Hearing him walking down the grass, Phillip pretended to be asleep. He watched through his lashes Father quietly going back to the sitting room; then drawing a deep breath, he snuggled down to enjoy the deepening twilight alone.

Through the dusk lights in the back rooms of houses up and down the road were visible. He imagined the people within going to bed. There was no light showing at the back of Turret House; Mrs. Rolls' cook-housekeeper and parlourmaid had already gone to bed, while Helena's bedroom was in the turret in front of the house. He knew this because one morning, at half past seven, as he passed the house on his way to the Hill, to earn twopence by retrieving balls for the early morning tennis players, he heard Mr. Rolls from the main bedroom opposite call out, in a master-of-the-house voice that seemed to come itself from bedclothes, "Helena! Get up!" a lazy, easy voice. Mother said Mr. and Mrs. Rolls were a perfect love match. Phillip knew that Mrs. Rolls was going to have another baby.

Something was moving near the hammock, in the corner of the garden, where the fence was low. It rustled, then grunted. Peering over the smooth edge of the slippery esparto grass, gingerly lest he tip himself out, Phillip watched a dark shape moving over the lawn, around the base of the tree. It was only Father's hedgehog, which he had had for years, sometimes feeding it with milk in a saucer.

Stars showed above the slated roofs and the black chimney stacks. He wondered how his men were getting on, in the gleam of the camp-fire just outside the tent.

The air was cool and clear to breathe, so much nicer than in the bedroom, even with the window wide open. Pleasantly tired by the day's exertions, he fell into a deep sleep, from which he awakened soon after dawn.

In this chill, steel-clear morning air Phillip got out of the hammock, dressed, and with boots in hand crept to the door by the back steps leading up to the porch. His bicycle stood in the porch. He had oiled the lock the previous morning, meaning to leave early, with no sound. Lifting his bicycle down the path between the rockery, he carried it over the lawn, and under the railing to Gran'pa's lawn. The reason was in the gates; No. 12 stood permanently open, held by a brick, while his own had a heavy coiled spring along the hinge to the post, to keep it always shut. It might go bang, and waken Father. Phillip was taking no chances of being stopped getting to his men for breakfast round the camp fire.

Boots tied round his neck, he cycled down the pavement to Randiswell, feeling himself like Mr. Mundy the vicar, only he didn't take off his boots and sling them round his neck. Feeling delightfully free, Phillip sat on the pavement by Hern's, and put on his boots. Then he cycled onwards, fast through the solitary clear morning, into the High Street and so to the main road damp with dew.

Smoke was rising from the rear chimneys of the big walled house at the corner of Whitefoot Lane, and sinking down broadly, like the grey chiffon scarf worn by Mrs. Rolls, among the cedars in the park on the right of the sandy lane. He passed the tall hollies in the hedge, seeing the haystacks across the paddock, on the other side, the field of Sheppherd's farm. Sheppherd was said to chase away all who trespassed on his farm with the aid of a very big and fierce dog. Sheppherd was also rumoured to shoot at boys' trousers, as they ran away, with a gun loaded with tintacks.

Phillip hid his bicycle just inside the wood, and having covered it with green leaves, he went forward along the path trodden among the trees, walking on tip-toe, feeling himself to be part of the silence of the new morning. He looked about him, ready to freeze if he saw any movement; perhap she would see a fox, stealing home with a rabbit in its mouth. He had gone fifty yards or so down the path when he stopped still, his nostrils expanded, every sense alert: for he had smelled tobacco smoke. Someone must be in the wood!

Remembering the wrinkle in *Scouting for Boys* how to find the wind's direction, he wetted an index finger and held it up. It felt cold to the east, from the direction of the low sun, shining direct into his face. He could see nothing in that direction, and could easily be seen. He dropped on hands and knees, and began to creep forward with extreme care, first picking up and removing any twigs on the path before him. He reached the shelter of a big oak, and looking at ground level to his right, saw a man in shirt-sleeves standing by an upturned bicycle, repairing a puncture. He had a big pink face, and wore dark blue trousers. With alarm Phillip saw a policeman's helmet and tunic hanging on a branch-stump beside him. Christmas, a bobby!

He lay on the ground, wondering if he would be seen if he crept back to his bicycle, to make his escape while he could. But supposing the patrol started to make a noise, singing, or Cranmer imitating a stoned dog? Would the tent be confiscated, if they were summoned for trespass? What should he do? Go back to the bike, or creep on to warn the patrol? Any moment Cranmer's idiotic yelping might come through the trees. Would his bicycle be confiscated by the policeman if he saw it, in order to force him to claim it, and so give himself away for trespassing?

The bike was well hidden, and nowhere near the gap by which the policeman probably had entered. With relief he heard him whistling the tune of *Three Juicy Juicy Jews*, a comic song the red-wigged funny man had sung in the Merry Minstrels; and though this might be a trap to lure him to be careless, perhaps after all he had not seen him. He crept on until he was well out of sight, then rising to his feet, went on tensely and fast, beginning to enjoy the adventure the more because he had been saved by his sense of smell and deduction, like a real scout.

With relief he saw that the tent was still where it had been the evening before. It was closed. The fire was out before it. He felt the ashes. They were cold. The robin was waiting for him, perched on a nearby branch. That seemed to show that all was well; and peeping through the flap, he saw that the others were asleep inside, all looking tumbled up as though bent, for the tent was only four feet in diameter. Cranmer's face with open mouth lay between the boots of Desmond and Jones. His face looked swelled.

Phillip pressed his hand, having read that this was the way to waken a man without giving him too much of a start. Cranmer opened his eyes and stared a few moments with what seemed to be misery in them, then he gave a sigh and said, "Blime, I was dreaming th' slops were arter me." He raised himself on his elbow, and grinned, looking pleased to see Phillip.

There was no time to be lost. Phillip awoke the others, who scratched and sighed dully, after their uncomfortable night, before creeping out and yawning.

"Quick, there's no time to be lost! Desmond, roll up the blankets and get them into the hand-cart! Cranmer, take down the tent and put it in too! Not a sound! We may be surrounded by a posse! Don't leave this place until I give the order! I'm going back to reconnoitre. If you hear me give the Bloodhound bay, then make off up that way"—pointing to the northern edge of the wood—"and follow the hedge to the sunken lane, which leads down to the main road. There I'll join you."

"What's up, Phillip?" asked Cranmer.

"Police are in the wood! It may be a posse! I scented their tobacco smoke just in time. I'm going back to spy out the land."

He felt a little alarmed by the thought that his invention of a posse might be true.

The two tenderfeet, Jones and Allen, their faces swelled and weary, looked frightened. Seeing this Phillip said, "No need for panic! On second thoughts I don't think they can be after us, else they'd have been here before now. Only keep absolutely quiet until I return."

Phillip was in time to see the policeman, helmet and jacket on, cycling away up the lane. He watched him out of sight; then after an interval in case it was a blind, and he should return, he went back along the path and reported that the coast was clear.

"A narrow escape, chaps, lucky I crossed his wind, sniffed his shag, and immediately lay doggo. You must always creep through a wood, and speak in whispers, if you *must* talk, but it is best to remain absolutely silent when you are on the trail."

"Yes, Phillip."

Soon the fire was going. Mess-tins were held out in acrid smoke and flame for the frying of bacon and eggs, the sausages having been eaten the previous day. Phillip knew how to fry eggs, and showed the tenderfeet how to avoid making them black underneath, after sticking to the pan. The secret, he said, was to fry them after the bacon, in the fat, and swish them about as soon as they were dropped into the pan, to get the fat well under them.

"An egg on roller-skates of fat," he said. "It's best to break the yoke at once, then this mixed in with the white makes a very nice pat of tasty stuff, and you don't then drop egg all over your lap or down your shirt."

Food and tea made them all feel better. They had not been able to sleep in the tent, except in snatches, said Cranmer.

"Trouble is the moskeeters, proper bloodsuckers they are. All night long they was 'ummin' and whinin', they 'atch art'v'r dirt, for when the flap was shut the 'ummin' and whinin' got mor'an' more. Wors'n bugs they is."

"You must all put on some of Mother's Zam-Buk, and rub it in," said Phillip. "Zam-Buk cures all complaints quickly, it says so on the lid."

The pale green grease certainly seemed to ease the itch of bites.

The patrol had an unexpected visitor during breakfast. This was Mr. Jones. His appearance was something of a shock, for he appeared suddenly from behind a tree and said in a deep voice, "You're all dead, wiped out in an ambush!" while pointing a finger at them, pretending it was a revolver. "Ha ha! Caught you all napping, didn't I, eh? So this is the famous Bloodhounds' camp, is it? Well well well," he said, in a jovial sneering voice.

Later he sat on a log by the fire and insisted on singing to them. He had a biggish red face, with a large black moustache waxed to points at the ends. The whites of his eyes were yellow and livery. Phillip could not help noticing his breath, since Mr. Jones held his face close to his and fixed him with his eyes as he rolled out, in a deep nasal voice,

Come, come, come to me Thora!
Come once again to me!
Light of my life, dream of my dreams

which made Phillip a little sad, despite Mr. Jones' awful breath, and his livery eyes.

Phillip had overheard Mrs. Bigge telling Mother that Mr. Jones had left Mrs. Jones, and when she was going to have a baby, too, poor thing. There was something about a court order, but Phillip had not been interested enough to listen; all he had cared about was that Mrs. Jones had given permission for Brian to join the patrol.

Mr. Jones' breath might have been beer, or it might have been sherry and smoking together, thought Phillip, trying to remember what his own breath had smelt like, when once he had puffed it into his hand and sniffed it after drinking Father's sherry and smoking an Ogden's Tab at the same time. Mr. Jones' voice was loud, and he wished he would moderate it. But after *Thora* was ended, Mr. Jones went on to sing a song that Uncle Hugh sometimes played on his cigar-box violin with the brass horn sticking out of it, only Mr. Jones sang it vulgarly. Uncle Hugh said it should not be sung as though you were calling the cows home. He wished Mr. Jones would not hold him by the arm, while fixing him with his brown-yellowy eyes as he waved his other hand with a diamond ring on the little finger.

Uncle Hugh played the song softly, like the breeze murmuring in the trees in *Alice, Where Art Thou.* Uncle Hugh had played it to him in his room so beautifully that the tears had run down Uncle's cheeks, and he himself had nearly cried, too. Thank goodness Mavis had not been there, for she laughed whenever she saw tears in his eyes. He hated Mavis for pointing at them, and jeering. She had not done it, however, since she had tried to run away from home, after Father found out about her going in the long grass of the Backfield with Alfred Hawkins. Once or twice since then he had seen tears in her eyes, when he came upon her talking with Mother on the sofa in the front room.

"Come on now, you boys, let's have a rousin' chorus. How about 'Out Went the Gas'? Come on, there doesn't seem to be overmuch spunk in the Bloodhound patrol! You fellers are too quiet by half. Come on now! 'Out Went the Gas.' When Harry Champion sings it, he brings down the 'ouse."

"We don't know how it goes," replied Phillip, quickly, to cover his confusion. *Spunk* was an embarrassing word, for it meant something besides what grown-ups meant when they used it, a word out of old-fashioned stories like *Midshipman Easy* and Harrison Ainsworth's books. Phillip tried not to giggle, as he stared into the livery eyes under the tilted straw hat with the red and yellow band around the crown, which Mr. Jones said were the colours of his cricket team, the Rushy Green Ramblers.

"Well then, now's your chance to learn! I'll sing the song first, then you can pick it up."

Mr. Jones sang the rapid pattering song about someone giving him a big cigar, and when he lit it out went the gas, so loudly that Phillip was sure he would be heard as far as the lane; and this was just about what did happen. For when Mr. Jones was about to finish, an alarming figure with a dog appeared, walking on the path through the trees. Phillip saw that it was Sheppherd the farmer, the rumoured tin-tack pepperer of boys running away.

"I wondered who it could be. Thought you had a phonograph with you," he said mildly. "Is that your trap with the pony tied to the tree, sir?"

Mr. Jones said it was; and the farmer went on to say something about not drinking from the pond across the lane unless it was well-boiled first, owing to mosquitoes there. The only safe drinking water was from the well in his farmyard.

"I didn't expect your boys until tomorrow, sir. I told your sergeant that these 'ere woods was thick with 'skeeters when he come and see me at Shrofften, about a camp in the paddock end of the orchard. You like the woods better, eh?"

"Good God, are there any more of you? Did you all squeeze in under that little brolly last night?" asked Mr. Jones, pointing at the tent.

"Oh, Peter Wallace has to go to the Unitarian chapel on Sundays," said Phillip quickly. He trod on Cranmer's foot to warn him not to say anything about them. Peter Wallace wore three stripes of silver on his sleeves taken from his father's old Volunteer uniform. Unobtrusively Phillip rolled his tell-tale Bloodhound pennant round the top of his pole.

When the farmer had gone, Mr. Jones said the woods were not healthy. Phillip agreed, thinking of the coming of Peter Wallace and the Greyhounds. He thought that they would leave fairly soon. Then, looking up, he saw a policeman coming through the wood; and beside the policeman was his father.

Phillip remembered all his life the details of that Sunday towards the end of August, 1908. First, the ride through the forsaken early morning along the empty tram-lines, then the open road to Whitefoot Lane corner, the quiet creeping into the wood, hiding his bicycle, and the smell of tobacco smoke across his nostrils; avoidance of the policeman; the closed tent and the robin peering at him; the frying of breakfast around the fire;

Mr. Jones appearing like a Jack-in-the-box; and then the awful shock he got when he saw Father with the policeman.

Father looked grave. He spoke to Mr. Jones apart, with the policeman. Then Mr. Jones said he wanted to speak to Basil. Basil looked very frightened afterwards, and began to cry. He left with Mr. Jones, in his trap. Then Father, when Mr. Jones had driven off, and the policeman had saluted him and left also, told him to see that the other boys got to their homes as soon as possible.

"No need to hurry, Phillip, but do not delay," smiled Father, giving them all a salute. "Mrs. Jones, you see, has been taken ill, so we came out to find Basil."

When Phillip got home he found Mother talking to Mrs. Bigge and Grannie in the front room. They all looked as though they had been crying. Then Mother told him that God had taken Basil's mother, and his little baby brother, too.

The baby had a tiny white coffin to itself, beside the big wooden one. This, said Mother, was because it had lived for a few hours after it had been born early on the Sunday morning, long enough for the rector of St. Cyprian's, a very good and broad-minded man, to baptise it in Mrs. Jones' bedroom. Mother told them about it at tea, on the day of the funeral. She cried as she told them, her face wrinkled up. Mavis and Doris cried, too.

"I was the poor little baby's godmother, you see, children. Mrs. Jones was all alone, and when Basil had joined Phillip's patrol, she confided in me. She told me"—here Hetty cried again, and her voice was stifled for a few moments—"that the reason why she wanted Basil to join Phillip's patrol was because she thought that Phillip was a perfect little gentleman, and she said she would like her little son to be called Phillip."

This was so surprising to Phillip that he began to cry too, before immediately leaving the room; and that night he said his prayers, for the first time for many weeks, telling God that he would try and be a better boy in future, and please would God forgive him for being so wicked in church in the past. Mrs. Jones' pale face, with her faint reddish hair and pale blue eyes seemed to be smiling gently at him in the darkness, as he hid his face in the damp pillow, feeling himself to be very small and clear, as he had when a child, when Father was Daddy, who was warm to lie upon, whose arms had kept the darkness from him.

Part Two

SOME SCOUTING FOR BOYS

"A Scout smiles and whistles
under all difficulties."

The Scout Law.

Chapter 13

ENTER MR. PURLEY-PROUT

One Friday evening in the autumn Phillip went as usual to return his library book. This one was called *Forty Years among Cannibals, by a Missionary*. He had changed the title round, but in pencil, so that it now read *Forty Years among Missionaries, by a Cannibal*. Having handed in the volume, which was disappointing since it had been very little about cannibalism—"over that we will draw a discreet veil"—he went into the reading room, to look at the newspapers.

Phillip's motive in taking out the missionary book had not been due entirely to a desire for sensationalism. For a week or two he had, after joining the Society for the Propagation of the Gospel, attended meetings held in St. Simon's Church Hall, and found them rather depressing. There were prayers, and talks, all in a subdued key, from which he learned nothing; for Mr. Mundy seldom appeared, though when he did, he was interesting, as he spoke about Roman Britain, and in particular the Hill and surrounding country, in the pre-Christian era. The other people in the meeting were rather doleful, Phillip thought; they made him feel sort of foggy. But what had closed his phase of semi-religiosity had been a rather scaring experience in the High Street one night.

He was passing the Salvation Army hall, when a salvationist spoke to him; and when he stopped, invited him inside. Rather fearfully Phillip went, to find a kind of bare little church or mission room where old people, one of them tipsy, were sitting on wooden chairs. There were prayers; each one present had to pray out loud. One old woman called Mary moaned and said, "I have slipped back", and she did not pray. Then the old tipsy man shouted out that his load was too heavy, so it must be transferred to the Lord Jesus. Then, to his horror, the salvationist who had brought him in knelt by him and said, "Now tell the Lord Jesus your sins, brother, and He will wash them all away." Phillip did not know what to say; so he knelt there, wondering if they were going to kidnap him, and would he ever see his home again? When he said nothing, the man kneeling beside him said, "This child's heart is too full, O Lord, for him to speak; but we will all say the Lord's Prayer together, and when he is stronger, he will be able to cast away sin, and trust in the Lord."

Then they all cried *Hallelujah!* several times; and at last Phillip got away; but not before they had asked for his address. Still in a flurry, he had given his name as Wilberforce Pye, with an address of a made-up number in Charlotte Road. That was a new worry he had added to his mind; which he had escaped by avoiding both the Salvation Army uniform and the meetings of the S.P.G. in St. Simon's Hall.

Another adventure was in store for Phillip, however. It began when, in the Free Library that night, he read in *The Kentish Mercury* a letter signed *Yours in Xt, Rupert Purley-Prout, Scoutmaster, The North West Kent Troop of Baden-Powell Boy Scouts.*

He read the letter eagerly. The writer invited all who were scouts already, or who wanted to be scouts, in the district lying within three miles of the Crystal Palace to write to him at his Mother's address in Sydenham. Phillip copied the name and address into his Scout's diary, and having said goodbye to Cranmer, hastened home. He intended to tell his news to Peter Wallace, with whom he had made a truce, after returning the brothers' subscriptions to the Tent Fund.

Bloodhounds and Greyhounds were now on good terms. Clad in proper uniforms, they had manoeuvres together on Reynard's Common, followed by camp fires almost side by side.

When Phillip got to the Wallaces' house he saw a hollow turnip, in the form of a skull, with a lighted candle flickering inside, hanging in the porch. By the noise within, the Wallaces were having a party.

"Come in, Phillip, come in!" cried Nimmo Wallace, opening the door.

Inside, the front room was lit by candles only. The Wallace girls and boys were trying to bite apples on strings, or hold oranges in their teeth as they floated on the water of a hip-bath. There were several pairs of hazel nuts roasting, like chestnuts, on the lower bars of the grate. These were to tell the fortunes of the bright-eyed lassies, said Mrs. Wallace.

The Wallace family consisted of, besides the parents, three boys and three girls. The youngest of them was Nimmo, whom Phillip liked. Nimmo was very thin and merry, with big teeth in front; he had blue eyes and fair curly hair, and was always laughing. He gave Phillip a handful of walnuts he had cracked for himself.

"Go on, Phillip, do have 'em, I've had lots already!" Nimmo was always giving things away.

Cakes, grapes, figs, dates, almonds and raisins stood on the table, with ginger wine and shortbread. Phillip was surprised to find that Mr. Wallace, a genial man with big white teeth and a curled black moustache, did not look a bit like a man who had thrashed Peter; though he had the scar of Peter's bite on the back of his left hand, as Phillip saw when Mr. Wallace put his arm on Peter's shoulder. They both seemed to like each other. Mr. Wallace said that boggles, flibbertigibbets, and wandering wullies were about on that night, playing tricks, for it was Hallowe'en. He suggested that Phillip should go and ask his Father for permission to join the party, which was to end at midnight. He and Mr. Maddison, he said, were members of the Miniature Rifle Association. "Give him my compliments, Phillip, and say I sent you to ask him."

"Yes, Mr. Wallace! Thank you very much indeed!"

Phillip ran all the way up Hillside Road, finally dashing up under the porch with a shriek, feeling a ghost was about to grab him.

In the sitting room Father and Mother were playing chess. Mother looked up and smiled at him, but Father continued to stare at the board, his beard resting on his hand, the finger up by his moustache as usual.

"Well, dashed if I know how to get out of this," said Father at last, looking up with a genial expression. "In two moves you will have me checkmate, Hetty. My word, I do not like the look of this at all!"

"I am very sorry, dear," said Mother, looking pleased. "I didn't mean to."

"O-oh!" replied Father. "Why spoil it by telling me? Surely you knew what you were doing when you moved that knight there?"

Mother was laughing now. She shook her head at Phillip, to mean she had no idea of what she had done. "I thought it might be a good move, dear, certainly. Isn't it?"

"You women are the blessed limit, 'pon my soul! Don't you want to win?"

"Yes dear, of course, naturally," replied Hetty, leaning back and smiling at Phillip, who winked at her. Father had tried to teach him chess, too, without result. "I don't really know what made me make that move."

"A ghost," suggested Phillip. "It's Hallowe'en, you know."

At this Father looked up at him, seeming to be quite pleased.

"Mr. Wallace sends his compliments to you, Father, and asks me to ask you to let me join his Hallowe'en party, until it ends at midnight. All the Wallace children are staying up for it."

"What do you say, Mother?"

"Why yes, Dickie, provided Phillip has done his homework."

"Yes Mum, I did it before I went to the library."

"Very well, I give my permission," said Father. "But mind you come straight home afterwards."

"Yes Father, thank you," said Phillip; and having washed, and flattened his hair with water and brush, he ran back to the house in Charlotte Road. There he told Peter Wallace about the letter in *The Kentish Mercury*.

The Bloodhounds were now up to full strength. After Basil Jones had left, his place had been filled by a boy called Ching, but only after a certain amount of bother. Phillip had never liked Ching. They were in the same form, and sometimes walked to school together over the Hill. Milton was an occasional third; he lived in one of the big houses of Twistleton Road, and sometimes walked over the Hill for variety. Ching, thought Phillip, was a hanger-on; he never knew when he was not wanted.

Ching's talk about girls, how babies came, and other such matters embarrassed Phillip when in the company of Milton. Milton never answered, or took part in Ching's talk. Phillip felt that Milton was far above it; for was he not a friend of the Rolls? Milton lived in the next house to Mr. Gould, the father of Mrs. Rolls.

Ching had a red round face with protruding eyes and ears,

and thick lips. Phillip had disliked him ever since, sitting with him in the bushes above the gully, Ching had showed him how to do something, and then, breaking off, had tried to do it to him. Being rebuffed, Ching had suddenly spat in Phillip's eye, and then run away. Phillip had refused to speak to him for a full week after that, not for what Ching had wanted to do, but for the beastly way he had spat; and then, tired of silence, Phillip had spoken to Ching again, but without shaking hands, as Ching would not agree to apologise.

When Ching joined the Bloodhounds he was tiresome. In Phillip's words, he mucked about all the time. He took no heed of orders on manoeuvres, he tried to trip up other scouts by putting his pole between their ankles, and was always inventing enemies who were not there. And when Ching did not pay his subscription for three weeks, Phillip sent him a postcard informing him that he could consider himself drummed out. He addressed the card to Mr. Tom Ching, M(ud) P(usher), afterwards smudging the ink across the face of the card, to give it a funny appearance —the sort of joke Ching would play on anyone.

To his surprise Ching called at his house the next evening, to complain. Mother went to the door, and from the kitchen Phillip heard Ching's doleful voice. He got up; and seeing him, Ching intensified his injured air, and asked to talk with him in private. Admitted into the kitchen, Ching demanded an apology for the insult done to him. Why had Phillip called him a Mud Pusher? What had he done to deserve such a slur?

"Can't you take a joke?"

"I don't call it a joke."

"I do."

"I know you do."

"Well then, what's all the fuss about?"

"You know very well."

"I don't."

"You do."

"You're a liar."

"So are you."

"Will you fight?" cried Phillip.

"Why should I?"

"Because you complain of a joke of the kind you play on people—only worse!"

"I don't!"

"You do! I can prove it!"

"Prove it then!"

"I will when I want to, not before."

"You can't!"

"I can."

"You can go to old Nick!"

"So can you, Brother Smut! You filthy spitter!"

"What about your postcard? You ought to apologise."

"I certainly will not! You never did, after gobbing in my eye!"

It seemed to be a deadlock. The two boys stood by the table, Ching with his injured air, Phillip with a suggestion of amused superciliousness on his face as he regarded the pale blue glass-bottle-stopper eyes, so pretending to be hurt, before him. The greasy hypocrite!

"Then Father says I ought to leave your patrol."

"That will be good riddance to bad rubbish. Anyway, you're drummed out already."

Richard returned home while they were standing there. After hanging up hat, coat, and umbrella, he entered the kitchen to change his boots.

To Phillip's silent contempt, Ching showed him the postcard, saying, in a very doleful voice, "I have asked your son for an apology, Mr. Maddison, but he refuses to give it."

Richard looked at the smudged address.

"Phillip, you should apologise for that piece of gratuitous rudeness!"

Phillip said nothing.

Richard waited. At length he said,

"Very well, I shall apologise on your behalf to your friend!"

"He's not my friend," muttered Phillip.

Mavis came into the room just then, and Ching, seeing her, licked his lips quickly, and brightened up. He would not go, after Father had picked up his slippers and taken them down to the sitting room, so Phillip, for a hint, led Ching to the front door, opened it, and said goodnight.

Still Ching would not take the hint, so Phillip pushed him out, and shut the door. He was doing his homework when Father came into the kitchen and said he must go round to Ching's house and apologise to Mr. Ching.

"If you use a householder's letter-box as a means of insulting others, at least you shall, while you live under my roof, express your regret to the householder in no uncertain fashion. Do you understand? There is such a thing as libel and defamation of character, my boy!"

"Yes, Father."

"And if you are punished tomorrow for not doing your homework, you will have only yourself to blame."

Scared about possible legal action, Phillip went round to Ching's house. Ching's sister came to the door.

"It's Phillip," she called over her shoulder. "Ask him in, dear, do not let him remain standing at the door," called a voice that he recognised as belonging to Mrs. Ching.

Phillip had been once before in that house. It had a peculiar musty smell, probably from Mr. Ching, he thought. Mr. Ching was short and rather toad-like, with wide mouth and heavy clean-shaven face. He had a shaking right hand like a fin, and spoke slowly, rolling his tongue round his wide mouth. He had had a stroke, Phillip understood, not knowing what that was, except that it was rather unpleasant to have to shake hands with a cold flabby hand working all the time like a flipper. He had dead sort of eyes, like Mrs. Ching's, and those of Tom Ching also. Mrs. Ching spoke dolefully, reproving him for calling her son a Mud Pusher.

"It isn't very nice, is it, Phillip, to call a friend of yours by such a term? It upset Mr. Ching very much, and he has had a lot to contend with in life as it is."

"Well, I have called to express my regrets in no uncertain fashion, Mrs. Ching."

"I hope you mean it, Phillip," went on Mrs. Ching, while Phillip tried to breathe as little as possible, owing to the smell in the room. "I hope you will never do such a thing again. Let this be a lesson to you."

"No, I won't, Mrs. Ching," replied Phillip, thinking of Tom Ching spitting in his eye, and running away, the filthy hog.

"Very well, Phillip, we will overlook it this time. Did your Father send you?"

"Yes, Mrs. Ching."

"It would have been better, of course, if it had come from you, then your apology would have meant what it said."

Phillip tried to look suitably chastened.

Tom Ching's younger sister, who had a brown pigtail down her back, looked at him with saintly eyes, he thought. She smiled. She was rather nice, though her face had the pale, greasy look of all the Chings. The room smelt as though the window was never opened. Mr. Ching was shaking like a jelly on one side, his hand moving all the time.

"Would you like a piece of cake, Phillip?" asked Mrs. Ching, after a pause.

"No thank you," replied Phillip. "I deeply appreciate your offer, but I must get back now. I promised to play chess with Father tonight. We are having a sort of tournament."

"Do you play chess, then? Fancy that! So does Mr. Ching, only he can't get anyone to play with him. You must come round one night and give him a game."

"Yes I will, thank you very much," said Phillip, with assumed enthusiasm for a game of which he was entirely ignorant; and then shaking hands all round, he departed.

The next morning Ching was waiting for him at the top of the gully. He asked to be allowed back into the patrol.

"I can't answer just now. I think we are full up."

Phillip took long strides away from Ching, and went on to school alone. Returning that afternoon, he found Ching waiting for him beside the mill over the Randisbourne, which made dog-biscuits of weevily corn.

"Half a mo', Phillip."

"What do you want?"

"I think we ought to try and understand one another better, Phillip. After all, we pass through this world but once."

"Speak for yourself," retorted Phillip.

Ching attempted to put his arm on Phillip's shoulder, but the other pushed it away, saying with distaste, "Don't paw me! I haven't forgotten that you gobbed in my eye, even if you have!" and once again he strode away from Ching.

Ching was persistent. He reappeared that evening at the front door, this time with a different manner. In the kitchen, as he rubbed his hands together, he said, "Have a sucker?" He pulled a quarter pound bag of American Gums from his pocket, the biggest pennyworth to be bought in any sweetstuff shop, and offered one. After hesitation, Phillip selected a black licorice gum.

"Take two, go on! Have three."

"No thanks, one's enough."

It was, too. Soon his teeth were locked together.

Phillip knew that Ching had come round, hoping to see Mavis.

He shut the kitchen door. Small hopes anyone like Ching had with his sister! If only it were Milton! Ching offered to pay his back subscriptions to the Tent Fund, so Phillip said, "All right, you can come back."

The sixth boy came through Hetty's "little woman", who sewed for her, Mrs. "Lower" Low. She lived in one of the small terraced houses near the Randiswell Lane cemetery gates. Hetty was sorry for Mrs. "Lower" Low, and often went to see her, to cheer her up. She knew her tragic circumstances.

Mrs. Low was a pale, fair-haired woman of about thirty, who had married a man twenty-five years older than herself, after a younger man she loved had jilted her. Hetty was in Mrs. Low's confidence, and knew that her son Lenny had been born eight months after her marriage to Mr. Low, who was a clerk in a Mark Lane corn-merchant's office. At first her husband had doted on the baby, said Mrs. "Lower" Low. Then one day he had remarked jokingly that the child's eyes were unlike both his own, which were dark, and his wife's, which were pale blue. Lenny's eyes were grey. Where did he get his grey eyes from? What was the colour of the eyes of the fellow who had jilted her? Grey! So that was why she had married him, was it?

What had started as an idle fancy, as time went on had become a dark figment of Mr. Low's mind. He accused his wife of being pregnant when she had married him; of putting the onus of the child on him. She had caught him. Periodically in fall and winter, when he came home from the City tired and dispirited with long delays in foggy weather, the doubt recurred in his mind, with the inevitable question: who was Lenny's real father? As time went on, he became captious and bitter; he kept her housekeeping allowance to the barest minimum, so that, to buy a winter suit for Lenny, which he greatly needed, Mrs. "Lower" Low one day had borrowed ten shillings from the money-lender in the High Street. Mr. Low had found out. He had never forgiven her; he had never spoken to her from that day to the present time. If he wanted anything, he wrote it on a piece of paper, and left it on the hat-stand in the hall. He took his meals in silence, afterwards sitting in a room of his own.

Now Lenny was ten, and so afraid of Mr. Low that he would say anything rather than incur his Father's displeasure, said

Mrs. Low. His father often punished him for telling untruths. Lenny was not really deceitful by nature, he was timid, that was all.

"Yes, I am sure that is so, Mrs. Low," said Hetty, thinking of Phillip when he had been very small. "But things will come right, one day. We must always look on the bright side."

"I do try to, Mrs. Maddison, but the worst of it is that I feel Lennie is being punished for my sin in borrowing the money without the sanction of Mr. Low," wept Mrs. Low. " 'Be sure your sin will find you out', my own poor mother used to say to me, and only too true, I have said to myself, time and time again."

Mrs. Low forbore to add that the times had occurred every month since the original loan six years before. She had paid a shilling a week interest on the ten shillings for six years; and the original half-sovereign was still owing.

It was Hetty's idea that Lenny should join Phillip's patrol. She was convinced that scouting had done a great deal for her own son, for it had given him ideas beyond his home and his school, both places wherein he was, she knew, never really free and happy. Still, that was the world, in which no one was, nor was it right that they should be, allowed to please himself or herself. God's law was one of continual self-sacrifice.

Hetty had some old clothes of Phillip's which she gave Mrs. Low; while Grannie, who had been told of Mrs. Low's little boy, on a visit to her grandson Ralph in Holborn, brought back a wide-awake hat, lest the child feel he was not good enough for the others.

Thus the Bloodhounds were up to strength—Phillip, Cranmer, Desmond Neville, Tom Ching, Lenny Low, and a boy called Allen. Cranmer had got hold of a real Boer War slouch hat somehow, which, with the brim trimmed a bit, looked almost like a scout's wide-awake. It was darker, heavier—somehow, Phillip thought, it was rather in keeping with Horace Cranmer.

A week or two after the Hallowe'en party Phillip went to fulfil an old ambition to be a choir boy. He had decided that St. Mary's was the best church to apply to, as several boys from his school sang in the choir there; and St. Simon's, where Milton sang the anthems, was too good for his voice, which was rather throaty. However, listening in the empty St. Mary's to the voices in the choir-stalls near the altar, he decided to come another evening, and went instead to visit old Mr. Newman in his little house opposite the Randiswell Baths. After some interesting talk with Mr. Newman, and half a glass of port with some biscuits, he returned home, passing a green bicycle standing against the kerb under the lamp-post outside Mr. Groat's house. The peculiar thing was that the bicycle was chained to the lamp-post.

Immediately he thought that this must belong to the new Scoutmaster, from whom he had received a brief letter, ending *Yours in Christ, Rupert Purley-Prout*, which had given him the idea, not a happy one, that perhaps Mr. Purley-Prout was a curate.

The bike chained to the lamp-post was a queer, freakish sort of machine, the kind a man-suffragette, a food-faddist, or an absent-minded butterfly-catching professor would ride. It had a sort of hammock instead of a saddle; and there was a big hump on the hub of the back wheel, where the gears were. Father had pointed out the make to him once by the Fish Ponds on Reynard's Common. It had been ridden by a hatless man with long hair like a girl's, who wore sandals, a shirt of unbleached calico with wide open collar, and leather shorts with flowers on the straps and braces. They were *lederhosen*, Father had said. The man was a crack-pot, said Father. When he rode off, the crack-pot slung on his back a small placard, saying VOTES FOR WOMEN AND SALVATION FOR ENGLAND.

"What did I tell you!" said Father.

Phillip hoped that the long-haired crack-pot would not turn out to be Rupert Purley-Prout.

When Mother opened the door she said in a whisper that Mr. Prout had called to see him. He was talking to Father in the sitting room.

Immediately Phillip darted into the front room, beckoning his mother to follow him at once. In the safe darkness he said, "Has he got long hair, and a whopping great adam's apple in a scrawny neck? If so, how can I get out of it? I said in the letter that my patrol would like to join his troop. I should have added 'E. and O.E.' to it, to make it businesslike."

"I think it must be someone else you are thinking of, dear. Mr. Purley-Prout is just like any other man."

"Is he tall and thin, rather saturnine? Does he look very stern, do you think?"

"No dear, he says he's at a Theological College, preparing to take Holy Orders."

"Oh lor', then he's a curate! Does he wear one of those round white collars?"

"No, he's in a tweed suit. But why not go down and see for yourself? I told him you had only gone to see about joining St. Mary's choir, and would not be very long. Was everything all right, Sonny? Did they try your voice?"

"No, they were practising, so I didn't disturb them. I went instead to say how do you do to Mr. Newman. He showed me his birds' eggs. He's got ever so many, Mum. I've only got a thrush's, a blackbird's, a robin's, and a sparrow's in my collection. What a pity you gave me that whippoorwill's egg you got from Canada, and the prairie hen's, when I was too young! Why did you?"

"Well, you asked for them so repeatedly, dear, so I gave them to you, although I was afraid they would be broken. Now you must go and see your visitor. Father is rather tired tonight, and Mr. Prout is so very enthusiastic, he talks quite a lot."

"I don't want to see him! I don't like him."

"But you might like him, when you see him."

"I don't like the look of his bicycle, somehow."

"Oh Phillip, what a thing to say! Now go down to the sitting room. I expect they have heard you come home."

Phillip tip-toed down the stairs and along the oilcloth to the sitting room door, and listened to the voice speaking earnestly within.

"There is, happily, a passionate minority, Mr. Maddison, among which I count myself. Briefly, we realise that in this work we have the best chance of equipping our young people with those principles, and what is more important, I think you will agree, their application in the formation of character, which, history has proved, are essential in the maintenance of a great nation. We see that we are in great danger, as a nation, in resting on our oars, of relying on our past achievements. Resting thus will not produce us men of intellect, or muscle, or character! All really thoughtful people realise that it has been in times of stress and strain that our great heroes and great men were produced. It was hardship and discipline and necessity that strengthened and tempered men's characters and uplifted their aspirations! While luxury and ease, such as are dominating Society today, are tending in the opposite direction——"

"Well, I would not altogether deny that there is a grain of

truth in what you are saying——" said Father, but the other voice went on at once, drowning Father's.

"Those who remember the causes which led to the fall of the Roman Empire, see the same deteriorating influences at work amongst us Britons today, sir. And the point I would make is very simple: in Boy Scouting we have a remedy, which, if applied properly, and sincerely used, will bring back the old nobility of character, the thoughtful and considerate behaviour, the chivalry and devotion, of the old days, which we are in such danger of losing irrecoverably."

"Well, I hope you are right," said Father.

"Our underlying principle," went on the other voice, "is 'Be prepared to do what is right'. The Scout's motto is brief and to the point: 'Be prepared to do God's will: to serve others at all times and at any cost: to be kind, loyal, obedient, cheerful, pure, thrifty, and manly: to face danger and to do any work, however difficult, uncomplainingly and successfully'."

Father said, "Oh."

Phillip's instinct was to creep away, to go into Gran'pa's and hide there until Mr. Purley-Prout had gone. How could he get out of it? He waited there in indecision, then listened as the voice continued,

"It must be emphasised, Mr. Maddison, that we are Peace Scouts. We would not fight in war. Our work is to *help*. The Scout requires devotion, and ability, because his work is often difficult, and needs great presence of mind."

"Oh," said Father, again.

There was a pause, then the voice went on, "The question may be asked, sir"—Phillip was pleased that his Father was called "sir"—" 'What kind of work do we perform that requires such qualities, and the exercise of such care?' Well, Scouts learn to track animals and each other, they are taught to observe and judge signs, distances, heights, numbers, objects, landscapes, etcetera; they are shown how to camp, cook, read maps, find their way in strange country, swim, row, and—most important of all!—to keep their tempers in *all* circumstances. They are instructed in ambulance work, to rescue from fire and drowning, and how to act in *any* emergency. Does this answer your question? I think it *does!* Just think for a minute of the vast difference there would be in the average modern Briton if he had been through a course of training as a Boy Scout! Why,

Britain would be a different country! There wouldn't be so much crowding to watch football matches or horse-racing. There would be less, far less, crime, and more brightness and cheerfulness in circles where there is now a dim kind of darkness."

"Oh," said Father, and there was another pause. Then Father said, "I wonder where the boy can have got to? I must not keep you waiting here too long, Mr. Prout."

"I'll give him another five minutes, sir, if I may. Now to sum up. I have not stated the disadvantages of scouting for boys, because if reasonably worked, there are none! If a boy neglects his school preparation for scouting, he is not doing his duty as a scout! He is only a tenderfoot! A greenhorn, as he would be called by our American cousins. Are there any questions you would like to ask me, sir?"

"I don't think so, thank you," said Father. "Well, the boy does not seem to be coming, but I will tell him you have called——"

At this point Phillip crept away, in agony lest he slip on the oilcloth polished by Mrs. Feeney that day; and opening the kitchen door, said with staring eyes to his mother, "Quick! Don't say I'm home! Take my cap off the newel post by the front door, quick! Hide it! I don't want to see Purley-Prout!" and disappearing into the scullery, Phillip took Timmy Rat from his box and went into Gran'pa's next door, to tell him and Grannie about his latest adventure.

When he got back, Father was playing chess with Mother in the sitting room. "I left some cocoa for you, dear, on the gas in the kitchen," said Mother. "Turn out both taps, won't you?"

"Well," said Father, looking up. "What did you think of your new scoutmaster, Phillip?"

Phillip stared at Father, before looking down. "I don't know, Father."

"Oh," replied Father, looking at the board again. When he looked up he said, "At least you know what you have to live up to, don't you?"

What did Father mean?

Later Phillip asked his Mother if Father knew he had been listening at the door.

"I don't know dear, he didn't say."

Phillip had a letter next morning, ending in *Yours in Xt, R. Purley-Prout*, asking him to attend a meeting at the Headquarters in Fordesmill on that afternoon, a Saturday, with his patrol, for swearing-in.

The Headquarters of the North West Kent Troop were in a loft over an old carriage works, now idle. Mr. Purley-Prout awaited them. In Phillip's eyes he was a powerful figure in khaki uniform, tanned of clean-shaven face, with clouded blue-grey gaze that never seemed to look at anyone directly. He had big bulging calf muscles under his brown stockings, and highly polished brown brogue shoes.

After what Mr. Purley-Prout called a pi-jaw, they were sworn in. They went for a march, the senior patrol, the Lions, walking in front. Then came the Kangaroos. After them the Greyhounds, with the Bloodhounds last of all. Phillip was disappointed that his was the last patrol, lowest in seniority, because the Bloodhound patrol was the first, and therefore the most senior, to be formed in the district. He was unable to say this to Mr. Purley-Prout. He had, too, an idea that the new Scoutmaster did not like him.

That Mr. Purley-Prout was indeed a very strong man became evident when, having returned from the march, they went into the loft, and the Scoutmaster, taking off Sam Brown belt and wide-awake, challenged them all to hold him down on the floor.

"Let us see who is the stronger, the entire Troop put together, or its Scoutmaster! I will lie down on the floor and you can pile up on me, as many as you like. Just to give you every chance, I'll lie spread-eagled. Now, hats off! Clasp-knives unswivelled!"

Mr. Purley-Prout rolled up his sleeves, so that all could see his mighty muscles. His calves were mighty, too. Phillip somehow did not want to get too near him, so he got behind the others who were waiting, with faint grins on their faces, for the coming contest. Phillip did not feel like grinning, but he grinned all the same, as though he were enjoying himself.

Mr. Purley-Prout, having fanned dust on the wooden floor with his wide-awake, skidded the hat away through the air to the side of the room, and lay on his back on the cleaned space.

"Ready? Now then, come on, the North West Kents!"

Mr. Purley-Prout let the boys lie on him, and get their grips on his arms, legs, and shoulders. Peter Wallace sat on his stomach.

"That's right, Peter, do your utmost! You won't hurt me," Mr. Prout said. "You could strike me in the solar plexus with a sledge-hammer, and make no impression. I am a Sandow pupil, you see! Now then, everyone got his grip? One to be ready, two to be steady, three to be off!" and with that Mr. Purley-Prout heaved himself up, boys tumbling off him in all directions, but Peter Wallace still clinging to his waist. Having scattered the boys, Mr. Purley-Prout rose to his feet and waltzed round and round, Peter's legs flying outwards as he clung on. Then Mr. Purley-Prout stopped.

"All right, Peter, well done! Let go now! I could have broken your clasp, of course, had I wanted to do it. Now boys," he went on, as he drew up a chair by the fire and sat down, "you have had an example of how a normally fit man can protect himself against what might have been, in different circumstances, a gang of toughs intent on battery and robbery. Come, sit on the floor around me, and rest for a few minutes before tea. Here you, what's your name? Lenny Low? Come and sit on my knee, you look rather cold."

Lenny Low sat on Mr. Purley-Prout's knee, and Mr. Purley-Prout put his arms round Lenny.

"Now boys, I want to say one or two things. One is, never forget you are scouts in the finest troop in Britain! If you don't carry your scoutship into your home-life, your schoolwork, your games, your friendships—you're not a scout, you're a mere tenderfoot! You must be prepared for calumny, too, there are many rotters always ready to—Phillip, are you listening?"

"Yes, Mr. Prout."

"Your eyes were somewhere up in the roof, Phillip. What was I saying?"

Phillip had been interested in a big long-legged hairy spider on its carpet web up by one of the glass tiles of the roof that let in light. The spider had run forward to a wasp—a big queen wasp, it looked like—on its back in the web, feebly struggling, as it was still half hibernating. Would the spider dare to seize it?

"A scout must always be prepared everywhere, in and out of doors, Mr. Prout."

"Be prepared for what, Phillip?"

"For rotters, Mr. Prout."

Mr. Purley-Prout shifted on his chair, moving Lenny Low on his lap with him.

"Now boys, I don't propose to give you any more 'pi-jaw'. I believe a great deal more in *deeds* than in words."

Phillip stole a look at the web up above in the roof. As he had thought, the spider had funked it. The wasp was crawling away. Good!

"What you must always do, boys, is to keep the ideal of the perfect gentle knight before you. Keep your thoughts and your bodies clean, then you will do always what is right, and noble, and splendid."

The boys were silent.

"We want to see the North West Kents setting a noble ideal of unity and concord before every district in Britain. Each scout shall be a paladin, a knight-errant, and while I remember it, don't forget to try and get all the recruits you can."

Mr. Purley-Prout put down Lenny Low, straightened his khaki shorts, and stood up.

"Now for those who have tuck to cook, the fire is available. It is a point of honour with every scout to clean up afterwards, and leave everything neat and tidy. I have to go now. I leave the Senior Patrol Leader, Watty Holdwich, of the Lions, in charge. Until next week then, at two-thirty parade, outside! Zing a zing! Boom! Boom!"

"Zing a zing! Boom! Boom!" the troop replied, and the leader of the Lions shouted,

"Een gonyama!"

The rest of his patrol cried, "Gonyama?"

"Ya bo, ya bo! Invooboo!"

Erect and tense, Mr. Purley-Prout gave them the salute, spun round, and bounded away.

Chapter 14

LEAFLESS DAYS

DURING the dull depths of the year, Phillip did not call his patrol together. It was a time of inactivity because the sun, though now climbing to the spring solstice, was unable to clear the vapours of London river, so that smoke and dust combined in a seasonal shroud, at times darkening to a pall.

Still, the days were lengthening, said Richard, settling to read *The Daily Trident* in his armchair, slippered feet before the fire, Hetty and the children more or less happy in the room with him:

Phillip working at his Stamp Book, Mavis making her new Red Riding Hood cloak for party-going, and Doris sewing clothes for her dollies.

The Maddison children had been invited to three parties that Christmas, not counting Gran'pa's and Aunt Dorrie's. The best of the parties was at the Todds, down the road. The Todds always had about a dozen children to tea and supper, with conjuring tricks, table fireworks, bonbons with toys in them as well as paper caps, and plenty of cream-puffs, jellies, mince-pies, blancmanges of various flavours, in addition to cold chicken and a ham.

Phillip secretly thought that Mavis looked very pretty in her Red Riding Hood cape with her hair up, and a sort of diamond comb stuck in it. It was half fancy dress, said Mother. Mavis had rubbed some petals of a geranium on her cheeks, and a little blue ink from her finger on her eyelids, like she did for the St. Cyprian's Hall charades, in which she had acted. Mavis' ears, he noticed, looked very neat and delicate. He felt secretly proud of her.

He wore his Etons, with dancing pumps and white kid gloves, in case there was any dancing at the Todds. It was just as well to be prepared, said Hetty. The last time they had gone, they had danced the Polka, the Washington Post, the Lancers, and the Barn Dance.

Mr. Todd usually had several of his friends as well, so that it was half a grown-ups' party. Mrs. Todd was a big woman, always jolly; and although Phillip was a bit wary of both her and Mr. Todd—who had a red face and a nose like a parrot's beak—yet they were both very nice to him, he thought. His wariness was due to a belief that they must consider him a bit of a hooligan, since they were friends with the Pyes up the road. The Pye children were there, but not Mr. Pye, for which Phillip was relieved. He was also relieved, in another way, that Helena Rolls did not come to the Todd parties, although they were friends.

Mr. Todd told them the same story every year, as he pointed with pride to a photograph on the wall of a bearded figure within an oval in the centre, with six younger men, each in a little circle by himself, around the Old Pater. Each son, declared Mr. Todd, had done well. Each had turned out to be a credit to the Old Pater, who was, he said, a partner in the Firm, Rice's Night-lights, Candles, and Motor Oil Ltd., on Thameside—and at this point in the annual Christmas party Mr. Todd, beaming, put his arm round his wife's waist, saying that he had married the daughter of the founder, Mr. Rice himself.

"Why, the candles you see on the Christmas Tree are Rice's!"

Then the grown-ups drank a toast to the Old Pater; and afterwards Mr. Todd, smiling hugely, asked Phillip to guess which of the six faces was himself. Phillip pretended to be puzzled, while Mr. Todd waited, delighted, until he pointed to the right face.

Postman's Knock, Hunt the Slipper, Charades, Musical Chairs, Consequences (Phillip's pencilled additions to the slips of paper handed round, folded up, varied from the grotesque and startling to the flippant and sarcastic)—all good things came to an end at ten o'clock, when after Auld Lang Syne and a final cup of cocoa, coats and mufflers and cloaks were donned, and with goodnights and thankyous, the guests departed, immediately after arrival home again to be told to toddle up to bed, to clean teeth and to make no noise; and so into cold sheets, still dazzled by the wonderful party.

At Mr. Jenkins' house there was a different sort of dancing. Mr. Jenkins, a comparative newcomer to No. 8, was different from the other people in the road. He always dressed up for his parties in yachting uniform, complete with cap, and he danced with each child in turn, while making the music himself by humming the *Merry Widow* waltz, *Waltz Me Around Again Willie*, or *Over the Waves*, generally making the party go, while tiny Mrs. Jenkins, despite a perpetual smile on her small round shiny face, seemed somehow always out of it. Nobody danced with her; but perhaps she did not mind, being the mother, thought Phillip.

The third party was at the other end of Charlotte Road, to some friends of Mavis. Thither the three children went, Phillip, as before, in his Eton suit, Mavis in her Red Riding Hood cloak covering her white frock, worn with black stockings and boots—changing into pumps inside the house—and Doris in a Kate Greenaway costume which Mrs. Lower Low had made for her.

It was a musical house, so the children took their songs. Phillip sang *In the Cathedral*, and *Love's Old Sweet Song* (which was his mother's favourite) helped out by Mavis; while Doris played her new piece, *Beethoven's Farewell to the Piano*; of which Uncle Hugh, after hearing her play it at home, had remarked, "And I don't wonder why"; to which Mother had replied, "Hush,

Hughie dear, she is doing her best." "So did Beethoven, poor devil", Uncle Hugh had said. Then he had said he was sorry, it was a caddish remark, and had tried to stroke Doris's head, but she had ducked down, and gone out of the room with a stony face.

When Hetty called to pay Mrs. "Lower" Low for the dress, Mr. Low came to the door. Mrs. Low was upstairs. Mr. Low invited Hetty into the front room. Then he wrote something on a piece of paper and took it up to his wife, instead of calling her down. Mrs. Low appeared, clutching the piece of paper, profuse in apology, and looking so crushed that Hetty had to restrain herself from begging Mr. Low to be kinder to his wife.

One day towards the end of the holidays Hetty said to Phillip, "I am just going round to see Mrs. "Lower" Low about making you some new nightshirts. Would you like to come for a walk with me first, Phillip, then we can call in on the way back, and she can take your measurements."

"No, thanks," said Phillip. "I don't want any new nightshirts. They always scratch me so."

"Well, I expect we can manage without special new measurements," replied Hetty.

Left alone in the house, Phillip went into his father's room and took his B.S.A. air rifle out of the cupboard there. He knew where the waisted lead pellets were kept, and helped himself to a dozen. Then he went into Mavis' bedroom—she was spending a week at Beau Brickhill with the cousins—and opening the bottom of the window, he loaded the spring and waited for starlings to fly to the elm.

Various mutton bones and lumps of fat hung from strings from the lower branches. Tomtits came to them, robins tried to cling on, starlings chittered about them. Phillip was after starlings, birds he did not like, as they were noisy and went about in mobs. He shot two, drilling through each bird a hole. The waisted pellet, spinning beyond the tree, struck the blind brick wall of a house beyond the Backfield.

Then cleaning the rifle, particularly any finger-prints on its stock and pistol-grip, Phillip put it back in the cupboard. By the time Hetty returned, the starlings had been skinned in the scullery, and a mixture of whiting, oatmeal soap, and alum rubbed on the skins, to cure them. These he nailed on a narrow board, afterwards hiding the board up the chimney of his bedroom, where the draught would dry the skins. Father would never think of looking for them there. The bodies of the starlings were to be put into the steak-and-kidney pudding Mother was to make the next day, to give it a sporting flavour.

One day in the new term, a Monday and washing day, Phillip took mutton sandwiches for what was called "free lunch" at school. He was unable to eat them. They were too salt. On coming home, he refused his tea, saying he had a headache. Alone in the kitchen, he settled to do his homework; but feeling seedy, he packed up his satchel and went to bed. There he slept fitfully, to awaken and see Father's face in candlelight, and Father asking him angrily why he had gone to bed without doing his homework.

"Up you get this instant! I know you very well, you know, you cannot deceive me! You are malingering!"

"I feel poorly, Father."

"I do not believe you!"

So Phillip put on his clothes again, and, after immersing his face in cold water to cure his headache, went downstairs, while part of him seemed to be floating off about the kitchen. Shivers of cold ran up his spine. He did his homework somehow, and was unable to eat any supper. Going to say goodnight obediently to Father in the sitting room, he listened to a lecture about honesty being the best policy, and that work was man's obligation upon the earth, to be undertaken as a duty, to be faced like a man, not to be run away from, self-indulgently. Phillip listened with his usual immobility and expressionless face, knowing that what Father said was true; all the same, he had *not* pretended to be feeling poorly.

The next morning his flushed face and feverish forehead convinced both parents that he ought to stay in bed until he had been seen by Dr. Cave-Browne. After the doctor had gone, Phillip was told to remain in bed. Several times he was sick. His head throbbed. His throat was swollen and sore.

In the evening Father came and sat on the edge of his bed, and speaking kindly, told him that he had scarlet fever; and if he remained at home, it would mean that he would have to have a nurse, that Doris would have to go elsewhere during the period of quarantine, and a considerable expense would be involved in the matter of the entire house being fumigated with sulphur candles, and the need to have it repainted afterwards, as when Mavis had had scarlet fever. Therefore, all things being considered, it would be best if he went to the Fever Hospital, where he would be taken proper care of, and quickly grow well again.

Phillip thought wildly for a moment that he would perhaps never again see Mother; but he remained still, and said huskily, "Yes, Father."

An hour or two later a horse ambulance came up Hillside Road. Phillip, wrapped in blankets, was carried down the stairs and out of the house. After saying goodbye to Mother, Father, and Mrs. Bigge from inside the ambulance, he was taken away in the night, an unspeaking nurse beside him, and an oil-lamp burning fitfully above his head. On arrival in the ward he was washed in bed, first on one side then the other, and tucked into rough sheets, with tight blankets. He cried silently for some hours, and the night nurse, in felt slippers, brought him a cup of gruel to drink. On the cup, in red letters, he read the words, *Metropolitan Asylums Board*, with silent terror.

After the first week, when the fever had died down, Phillip began to behave oddly in the ward, sometimes not wanting to open Mother's letters, but keeping them under his pillow unread, while he set himself to think that he did not want to see her ever again. When at last he did read the letters, he hurt himself further by not replying. When eventually he did so, it was a brief little letter, beginning *Dear Mrs. Maddison*, and ending up *Yours Truly, Phillip Maddison*, in his best writing, which resembled Richard's in the painstaking correctitude of each stroke, pot-hook, crossed *t* and dotted *i*.

He became the clown of the ward as the fever and pickled-crimson appearance of his body abated. At any moment he was liable to jump on his bed, wave his arms in the thick flannel nightshirt, waggle his head about like an imbecile, and then to imitate bagpipes by holding back his head, pinching his nostrils, uttering prolonged bleating cries while tapping his adam's-apple with the stiff fingers of his other hand. After finding some sort of appreciation in the ward, among the nurses and the other boys, he looked forward to his mother's letters with less anguish, and replied to them in pencil, saying that he was enjoying his holiday very much, and that she need not fear infection from his "missives", as they were "all well-baked before leaving the premises of the Metropolitan Asylums Board".

"H'm," remarked Richard, after reading the "missive" in his armchair. "The iron seems to have entered into your best boy's soul, Hetty."

After three weeks in the hospital, Phillip and some other boys of the ward, dressed in blue suits, went away to the convalescent home at Dartford. This too belonged to the Metropolitan Asylums Board. The building was on a small hill, and surrounded by the usual high spiked railings of authority. It adjoined a real Lunatic Asylum. From the slope of the hill there was a view of the Lunatics' Graveyard just beyond the railings, and several times a week there were funerals to be watched from the distance of a hundred yards or so. The boys and youths of the convalescent home stood and stared in silence while relations wept around the pit, all clad in black. Every time he saw a lunatic being buried Phillip thought of Mother's face, should he die, and be buried there. The thought of the utter sadness of Mother's face was almost unbearable; but he kept his feelings, as usual, to himself.

Never once since he had left in the ambulance at night, lying in thick warm blankets in the light of a hanging oil-lamp, had Phillip thought of Father.

The day approached when he would have his own clothes again, and meet Mother. He dreaded the meeting. Since being away, he had lived another life of his own, making friends with two boys. He no longer cried at night; he enjoyed the meals, at the long tables, except one tea-time, when someone gave him bread and butter, for a joke, which was the equivalent of those chocolates, called hypocrits, which some boys at school gave to others—filled with a peppery liquid which burned the tongue for hours afterwards. Phillip did not know that the "butter" on the bread on his plate was yellow soap until he had taken a good bite, which filled up some of his teeth; and though he scrubbed them at once, retching once or twice, in the wash-house, the soapy bubbly taste remained until the next day.

When at last he met Mother again, he felt somehow ever so small, whereas in the convalescent home he had not been conscious of being any size. Mother smiled her usual smile, gay but also a little sad. He felt rather sad, too. It was a queer train journey to Brighton. He did not feel able to kiss her, but read *The Boy's Own Paper* in his corner, by himself.

They had tiny little lodgings near the front, with a fire in the smallest grate, curved like a shell and half way up the wall. A kettle steamed on the side. After tea he went to bed, sleeping on a couch in Mother's room. In the middle of the night he awakened, after a dream in which he had been trying to claw himself out of a grave, and on awakening, the unfamiliar dark room appeared to be the grave.

Hetty found him standing up in his nightshirt, running with perspiration, and trying to speak in a choked voice. She soothed him when he got back to bed, promising to leave the candle alight. After he had cried, he felt better, and gave her a good-night kiss; and the effects of six weeks in the fever hospital and convalescent home began to recede, and he felt suddenly happy.

They went for walks on the front, and to a concert, where a fat man sang *I'm afraid to go home in the dark*, rather on the lines of the Merry Minstrels on Hayling Island; but this lot was not in holiday mood like the Minstrels. There were only about twenty people in the audience, and it was raining on the windows.

At night in the little room, with the small fire glowing, he and Mother played Ludo, and whenever he or she turned up the Prince of Wales feathers on the dice, Phillip cried, imitating Cranmer, "Fevvers!" and they laughed until their sides ached.

"Fevvers again! *Fevvers!*"

It was the funniest word, and Ludo was the best game he had ever played, he and Mother together in the tiny old-fashioned room over a shop in Old Brighton, where the cobbled street was so narrow that only one horse and cart could proceed at a time. It really was a wonderful week, thought Phillip, when at last they were home again.

Chapter 15

THE PALADIN

"So you're going to the Crystal Palace, are ye, m'boy?" said Thomas Turney to Phillip, early one Saturday afternoon towards the end of March. "Well, that is an interesting place.

I remember my mother taking me to see it soon after it was opened by the Old Queen. M'brother Fred came, too, and a sister—let me see, was it you, Marian?"

"You know it was, Tom," replied Great-Aunt Marian, who had left her apartments at Greenwich to keep house for Gran'pa while Grannie was away for an operation. "Do you not recall that we saw the Duke of Wellington, and heard him telling another gentleman that the way to clear the flocks of sparrows living under the glass was to use sparrowhawks? It has always remained in my memory as an example of a clear and practical mind. O, I did so admire the Duke! And he gave me a glance as we passed! Only at a distance, of course, you understand, Phillip," said Great-aunt Marian, "for we were very ordinary folk."

Phillip liked Great-aunt Marian. She did not seem like a real aunt, like Aunt Belle, Aunt Viccy, or Aunt Dora, although she was ever so much older. Great-aunt Marian was very alert and upright, she had a nice clear voice and said things direct, she never told you how you should behave, like the Aunts who were Father's sisters.

He had gone next-door, in uniform, to tell them of the Great Review of all London's Boy Scouts that afternoon in the grounds of the Crystal Palace.

"And there is a mock battle after the review, you know!"

"Fancy that!" said Gran'pa. "Well, the Crystal Palace has seen some rare occasions, m'boy. Once I saw Blondin, the Swiss, walking on a tight wire stretched between the two water-towers. Half way across he stopped to cook and eat an omelette, he-he-he! He was three hundred feet above the ground."

"Did he fall, Gramps?"

"No, fortunately for him! He would have gone through the glass if he had, and dropped among the stuffed animals and statues down below. Blondin was a remarkable man. Your Uncle Charley, when he was in Canada, saw him walk over Niagara Falls, with a hoop around his ankles. But the distance he walked then would be less, I fancy, than between the two towers at the Crystal Palace. They must be over a quarter of a mile apart."

"I would like to have a sparrowhawk, Gran'pa, to train it to catch spadgers. But I would have to keep it well away from Timmy Rat. Although kestrels go after mice and rats, rather than sparrowhawks. I suppose Sparhawk Street, where the Firm is, came from sparrowhawks?"

"Yes, Phillip," replied Thomas Turney, surprised and pleased at his grandson's reference. "It's a corruption. There were trees in High Holborn not so long ago, and what the Cockney calls 'Spar'r'awk' probably nested in them, or on the roofs of houses. D'ye know, when m'Father was a boy, rooks used to nest in the trees of what is now called Trafalgar Square? They called it Porrige Island in those days, after the mud, he-he-he! That was before Nelson sunk Boney's fleet. You may be interested to know that my Father's father, that is your great-great-grandfather, Phillip—are ye listening, hey?—I said my Father's father was a Navy man then, and commanded a frigate. How would you like to be a sailor when you grow up, eh?"

"Not very much, Gran'pa. I am very easily sea-sick."

"Well, so was Nelson, Phillip."

"All the same, I wouldn't mind being a fisherman. I could hold the rope on shore, like one man does at Hayling Island. I think I might like to be a farmer, too."

"Well, farming's done for in England, Phillip. It's a thing of the past. You can't put back the clock, m'boy. Your other grandfather tried, you know, and more harm than good came of it—you can't go against the times, you know."

"Well, I think I'd better be going now, Gran'pa. I hope Grannie will soon be better. Goodbye, Aunt Marian." He shook hands with both, and left the room: but came back to say, "I hope there is a balloon race from the Crystal Palace this afternoon! I would like to see one close to. Goodbye once more."

It was a fine clear day, with an abatement of the east winds which had been drying the streets of the soddenness of winter. Phillip had told his men on no account to be late on parade, for the honour of the Patrol. All must bring their own sausages: this was for Ching's benefit, as Ching was a bit of a cadger. Boots must be polished, Mr. Prout had warned them, faces and hands clean, poles scrubbed, hair cut, neckerchiefs washed—for the honour of the Troop.

The Bloodhounds set off to time, following the Greyhounds at an interval of about two hundred yards. They arrived in time, to see the other patrols marching to Headquarters.

Mr. Purley-Prout did not make his pi-jaw so long this time. He said that it was on the cards that Lt.-General Sir Robert Baden-Powell—which he told them should be pronounced

Barden-Pole—might be present, and so the North West Kents must shine as the best troop there. Phillip had even cleaned his teeth after his dinner, borrowing some of Father's precipitated chalk from the box hidden behind the hot-water boiler.

He long remembered the excitement of waiting, with the rest of the Troop, at Perry Vale Fire Station, and seeing what looked like an endless column of Scouts, some with drums and fifes and bugles, passing up the cobbled road towards the hill on which stood, unseen as yet behind shops and trees, the building he had never been so close to before—the Crystal Palace.

There were many sorts of people beside the Scouts. There were men of the Legion of Frontiersmen, all looking like Buffalo Bill; Boys Brigade companies with pill-boxes on one side of their heads; cadets in khaki; and boy sailors pulling a waggon by two long ropes. All sorts of motorcars banged and honked past as they joined the procession through Sydenham and West Hill, cameras going all along the route; people standing on the pavement, dogs barking, aproned shop-keepers, shop-walkers in frock coats, girl assistants with white faces and black dresses looking through windows, hundreds of small boys running alongside, bands playing—and at last the huge towering mass of grey scaly glass rising with cold glitter high into the sky above them—through the iron gates—and there was Father in the crowd, standing by the Sunbeam, smiling at him.

Phillip felt proud that he was patrol leader of the Bloodhounds, the first patrol in the district to be formed.

Inside, the place was noisy with shuffling feet, whistles, orders, and shouted commands. At last they were all formed up in the Centre Transept, and were addressed by an old man that Mr. Purley-Prout said was Sir John Campbell, whom they saluted while the band played God Save the King.

Then the great moment: out into the grounds, through the North Tower Garden, and down to the Balloon Ground to divide for the Sham Fight. The Troop, with the Bereshill, Fordesmill, and St. Anselm's Troops, were, under Mr. Purley-Prout, Phillip heard with pride, to form the main attack.

What were the scoutmasters arguing over, for so long? Phillip felt quite cold with the long wait.

At last Mr. Purley-Prout came to them, and said hurriedly,

"Peter, I want you to take your Greyhounds and be the extreme right wing of our outflanking movement against the main body. Phillip, go with Peter. I am putting Peter in charge of the right flank force. What you have to do is to move, unseen by the enemy, to beyond their extreme left wing, and encircle it. Get behind them, without them seeing you. Meanwhile, the Lions and the Kangaroos will do the same thing on the left flank, at the other end. Thus you will turn both flanks of the enemy's position at the same time. When you are behind them, capture their headquarters flag, and so end the fight! This is an occasion to show everyone what the North West Kents can do! I will remain here, with the main body, and when I see through my binoculars that you have got round the flanks, we will charge forward, and so create a diversion. The enemy will think this is the main attack; and while repelling it, will not realise that their flanks are being turned and their flag taken! We must hurry."

He looked at his watch. "The time-limit is almost up! There had been far too much jawing and crabbing of my plan of attack. Now to your positions! At the double!"

"Follow me," said Peter Wallace.

Phillip did not feel enthusiastic, having to be under Peter. After all, the Bloodhounds were before the Greyhounds. He decided to attack in his own way, once he had lost Peter.

There were a number of old cracked statues lying about the place. Brambles grew among the shrubs. The place looked a bit neglected, he thought. They passed some fountains without water in their rims. An old boot lay in one. Nearby, among some nettles, was part of a concrete alligator, or prehistoric monster. This gave Phillip an idea. In the main building, he told Peter, were some imitation stuffed prehistoric beasts: why not get inside one, and move slowly towards the flag they were going to capture? Perhaps they could get some workmen to carry it, while one of them hid inside?

"Don't talk daft," said Peter Wallace.

He led them what seemed to be miles and miles round the flank, so that the Sham Fight was over before they could even start to move towards the Terrace where the rival flags were.

They went back, hearing the Umpire's bugle, and saw that Mr. Purley-Prout was arguing with the scoutmaster of the 1st Fordesmill troop, on the Terrace.

"My lads are cold, waiting here for nothing to happen, let me tell you! Your plan was only for the glorification of your own so-called North West Kent Troop, that was obvious from the start!"

"Have you ever heard of the team-spirit, sir?" said Mr. Purley-Prout.

"We've all heard about *you*, if that is what you mean," retorted the other.

"Hardly the remark of a true Scout, rather that of a glorified Tenderfoot," said Mr. Purley-Prout. "In future kindly keep your distance, if you cannot exercise the art of manners."

"I shall and all, don't you fret! We all know what you are!"

"Be careful! I warn you that any slanderous statement will instantly be challenged in the proper Court!"

"Faugh!" ejaculated the Scoutmaster of the 1st Fordesmills, as he turned his back on Mr. Purley-Prout.

"The trouble with you is that you are not a gentleman," Mr. Purley-Prout called after him.

Phillip saw that Mr. Purley-Prout was white under his tan.

"Faugh!" said the 1st Fordesmills scoutmaster again.

Phillip saw Mr. Purley-Prout's nostrils open wide as he breathed.

"Fall in, the North West Kent Troop! Let us ignore such evidences of bad-breeding and ignorance."

They marched to the lake, where they were allowed to light camp fires. While scouts of the other patrols went off to look for firewood, Phillip squatted on his heels to make his patrol's fire of wood which he, Cranmer, and Desmond had brought in their haversacks. Seeing their store beside the fire, Mr. Purley-Prout immediately suggested that Phillip should hand over some of his sticks for use by the Lions and Kangaroos.

"But we brought it with us, Mr. Prout!" he protested.

"The Scout's code is based on service, which means unselfishness, Phillip. You should be glad of this opportunity to help others. To be selfish, to think only of yourself, is to reveal the spirit of a tenderfoot."

"I am the senior-est scout here, Mr. Prout, and if I am a tenderfoot, at least I did think of bringing wood for my patrol, which is more than the other patrol leaders did."

"Argument with your Scoutmaster is hardly good manners, Phillip, and such constitutes the mark of a tenderfoot," said Mr. Purley-Prout, as he bent down to take a double handful of the wood. He walked off with it, distributing a few sticks each to the Lions and Kangaroos.

Peter Wallace had brought his patrol's wood, too, but while Mr. Purley-Prout had been talking to Phillip, Peter hid his spare sticks by sitting on them until Mr. Purley-Prout had gone.

"It's not fair," said Phillip, "to pinch our wood! Any fool knows that with a mob like this about, it's hopeless to look for firewood. Faugh!"

Twilight blurred the outlines of the tiers and terraces of cold grey glass: trees began to look black against the sky; points of fire flickered all around and across the lake, where hundreds of boys squatted with billy-can, mess-tin, fitted knife and fork, and folding frying pan. From out of the vast glassy shell, lit in patches with yellow lights within, a rumbling sound came, seeming to quiver the windless skin of the water of the lake; the very ground seemed to be trembling. What could it be? Was it only his fancy? Phillip asked Desmond if he could hear anything. Desmond, with whom Phillip had become intimate, after several visits to his mother's flat for tea, said he thought he could.

"It is the Willis organ, playing the Hallelujah chorus, with all stops out," exclaimed Mr. Purley-Prout, standing, a Greek-god-like figure, hat brim over eyes, on the edge of the lake. "This is a solemn moment," he added.

Phillip was thinking that there would not be enough wood to fry his sausages nice and brown outside, as he liked them, when Cranmer suddenly appeared, dragging a long dry branch.

"I half-inched it from a Kestrel, one'v old Whazzisname's lot what gave Mr. Prart some of's lip," said Cranmer.

"Good for you!" cried Phillip. "We'll have a decent fire after all!"

When they had smashed it up, and the fire was blazing brightly, with tea and potatoes and sausages inside him, Phillip joined in the troop sing-song, while the lower night was ringed with fire, the stars shone above in the cold air, and the surface of the lake was a reflection of the mingled lights of earth and sky as it carried the singing voices of a thousand boys.

At last, like all good things, it came to an end. The fires went out, the singing ceased. Bugles sounded, mysterious in the night. Phillip thought of Gran'pa, years ago, just before Uncle Hugh and Uncle Sidney went off to the Boer War, reading from

Shakespeare's *Henry the Fifth.* It was rather like it, all the fires, and now the bugles.

"Fall in, the North Western Troop!"

It was half past eight. This time the Troop was near the head of the procession, and marched to the music of the band. Phillip put his wide-awake strap under his chin, like Mr. Purley-Prout did, to give him a feeling of being strong and resolute with the band playing so near. He stuck out his chin, so that people standing on the pavements in the lights of the Saturday evening shops might take him at his own valuation: the first to form a patrol in the district.

Phillip did so hope that Father would give his permission to go to camp at Easter that year. Mr. Purley-Prout promised to come and see Mr. Maddison about it. He had managed to buy a real tent after all. For seven shillings and sixpence a grey canvas bivouac, six feet long and six feet wide, had been ordered from Murrage's. It had been used during the Boer War: broad black arrows stamped on it in one corner showed it had been Government property.

When it arrived by Carter Paterson, in great excitement Phillip put it up on the lawn, and sat in it for a while in silent wonder; then he lay down on the wrinkled rubber groundsheet, and hoped for rain. The canvas had a funny musty smell, which he thought must come from the troopships in which the army had returned.

The half yearly payment of the scholarship grant into his Post Office Savings Account had enabled him to buy the tent, as well as a new Swift bicycle, with three-speed gear, on easy payments, from Wetherly's opposite the Fire Station. It was black, lined out in gold. He kept it oiled and clean, like the Sunbeam, which stood on one side of the downstairs lavatory, while the Swift stood on the other.

"Oh, if only Father would give his permission for me to go camping at Easter!"

Mr. Purley-Prout called one evening, when Phillip was in bed. Phillip put his ear to the floor of his bedroom, hoping to hear what was said down below in the sitting room; but all he heard was the long murmuring of Mr. Purley-Prout's tenor voice, followed at intervals by Father's deeper rumbling, which sounded through the floor like grumbling, but was not, Mother had often said. "When Father speaks in the kitchen at breakfast, your grandfather in the bathroom hears the rumbling of his voice, and mistakes it for grumbling, dear," she had said many times. Was Father's voice rumbling now, or grumbling? Pray that it was not grumbling before Mr. Purley-Prout.

When Mother came upstairs, after Mr. Purley-Prout had gone, Phillip was feeling almost sick with suspense.

"Oh, I knew Father would never let me camp out," he wept, on being told the news. "I have recovered fully from scarlet fever! I am not delicate any longer!" and he hid his face under the clothes.

Phillip was allowed to cycle out to the camp beyond the Fish Ponds by day, but he had to be home by six o'clock every evening. Thus he missed all the fun, he told his mother. Mr. Purley-Prout was a hero. He was out all night, raiding the camps of the Bereshill and Fordesmill troops, returning with their flags, after they had raided the North Western's camp and failed to take their flag.

"The chaps get no sleep at all at night, Mum, as the raids go on all night. Oh, why didn't Father let me go?"

"Perhaps he will at the Whitsun Camp, dear, when the weather is warmer. But surely Mr. Prout allows the scouts to have some sleep? It must be very bad for growing boys to be on the go all the time."

"It's not his fault, Mum. It's those awful Bereshill and Fordesmill roughs. Their scoutmasters simply hate Purley-Prout. He says it's due to envy, as he has the smartest troop in the district. I say, don't tell Father about the lack of sleep, will you? You know what he is. Else he'll say 'No' to the Whitsun Camp. He's a spoil-sport."

"Phillip, that is most unfair. Your Father has only your good at heart."

"Well, then, try and persuade him to let me go at Whitsun."

"You must ask him yourself, dear."

It was a fine Whitsun; and Phillip's anxious request was duly granted. With wild enthusiasm he set about rebuilding the baggage waggon. The only wheels he could get were old, but with care they would last out.

The great moment arrived at last.

On Friday, May 28, just before 6 p.m., the Bloodhound Patrol, in a somewhat hot condition, after carrying the baggage waggon (which had broken down *en route*) arrived upon the parade ground of the North Western Troop near Fordesmill Bridge Station. Richard had made one stipulation: that the faulty groundsheet be replaced by the remains of a roll of oilcloth, "which I will lend to your patrol, provided you return it in good condition."

Phillip was rather ashamed of the roll of oilcloth, which had had to be carried with the waggon, from the Fire Station onwards, by Cranmer and Desmond. Half way to Fordesmill, after a taunt of "Doin' a moonlit?" from some boys, they had stopped to wrap the tent around the roll, to disguise it. The patrol arrived a quarter of an hour late.

"Where have you been? Do you want to be left behind?" asked Mr. Purley-Prout, when they halted. "Phillip, the eternal tenderfoot, I see! Whatever is in that bundle?"

"It's to keep the patrol dry, please sir," gasped Phillip. They had run the last quarter of a mile.

"Fall in behind the others!"

Excitement started early. While they were waiting on the platform for the train to Reynard's Common, a bowler-hatted head and shoulders, with big white moustaches under its bushy eyebrows, stared down at them from the parapet of the road bridge above. This was Captain Blois, from St. Anselm's College. The St. Anselm's Troop were rivals of the North West Kents, who had ambushed them more than once. Captain Blois was considered to be spying as he stood there. Phillip did a little jig on the platform towards the bowler hat, taunting it. Cranmer let go his terrific four-finger whistle. Captain Blois glared down revengefully, he thought, before disappearing. He had obviously come to find out their strength, and in plain clothes!

The train puffed in, just after a quarter past six. The troop rushed for carriages. Mr. Purley-Prout had cycled on with some of the other scouts. They wanted their bikes for midnight raids, explained Mr. Swinerd, in charge of the train party. St. Anselm's Troop were camping around Reynard's Common, as well as the Fordesmills and Berehills, he told them. Oh, there would be some sport!

The railway terminus was a familiar place of pleasure: here the Maddison family had arrived in past times, for Sunday picnics on the common, Father joining them there on his bicycle, finding them by the family whistle.

The engine turned round on a wooden turn-table at the end, in order to go back the way it had come. It was the end of the ordinary world. This was the real country. There were roses growing along the platform fence, and large oil lamps on wooden posts. Phillip felt very happy as they jumped out on the platform and saw the cyclists coming in, led by Mr. Purley-Prout, half a minute later. The train had raced them!

"Fall in, the North West Kent Troop! Leave the baggage, a cart is coming for it. Peter, detail a scout from your patrol to remain as baggage guard. He can ride on the cart."

They marched across the common, with its silver birches and clumps of gorse giving out a sweet scent of blossom, its linnets and stonechats and warblers among the rising honeysuckle bines and plants of foxglove. When they rested, Phillip could hear the chirp of grasshoppers and crickets in the sun. There was a low line of dark clouds on the horizon of the west, which Mr. Swinerd, a man with a dull face and loose mouth, said he did not like the look of. While they were sitting there, he told them a story about a man who asked at London Bridge station for a return ticket to the Crystallised Palace, meaning to cheat the railway company by not going back by train. The same man spat on the carriage floor, while going to the Crystallised Palace, and someone else in the carriage said, "You cannot expect to rate as a gentleman, if you expectorate on the floor."

Mr. Swinerd had to explain what the long word meant, then they laughed.

Mr. Swinerd continued to be a funny man. When they fell in again, he said, "Now for another amble onwards, forward my merry men, to honour, glory, and bags of mystery for supper!" They could laugh at that, knowing that he meant sausages.

They reached camp at eight o'clock, and set about putting up the tents. The camp was in the same paddock as at Easter. It was about an acre, with tall fir trees rising along three sides. The fourth side had a hedge growing over posts and rails, to keep sheep and cattle from dropping to the road below the steep bank. The subsoil was chalk; the road dipped down and rose again some distance away, to Farthing Street. There was a quarry below the lower end of the field, and in this were cow-sheds and a piggery. Phillip knew that it was the home-farm of the

Dowager Countess of Mersea, which the bailiff, a small neat man in cord jacket and breeches with cloth gaiters, managed for her.

The bailiff's cottage was across the road, on the corner of the other long white road which ran under the cleft-oak fencing of Knollyswood Park. The bailiff came to see if they wanted anything beside the milk and eggs he had already brought.

"It looks like rain," he said to Mr. Purley-Prout, and Mr. Prout said, "Oh, do not be a Jeremiah, Mr. Wilson." The bailiff laughed a short laugh and said, "Well, I can't control the weather, sir, and a little rain just now will bring on the malting barleys nicely. They need it."

"They are never satisfied, those horny-handed sons of toil," Mr. Purley-Prout said to Mr. Swinerd, when the bailiff had gone.

Phillip laid out the patrol tent and knocked in the pegs, then unrolled the linoleum. It was nine o'clock before they had their supper. Then they had to turn in, as they had a long day before them on the morrow, said Mr. Purley-Prout. Prayers first. After prayers, a scout was put on guard at the entrance, at the five-barred gate under the pine tree at the road junction. Mr. Purley-Prout told them that the Greyhounds would provide hourly guards for the first night.

"The Bloodhounds can try their mettle tomorrow night, when we can expect attempts to capture our Flag." It was wonderfully exciting.

Each of the six Bloodhounds had twelve inches of lateral space for his bed. Each had a blanket. Rolled capes were used as pillows. Hardly had they taken off their boots, and were trying to settle down, when it began to rain.

"Lucky we put up the tent when we did," said Phillip.

The sides of the tent were open; and Phillip, lying on the outside, towards the west, soon felt drops on his face. He tried to get farther into the tent. The need for adjustment passed from boy to boy, until the one at the other end, Ching, exclaimed, "Don't push, Cranmer! You're deliberately shoving me out!"

"I ain't! I was shoved, see?" replied Cranmer. "Move up, Lenny."

"I can't, my ribs are almost crushed!"

"Silence everyone!" said the voice of Mr. Purley-Prout.

He occupied a small khaki bivouac between the Bloodhounds and the Lions and Kangaroos who were in a large bell-tent. Beyond the bell-tent was another small tent, in which the

Assistant Scoutmaster, Mr. Swinerd, slept. Then came the Greyhounds, in their tent.

The rain pattered down. After a quarter of an hour's sleeplessness, writhing, and muttering, Ching suddenly cried out, "Aow! It's raining down my neck! You've pushed me outside again, Cranmer!"

He struggled to sit up. His head touched the canvas. "I thought so! The tent's rotten!"

"Be quiet," whispered Phillip.

"I'll get pneumonia!" wailed Ching.

"Well, you insisted on being on the outside, you know," said Phillip.

"Yes, to get away from the smell of Cranmer's toe-jam."

"I washed me feet 'smorning," protested the corporal.

"Shut up, everybody," said Phillip. A few minutes later he rose on his elbow and said, "The tent is wet down the inside everywhere! I told you fools to be careful not to touch the canvas."

"The splashes from the trees are coming in my end as well. I wish I hadn't come," moaned Ching.

Phillip flashed his electric lamp. The interior certainly was glistening in places. "Don't touch it above your head, Ching, whatever you do!"

At once Ching's fingers went up. A dribble of drops pattered on his head.

"You damned fool, I told you not to! I hope you like it!"

"Phillip, let your voice be silent from now onwards!" called the voice of Mr. Purley-Prout through the rainy darkness.

Phillip rested disconsolately on his elbow, after he had switched off the lamp, to save the battery. A battery cost 4½d., and did not last for many flashes.

"Did you hear me, Phillip?"

"Yes, Mr. Prout."

"Then say 'Yes', the next time."

"The rain's coming in where I am, too," whispered Desmond.

"Did you hear what I said, Phillip?"

"Yes, Mr. Prout."

"Then don't you consider it a matter of common courtesy to reply when your Scoutmaster is speaking to you?"

"I thought you told me to say 'yes' the next time, so I was waiting for the next time, Mr. Prout."

"Don't split hairs. Now, understand this, there will be no further talking among your patrol. Shut up, you Bloodhounds!"

"Yes, Mr. Prout."

"And shut up yourself, Phillip."

"Yes, Mr. Prout."

Ching whispered, "My blanket's covered with wet! Oh, why did I come? Curse you, Cranmer, take your bony elbow out of my stummick!"

"You take yer stummick, Ching, and put it where v' monkey puts v' nuts!"

"Aow! Something walked over my face," Ching complained next.

"Phillip, I hope I shall not have to tell you again to keep your men in order! For the last time, shut up!"

"Stop talking, men!" Phillip cautioned his unhappy patrol.

"Shut up, yourself, Phillip! How can you expect to be obeyed, when you set a bad example?"

"Ask Old Nick," muttered Phillip.

An uneasy half hour followed. Then complaints began to arise once more from the cramped boys lying under the dripping canvas. Phillip felt unhappy, that a real Boer War tent should have behaved like that. "I hope the rain stops before long. I expect it will," he encouraged his men.

"For the last time, will you keep your men in order, Phillip!"

"I'm doing my best, Mr. Prout."

"Then your best is not good enough, Phillip! How can you command without having learned to obey? For the very last time, will you be quiet! Can't you keep your men in order?"

"Shut up, everybody!" said Phillip.

From inside the dry bivouac tent of the Scoutmaster came a dreadful command.

"Phillip! Go home!"

The patrol lay silent in the open, leaky, dark tent. Phillip reached for his boots. He felt them to see if there was water inside, then put them on and laced them up. Water splashed on the back of his neck. He unrolled his thick dark grey cape, which came down to the elbows, and fastened it by the rusty chain at the throat. He put on his wide-awake with the strap under his chin, as the wind was now blowing. Then rummaging in the wooden box which had been taken off the chassis when the waggon had broken down, he selected the rations, which Mother had given him. There was his loaf of bread, his half pound of streaky rashers, his blue paper bag of sugar mixed with tea, his pot of apricot jam, his quarter-of-a-pound of butter, his tin of condensed milk. He put these in a sack; twisted the hessian round the bundle to sling it over his shoulder; then whispered, "So long, men, see you another time," and crawled out. He took his pole and started to trudge across the wet grass.

At the gate his flash-light revealed a huddled figure on guard under the pine tree. It was David Wallace. Silver streaks of water fell in the rays of the carbon-filament bulb. David was shivering.

"Are you relieving me, Phillip?"

"Old Purley-Prout has sent me home. How far is it? Nine miles?"

"Just about."

"It's cold, isn't it?"

"It is, rather. Mr. Prout lent me his cycling cape."

"Seen anything of the raiders?"

"No."

"I don't suppose they'll come in the rain."

"You never know. What's the time?"

"About eleven, I should think. It will take me till three o'clock to get home." He would wait in the porch when he got back. He would not dare to wake up Father.

"Where's your black rubber cycling cape, Phillip?"

"I lent it to Cranmer. Well, so long, David. Goodbye for now," said Phillip, trying to stop his voice quavering.

He started walking on the gritty, running surface. He began to whistle *Alice, Where Art Thou?*, and had gone less than fifty yards when Cranmer's shrieking whistle came through the black night.

Stopping, Phillip heard David Wallace calling out to him, "Phillip, come back!"

He went back, as slowly as he had set forth, whistling softly to himself, sack over shoulder. He returned to the patrol tent. Crouching down, among silent men, on the cold wet oilcloth, he took off his sodden cape and boots. There was more room in the tent now, for Mr. Purley-Prout had taken Lenny Low into his bivouac, said Desmond.

Chapter 16

ALARUMS AND EXCURSIONS

PHILLIP did not know when the rain stopped, although it must have been after dawn, for the cuckoos were calling while drops were still pattering on the canvas from the pine trees above. There was a mist over the paddock when he did leave the tent, on hands and knees, feeling cold and pale. A voice in the quarry below called to a cow, and pigs made shrill squealings, which suddenly stopped. Many birds soon were singing. One by one his men crawled out. They began to look about for firewood, but only sodden sticks lay on the ground. Mr. Purley-Prout crawled out of his bivouac, followed by Lenny Low.

Mr. Purley-Prout said another troop was coming from Croydon that day, so the troop must hurry up with breakfast, as they had to go and meet their guests and help carry their baggage. This would be reckoned a good turn for the day for everybody. There was no camp fire, each patrol was left to make its own as best it could.

Phillip had been lent a double-cooker for the patrol's porridge, by his mother. After many matches, kneeling in the wet, blowing and coughing, he managed to start a hissing fire which, with damp sticks, was no flame and all smoke. The porridge pot had just been put on when Mr. Purley-Prout told them that in five minutes they must leave. As there was no time for oatmeal, attempts were made to fry eggs. The wet sticks picked up below the pines being rotten, were saturated with water; the fire required constant blowing to make the smallest flame appear in the steam. So the Bloodhounds, together with the others, had to leave without any breakfast. Mr. Purley-Prout had eaten some dates, nuts and figs, while Mr. Swinerd munched sandwiches left over from the night before.

"Fall in the North West Kents!"

Soon after they had set out, the sun appeared, and dried the puddles in the road. They took an unfamiliar route. On and on they marched. It became hot; dust arose as they straggled on, pallid with sleeplessness and no breakfast. Phillip felt thirsty, but the water in his wooden bottle tasted too bad to drink. The others, too, wanted a drink, but Mr. Purley-Prout did not stop. After two hours they arrived outside a strange station, where stood a solitary waggonette.

Mr. Purley-Prout looked at his gold watch. "We've got two minutes to spare," he said. "Bravo, the North Western! Never let it be said that we kept our guests waiting!"

Oh, for a drink! Would they all march back as soon as the train came in? A distant whistle and a chuff-chuffing told that it was coming. Mr. Purley-Prout called the Troop to attention. The Flag was held up by his personal Standard Bearer, Holdwich, patrol leader of the Lions.

The train came in and stopped. Eight old people alighted, led by a clergyman. Mr. Purley-Prout spoke to them. They were Ramblers, they said. They were going in the waggonette to visit Caesar's well, which fed the Fish Ponds, the source of the Randisbourne, and look for relics of Roman pottery on the common. No, they had seen no Boy Scouts in the train.

"The blighters have obviously missed it," Mr. Purley-Prout said to Mr. Swinerd. "Well, we've done our part. We shall have to hang on for the next train, that's all."

Mr. Swinerd told them that meant two hours to wait. There was a shop near the station, and Phillip bought some oranges and a loaf of white bread, with fourpence of the sixpence Mother had given him for emergencies. He gave an orange to each of his men, and kept two for himself. He hacked slices of the bread with his knife, and they ate it. An old woman in a cottage gave them a jug of water; two jugs of water; three, four jugs. Mr. Purley-Prout thanked her on behalf of the Troop.

To employ time usefully, said Mr. Purley-Prout, they would have an abbreviated field exercise in the lanes. The Greyhounds were sent out to get through a line held by the rest. While waiting, Phillip went into the shop and bought four more oranges, he was so thirsty. He ate these, sitting behind a tree by himself, and then some more bread.

"You want to be careful," said Mr. Swinerd, coming suddenly round the tree. "Orange juice might very well work on the dough inside you, and cause gas to press upon the heart, and suddenly stop its action. *Six* oranges? Well, look out, my boy! The bread you've eaten may suddenly swell bigger than your stomach. Any moment you may blow up!"

He said this in a serious voice, and Phillip believed him.

Listening to his heart, he felt it beating loudly in his ears. Was he going to die? He might never see Mother again! Any moment his inside might swell up, and choke out his life. He waited for something to happen, trying not to utter his terror. His heart thumped in his ears.

When they marched back to the station, it was hotter than ever. He felt thirsty once more; but dared not drink any of the water brought out by the old woman.

The guest Troop arrived in the intense heat, which caused a watery waver on distant trees. Mr. Purley-Prout insisted that the hand-cart, containing all their gear, including four bell-tents, should be pushed by his own Troop.

"We, as gentlemen, have that privilege towards our guests. The Bloodhounds, for having been so noisy during the night, will push it the first leg, up the hill to the Common. That will sweat the vice out of them, and enable others to have a proper sleep during the coming night."

The Bloodhound Patrol managed, somehow, to get the cart to the top, after several rests for thudding hearts and wet red faces on the way. Mr. Purley-Prout was waiting for them at the edge of the common.

"The others have marched on, but I have remained to give a hand."

He pushed the cart by himself, his wide calf muscles bulging, Phillip noticed with envy. His own calves were very thin, with scarcely noticeable muscles, as he had observed many times in Mother's dress-cupboard glass in her bedroom.

The rest of the Troop were resting further on, lying on the grass by the road. When they got there, Phillip and his patrol flung themselves down, faces red and prickling, being tired out. Mr. Purley-Prout, lying on his back, did some exercises to strengthen his stomach muscles.

"How are you feeling?" said Mr. Swinerd, with apparent concern, coming to where Phillip lay. "Heat adds to the chances of blowing up, you know."

"Are you serious, Mr. Swinerd?" asked Phillip, faintly, as he felt himself suddenly far away from them all. Was he dying?

"Well, what do *you* think?" replied Mr. Swinerd, over his shoulder as he went away.

Phillip thought Mr. Swinerd was offended by the question. If only God would spare him, he would never again eat more than one orange at a time, and always wait a long time afterwards before adding bread. He would say his prayers every night, too, and be very kind always to his sisters.

It was only when they had got back to camp, dusty and fearfully hot, that Mr. Swinerd told Phillip he had been ragging him in a friendly spirit.

"You ought to know me by now, my boy, that I am a joker."

So relieved was Phillip that he decided to play a joke on Mr. Swinerd later on.

Desmond Neville, who as one of the youngest had been left behind with others to guard the camp, came to Phillip, his face tear-stained, with a sad story of having felt for a nest in the hedge, and all the eggs had rolled out and broken. He had only meant to feel in the nest, he said, not to tip it up.

Phillip went with him to look at the remains of the shells. The eggs were unfamiliar; they were a yellowish grey, with browny spots and blotches on them. The nest was about the size of a thrush's, but taller and built of twigs and grasses. While Phillip was wondering what it could be a bird flew to a branch in the thorn hedge and looked down at them. It was a browny sort of bird, with a large eye, blackish whiskers, and a strong bent beak.

"It's a butcher bird, I do declare!" he cried, in a voice like that of his cousin Percy Pickering. "I saw one once at Beau Brickhill with Percy! Coo, I wish I had got an egg! The red-backed shrike is its real name. It's a cruel bird, sticking bees and little birds' nestlings on a thorn, like a skewer, for its larder."

"I'm very sorry, Phillip, I tipped the nest. I slipped when my hand was just touching it."

"Oh, it doesn't matter. It's done now, anyway. This is a wonderful place for nests, isn't it?"

Desmond looked happier. Behind his rather stolid-looking face he was a sensitive boy, anxious to do the right thing, the more so as he had no father living at home. Hetty had told Phillip that he must never ask questions about Mr. Neville, as it was not polite to be curious about other people's affairs.

It was now the middle of a scorching afternoon, and Phillip's turn to be sentry at the gate. The rest of the Troop were in the shade of the pines at the farther end of the paddock, where the smoke of fires arose, preparatory to cooking dinners.

Phillip was watching a spotted flycatcher flying off its perch on a post to take a fly, when, absolutely silently, a black carriage without a horse came round the corner of the road and stopped. It was not a motorcar, for it had no engine; its silent approach was most mysterious. What could it be? The driver held a black enamelled stick to steer by. He had a big face and moustache, and wore a bowler hat and black suit. An old lady sat beside him, wearing black silk widow's weeds, which rustled as she moved. She had on a black hat, made of a sort of lace, which hung down over the frame, like a small short curtain all round.

Mr. Purley-Prout had seen the silent carriage, and came running over the paddock. He vaulted over the gate, and stood to attention to salute the people. He bowed over the lady's hand as he shook it. After some words he saluted again, and the black-spider carriage turned round and glided off in the direction it had come, again without any sound, except for the slight slur of its thin rubber tyres on the white chalk and flinty dust, which was glaring in the heat.

Mr. Purley-Prout said to Phillip that the driver of the electric brougham was the Earl of Mersea, the owner of all the land round about, and one of the richest noblemen in England. With him was his Mother, the Dowager Countess. In their family, said Mr. Purley-Prout, there had never been a scandal throughout its long history.

"Lady Mersea has asked twelve of the Troop to tea tomorrow afternoon. I shall probably take three from each patrol, and leave you in charge during my absence, Phillip."

Phillip was pleased to have this trust. Also, it would mean that he would get out of cleaning his boots and having to behave properly all the time, like on church parade. He might even raid one of the other camps all by himself, and pinch a flag! All sorts of things might happen!

After eating—the Bloodhounds finished cooking their belated breakfast of porridge and half-fried burnt eggs about 4 p.m.—Phillip told his men about two jokes he had thought out while on sentry-go. The first to be played on Mr. Swinerd. He would wrap a lump of chalk in grease-proof paper, pencil the word cheese on the package, and put it in Mr. Swinerd's food-box just inside his bivouac. The second joke was intended to prove to Mr. Purley-Prout and the others that the Bloodhounds were not the tenderfeet he had declared them to be.

Two birds could be killed by one stone in this second joke, Phillip whispered. The patrol wanted some more bread, so if Ching sneaked off to Farthing Street and got some, and some buns as well, without anyone seeing him go, they could wait a bit, and then raise the alarm that he had been captured by some other Troop. This would lead to counter-raids, and a fine old schemozzle!

A week or two later, Phillip got some satisfaction in reading to his mother what Mr. Purley-Prout wrote about him in *The Paladin*, the Troop magazine.

" 'Splendid weather was our portion at Whitsuntide. We paraded at Headquarters at 5.45 p.m. (less one patrol, which was late) on Friday, May 28th, and all except the cyclists entrained at Fordesmill Bridge with tents, flag, and other camp paraphernalia at 6.17. The cyclists, with Mr. Purley-Prout, reached Reynard's Common later, a cart having been sent to convey the tents, etc. The night proved very wet, and sleep was rather difficult on account of this and the talkative mood of a certain patrol-leader, who disturbed everybody, in spite of threats and warnings.'

"That was me," he said to his mother, with pride.

" 'Saturday saw us off early to West Lennards, to meet the 1st Croydon Troop, who did not appear till noon, making our numbers up to 43 scouts and 4 officers. On the return to camp, a certain unauthorised and unofficial ambush party made itself notorious by harassing other Troops who passed by, and prisoners were continually being brought into camp without any apparent reason. But as we heard from the patrol leader of the harassing party in question that one of his men was lying bound and gagged in a rival camp, we thought fit to detain our prisoners.'

"That was our joke, Mum."

" 'Tea was made at 6.0, and a pleasant time was spent round the camp-fire from 7 till 9, Mr. Purley-Prout telling us a ghost story with a moral.

" 'Supper was at 9.0, followed by prayers. "Last Post" went at 9.30, and "Lights Out" at 10.0.

" 'Whitsun Day saw us early astir, Reveille being at 6.0. Everybody, except the guard, went off at 6.30 to the Fish Ponds to wash. Church Parade for Communicants was at 7.50, the service being at 8.0 in the church. Breakfast followed at 9.0. We marched off again to church at 9.55, the service having been arranged specially for the Kent Guides under Lieut. Oakfall (who were camping near by) and ourselves, at 10.0. The Rector, in his address, extended a hearty welcome to us, saying, amongst other things, that war had in the past brought out many excellent qualities in those taking part. The hymns were lustily sung, and we returned to camp feeling much elevated in spirits.

" 'A march to Farthing Street village in the blazing sun, and a visit to the Bereshill's Camp followed. We found that the troops (1st Fordesmill and 2nd Bereshill) had just gone off to Farthing Street Church. On our way back we met Mr. Maddison, who had cycled out to see us. (We are always glad to see visitors.)'

"A pity Father didn't arrive in the middle of the big attack, Mum, on the Bank Holiday. Coo, that was exciting! Captain Blois lost four front teeth!"

"What, were they knocked out by force, Phillip? Surely Mr. Prout——"

"Just a mo', Mum. I'll come to it later. First, listen to this——

" 'Whitsun Monday was but a few minutes old when in the darkness we were attacked by rivals from the Bereshill Camp, who, in the endeavour to seize our Flag, were surprised and discomforted at the lightning return attack, some of our chaps going up to the Bereshill camp, unknown to those who had attacked us. Skirmishing went on until dawn. In the morning we escorted our Croydon guests to their station, helping them with their "waggon", and on our way back (the required notice of attack having been given) we attacked the camp of the combined Fordesmill and St. Anselm's Troops. In the words of the Camp Chronicler:—

" 'Having been apprised of our intentions, the camp was on the *qui vive*. We had the sagacious company of Lieutenant

Oakfall, of the Kent Guides, and it was decided to make a false attack, and retreat, to draw the defence away from the point of final effort. This was partially successful, and our doughty leader penetrated nearly to the centre of the camp, where Captain Blois, perceiving the ruse, recalled his men by whistle just in time to save the day. Whether the camp should have been considered captured by our troop must remain a moot point. Our gallant Scoutmaster appealed to the opinion of an umpire, but none was forthcoming.

"'On the contrary, the only reply vouchsafed to him was capture by six Territorials who were augmenting the hard-pressed defence. Our doughty Scoutmaster was over-powered only after a great struggle, which did not succeed in putting him on his back, as was the obvious intention. With this incident the engagement ceased, three mighty cheers being raised for our Scoutmaster on his release. Considering the impregnable position of the camp, and the strong chain of sentries with which it was surrounded, great credit was due to our Troop.

"'In the afternoon, Mr. Purley-Prout took picked scouts to tea with the Dowager Countess of Mersea, as they had been graciously invited on the Saturday. While they were away our camp in the Home Farm paddock was the scene of some excitement. The vigilant Bereshill and Fordesmill Scouts, soon discovering that only twelve men were left in charge, resolved on a counter attack in force. Their approach was quickly seen, but our sentry was over-powered by four to one, and, it being impossible to defend the whole area of the camp, the patrol leader in charge, Peter Wallace, ordered a concentration around the Flag, and with his men, outnumbered by five to one, hurled defiance, and prepared to fight to the bitter end. The enemy halted some twenty paces from the little band, and held a consultation. Whether it was the firm mien of the defence or some other cause which decided the invaders is not known, but they retired, leaving the defenders in possession of their Flag, and defiant.'"

Phillip thought that a fine bit about Peter. All he and his men had done, actually, was to stand still. Cranmer had put his fingers in his mouth and let out a terrific whistle—but Mr. Purley-Prout had not put that bit in *The Paladin*. What was thrilling was the night that followed, after it had rained, and the stars came out.

Owing to a mighty attack pending, Mr Purley-Prout took

them into a loft, up some wooden steps, in the bailiff's yard. Mr. Purley-Prout went off on his bike, without a light, meaning to capture the Fordesmill's Flag, while they were attacking the paddock with only the tents in it. Owls sometimes hooted in the dark mysterious woods; nightingales sang far away in the valley; and while they waited, yawning and shivering, at the top of the steps, they saw someone up the road strike a match.

There was no sound; only the light, a signal, and then darkness. For a very long time they waited; then cheers came from the paddock. It was the attack! And no one there, the Flag was in the loft! Then, at two o'clock, Mr. Purley-Prout returned, his hat down over his eyes, and with the Fordesmill's Flag!

"He had wormed his way past their sentries, Mum! After showing us the Flag, he went back, all alone, with a paper notice, 'Be Prepared!', pinned by a safety-pin to their old Flag; and stuck it in its place again, without anyone seeing him do it!

"When we lay down to sleep the dawn chorus was just beginning, with the cocks in the farmyard crowing. I was very tired when we got up again at six o'clock, for a wash in the Fish Ponds, which were two miles away, there and back. Then, before we could properly cook breakfast, we had to go off again, for miles and miles, on manœuvres with other troops. Now listen to this account, Mum! It's the big attack!

"'The next afternoon, scarcely had the main body of the troop returned, hungry and weary, after their ten miles march and skirmish, and settled down to prepare their well-earned meal; scarcely were mess tins opened, and wood smoke arising, when the Alarm was sounded, followed by the order to fall in and defend the camp. The Fordesmill and Bereshill Troops, reinforced by the 2nd Sydenhams and St. Anselm's, to a total of probably over a hundred, were seen to be swarming down behind every hedge, for a grand attack. The defenders, numbering about forty, were posted to the best advantage, and shortly afterwards the camp was surrounded on all sides, and a battle-royal began.

"'The attack was fierce, the defence stubborn; but at last sheer weight of numbers bore the attackers through the gate, and a rush was made for the Flag, around which a furious tumble ensued. A guinea was to be the prize of the attacking scout who captured the trophy, but all who essayed were hurled back, and the guinea went a-begging.'"

Phillip had been squatting by the double-cooker, which was beginning to puff steam from the oatmeal in the pot, when the whistles of warning went. Cranmer cried, "Billo! Oley-oley-oley! Crikey, nah su'fun's comin', strike me pink if thur idden!" He threw his hat into the air. Then he blew his four-finger whistle. Phillip, feeling no excitement (he was very tired) stood up, forgetting his pole. A bugle sounded the alarm; he felt a little excitement then.

He saw, spread out across the chalky down-sloping field in the direction of Farthing Street, scores of advancing scouts. Others were running from the narrow strip of woodland beside the road under the oak fence of the park. Still more were scrambling up the steep bank above the quarry. There was a lot of shouting. He felt slightly dismayed.

"To your posts!" cried Mr. Purley-Prout, rolling up his sleeves. "Every man to his post, for the honour of the North West Kents!"

Seizing the bugle from the boy on guard, he blew a loud defiant blast. Phillip picked up his broomstick, and watched what was happening.

Soon poles were beating on the barb wire fence all around the paddock. Enemy scouts got over the gate, wrestling with the picket there.

"Concentrate around the flag, defend it to the last!" cried Mr. Purley-Prout.

Phillip watched them, doing nothing himself. Most of the scouts did the same. Only a few stood around Mr. Purley-Prout, grasping their poles. Phillip had no wish to fight, or defend any Flag.

Then Lieutenant Oakfall suddenly appeared on his bicycle, followed by the two other Kent Guides who were camping with him near the Fish Ponds, and cooking on an oil-stove with a smoky wick. With the Guides were two Legion of Frontiersmen, each with a big grey moustache and big brown gauntlet gloves. They wore Stetson hats, Sam Browne belts, leather shirts with red neckerchiefs, khaki breeches, leggings, and spurs on the heels of their brown boots. Like the Kent Guides, they had no horses, but rode bicycles. Phillip thought they had been heroes, somewhere or other in the past.

Lieutenant Oakfall did not look like a hero. He had one eye which bulged. It looked in a different direction to his other eye, which was small and sunken. He spoke with a lisp. His flat khaki cap, which had a leather peak, had the band down, under his chin. Like the two other Guides, and the Frontiersmen, he wore big gauntlet gloves. Lieutenant Oakfall had tucked his gloves into his Sam Browne belt, Phillip noticed. There was a revolver holster on his belt. He had steel chains on his shoulders, and big swan-neck spurs on his boots below the strapped leggings.

" Three cheers for Lieutenant Oakfall and his Guides, and the Legion of Frontiersmen!" cried Mr. Purley-Prout, as the new-comers joined them round the Flag. Only a few of the scouts cheered. Peter Wallace had taken off his spectacles, Phillip noticed. Crikey, would there be a scrap?

"Let them all come!" cried Mr. Purley-Prout. "We are ready for them! I offer a guinea to anyone who can take our Flag!" Mr. Purley-Prout then rolled his sleeves higher, and braced his iron-studded brown brogues.

The invaders walked nearer, poles held out. Soon broomstick was knocking on broomstick. Phillip got behind a tree. The troop pressed closer round Mr. Purley-Prout, Mr. Swinerd, the Kent Guides, and the Legion of Frontiersmen. Phillip did not want to fight; he wanted to watch what the others did, so he kept behind the tree.

Two enemy scouts ran forward. Mr. Purley-Prout seized them by their arms and swung them round, so that they fell on the ground. Others took their places. More were hurled back, tumbling, wide-awakes falling off.

While this was happening, the Fordesmill Scoutmaster stood and glared at Mr. Purley-Prout.

"Who's using force now?" he said grimly.

"You aren't!" shouted Mr. Purley-Prout. "Come on, if you dare! A guinea for you if you can take our Flag!"

Phillip hoped they would fight. But after glaring at Mr. Purley-Prout, the Fordesmill Scoutmaster turned his back.

Then Captain Blois walked across the paddock from the gate. At this, Lieutenant Oakfall, to Phillip's awe, withdrew his nickel-plated revolver from his holster. Surely he was not going to shoot Captain Blois? Lieutenant Oakfall had a grin on his face, while his bulging eye twitched. Pointing the pistol into the air, Lieutenant Oakfall pulled the trigger. A sharp crack followed. Golly, he was a hero after all!

"What are you doing, sir?" cried Captain Blois, brushing his white moustaches with his gloved hand. "Who do you think you are? I order you to put down that lethal weapon this moment!"

"What authority have you for demanding such a thing?" smiled Lieutenant Oakfall, his bulgy eye twitching. He was a small man, about as high as a broomstick.

"As the senior officer holding His Majesty's commission present," replied Captain Blois. "Indeed, as the only commissioned officer present, I repeat my order. Firearms, even with blank ammunition, can be dangerous!"

Lieutenant Oakfall's answer was to fire two more shots into the air.

"I challenge you on the point of *your* commission, Mr. Blois!" said Mr. Purley-Prout. "I understand that you are a Cadet Corps officer, with honorary rank while you hold that position at St. Anselm's College, and not outside its precincts!"

"At least I did not design my uniform myself, from no known or authorised pattern!" barked Captain Blois, fixing his eyes on Lieutenant Oakfall, who was twiddling his plated revolver on his finger.

"Bluff!" cried Mr. Purley-Prout. "Sheer bluff! Imitation of Napoleon at Marengo! You find us prepared, and you cannot, with all your numbers, take our Flag! The offer of a guinea is still open!"

"As Umpire, I consider you are militarily overwhelmed and defeated, but have not the grace to acknowledge our moral superiority," retorted Captain Blois. "Gentlemen, let us withdraw!"

Putting his whistle in his mouth, he turned round to face the assembled attackers. At that moment he stumbled on the white and black flints around the Greyhound patrol fire, which Peter Wallace had brought from below the quarry; and falling on his face, Captain Blois appeared to be knocked out. Phillip ran forward to look at him, with the others. He was groaning, and holding his mouth.

"'We greatly regret,' read out Phillip, 'that the day did not pass without a serious accident to Mr. Blois, who, turning to give the signal for withdrawal after the unsuccessful assault, with his whistle between his teeth, tripped on some newly-laid flints around a fire, and lost four teeth. We offer him our sincere sympathy. Luckily no bones were broken, and beyond very severe bruises and cuts, and the loss of teeth, he was not dangerously hurt, as was at first feared.

"'And so it came to pass that a truce was called, the honours being fairly even. The camp was forced, but the Flag remained intact.

"'Several scouts went back on Monday evening. Nothing further of interest happened.'"

Having read the account to his mother, Phillip ran down with his copy of *The Paladin* to Desmond's flat, where Mrs. Neville had told him he was always welcome. He read the printed account again, to the accompaniment of several ho-ho's and ha-ha's from Mrs. Neville.

"Like the newspapers, print seldom tells the truth. Your Mr. Purley-Prout, from all I hear, is quite a character," the fat woman remarked, blandly sitting in her armchair, and pouring out tea on the tray before her, after Phillip had finished.

Phillip liked having tea in Mrs. Neville's flat. You did not have to sit up at the table for it, unless it was in the kitchen, where anyway it was just as free and easy as in the drawing room up the stairs.

"Look at this," she said, while Phillip ate his third doughnut. "Mr. Purley-Prout's letter at the end of the magazine. Oh ho, he's a downy bird, is your Mr. Purley-Prout, if I know anything about men!

"'The resolve to do "good turns" wherever possible, must ever be in our minds: we must "be prepared" for jealousy, ill-treatment, enmity, but we must remember that a scout has promised to help others at any cost to himself, and the memory of that promise must make us set a good example to our enemies by our patience, tolerance, forbearance, and kindness. Don't do this because in doing so you will "heap coals of fire on their heads"—that's not a very great or a good motive—but do it because it is right and noble, and splendid.'

"H'm," she said, putting down the little green-covered magazine. "I wonder what's in the back of his mind to write like that? Your Mr. Purley-Prout has got something on his conscience, I should not be at all surprised! And dear me, after what you and Desmond have told me—just listen to what he has to say next!

" 'Don't think that every other scout in every other troop is your sworn foe. Remember that you are a *peace* scout: and if the other fellow seems to forget this, you can remind him of it by your actions—don't jaw! The other Troops are not enemies of ours—they are friendly rivals: and I want all my North Western chaps to treat them as such, and as gentlemen. You must particularly remember to show great respect to the Scoutmasters of other Troops—just as much as if they were your own officers.

" 'We want to see our North Western setting a noble ideal of unity and concord before every district in England. And why shouldn't it?

With every good wish,
Believe me,
Your affectionate friend and Scoutmaster,
Rupert Purley-Prout.'

"H'm," said Mrs. Neville, putting down the little magazine, "I don't think there's much affection about that gentleman. Why, when Desmond came home, he was starved, all skin and bone! There were dark rings under his eyes. And the grime on his body! If this Mr. Purley-Prout thought less of the soul, and more of the body—but perhaps he does, from all I hear," she added, nodding significantly. What could she mean? But it was a grown-up's remark, and Phillip thought no more of it.

After the Whitsun Camp he was not so keen on scouting as he had been. He did not know that this was due, in part, to fatigue. The boys had hardly slept during the four nights. Instead, he played cricket on the Hill; and sometimes, when it was wet, he and Desmond went to the twopenny seats of the Electric Theatre in the High Street. After the holidays, on fine Wednesday and Saturday afternoons, they cycled out to explore Reynard's Common and the surrounding country, finding perfect companionship in viewing external objects together.

Desmond had a machine with dropped handlebars which gave it a racy appearance. Its badge was a red hand on the front pillar, while Phillip's was a swift in flight. Phillip knew every speck on both badges: his eyes seemed to illumine every aspect of the marques. There were hundreds of other interesting things to be seen on their rides together.

Some of them were funny, such as the two horses in the lowest of the Seven Fields, where the rifle range was. Near the post-and-rail fence at the bend of the road the two animals stood, necks crossed, nibbling energetically at one another's hair. The boys watched for five minutes, wondering when the horses would stop; they left only when a Vanguard 'bus came along, steam blowing from its radiator, to race it up the hill.

The Vanguard, like the red General that sometimes came that way on Saturdays, could not do more than twelve miles an hour; the Swift could pass it, even if Desmond's Rudge could not—just. But up the hill leading to Brumley they both won easily, as usually buses had to stop half-way up, after creeping at three m.p.h., their engines boiling furiously.

Chapter 17

EXIT MR. PURLEY-PROUT

One early evening when Phillip returned, he found Mother and Mrs. Lower Low in the front room. Mother closed the door quietly as he stood wiping his boots on the mat. Phillip wondered what was up, for usually when Mrs. Lower Low called with her work she and Mother went into the kitchen.

"Phillip," said Hetty, when Mrs. Low had gone, "could you spare me a minute, dear, from your homework?"

Since Mum could see that he was reading the latest number of *The Scout*, Phillip thought this hint a little too obvious. What had he been found out about, now?

"You know I'm not doing it, so why pretend I am, Mother?"

"Oh, it was just a figure of speech. Politeness costs nothing, my son." Then feeling she might have been too severe, Hetty kissed him on the top of his head. He wriggled away from the caress. How like Dickie he was sometimes, she thought, feeling rebuffed.

"Well, what is it? Come, speak out!"

Yes, it might have been Dickie speaking.

"Phillip," said Hetty, taking a chop out of the safe in the larder, and putting it in a pan, "I would like to speak to you in the strictest confidence, dear. You are now fourteen, and soon will be growing up towards manhood. Are you listening, dear?"

Phillip seemed intently to be reading something in the paper; but he was thinking rapidly. Had anyone told her that he and

Desmond sometimes went into the Randiswell Recreation Ground on Thursday nights, for the thrill of passing by the dark waiting figures of toms by the rustic bridge leading to Rushy Green—to hear the low-spoken, rather fearful invitation, *Want a sweetheart, dear?* He and Desmond had pretended to be on their way to Troop Headquarters, but they had walked about instead, not wanting to see the brassy-haired Mr. Purley-Prout.

"Well, Mum, go on! I'm listening! I can't wait all night!"

"It's something to do with Lenny Low, Phillip. But first, will you give me your word of honour not to say anything to anyone else about what I am going to say to you?" Hetty lit the gas under the frying pan.

Phillip looked up, with puzzled expression. "Is that why Mrs. Lower Low came just now?"

"Yes, dear. Do you know anything about it?"

"About what, Mum?"

"Are you sure you don't know, Phillip?"

"About *what?*" he cried, in exasperation.

"Phillip, will you give me your word of honour to regard what I am going to say in the strictest confidence? It might cause very great trouble if you told anyone else, you see."

"All right, I promise. Cough it up."

"First, I must ask you if you knew anything about the money Mr. Prout gave to Lenny Low after the Whitsun camp?"

"Money? What money?"

By his face Hetty could see that he did not. She felt relief. How could she tell him about the very terrible thing Mrs. Low had confided in her? If Phillip's Father knew, he might put his foot down, and cause all sorts of trouble. Ought she to confide in Mamma first? But Mamma was not well; Dr. Cave-Browne had said she had a clot of blood from the varicose veins on her legs travelling about, and she must on no account be worried. No, Phillip was old enough to be warned, at least, of the dangers that beset him along the road of life.

"What money, Mum. You do beat about the bush, so!"

"It was a very considerable sum for a little boy, Phillip, for that after all is what Lenny is still. Mrs. Low said it was a half sovereign."

"Yes, Mr. Prout gave Lenny that, to do his good turn, in secret, to help Mrs. Low."

"Then you do know about it then, dear? Who told you?"

"Lenny did. You told me yourself about the money she owed the money-lender, who charged her all that interest, ten per cent a month, or a hundred and twenty per cent per annum."

"Is that all Lenny has told you, dear? I mean, was there anything else between him and Mr. Prout, that you know of?"

"No, Mum."

Phillip looked puzzled, to Hetty's relief.

"Well dear, perhaps that was the reason. Only Mrs. Low was very worried, you see."

"Did she think Lenny had pinched the money?"

"Oh no, Phillip, nothing like that! Don't you go saying anything like that, I beg of you." Hetty hesitated. "Perhaps I should ask you one thing more, dear, though I am sure a son of mine would never do anything with anyone of which he would be ashamed, would he?"

Phillip wondered if his Mother was by chance referring to the remarks he had inked into *British Birds*. He pretended to a naïve innocence. "In what way d'you mean, Mum?" as he opened his Algebra book.

"In any way, dear," replied Hetty. She was unable to express her thoughts in words, "beating about the bush", as Dickie often said. At the very moment that she thought of him, a key jingled in the porch. It was like telepathy!

"Now dear, I must see about your Father's dinner."

Hetty turned up the gas. The chop in the frying pan began to hiss more noticeably.

"And I must get on with my beastly Algebra," said Phillip, sliding the folded *Scout* into his satchel. "Algebra—Algebra—it sounds like teeth being pulled out."

When Father had gone out for his cycle ride, Phillip slipped through Gran'pa's house and up the gully and through the thorns to the grass below the sheep-fold, and down behind the Grammar School to the cemetery lane, to find Lenny Low.

A green Dursley-Pedersen bicycle stood against the kerb outside Lenny's house. Seeing it, Phillip at once turned and walked round the corner. To his relief he saw Lenny coming along by the railings towards him, a library book under one arm.

"Don't recognise me," Phillip hissed as Lenny walked slowly past him. "Follow me to the turning to Joy Farm."

He went on slowly as though he were out for an ordinary stroll.

Out of sight, in the farm turning, he waited for Lenny.

"Mr. Purley-Prout is at your house! I saw his bike outside!"

Lenny looked afraid.

"What's up, Lenny? You can trust me. I know about the money he gave you. Tell me, on your Scout's honour, did Old Prout give it you, or did you sneak it?"

"Mr. Purley-Prout gave me it, Phillip. Only it isn't that so much." Lenny looked ashamed.

"Come on, out with it! I won't split."

"It was when I was in his bivouac."

"What was?"

When Lenny had explained, Phillip said,

"Fancy Mr. Purley-Prout doing that! I didn't think men did that, only boys. Ching tried to do it to me, once, under the bushes above the gully, but I told him off. It was then he spat in my eye. They say if you do it a lot, a long hair grows out of the middle of your hand. Do you believe it?"

"They say it gives you the palsy, too," said Lenny, unhappily.

"My Father started to tell me about it once, when he said he'd seen something on the sheets of my bed. He couldn't have done, because I can't get anything yet."

"Nor can I."

"How did your mother find out about you and Old Prout, then?"

"She saw me in the bathroom, in the mirror on the wall, when she looked from her bedroom window."

"Ah, you see, light reflects in equal angles! You want to be careful of mirrors, for if anyone can see *you*, you can see *them*, since the rays of light pass between you. Was your mother angry?

"No. Only when she asked me where I learned it from, I had to tell her. Then she asked me if Mr. Purley-Prout had promised me the money for that."

"*Money for that?*" said Phillip, incredulously. "I don't believe it! And half a sovereign, too! When did he give it to you?"

"On the station, just before we came home by train after the Whitsun camp. I told him before that, you see, about the money my Mum owed, when he asked me to tell 'im all about myself, after he'd taken me into his bivouac, that wet night at camp."

"Well, I think it was rather decent of Old Prout to give you the tin, anyway. Your mother won't be worried about owing money any more."

"My Father found out from my Mum, and created a terrible scene."

"How did he find out? I thought he didn't speak to your Mother."

"Nor he does, usually, but he told my Mum this time he knew all about what she had been doing. My Father told my Mum he used to call in and ask the moneylender if she had paid the interest, so he knew all about it, and it served her right."

Lenny was now crying, remembering the shouts at home, and his father's angry face as he shook his fist at his mother.

"Well, Old Prout's at your house now, Lenny. Let's come and see him. Only let me explain."

Phillip quivered as he said this, though he was not in the least frightened. He was rather enjoying the thought of standing up for Lenny Low. Perhaps Mr. Purley-Prout would see him, too, in a new light.

The two boys walked down to the cemetery gates. As they turned the corner, they saw Mr. Purley-Prout cycling towards them. He swerved over the road, leapt off his bicycle, and stopped. He wore a tweed suit, without a hat. His fair hair was ruffled. Phillip thought that his face looked rocky. His forehead was wrinkled up as well as his cheeks. His eyes had a faraway look.

"Good evening, boys," he said hurriedly, "just the two I wanted to see. Phillip, can you spare me a minute or two? No, don't go away, Lenny. Just wait here and guard my bike, will you? I want a word with your patrol leader."

Mr. Purley-Prout set the pedal of the Dursley-Pedersen upon the kerb. Then he took Phillip's arm and walked with him along by the cemetery railings. With head bent down, he spoke in a low voice close to Phillip's ear.

"What's the matter, Phillip, what's the matter? Have you heard anything? My enemies are trying to ruin me, Phillip. They are jealous of the superiority of the Troop, you see."

Phillip trembled, but his mind remained apart. He knew Mr. Purley-Prout was just saying that. It was strange, and rather enjoyable, to feel upright and confident, while Mr. Purley-Prout was bent and afraid.

"Is it about Lenny, Mr. Prout?"

"What about Lenny, Phillip, what about him? Tell me, quick. The future of the Troop is at stake. What do you know about Lenny, Phillip?"

"Well, *you* know, don't you, Mr. Prout?" replied Phillip, in a kind of wonder that he seemed so weak and frightened.

"What do you mean, Phillip? Why *should* I know anything? I gave Lenny that half-sovereign to help his poor Mother! I swear that was all! It was my good turn, Phillip. Don't you believe me?"

"Yes, Mr. Prout, I do."

Mr. Purley-Prout looked into his eyes. Even then, his eyes did not seem to be seeing him. "You are a good Scout, Phillip," he said earnestly. He put his arm around Phillip's shoulder. "Are you my friend?"

"Yes, Mr. Prout."

"Then help me, Phillip! A man like me has many enemies! Tell me what they are saying? Has anyone been to see you?"

"No, Mr. Prout. I heard about it from Lenny."

"What did Lenny say, Phillip? What did Lenny say?"

"He said you wanked him, Mr. Prout, in your bivouac."

Mr. Purley-Prout held Phillip's arm tighter, and bent his head more as he said, "I don't quite follow you, Phillip. What does that expression mean?"

Phillip felt awkward.

"Well, it's what they say—only no one believes it—well, you know—a long hair growing out of the middle of your hand, Mr. Prout."

"I am afraid I don't understand, Phillip."

"It's what's supposed to be bad for your health," said Phillip, lowering his gaze.

Mr. Purley-Prout took his arm off Phillip's shoulder. After a few paces he said. "Is that all Lenny said?"

"Yes, Mr. Prout."

"I see. Now I want a frank reply to my question, please, Phillip. Do you think I would do such a thing as that, Phillip? On your Scout's honour, now!"

Mr. Purley-Prout was now upright.

Remembering what Mother had told him—to be very careful what he said—Phillip began to feel anxious.

"I don't know, Mr. Prout."

"Lenny is imagining things, Phillip. He is younger than you, and probably got an idea into his head from someone else. Do you know if anyone has been questioning him?"

"Only his Father, Mr. Prout."

Mr. Purley-Prout thought again. "Ah, I begin to see daylight at last! It was a very stormy night, and I was worried about more than one thing, if you remember, Phillip. We were liable to be attacked at any moment. The other Troops envy us, you see. Also, I wasn't sure of the water supply, it had to be boiled before you scouts drank it. Then again, the heavy rain would mean no fires in the morning. All sorts of responsibilities weigh upon me, as Scoutmaster, Phillip. Knowing you were overcrowded, I offered a share of my bivvy to one of your patrol, hoping among other things, to keep you quiet! I expect as I tossed and turned in the flea-bag, half asleep, Lenny put a certain interpretation on it. So if anyone asks you questions, you will tell them the truth of our very disturbing night, won't you?"

"Yes, Mr. Prout," said Phillip, thinking that Lenny's side of the case was the true one, all the same. He had seen it in Mr. Prout's face. Mr. Prout was not really what he pretended to be.

They went back to Lenny Low, who was subduedly standing on guard by the two bicycles.

"I would like to give every one of my scouts a bike like your new Swift, Phillip, if I had the money. But I suppose that good action would be misconstrued, without the shadow of a doubt! Well, Lenny, I have told your patrol leader the truth, and he believes me, so don't—for you are only one against many, you know!—please don't, for all our sakes, repeat what you have been saying any more. Some people might misconstrue it as blackmail, you know, and that is a very serious thing, indeed. Now if you, Phillip, had exercised proper judgment in buying your tent, we would all have enjoyed a good night's sleep in camp that first night, and none of this storm in a teacup would have happened!"

Turning to Lenny Low, Mr. Purley-Prout said, "Now, Lenny, we have a duty to your parents. This is a moment for courage of a high order. You must come with me to your Father and Mother, and tell them that you imagined the whole story, then we can all forget it. Phillip here will bear me out, won't you, Phillip?"

"Will I get into trouble, please, sir?" said Lenny Low, scarce above a whisper.

"No! For I will, of course, as your friend and Scoutmaster, stand by you. Come on, a mistake has been made, so let's all face it with true British grit! Like having a bad tooth out, that's all! And when it's all over, we'll forget the whole business!"

Mr. Purley-Prout was like his old self again. Phillip could not look at his face. He could not look at Father's face either—

Father said it was because he was shifty. Phillip felt that if he was shifty, so was Mr. Purley-Prout.

They walked in silence to Lenny Low's house.

In the front room, Mr. Purley-Prout said that he had thought the whole matter out, and really, it was all a storm in a teacup. Boys, he said, sometimes dreamed, and, when awakening, felt great relief that it was, after all, only a bad dream. The human mind had been a mystery to even the greatest savants; men knew little about the human mind even in the present advanced age, when the ether had been pierced by wireless telegraphy, and the air conquered by flying machines and dirigibles. Illusions were common amongst the most intelligent as well as among ordinary, everyday sort of people like themselves. People would swear to their beliefs, and sincerely, even though they were proved to be based on imagination. There was the case of William Blake, the great metaphysical poet, who was thrashed as a child for saying he saw angels on a tree. The eighteenth century was a barbarous age, but today men knew better than to punish little children for the fantasies of their minds.

Then, looking up from the carpet of the front room, Mr. Purley-Prout said earnestly, holding his hands before him,

"Mr. and Mrs. Low! I swear to you on my honour as a Scoutmaster, as I am prepared to swear my oath in court to defend the good name of the Troop—and I most sincerely hope it will not be necessary—I swear to you that I gave your son money simply and solely because of a humble Christian impulse to do a good turn to others. Now Lenny dear, answer me this before your parents. Did I, or did I not, promise you the money before, or after, you had told me about the debt that hung like a dark cloud over your home?"

"After, Mr. Prout."

"Thank you, Lenny, for your courage in telling the truth. I am far from being a rich man," went on Mr. Purley-Prout. "Indeed, I am a poor man, but when I decided to form the North West Kent Troop of Baden-Powell's Boy Scouts, it was with a determination to do all in my power, to spend every penny I possessed to help the youth of England. God knows I am no paragon, indeed in many ways I consider myself a failure, but when I heard from Lenny the sad story, it——"

Mr. Prout's voice broke. He turned away, and blew his nose with two trumpet notes. He dabbed his eyes.

"Mr. and Mrs. Low, I have opened my heart to you! I can only hope, humbly, for your understanding. I ask you to consider just this one thing more. Would a man in my position, were he guilty of the unspeakable crime that has been whispered abroad simply and solely because of this money—I ask you, as I would ask any British court of justice should it be necessary to clear my good name—I repeat, I ask you, would any man in his senses, any guilty man that is, give any boy he had injured a half-sovereign, knowing that such an act would suggest the very thing that, if he were guilty, he would want to hush up?"

Mr. Purley-Prout looked from Mrs. Low's face to Mr. Low's face, then quickly back to Mrs. Low's face again.

"I can only say to you, Mrs. Low, that if my generosity were misdirected, I am humbly sorry, and well have I paid for my impulsiveness. In future I shall think twice before I leap, in a world which so easily can miscontrue a generous act. And if this little storm in a teacup has served to allow us to know one another better, well then, it only fulfils the old adage, that it's an ill wind which blows nobody any good! Phillip, thank you for standing by your Scoutmaster! Mrs. Low, I hope you are now in some way less a prey to anxiety. Mr. Low, I hope you will not think too hardly of Lenny, who will, I am sure, grow out of his functional hysteria—I had some training as a medical student before I decided I could serve humanity in other ways—and develop into a fine young man."

"I'm sure I don't quite know what to say, Mr. Prout," began Mrs. Low; but Mr. Low interrupted and said, his jaw almost clenched,

"I do! Here is your half-sovereign back! I thank you for that part of your actions which were concerned with your good intentions."

Mr. Purley-Prout looked at Mr. Low, as though puzzled. Mr. Purley-Prout seemed about to say something. Then he held out his hand to Mr. Low.

Mr. Low looked Mr. Purley-Prout in the eye, ignoring his hand. Then Mr. Low went to open the door. Mr. Low looked very grim, thought Phillip. He looked as though he would never speak to anyone ever again. Mrs. Low was crying, so was Lenny Low.

Mr. Purley-Prout rode away on his Dursley-Pedersen. Feeling lost for a moment, Phillip wandered into the cemetery, then he went to tell Mrs. Neville all about it.

The patrols scattered when the North West Kent Troop came to an end. It was said that Mr. Prout had gone to Rome, to live in a monastery.

Phillip decided to join the troop attached to St. Mary's church. They had two buglers, a drum, and the parish hall every Thursday for lectures, games and *soirees*. Thither he went, and met a tall, dark, tight-lipped scoutmaster called Oscar Blackman, whose sallow face was adorned with an incipient moustache. With hardly a word of greeting, unsmiling, this authority ordered him to report with his patrol at the next Saturday afternoon parade.

When Phillip turned up, with Cranmer and Desmond, Mr. Blackman said, as Phillip saluted him, "Is this your patrol? What do you call yourselves?"

"The Bloodhounds, sir," replied Phillip, standing to attention.

"Oh," murmured Mr. Blackman, through pursed lips. Then he muttered, "Shades of Sherlock Holmes."

Phillip thought that perhaps it was not a very favourable remark. Mr. Oscar Blackman, who was an Old Boy of his school, somehow seemed to be different from other scoutmasters he had seen. Cranmer remarked, when Mr. Blackman had gone away, that he looked "a bit of a black 'isself, wiv 'is gloomy fissog, bloomin' great cape and sewerman's boots."

The new scoutmaster's uniform was rather different, certainly. Mr. Oscar Blackman wore the same sort of cape that the Bloodhounds had, but not cut down. It was fastened by a chain at his throat, and when he cycled fast along the High Street on his Humber bicycle, in top gear, pushing with his black leather riding boots, the cape fluttered behind him.

"This bloke fancies 'isself as Dick Turpin," said Cranmer, adding that he must have swiped the boots from a mounted copper. In this Cranmer was not far wrong, for the boots, together with the cape, had been bought at Murrage's, old City of London mounted police gear.

"Dick Turpin" became his nickname among the three friends. After the first day, Dick Turpin said that they would have to join the other patrols, and become either Wolves or Kestrels. That was devastating news; but before Phillip could decide for himself, an occurrence at the next Thursday evening meeting in the Parish Hall decided for him.

The senior patrol leader, a younger brother of the Scoutmaster, a big, red-faced, curly-haired boy who went to Phillip's school, took the meeting. He addressed them all, saying that his brother was very ill. Very ill indeed. He walked up and down dramatically on the platform, before the scouts waiting in silence to hear the news.

"Worn out by constant work for St. Mary's Troop, on top of his day's work in London," declared the patrol leader of the Wolves, "my brother Oscar has finally succumbed to what at first was feared to be brain fever."

The boys listened in silence.

"On Monday morning," went on the Wolf leader, dramatically, "we found Oscar in his bedroom, wandering about in his woollen combinations. He had a dazed look in his eye, and a thermometer in his mouth, upside down."

At this, Phillip could not help laughing.

The Wolf leader scowled as he pointed at the offender.

"Oh, it's *you!*" he said, sarcastically. "It *would* be, you bloody little hound!" He looked so angry that Phillip was scared. "Get out!" he shouted, in sudden rage. "Clear off, before I boot you up the backside, you little rough, you scholarship kid!"

Phillip hurried to get out. At the door he turned and said, "Coming, Cranmer?"

"Yes, take your guttersnipe pal with you. We don't want you, either!" pointing to Desmond. Desmond hastened after Phillip.

"Brain fever my eye!" taunted Cranmer, at the door. "Dick Turpin ain't got no brains to get 'ot!"

"I'll smash you for that!" shouted the Wolf, leaping off the platform. "My brother is to have an operation for appendix tonight!"

"That won't put in what wor never there!" retorted Cranmer, before he darted off among the tombstones.

"They're all sissies in that there lot, if you arst my opinion," he remarked, when Phillip and Desmond met him in the Rec. a few minutes later. "Good riddince ter bad rubbage!"

Which was, it must impartially be recorded, more or less what the senior patrol leader had just remarked about the Bloodhounds.

Despite his experiences, Phillip still dreamed of ideal scouting. At school he heard of a troop on the Heath that wanted recruits. Milton gave him the name and address of the headquarters.

There he went the next Wednesday night, for the mid-week meeting. It was held in a house in Tranquil Vale, near a pub called The Three Tuns. Phillip remembered the name of the pub because Uncle Hugh was sitting outside it, in the dogcart he sometimes hired from the publican who kept the Randiswell. Uncle Hugh's man, called Bob, who came from a family living in Railway Terrace, was with him. Uncle Hugh offered Phillip a bottle of pop, but Phillip said he was going to a patrol leaders' meeting, and must not be late.

Determined to make a good impression, he put on a happy face as he sat with the other patrol leaders—including Milton of the Peacocks—round a big mahogany table. He paid the closest attention to what the presiding scoutmaster said. The others wore their everyday clothes, but Phillip had changed into his Eton suit, with gloves. He listened with apparent great attention, a wide smile fixed across his over-soaped face. He wore a new collar and tie, both borrowed from his cousin Hubert. Determined not to make a fool of himself by talking too much—his mother had often told him that he had no reserve—Phillip sat silent during the entire discussion, except to say "Yes", or "No", as occasion demanded.

At the end of it, the scoutmaster said to Phillip that he could join the troop if he cared to, but not as a patrol leader.

"We have enough patrols for the present."

Concealing his disappointment, Phillip continued to smile widely.

"By the way," said Mr. Peacock. "Do you attend Dulwich College?"

"No, sir," replied Phillip, surprised. Milton winked at him.

"Oh, I see. I asked only because you are wearing the school tie. You see, I happen to be an Old Alleynian."

"Oh, this one?" said Phillip, pointing with a gloved hand. "My cousin Hubert Cakebread lent me this, as mine had a greasy mark on it, sir." He smiled at Milton. He would not mind being in his patrol. He would do his very best, if Milton would have him. Was he not a friend of Helena Rolls?

What was left of the Bloodhounds—Phillip, Cranmer, and Desmond—paraded with the new troop on the following Saturday. Alas, there was no room in the Peacocks. But the Rattlesnakes needed men. Their call was a pebble in a small potted-meat tin. The other Rattlesnakes did not like Cranmer. Cranmer made the rattle with his throat. They looked at him as though he were quite different from themselves. To Phillip the new troop seemed tame after Mr. Purley-Prout's way of doing things. They marched about and scouted over the Heath, signalling with flags, or pretended to be hiding in the open, with golfers moving past them, or calling "Fore!" from the distance. Worst of all, there were no camp fires. And as they obviously looked down on Cranmer, Phillip said, "I votes we don't turn up in the mouldy old Rattlesnakes again."

Anyoldhow, declared Cranmer, he had to start work on Monday, in a tanning yard at Bermondsey; which left only Phillip and Desmond.

And that was the end of the Bloodhound Patrol.

Part Three

THE WIND'S WILL

"Not I, but the wind——"

D. H. Lawrence

Chapter 18

SPRING FEVER

DURING the winter Phillip discovered a big red book in the Free Library which had a list of all the villages of Kent, with their populations, industries, and principal landowners. The first place he looked for was where he had camped at Whitsun. The lord of the manor and principal landowner was the Right Honourable the Earl of Mersea, K.G. Knollyswood Park was the residence of the Dowager Countess of Mersea.

Reading the description, Phillip thought of writing to the Dowager Countess for permission to photograph birds in the park with his camera. Peter Wallace had got permission to go in Whitefoot Lane woods, so why shouldn't he, in this ever so much better place?

In another volume among the thick red reference books he read how to write a letter to a peer or peeress of the realm. He copied out the specimen letter carefully upon a piece of paper; then returning to the Gazetteer, he searched for other names of landowners in North West Kent. Excited by the idea, he imagined Desmond and himself, with his Christmas-present five-bob Brownie, exploring far and wide in their secret preserves. They would study Nature and take wonderful photographs!

Obsessed by his idea, he hastened to the lending section and took out a book on the topography of North West Kent. It had several maps and photographs. He spent the next hour looking up villages on the map within a dozen miles of his home, where woods and streams were marked, and in transcribing particulars from the large red Gazetteer. Why not fishing, too? But perhaps he had better not ask for too much at once, in case it looked greedy, and permission therefore be refused.

There was no Cranmer to be met at the Free Library nowadays; so with his information he hurried home, and copied out the names and addresses, in code, into his *Schoolboy's Diary*. This had been another Christmas present: it had sketches of birds and animals in the corners of some of the pages, with brief descriptions. He knew them all by heart—fox, otter, badger, deer, hare, rabbit, stoat, pine-marten—capercailzie, pheasant, partridge, wren, ring-dove, owl, eagle.

Phillip had entered the most important things of the New Year in code. Therein were the names of rare motorcars; the times he had seen Helena Rolls in the distance; and when he had met Cranmer, one Sunday afternoon, down in the Warm Kitchen, below where the promenaders walked by the bandstand. In code, now, went the names and addresses of his preserves, as he thought of them.

The Rt. Honble Dowager Countess of Aesrem. Doowsyllonk Park, Vulpine's Vulgar, Kent.
Major Sir H.A.H.F. Drannel, Trab. Lampbacon Court, West Lampbacon.
Henry Souman Esq., The Swizzery, Bee Yoho ley Common.
The Dowager Lady Ynasnud, Finished Stall Priory, Poemoaks.
The Honble Mrs. Edraw, Sq Norfolk Broadses Court, Easterbacon.
The Lord Yrubeva, Tall Yellow Leaves in Autumn, Close-n-borough.
The Earl Epohnats, Drofsnye, Kent.

These precautions would conceal the whereabouts of his preserves should he lose his diary, and some spy such as Ching find it and try and copy him. However, even if Ching found out that some of the names were spelt backwards, he would have to think very hard to puzzle out that when you were swizzed you were rooked, that Tall Yellow Leaves in Autumn meant *High Elms*, Lamp was *Wick*, Bacon *Ham*, Yoho—fifteen dead men on a dead man's chest, Yoho for a bottle of *rum*—Finished was *Dun*, Close was *Far*, and hardest of all, Norfolk Broads was wherries, or the Old English spelling Uerries.

Phillip's handwriting in his diary was almost of a copperplate engraving care and precision: in his diary was his pride of life, his passion, expressed in the regularity of the lettering made with firm strokes, and careful forming of loops and circles. This was his writing when he lived in what he was recording; in contrast to the formless and irregular scrawl of perplexity and distaste, the deadness in his school exercise-books. The letter he wrote that evening in the kitchen would have pleased, and certainly surprised Richard, had he seen it before Phillip slipped out to catch the half past eight collection in the red pillar-box in Charlotte Road.

The letter was not entirely of his own composition. Mr. Newman, in his little cottage opposite the Randiswell Baths, had made some suggestions as to how to make the best impression on so great a lady as the Dowager Countess of Mersea. Phillip borrowed a piece of Gran'pa's best rag-made grey writing paper for the copperplate final draft.

Lindenheim,
Wakenham,
Kent.

2 March 1910.

To
THE RIGHT HONOURABLE THE DOWAGER COUNTESS OF MERSEA
Madam,

I have the honour to present my Compliments to your Ladyship, and to request that the cause of scientific knowledge be advanced by permission for myself and my friend to roam your Ladyship's land, both arable, grazing, and park, for the purpose of taking photographs of wild birds and their nests *in situ*, without disturbance or in any way causing distress to the feathered songsters for which the writer has the greatest regard. I have some knowledge of the art and mystery of farming, and would in no wise cause damage or leave any gates open, so to cause possible straying of cattle, horses, sheep, or other live stock. I am fourteen years of age, and a student at Heath School, founded in Elizabethan times by the famous donor of our local Almshouses.

I have the honour to be,
Madam,
Your Ladyship's Most Obedient Servant
PHILLIP MADDISON.

The envelope of this missive, as he called it to himself, was sealed with red wax, and impressed with a signet ring he borrowed from a drawer in Father's bedroom.

When a reply came two days later, in a grey envelope with a thin black band all round it, and a crest with motto on the flap, he opened it with trembling fingers holding the bread-knife to cut the top carefully; and taking out a white card, also lined with black, read first the signature beneath, *Constance Mersea*, then the word *Permission* on top, in shaky slanting writing. Permission for Mr. Phillip Maddison and friend to enter the woods!

"Hurray, hurray, hurray!" he shouted.

When he had told Mother she said, "Finish your tea, dear, before going down to see Desmond. And be sure to write a note and thank your benefactor for her great kindness, won't you?"

Phillip was too excited to listen; and pressing two pieces of bread and beef dripping together, he gulped his cup of tea, and with cheeks bulging ran down the road to give the wonderful news to Desmond. There he had a second tea, before going on down to tell the news to Mr. Newman.

The housekeeper, shawl over shoulders, small round wrinkled face and white hair scrimped up in a wispy bun at her neck, opened the door to him, and with her smiling little bow stepped back for him to come in. Mr. Newman was sitting in his parlour, the walls of which were lined with all the same kind of pictures. Blue and red predominated. In each one a volcano was erupting above the sea, while below ships were at anchor in icy cold water. There were seven such pictures, two on each of the three walls side by side, while the largest was alone, over the fireplace.

Phillip thought that Mr. Newman's treasures represented his past life. If this was so, he must have spent some time at anchor, canvas furled so closely that he had never been able to sail away in time from those great eruptions of flame, steam, and cinder. Mr. Newman had told him about his visits to Italy, Japan, Iceland, and Mexico; and Phillip had assumed that he had been a sailor, as sometimes Mr. Newman wore an old peaked cap, while sitting by his iron grate shaped like a sea-shell. What adventures he must have had! The largest picture over his chimney piece was one of the Great Fire of San Francisco, while his frigate, every stitch rolled, lay at anchor in the bay.

Mr. Newman must have seen some fighting with cannibals, too. On the wall hung a cutlass with its golden hanging knot;

next to it a Polynesian painted mask and two crossed boomerangs; a jagged-bladed fishing spear with a light wood shaft. There were models of wooden ships in bottles, all with sails flying; and beside the hearth, by the bellows, a funny brown velvet cap, a pill-box hat, with a tassel hanging from it. Mr. Newman said it was a smoking cap, from Heidelberg in Germany.

Then there were the cabinets, shells, and bird's eggs which lay, some in cotton wool, in many tiers of shallow drawers, around the walls.

"Ah, it is my little friend!" exclaimed the thin old gentleman, rising from his tattered leather armchair to bow and take Phillip's hand. "What a pleasure to see you again. Pray take a chair, and draw up to the fire. I have wondered since last we met how you have fared with your letter writing. Ah, I see you have something to show me," as he felt for his glasses in his breast pocket. To his housekeeper he said, "The tray, if you please, and the barrel of biscuits."

Mr. Newman always said this whenever Phillip called; and his housekeeper always half-curtsied before withdrawing behind a curtain, to reappear with a silver tray on which was a decanter of wine and two glasses. She took the biscuit barrel from a shelf, and put it on a hassock beside Phillip. Mr. Newman was reading the card Phillip had given him.

"Permit me to congratulate you, dear boy, and to say that I am sure you will prove worthy of such a privilege. Now may I offer you a little port wine, with a biscuit?"

"Thank you very much, Mr. Newman."

Phillip liked Mr. Newman's port wine. It gave him a rusty-stinging warmness as it went down his gullet, to lay warm in his stomach. The biscuits were Osbornes, oval and crisp. He ate two; and after looking at some of the birds' eggs in their trays, he said, unconscious of his abruptness, "I must go now, I think," and shaking hands with Mr. Newman remembered the half-mechanical "Thank you for your hospitality, sir," and hurriedly left the house to hasten back to Desmond.

Exhilarated by his success, Phillip borrowed more writing paper from Gran'pa, and sent his requests to the owners of woods and coverts at the places he had recorded in code in his diary. The baronet of "Lampbacon Court" replied in clear but shaky handwriting, giving permission; but asking Mr.

Phillip Maddison kindly to see the keeper before entering the coverts. The squire whose Queen Anne red brick house was behind the noisy and extensive rookery set back from the road along "Bec Yoho ley" Common also gave permission to Mr. Maddison and friend to walk over his estates. The chatelaine of the big house at "Easterbacon" likewise gave her consent, adding that fishing in the mere was permitted only after hay-making; while his Lordship of "Tall Yellow Leaves" wrote that he would be most pleased to give permission for Mr. Phillip Maddison to pursue his Nature Studies on his property.

Phillip swore both Desmond and Mrs. Neville to secrecy, before he showed them these replies. After tea, he and Desmond sat at the kitchen table, when it was cleared, and experimented with Desmond's electrical apparatus. There was a coil of green-silk-covered wire, which when connected with Desmond's curved pocket accumulator, with its transparent celluloid case, buzzed almost evilly with a hard little star-like spark. Two hollow brass handles extended on wire from the terminals; and when you touched these you got a shock.

So far Phillip had been afraid to hold them while the blue spark was buzzing like a little fly of hell that would never die under a spider's fangs. Sometimes the blue spark turned green and threw off a wisp of smoke about a red speck; it was eating the brass spring away. Now, emboldened by his good fortune, he held the handles firmly while the coil was switched off, and said, "Try me!" Desmond moved over the switch, and the next moment Phillip had fallen sideways off his chair, with a loud and surprised shout. Picking himself up, he asked Desmond in an anxious voice if he supposed his Mother up in the drawing room had heard the word he had used, and been shocked? In case she had, he went up to apologise.

Mrs. Neville, crochetting in her armchair by the fire, showed surprise on her large face at the subdued question. No, she had heard nothing to shock her, she said gently. Had Neville's experiment been a little strong? Oh no, replied Phillip, it had caught him on the hop, that was all; and after showing an interest in her work, he withdrew, with a slight bow, leaving Mrs. Neville with her face as straight as his . . . until he had gone out of the room, when the fat woman began to shake with silent laughter. There was another shout soon afterwards, when Desmond held the brass handles in order to do what Phillip could do.

After that, it was time for Phillip to leave, to do his homework. He had given up taking *The Scout*, *The Gem Library*, and *The Magnet;* and in their place he bought the week-old copies of *The Field* and *The Autocar* from the Public Library, for twopence. The only trouble with the copies was that they were dirty, particularly at the bottom corners of the pages, where the print was usually rubbed out by the grimy fingers of the Dog-eared Brigade.

One Wednesday afternoon in Eastertide two boys on bicycles, each wearing a haversack containing a packet of banana sandwiches and slices of plum cake, crossed the familiar flint and gravel road across Reynard's Common. It was a warm day; the wind of morning had dropped; sunshine lay over the linnet-haunted heath.

They entered Knollyswood Park by three oak steps, which led up to a swing gate, built in the long oak-cleft fence. Lifting over their bicycles, they hid them in the bracken growing below silver birch and other trees within. Walking away, eager to explore the new hunting grounds, Phillip was startled to hear a laughing, almost mocking cry in front. He stopped, his hand on Desmond's shoulder, as a bird of many bright colours seemed to dive up in its flight over the greensward and stick to the white bole of a big birch in front.

"A green woodpecker!" he whispered. "I saw one on the Socialist Oak on the Hill once, just like it!"

The woodpecker looked at them round the bole, its red head moving snake-like; then it moved back and hid. Phillip could hear its claws on the bark. Again came the wild mocking cry, then it was flying away from the top of the tree, rising and falling in a series of half-loops.

"Come on, man!" said Phillip, and they ran to the tree.

The birch was a thick one, with many chippings spread around its base. One of the upper branches was snapped off, and lying below in the ferns. The wood had rotted, becoming tinder, but the white bark was still round and firm.

"It's the oil in it that preserves it, Desmond. And look, can you see the holes in the trunk up there?" he pointed. "That's where it chisels out insects in the wood. And golly, that round hole among them is its nest! Here, give us a bunk up!"

He started to climb. Desmond pushed him up until he

reached the lowest branch. The nesting hole was about twenty feet above. Phillip reported, as he clung to the trunk, that it went in about three inches before it turned downwards. "It's the nest, all right. But it is too early for eggs. We ought to leave it, in case the bird deserts. You can have a look next time." He climbed down, dropping the last six feet upon the sward. "Come on, man, isn't it a wonderful preserve?"

The next nest they found was in a holly tree, out of which a woodpigeon clattered noisily. There was a small platform of crossed black twigs on one of the branches. It was Desmond's turn to climb up. The tree was easy.

"Careful of any eggs" called up Phillip. Desmond reached the nest, and said, "Two white eggs."

"The ring dove is the farmer's enemy, but we will leave them, for a photograph later on. Some people tie the young pigeons, called squabs, by their legs to the nest, for their parents to feed long after they are fledged, Desmond. Can you guess why?"

"For pets?"

"Well, hardly. To get them nice and juicy, for cooking. It's rather cruel, don't you think?"

"Yes. I would like to keep pigeons in my garden."

"Well, we'll see. Come on, my ambition is to get a young hawk, to train it for sparrows in the Backfield, but it's too early for them nesting now. Jumping Jehoshafat!"

A mottled brown bird, with a long beak and liquid dark eyes, had flown up with a whirring, clicking noise from the dead leaves of the woodland, seeming to dart away through the trees.

"A woodcock! Father saw one here once, he told me. They don't usually nest in England, but a few stay behind in the migration, and lay their eggs on the ground. Carramba, this is a wonderful place! Come on, let's explore!"

Phillip felt that they must miss nothing. Here was the world he had dreamed about during foggy evenings with the soiled copies of *The Field* before him on the kitchen table; while sitting quietly behind Father's armchair later in the evening, reading library books (none of them glossed nowadays) about birds, animals, fishes, and rural customs. He had searched through the bound copies of *The Gentleman's Magazine* in Father's glass-fronted bookcase, and lived in the accounts of fishing and collecting birds for stuffing in Norway and other foreign countries; and best of all, descriptions of English fields and village people. He had put up nesting boxes in the elm in the garden, and watched through the window tits and starlings inspecting them at the beginning of spring, determined never to shoot at the starlings in the close season. All that he had read and seen, together with what Father had told him of his own boyhood doings, during Sunday morning walks, now seemed to be coming real in his own life.

A flattish nest made of brown beech leaves in another holly was recognisable from one of the engravings in an article in *The Illustrated London Magazine*. He was sure it was a squirrel's drey, but said nothing, in case of disappointment.

Trembling, he told Desmond to climb up, and feel in a hole he would find in the side. He felt too weak, almost too dreamlike, to climb up himself.

Desmond picked his way up through the spiny leaves of the holly, which surrounded the base of the tree. Phillip had read that holly leaves often had no spines on them above the reach of grazing cattle. He told Desmond this; and Desmond called down, "You're quite right, Phillip, the leaves are quite a different shape up here, more rounded and smooth." He reached the nest. "I can't find the opening."

"Feel very carefully all round it. Don't pull it, whatever you do. Feel carefully, and something inside might feel warm, like Timmy Rat in his nest."

"Oh!" cried Desmond. "Look!" He held out a fawn-coloured animal, with short working legs and stump of tail. "What is it?"

"I thought so, you know!" cried Phillip, in triumph. "It's a drey of young squirrels. Bring it down, for a photo. Put it in your shirt, for safety."

Desmond did so. He climbed down carefully. "Oh, it tickles! It's trying to crawl away!"

The baby squirrel was about five inches long, very soft, with fine silky hair, a blunt head and rounded tags of ears. It had long claws, as yet soft and unpointed. The boys admired it, holding it against their cheeks in turn.

"Father had one as a pet when he was a boy, as well as ferrets, a white rat like mine, and other things," said Phillip. "Only his squirrel was a nuisance when it grew up. It used to prance around the rooms, leaping from particular places every time, so that its claws wore them out after a bit. So he had to let it go. It used to drink the cream off the milk in the larder, and also suck hen's eggs. Hold it in your two hands, will you, while I take a photo."

Phillip went back two paces, and shaded the view-finder with a hand. The Brownie box camera, with its fixed focus, clicked. "Good! That's our first photo! Five more, and I'll be able to develop the film. Have you ever done any developing?"

"No, Phillip."

"It's quite easy. You want some black cloth over the window, a lantern with red glass in it, a tray with developer, and when it's done you wash the negative in the bath under the tap for an hour, to stop further oxidisation of the silver nitrate on the film, which turns black in light. That's all. Only when the film is wet, you have to be jolly careful not to nick it with your nail, for it's soft like jelly, and a nick comes out black on the print afterwards.

"My first camera was a penny pin-hole one," went on Phillip. "It was a tiny little cardboard one, with a pin-hole instead of a lens. It took about a minute exposure. For the penny you got also a glass plate, chemicals for the developing solution, a piece of sensitised paper for the print, and a screw of hypo for fixing. I took a photo of Father holding his bike. The bike came out very well, but instead of Father's face and body only my thumb-mark was there. I must have touched it with chemicals, before I developed it."

They talked under the tree, sitting on the ground among the primroses and rising shiny leaves of wild arums. Rooks were cawing in a distant rookery among the beeches. They heard again the laughing cry of the woodpecker, and the thin singsong of a chiffchaff.

"Soon all the migrants will be arriving, Desmond. They come from Africa, many of them. My Lord, we're going to have a wonderful time in our woods! It's a damn sight better'n scouting, don't you think? Though those days were fun, weren't they? I am glad I didn't miss them!" He rolled over with delight, and pressed his face into the drift of dead leaves under the holly. "I say, smell this earth! It's all fresh leaf mould. And just look at these skeletons, aren't they lovely? You wouldn't think that every leaf had all these ribs and veins in it, would you? It'd take years to make, if you tried to do it yourself. It's finer than any lace-work. Yet on the tree they just grow! How? Who makes them, *really?* Have you ever tried to think about why the stars are, and everything on the earth, Desmond? I can't think about the stars for long, it makes my head simply reel."

"Well, God made everything, Phillip, didn't he?"

"I suppose so, but *how?* Don't tell your Mother, will you, but my Father doesn't believe in God. That's why he never goes to church. I don't believe in church very much myself, either. Do you?"

"My Mother and I are Catholics, and Mother says it is not for man to question Holy Mystery," said Desmond, in a quiet voice, with a slight quaver in it.

Phillip hastened to say that his mother liked the Catholic Church.

"I went once with her to the church at the top of Comfort Road, almost opposite where I was born, and I preferred it to St. Cyprian's or even St. Simon's. I liked the singing of the Gregorian chants, and the smell of the incense. It was like those joss-sticks my uncle Hilary had burning on the shelf at Epsom, when I was a child. But Father doesn't seem to like the Catholics. He talks about Catholic countries being priest-ridden. Is your Father like that, too?"

Desmond went pale, and then slightly pink. Phillip pretended not to see, as he examined an empty case of beech-mast. He felt awkward, remembering that Mother had told him never to ask personal questions, or about other people's affairs.

Desmond climbed up to put back the baby squirrel. Afterwards they walked over the pasture, among ewes with their lambs, to the gate leading to the bailiff's cottage, and the paddock where they had camped.

Desmond produced a penny. "Mother said I must get a glass of fresh milk if I could, Phillip. Do you think Mr. Wilson would let me have one?"

"Let's try, and see. Only I haven't any money." The bailiff's wife gave them each a glass of milk, and refused to take any money for it. Rejoicing in their luck, they left, caps politely raised, and went across the road into the paddock, to search for marks of their camp-fires of long ago. Round the hedges they found two thrushes' nests, each lined with cowdung and tinder-wood mixture, and holding four blue, warm black-spotted eggs; a hedge-sparrow's with sky-blue smaller eggs; a blackbird's with its faint rusty freckles; and a wren's building in the side of a haystack.

"I'll make a map, and put them in, tonight," announced Phillip.

Down in the quarry farmyard there was much to interest them, including a pink white pig with a big pouch hanging below its hind legs. It was so big that Phillip said there must be something wrong with the pig.

"I wonder if it's deformed, Des. I think it must be. Perhaps it has been put in this pen, alone, in case the others bully it, as they always do a weaker creature," he went on, recalling what Father had once told him. "Poor devil, its insides must have fallen out! That pink bag must be part of its intestines. You see, the pigs in the other pens aren't like that."

"I expect it's ruptured itself, and is going to be done away with," suggested Desmond. They scratched its back with their sticks, to give it a little happiness, poor thing, before its sad end.

Cows were in another building; and looking in the open upper halves of the doors, Phillip pointed out the grey mudded cups, over which feathers and grasses showed, on the rafters. "Swallows!" he cried, recognising them from a photograph in his Kearton bird book. "They'll be home again soon. I say, isn't all this simply *wonderful?*" He ran round in a circle, pretending to be a dog, panting, with tongue over teeth, hands on both sides of his head for ears. "Aough! Aough! Aough! I know how a dog feels when it's off the lead. My Lord, I'm glad I wrote for our permit! How about some tea, are you peckish?"

They sat in the only patch of sunlight near the entrance, to be warm. While they were there, eating their banana sandwiches, the crunch of boots came down the road, and immediately a shrill squealing arose from the pig-houses at the lower end of the quarry. They wondered what the row was about, and went down to see. The pigs, including the deformed one, were all standing, snouts held still, small glassy bristled eyes staring, hairy ears raised as though listening. Suddenly they all began squealing again.

When a labourer walked down the cart track, with two pails of swill fixed to chains from the wooden yoke over his shoulders, Phillip asked him if the pigs were hungry, and was told it was their feeding time. A thought came to him. "Did they hear your footsteps, do you think?"

"Aye, they listen, their bellies is their clocks, young sir," said the pigman.

Phillip thought that the man had mistaken him for perhaps a relation of the Dowager Countess, because he had called him "sir". How awful when he found out that he was only a nobody! He decided to bring him a packet of Ogden's Tabs when he came next, so that the man would not be too disappointed in his mistake, and feel he had been cheated.

The boys watched the feeding. What a jostling, grunting, slopping of chops and greediness there was! Some of the pigs stood their front trotters in the troughs, to keep others away, like staking out an extra claim, while they sucked and gulped the swill as far away as possible from their feet. It was like Ching, who if he had a bag of sweets, would hide it in his pocket (unless he wanted a favour done) in order to cadge a sucker from someone else. Phillip thought that he had done that, too, when he was at the dame school. He asked the pigman about the deformed pig. Was it going to be killed?

"That one? Not likely! That's one of the best boars us ever 'ad, sir! His sire took the blue ribbon at the last show."

"Then it's not deformed?"

"Deformed? Not likely! Whatever made you think that?"

"Well, he was all by himself," said Phillip, lamely.

When the pigman had gone again with his buckets, Phillip threw little pieces of chalk on the boar's back, because he had been deceived.

"Fancy having them so big as that," he reflected aloud, feeling a half-guilty pleasure in the sight. "Sows have a lot of pigs at a time, and I suppose that's why, don't you, Des? Don't tell your Mother, or anyone else, what I said, will you? I don't want it to get back to Old Pye, who lives at the top of our road, in case he thinks I have an unclean mind, and tells the Rollses. It isn't true, for I don't like smutty yarns. Do you?"

"No," said Desmond, turning a faint pink.

"They are vulgar without being funny," said Phillip. "I like this old boar now. I know what I'll call him—Squire Bigballs."

Boys who had unclean minds were severely punished when they were found out, Phillip knew. There was the case of Jack Hart, who had had to leave school for going out at night with girls, despite many thrashings given him by Mr. Hart, to cure

Jack's brazen ways. Jack was now a cadet in a training ship, preparing for the merchant service.

There was a story that Jack had been expelled after being found, one Wednesday evening, with two girls in the sheep-fold on the Hill. According to Ching, Jack Hart had lured them into the fold. His father, Mr. Hart, had seen the clay-stains on Jack's knees when he got home, and accused him of misconduct with the girls, one after the other. Jack Hart had not denied it, but refused to say who the girls were. According to Ching, Jack Hart had been brazen. When his father had said to him, "I know all about one of those girls you were with! She is a bad lot, and wears a blouse that shows her chest!", Jack Hart had replied, "That wasn't her chest, Father, that was her belly!" So Mr. Hart had tried to give Jack a thrashing, but Jack had not only refused to take his trousers down for his father, but had given him a black eye as well, and then run away from home.

Mr. Hart was a squat man in a brown suit and broad brown face, rather ugly. He was known to be very bad tempered. Phillip was frightened of him. Mr. Hart, said Ching, had reported his son to the Police Station. Mr. Hart had been heard to say—the Harts lived two doors down from the Chings—that he would break his son for having struck him. The police sergeant had told Mr. Hart to control his temper. So Mr. Hart had gone to see the Magister, saying that his son was beyond his control. The Magister had sent for Jack's house-master, and then for Jack, in his study. There, according to Ching, Jack Hart had still been brazen; so he was expelled.

Phillip felt a fascinated admiration whenever he thought of Jack Hart, as well as a slight fear of his badness. He had met Jack in the High Street a day or two after he was expelled, when Jack had asked for a loan of his bicycle pump. Jack said he did not care a hoot about being expelled. He was really awfully brave, like Peter Wallace; and the funny thing was that both of them wore glasses, while all the boys with spectacles in *The Gem*, *Marvel*, and *Pluck* libraries were sort of milk-sops and swots, interested in butterfly-catching and poetry and stuff like that. Since then, a year ago, Jack had joined the merchant navy.

Jack Hart's photo in his cadet's uniform was side by side with his own in the window of the shop in the High Street where he had had his taken, in Eton suit and gloves, and his lower front teeth over his upper teeth, to give the effect of an outjutting jaw. Jack Hart was grinning in his photo. Phillip looked at them whenever he walked that way, for a change, home from school.

How he would like to be bold, like Jack Hart! Jack had been, not only not afraid to speak to girls, but brazen enough to ask them to go for a walk with him. As for anything further, oh, that was unthinkable——. And yet——

When Desmond went away with his mother for part of the holidays, Phillip felt lonely. He seldom saw Cranmer now; cousin Gerry had his own friends at St. Anselm's; and the only friend he had, if he could call him a friend, was Ching, who hung about because of Mavis, who disliked him, thank goodness.

On Saturday afternoon, too wet to cycle out to his preserves, Phillip was looking at the new motor fire engine, all polished brass and red paint, when several dogs on the pavement took his attention. They were jumping on one another's backs in turn; a common enough sight in the streets and recreation grounds, but one always of furtive interest to Phillip. While he was watching them, pretending to be examining the fire engine, someone touched his arm. It was Jack Hart.

Jack Hart invited him to the cook shop over the road, and they went inside to eat a penny plateful each of the tasty yellow pease-pudding, which had little bits of boiled bacon in it.

"Well, thanks for treating me, Jack," said Phillip, when they went outside. "I was going to the Electric Theatre, I've only got tuppence, else I'd treat you."

Phillip had lost some of his nervous fear of Jack Hart, after he had told him about his training ship: the rigging they climbed up, boxing and sword-stick games, celestial navigation, the model steam engines which worked, the magic lantern lectures with slides of foreign ports.

"That's all right, you can treat me another time," replied Jack Hart. "It's my treat this time." They went into the dark hall, and found seats on the fixed forms, halfway down.

When their eyes were accustomed to the flickering light Jack Hart turned round to look about him. "We might find a couple of birds," he said. "Wednesday afternoon is the best time, when the shop girls get their half-day. If you can get in the corner seat at the back, you can't be overlooked."

Phillip did not want to meet any girls; yet the idea fascinated him. He forgot it in the wonderful film on the screen. There was a train robbery, the hero on a horse racing the train, and leaping on it to fight the bad men. He was standing on top of the train, which was about to enter a dark tunnel, looking the other way. Oh, what relief! He saw it and ran back just in time, leaping from roof to roof of the coaches. But the end of the train was near. Would he fall off? Ah, there was his faithful horse, racing alongside! The hero leapt sideways, right into the saddle, and pulled up just in time to save the horse from crashing into the wall of the tunnel. Then, climbing up a path and galloping down the hill again, he forded a river, swam the torrent, and pursued the train again, which was crossing a high wooden bridge over a gorge. Jack was staring at the picture now, his peaked cap on the back of his close-cropped head.

When they had seen the programme through once, Jack Hart wanted to go; but Phillip said he would like to stay and see it through once again. Before leaving, Jack Hart went down to the girl playing the piano behind the curtained rail, below the screen, and Phillip watched him speaking to her. Then he came back, slid into the seat beside Phillip, and whispered that he had fixed up to see her home after the place closed.

"Is she very hot?" asked Phillip, greatly daring. He did not want to be thought backward in knowledge, even if he was under-developed.

"She will be, if she isn't now," replied Jack Hart, with a grin, biting his nails with a kind of glee. Phillip wondered why Jack Hart bit his nails. Mother said biting your nails was a very bad habit you got into in childhood, and one very hard to break. She used to do it, she said, but going to the Roman Catholic church on Sunday evenings had helped her to stop the bad habit.

"Well, so long, Phil. I might be seeing you again this leave. I might come up and see some of the chaps after school one day."

"Yes, I hope so," replied Phillip, hoping he would not see Jack Hart if he did come. He was rather scared, once more.

On the Monday night he met Jack Hart, again by accident, in the public library, where he had gone to collect his *Field* of the week before. It was a fine night, with a new moon, and they went for a walk. They walked through the Randiswell Recreation

Ground on the way to the Roller Skating Rink at Fordesmill. Phillip had learned to skate, down Hillside Road, on one roller skate, a year or two back, crouching down to sit on the skate with the free leg held out in front, parallel to the pavement, for balance; but he had never tried two at once. The composition of the skate wheels, said to be made of ox-blood and sawdust, soon wore out on the asphalt. Cousin Gerry sometimes went to the Fordesmill Rink.

"You can hire a pair for twopence an hour," said Jack Hart; as, feeling very daring, for the rink was known to be a hot place, Phillip set off with him.

The Rec. was a dark low flat grassy place beside the river. There was a path beside the river, and several wooden rustic bridges, where the fearful figures of the toms lurked. With Jack Hart beside him, Phillip did not feel so scared of them as when he and Desmond had hurried by, never daring to speak.

The toms, called whores in the Bible, were terrible women. They were said to drop unwanted babies, wrapped in brown paper and tied up like a parcel, over the bridges into the river, where they floated down into the Thames. They were murderers!

As they approached the rustic bridge, three or four figures were to be discerned in the moonlight by the low railings under the weeping willow tree. Phillip nudged Jack Hart and whispered, "Don't say anything to them will you, if they speak to us?"

"Who the hell wants to speak to them?" replied Jack Hart with his rough laugh, "They're only fourpenny bits. They'll take a boy for nothing, as a change from the usual beery buck navvy."

Phillip began to wish that he had not come. It would be awful if Jack Hart went with one, and he was left on his own to face the others. He would rather die than do the horrible thing of which he had first heard from a bully called Mildenhall before he had got his scholarship. Mildenhall had said he was a tool-greaser to his Father, and thinking of Mother, Phillip had felt unutterable horror and shame. Fat-lipped Mildenhall, big red face with little pig-eyes, and his heavy, cold way of sitting on smaller boys, grinding their bones beneath him on the hard playground until they shrieked! Ah, in the end Mildenhall had turned out to be a funk, when he had punched him on the nose and tapped his claret! How strange that Mildenhall had been afraid, in the end, of him, Phillip!

Trepidant beside Jack Hart, Phillip came to the figures; passed by without any words being spoken by them; reached the near-safety of the bridge. There the reason of silence was startlingly obvious. Darkly upon the bridge, distinct in the amber light of the declining crescent moon, was a helmeted policeman. Phillip nearly said, in his relief, "Good night, officer," but another kind of fear, that of the policeman himself, kept him from speech.

As they came near the exit gate, Jack Hart said, "I know who that slop was. That was Garrott. He gets money from those old horse-collars. He waits to spy on chaps sitting on seats with girls, creeping up on 'em, hoping to catch them. He's a hypocrite, for in plain clothes he's no better'n anyone else. I tell you, one dark night somebody'll wait for Garrott and he'll get a bloody good hiding, and serve him right."

The Fordesmill skating rink was near the Bull Inn, whence came a mild roar as a door opened. The Rink beyond roared, too, with a roll of wheels on the boarded floor almost hidden by a swirl of skaters, some old (quite twenty) but most of them boys. Phillip noticed at once two girls wearing red woollen caps with pompoms, white jerseys, blue skirts, and brown high-laced boots. They swung round the circular floor, holding hands crossed behind them. They were ethereal!

Jack Hart offered to pay for his skates, but Phillip was afraid of falling. He sat behind the wooden fence, and after a while, to his excitement, the two girls came to sit near him while they took off their skates. He caught the dark one's glance, then looked steadily away, to show he was not rude. Then they were going out . . . ah! the dark one, with swing of plait, had glanced back, at the door. His mouth went dry, as he got up to follow.

Outside the Bull they stopped and looked back. He stopped, too. They went on; he followed at fifty yards. They stopped again at the next corner. The fair one beckoned. He trembled, feeling in a fume. They went on up the road. He followed, until, with anguish, he saw them entering their gate.

When the door was shut, he dared to walk past, but not to look at the number. He wanted to write the dark girl a letter; but he walked on, back to the High Street, to the bright lights of shop and tram, which made him feel more lonely than ever, as he returned to his home.

Chapter 19

WOODNOTES WILD

Now there was something to live for, in the woods and coverts, where the new leaves speckled the sunlight upon the old skeleton leaves below.

The nightingales had arrived, and were in full song among the bluebells and windflowers. The boy cycled through yellow shadow-slanting evenings to where the white owl flew over springing corn, and the smaller spotted woodpecker drummed on dead branches of oak trees. Rooks cawed across the lake in the new place he and Desmond visited one evening for the first time, on their way back from Knollyswood Park. This new place, on Shooting Common, was only five miles from his home.

The coverts were planted with hazel and sweet chestnut. Long grassy rides bisected them, all imprinted with the nob-nailed boots of the under-keeper. There were thousands of footmarks, all firm and going the same way, just as he remembered from the wood he had explored with Joey the old dog when, many years ago, he had run away from Aunt Viccy's house one Derby Day at Epsom. The coverts stood between fields green with rising corn, enclosed in a wire-netting fence about four feet high. The fence was to keep vermin out, and rabbits in, the under-keeper told them. From what Father had told him, Phillip knew about vermin; and to show his knowledge, he enquired where the gibbet was to be found. The under-keeper, a dark man who grinned and nodded usually instead of speaking, pointed with his stick to the corner of the covert they were approaching.

There was an ash sapling resting horizontally to the ground between the forks of two small oak trees, near the ditch which drained both field and wood. From the pole hung scores of bedraggled stoats and weasels, some very old and falling to bits, others put there so recently that the brown congealed blood was visible on nose and paw. They hung by the neck, on pieces of string from the pole. Among them were hedgehogs; rats, carrion crows; brick-brown, black-striped kestrels; and jays, the inquisitive ones of the forest, Father had said, their crests still raised as though in a last surprise.

Phillip and Desmond stared at the hanging corpses long after the under-keeper had left to continue his search for nests. He was collecting pheasants' eggs to put them under broody hens in coops.

There were planks laid over the ditches at each corner of the coverts. In the middle of the planks were traps, concealed under wire-netting threaded with reeds. There were also drain-pipes near each gibbet tree, with sods on them, and inside each was a trap baited by pieces of rabbit. A weasel or stoat, the keeper said, could not resist going down a drain.

Phillip collected skulls of both hawks and owls, to take back for his museum. He felt no pity or regret for the dead hanging there; only curiosity to examine the teeth, all bared, of the stoats, who were thrice as big as the weasels, and had black tips to their rather thin little tails. The weasels seemed to have died biting, too, or trying to bite. But what harm did hedgehogs do, asked Desmond. They suck pheasants' eggs, said Phillip.

Across the oat field was a pond, into and out of which a small brook ran fast.

"Good Lord, this must be the Randisbourne on its way to the Thames from Caesar's well above the Fish Ponds!" cried Phillip, astonished by his own discovery. "Fancy, this goes all the way from here to Cutler's Pond; then through those meadows beside the main road where Jack Cade hid after his rebellion had failed, and they cut off his head; under Fordesmill Bridge, through the Rec.; behind the houses you see from the train, and then by the dog-biscuit mill I pass on my way to school! But it's filthy there now, all the fish are dead!"

After the holidays, when Desmond had gone away to a preparatory school, Phillip went alone to the woods, seeking for new nests, and revisiting the ones he had found already. In hedge and hollow tree, hanging branch of fir, arching bramble, and in the reeds of the lake before the big red Queen Anne mansion, he had his places of call. A softer look came in his eyes, his face lost its furtive strain of fear, its expression became clear and simple in the sun, though in moments of memory the melancholy (the hunger for the mammalian warmth of love which had come upon him since his earliest years, from his aloneness) was to be seen upon his face. Thus he grew in secret love for the birds he watched in their nests, away from the constrictions and denials of home and school.

The woodpecker's nest in the silver birch just inside the footpath gate leading off from the common had been completed, judging by the increased number of chips lying on the grass below. The hole leading down into the wooden-water-bottle-shaped interior was too small for his hand, so he tried to get at the coveted white eggs within with a bent spoon. This proving useless, he thought to chop the hole bigger, using the small axe from the chest of tools Father had given him years before. It was very blunt, with a rounded edge; and after hacking for ten minutes, when he had not got so much as a finger's width in from the bark, he gave up the attempt; reflecting how strong the bird's beak must be, and its neck, to be able to chip and break off dozens of splinters of living wood as long as his little finger, while with his axe he could make but little effect.

Would the bird desert the eggs which must be inside, now that the hole was disfigured? He hoped not. There was another aspect, too: would his chopper marks around the hole be noticed? He found some clay and smeared it over the mutilated circle, which had been so round and neat before, half-ashamed of his work.

Apparently his house-breaking efforts had not frightened the bird too much, for on the next occasion, as he approached the nesting tree, he saw a starling fly to the hole, straw in beak; and, clinging to the rough bark, it made as if to enter the hole. The next moment the starling fell back with a squawk, as a long beak and red cap poked out, and looked about it. Phillip wondered if his clay plastering had deceived the starling into thinking that it was just any old hole in a tree. If so, Mr. Starling had got a shock!

The squirrel's drey of light buff oak-leaf sprays was deserted. Phillip decided that the mother had taken her young away to one of her spare dreys. He was disappointed that she had not trusted him, though of course, as he wrote to Desmond, the dam could not possibly tell the difference between him and an ordinary human being.

He came to feel with the birds, with their delicate and joyous ways. Each egg was a miracle: creamy pale blue of the starling in hole of tree; grey speckle of wagtail in chalk-face of quarry; frail white, faint with pink speckles, of blue titmouse who would not leave her eggs, but puffed herself up and hissed as he peered in her cranny in a tree; the almost spotless pale white of the wren. Starlings were noisy, workmen-birds, their nests a jumble of straw, dropped anyhow: yet so glossy, so summer-skiey, those wonderful eggs. The wren's nest in a haystack was made of hay, lined with feathers and round with a hole in the side; or of green moss if in ivy, and of dead leaves when placed in dead ivy. Fingers gently inserted into a nest; a hot soft flutter within: the mother bird was on the eggs: oh, gently, gently stroke her neck with top-side of finger, and then quietly withdraw, so that she would have no need to fly out like a moth and drop her beady notes of alarm as she drew her brown wool through the tapestry of the woodland. Or the chaffinch's nest, with its brown-stained grey-blue eggs, in the marvellous cup of horsehair and feather lining within the moss and lichen mould. Everything in its place in the chaffbob's nest. And the bullfinch's, so frail-looking, rootlets and black horsehair: yet strong, like the whitethroat's built in the nettles, all grass, only a little horsehair inside, almost transparent, weighing perhaps a tenth of an ounce. He saw them all for the first time, a new and secret and miraculous world, and began to think why the varying colours and patterns, and how had they come to such patterns? They were not all for protective coloration; they were perhaps beautiful just to be beautiful, in the eye of the bird who *knew* what they were for.

Phillip was sure that birds knew as much about their eggs and young as human mothers felt about their children; he once watched a thrush get off her eggs and listen to hear any movement of tapping within the shells—they were hard set—and while he lay hidden, watching, he heard her give a little trilling talk to herself, or the air, by which, he knew, they were starting to hatch. The thrush's eye, over the rim of her cowdung-plastered nest, while she had been sitting with only tail showing and throat and beak and head, had had a look of his mother about it; the same look in the eyes. Mother said the thrush was her favourite bird, so she must have a sort of affinity or soul-likeness to it. If she were a bird, she would make a thrush's nest; she could never make a chaffinch's, or a goldfinch's, but a rough and ready thing like a thrush's, good enough, but not much skill in it.

There was an area in the upper side of the park, adjoining the common, which was more or less open, bracken on the floor, and old oaks, most of them hollow, growing there, where white owls lay up by day: the mysterious barn owls which floated dream-silent at twilight and mused by day inside hollow limbs and holes from which old branches had fallen. If only one would be his friend, and perch on his shoulder, and let him stroke it! They would have a secret friendship of the forest, he and the lovely bird of evening, of the sad still hours of twilight in the glade of the oaks, in the silence and peace of the wild Kent country. But perhaps he would have to die before he could know the birds as they really were.

It was always a sad moment when he had to return home, to the noise of trams and omnibuses, raucous cries in the streets, and the deadness of school books and lessons. At home and at school he was someone else, doing and saying things that had nothing to do with what he really was.

During the past month, in the evenings at home, he had been training for the school sports, which were to take place in the second week in May. Three times a week, at night, he had been running in shorts, singlet, and plimsolls round the Hill, four and five times without stopping. He was no good at sprinting, but he could run long distances without getting puffed, at least when by himself. On the track near the Crystal Palace, where the school had held their sports the previous year, he had come in last in the junior mile, as his throat had dried up with nervousness before the pistol fired; and he had started off as though the race had just ended, instead of begun. This year, he would do better, after hard training.

Sports Day was on a Saturday, in the afternoon. In the morning there was no school; and when Father had left for the office, Phillip went into the Backfield to watch where the skylarks dropped, hoping to find a nest. He was sitting in his camp near the red ballast heap when a peculiar sound came from over the ragged grassy crest above, beyond which were the unseen spiked railings enclosing the south-east limits of the Hill.

Getting up, he crept through the grasses, Indian style, to avoid being seen as he went to the railings.

On the path, walking slowly forward, was a kilted Scotsman, playing the bagpipes. Phillip had occasionally seen him on the

Hill, wearing his tartan. Sometimes he was to be seen in the High Street, on Saturday nights, playing outside public houses. The Scotsman was now playing a tune that he recognised, from a gramophone record of Father's, as *The Flowers of the Forest.*

Phillip climbed over the fence, and walked towards the figure in uniform, striding forward with head erect and cheeks blown out.

Except for the bagpipe player, the Hill seemed empty. It was early for children and old men to be about. Phillip followed the Scotsman, past the tennis courts, past the public lavatory, and so to the main path which led to the elms in the distance. What was he doing, playing all alone, in the quiet sunny morning?

Phillip saw another figure coming towards them. It was Uncle Hugh, moving slowly with his two sticks. As the Scotsman came near him, Uncle Hugh stood to one side, and balancing on his legs and one stick, removed his straw hat. The Scotsman passed without looking at him, playing all the time.

As he came to Uncle Hugh, Phillip saw that he was crying. What was the matter? Uncle's face was working. Uncle glanced at him, then looked down, as though trying to speak. Phillip felt shaken, why, he did not know. Then he heard the sound of a distant gun.

"Well, Phil," said Uncle Hugh, at last, "this is the end of an age." His voice quivered. "He was a good fellow, was Teddy."

Another gun boomed from far away. And upon the flag staff of the Grammar School roof Phillip saw that the Union Jack was flying half mast. "And Halley's comet, the great oriflamme, doth blaze across the heaven!" recited Uncle Hugh, like an actor.

Phillip ran home to tell the important news to Mother. Then he rushed in to tell Gran'pa; then Mrs. Bigge. The King was dead! While Halley's comet was blazing!

Afterwards, he decided that the School Sports would not be held; and with relief set out for his woods instead.

As it happened, the sports were held, after some discussion by the authorities; but Phillip spent the time in Knollyswood Park, visiting his nests.

In the afternoon heat he sought cool solitude of sun and shadow under the beech-wood near the Home Farm. Here were very tall trees, growing out of the chalky slope, some of them old. The dry ground beneath was littered with beech-mast covers. It was a mossy place where the sunlight fell in little pools and patches from the pale green canopy far, far above, as he lay on his back, hands held like opera glasses before his face as he watched the woodpecker holes along a grey trunk, and wondered if he would see one of the many-coloured, laughing birds pushing itself up by its tail, as it clung to the bark and listened for the boring of grubs within.

Keeping still, he saw what he had waited for. Round the bole the green and red bird came, moving with a series of jerks; its head held sideways as it listened, while the forest seemed to pause. Even the rooks were for a moment silent; then furiously the woodpecker threw back its head and struck again and again, tearing away bits of tinder wood, which floated down from the great height above. It seemed to get what it was after, as it swallowed upon prods with its beak-tip, and then suddenly an amazing thing happened. Another woodpecker flew up with a loud ringing *yaffle-yaffle-yaffle*, and clinging to the bole fluttered its wings like a fledgling and begged to be fed. It looked like a cock bird, judging by the brighter colours on its feathers. While it was still begging, the first bird dropped away and flew down the sun-dappled glade, followed almost at once by the begging bird. What could be the explanation? Had someone or something robbed the hen of her eggs or young, and so the father bird begged for the food?

Lying on his back, knees crossed, one foot idly lifting, Phillip pondered what he had seen. Birds did do queer things sometimes. There was the robin who had the nest in the steep bank in the Backfield, immediately behind Mrs. Rolls' garden fence. One morning it had flown with food to its nestlings, who were asleep. They were not hungry, so slept on. The robin spoke to them, they took no notice, so the mother bird had flown away over the spiked railings above the Rolls' fence, where the Hill began. There were may bushes there; and from one of them had come the noise of hungry nestlings, chirruping with open beaks. Could the robin have two nests?

When he had shinned over the railings to search, the nest had turned out to be that of an accentor, as the books called the modest little hedgesparrow. What a wonderful discovery! The mother robin had given away the food her own young did not want! And yet the books said birds acted only and solely from instinct, and could not think for themselves!

It was heaven to lie on the chalky earth, among the slightly prickly beech-covers, far away from all people. He picked up one of the covers, from which the brown seeds, shaped like wedges, had fallen. What ate them, besides woodpigeons? Was it mice that had made stores, which he had found in cracks and crannies of trees, or was it birds? It might be squirrels; though those cranny-stores looked more like trickles than mast packed in. Perhaps they had dropped in as they fell from the tree-tops, and had become chance stores of gravity? That sounded rather nice, *chance stores of gravity*. Everything fell, sooner or later, back to earth again. He repeated the phrase to himself. It sounded like *wind-borne*. Dandelion and thistle seeds were wind-borne, drifting on the wind, riding airily in little spheres of light, glistening as they turned slowly over in the blue sky under the high invisible larks, their destiny unknown, *wind-borne*, to fall to earth by chance. Yet not a sparrow fell to earth, frozen dead in a hard winter such as the one Father had told him of, before he was born, without its Maker knowing of it.

Did the Maker know everything, then? Even a pebble from his catapult whizzing through the air and falling on the slate roofs of the flats in Charlotte Road? Mother would say that was coming from the sublime to the ridiculous. She would say *Hush Phillip!* She often said that to him. The best thing was not to tell her anything. Father objected, and withheld his permission; Mother tried to hush him. O, why was he thinking of things at home, out here in his hunting grounds? He felt his cheeks to be thin again.

Wood-pigeons were cooing in the glade under the high cathedral beeches, a lovely spring sound, like the cry of lambs running and leaping at play in the field below. Many of the holes of the gally-birds, as the woodmen called them, so high in the beech bough above must be old ones; perhaps they did not nest in thoroughly rotten wood, knowing it to be unsafe. Did grubs feed on quite rotten wood, or did they need sap? If so, by the time a tindery bough was ready to fall, heavy and sodden with rain, the last grub would have left it. Could wood-lice climb so high from the ground, sixty feet or more? If so, would the gally-birds eat them? Spiders did not like wood-lice, they cut the silk to drop them off when he put them in their webs.

He got up, brushed the dry prickly mast-covers off his knickerbockers and Norfolk jacket, and walked down to the edge of the wood. Strands of wire kept the sheep in the field from straying among the trees; and getting through the fence, he went to his next place of call, a spinney beside the road, at the edge of which stood the cottages of the woodsmen and farm labourers. Here the trees were thinner, being larch and ash-pole. The ground was covered with ivy. In places old rusty tins lay, half overgrown: and in one of them, an ancient biscuit box standing on its side, the paint on it nearly obliterated by exposure, was a robin's nest. Near it was a thrush's, on the ground at the base of a larch. These were duly photographed by the Brownie.

There were long gardens, filled with cabbages, between the border of the spinney and the cottage back-doors, which was pleasing, for then no-one could overlook what he was doing, and find his nests. A row of pollarded elms ended the gardens, and Phillip was peering into one of these, which was hollow, when he jumped back, thinking he had disturbed a snake: for the spitting, hissing noise had come as he was about to put his arm into the hole. Then he noticed a rat's tail, and some feathers. Could it be an owl? His heart beat wildly with excitement. An owl's nest! It would be as wonderful as finding a hawk's! He retired to sit down in the ivy, in a circular and waving patch of sunshine, and delay the pleasure of exploring further.

He was watching the side of the hole, when a furry ear appeared, then a whisker, and finally part of a kitten's head. His disappointment was great; still, it might very well be a wild cat, judging by the renewed spitting and yowly noises which greeted his face at the entrance of the hole. Accustoming his eyes to the darkness within, he counted five faces, all crouching against the far end. Well, it was quite an adventure, and something to write and tell Desmond about.

Creeping to the next of the old trees, which was covered with dead ivy, he found a robin's nest about four feet from the ground, built between three intertwisted bines. It was made of the usual dry grass, and lined with moss and black horsehair; the eggs were a pale greyish-yellow faintly dappled all over the brownish-pink; there were five of them . . . but wait a minute! One was larger than the others, wider, less pointed, more rounded, faintly lavender-purple mottled . . . could it be? It was, it *was* a cuckoo's egg! Value two shillings, in Watkins and Doncaster's catalogue! Not that he would ever think of selling such a treasure; but such a very high price showed just how rare it was. None of the boys at school who collected eggs had ever found a cuckoo's.

Putting it back in the nest with extreme care, he walked away, making his mind a blank, pretending not to have been near the tree, or that any nest was built in the dead ivy. It did not exist.

After wandering around as though aimlessly, while trills of happiness ran up his body, he approached the tree once more, as though casually; and re-enacted the surprise of seeing the larger egg with the pinky-brown robin's eggs. At length, taking out the egg, he strolled away in the direction of the gate, where his bicycle was hidden. Then, removing the tools from his tool bag, he put them in his pocket; and again holding up the egg to the light to confirm that it was fresh, he wrapped it in his handkerchief, and with the greatest care placed it in the leather bag.

He decided to go to Farthing Street, and the village beyond, where Charles Darwin's house stood. Charles Darwin was dead, of course, but it would be nice to see where the author of *The Voyage of the Beagle* had once lived. Also in that village was a shop which sold very good buns, with more currants in them than ordinary ones, and flavoured with some sort of spice. They were a halfpenny each; one would do for his tea. That left a halfpenny for a spill of broken biscuits at the old dame's shop on the way home.

Cycling onwards, he came to the gate of the drive leading up to the explorer's house, and passing it, got off and crept through the hedge. On the edge of a wide lawn stood a thin cypress tree, and peering into its close, upright branches, he found a nest. It had young, but an egg lay under the nestlings. Lifting it out between two fingers, he shook it by his ear. It was sloppy, infertile. Now he had a greenfinch's!

He crept back to his bicycle, and ate his bun while listening to nightingales in a green shade, while waves of happiness rose in him so strongly that he could scarcely stop himself from warbling with joy.

That night, in the height of the sky, he saw the comet—a silver bird with a great sweeping tail. The world was a wonderful place!

So the spring advanced for Phillip, two half-days of freedom a week in the country, in his own especial private places; five days of tedium, evasion and passive resistance in the classroom, wherein the spirit was never moved by wonder or beauty, but where, in periods of rumination, the psyche could wing to its true or natural habitat, by way of pictures in the mind: of chestnut and hazel coverts, white-starred with wind-flowers growing out of the layers of skeleton leaves which fed them, as a mother her children; and the dead-leaf pattern of the hen-pheasant's back, on her eggs in the nettles, her back sun-dappled. Nature was a relation of all life, said Father, when he had brought him, once, some leaf-mould from under the elms in the Backfield, for the garden-bed. Leaf fed root, as the rabbit the stoat, and spring became summer.

It was sad that everything had to pass away; that it was no longer spring, that the nests were forsaken, the young birds flown—or dead. Phillip felt sad; all things had changed, except himself. He was left behind. A tear dropped on the History book, momentarily magnifying part of the print which gave the date of the burning of Joan of Arc by the English at Rouen.

The corn was high in the third week in June. Hundreds of little pheasants in the big wide cage in the heathery clearance of an old covert, where the stubs of oak and ash were sprouting again, ran to the keeper when he appeared out of his hut with a pail of mixed maize, wheat, and barley. The cage was of wire netting, top and sides. Rats, foxes, stoats, weasels, and other vermin moved round it by night and by day, in vain said the keeper. Only the nightjar sang now, reeling its song, like bubbles blown in water from a hollow grass-stem, in the calm summer evenings when the moths were about. From the gibbet trees most of the bird and animal corpses, shrunken thin and nearly shapeless, had fallen to the ground, where the plants of dog's mercury were a deeper green, thicker in stem and leaf.

Phillip saved up to buy a packet of twenty cigarettes for each of his new friends in his preserves. It was already July when he cycled out to give a present to each of the two keepers, a woodman friend, and the man who looked after the livestock at the Home Farm. Dare he call on the Dowager Countess, to thank her also? He dared not. A last visit to his favourite places—the birch tree whence the young woodpeckers had flown, the silent rookery, the spinney where the two robins' nests were worn shapeless, the quiet swallows' cups in the cowhouse, the empty paddock where once the Troop had camped, and grass had grown over the charcoal patches of ancient fires.

As he cycled away, he saw a gipsy sitting in the wood beside the road. He was singing a plaintive song, all by himself, about lavender. *Who'll buy my sweet lavender?* Phillip remembered hearing it in the streets, when he was very small, before the elms were cut down in the High Road, before he had gone to his first dame school. It was the time when the ningaring man came with his barrel organ, the Italian man with his little girl, who played the tambourine and danced, for the penny Mother gave him for her.

He stopped at the bend of the road, and heard the gipsy still singing. There was no other sound in the air, except the buzz of flies shooting past, above the glaring white dusty road.

Goodbye, he said to himself, goodbye woods, goodbye birds, until another spring.

Chapter 20

THE OLD MEN ON THE HILL

THE midsummer hum of insects—most of them blue-bottles bred in dustbins, and an occasional green Spanish fly from the sheep-fold—was upon the Hill, idly heard by Thomas Turney sitting on his usual seat, with other elderly and retired *habitués* of the Open Space.

Most fine mornings, upon that seat, conveniently near to one of the rustic shelters built of herring-bone brickwork in a timber frame, Thomas Turney was to be seen with any number up to three of his regular acquaintances. There was the tall, thin white-whiskered figure of Mr. Newman, in grey frock coat and trousers and either tall grey (called white) hat, or less formal Panama; beside him, Mr. Krebs, a large man with shaven head and pendulous cheeks, jowl, and neck, all as pink and as clean as the carcass of a scrubbed pig. Mr. Krebs was a south German who lived on the other side of the Hill with his English wife. Krebs was a name understood to be the equivalent of Crabbe.

Since Mr. Turney and Mr. Newman often appeared to be on the point of irritating one another—being different types of men—the presence of Mr. Krebs was helpful to both: he was an excellent listener and sympathiser, as ugly, bare-headed, with his hat on his knee, as he was invariably courteous.

There was a fourth man of the little group; but he never sat down with the others on this particular seat. In the first place, although intended for four people, the seat could not possibly hold more than any three of them, and then only with considerable restraint—a condition second-nature to thin Mr. Newman and fat Mr. Krebs, but not to Tom Turney. As for Mr. Bolton, the fourth man, he never wanted to sit down; he came up from his house in Charlotte Road for a constitutional, with his fawn-coloured dog. Invariably affable, Mr. Bolton nevertheless was a man apart, a man aware of all men, but attached to only two—His late Majesty the King; and his son.

Mr. Bolton was always most circumspectly dressed. He wore, in the hottest weather, a high-lapelled tweed jacket, a Gladstone collar with wide starched wings and a satin cravat tie, in which was a gold pin set with pearls and diamonds in the shape of a horse-shoe—gift, of which he was modestly proud, of the Earl of Mersea. Mr. Bolton's narrow trousers were always freshly sponged and pressed, his boots boned and polished under their protecting spats. Even on the brightest days he arrived in a Covert coat of pale brown melton cloth, with velvet collar, and carrying his gold-topped clouded cane in one hand, and the lead of Bogey, a pug-dog, in the other. Mr. Bolton, bowler-hatted by Lock of St. James Street, wore his grey beard and moustaches in the style of the late King Edward the Seventh, from whom, it was understood, he had received many a confidence.

More than once Mr. Bolton, in a shadowed background, and with appropriate deference, had bowed the Royal Personage into the London club of which he had been the steward. Mr. Bolton, now retired on pension, lived with a housekeeper and his only son, a clerk in the Bank of England. Beside his pension, Mr. Bolton enjoyed an income of six per centums from his investments —life-savings of presents from the gentlemen of his Club, as well as commissions from purchases of food and wine; the latter, of course, having been shared with Chef and Wine Steward.

"Good morning, gentlemen, I trust I find you well," was Mr. Bolton's invariable greeting, as it was usually Thomas Turney who replied,

"Good morning, Mr. Bolton, come to join us, eh? I was just saying to Mr. Krebs here, that——," while he made but the least pretence to shift up on the seat. After the gesture, he sat as before, knees apart, dressed in one of his numerous blue serge suits—he bought new ones every year at the January Sales, and never gave away any of the old ones—Panama-hatted, tie passed through a diamond ring, both hands clasping his oak walking stick, to help distribute his weight.

"Thank you, gentlemen, but I am about to take my morning stroll upon the grass, to exercise Bogey here."

At this point Mr. Bolton would lean down carefully to give Bogey his expected reward for climbing the steep gully—a rub under the collar with his gloved hand.

"I was saying to Mr. Krebs, Mr. Bolton, that I had a letter this morning from South Africa, from me eldest son Charley, coming home for the Coronation, he says."

Mr. Bolton had never travelled; he had always had to work to maintain himself, while looking forward to seeing the world after his retirement—when he had felt himself to be too old. However, he had a fund of travelling memories gained at secondhand during more than twenty years of sharing, at a correct distance, and with perfect discretion, many lives in the famous Voyagers.

"Yes," Tom Turney continued, "the news came only this morning, by letter, that m'eldest boy, Charley, is already on his way home from South Africa, with his wife and little family. He'll be a stranger, we haven't seen him for twenty years, since Hetty and I went over to pay him a visit in Manitoba. He was trying his hand at farming, shovelling muck all day on to sledges, at the dungstead, he-he-he, he didn't seem to relish the work very much."

Tom Turney's cat usually accompanied him from his house up the gully to the crest of the Hill, every morning. It was a neuter cat; it had a truculent tail-swishing attitude to the tame dogs it saw during the walk behind its master. Once on the Hill, it contented itself by sitting under the seat, behind the boots of the elderly men. It had a guarded friendship with Mr. Bolton's pug, and allowed it to share the shade beneath: the one watching movement upon the gravelled path, the other, despite its snivelling nose, regarding the smells which were wafted under the galvanised iron frame. The animals, like the men, knew their places, and kept them.

"I perceive, or rather I hear," quavered Mr. Newman, "that the cuckoo in the cemetery is already out of tune. How the days slip by! Why, only yesterday it seems, your grandson Phillip came to show me his cuckoo's egg. But to my amazement, he told me that it was last year! How time does fly, to be sure."

It was peaceful on the Hill during the summer mornings. The few figures to be seen there were quiet: nursemaids in uniform with perambulators; small servant girls with mail-carts; an occasional three-wheeled invalid's chair pulled or pushed by a hired man; a keeper in the brown livery of the L.C.C. picking up paper and cigarette packets on a steel point; and transferring the litter to a brown canvas side-bag; odd figures taking their constitutionals, among them the lonely figure of Hugh Turney, walking slowly with the aid of two rubber-ended sticks. He never went near the four old men, if he could avoid it.

A quietness lay upon the Hill, for those others who had managed to get out of the main stream of life and business without undue maiming of body or spirit—and this quietude would remain for another fortnight or so, until the schools broke up, and the green tranquillity of the Hill would be adorned with coloured kites of many shapes and designs, model aircraft powered by elastic threads—some with aluminium frames, others of wood, all monoplanes—and remotely interrupted by the smack of cricket balls and the softer thud of tennis: and among these quieter pursuits of the young, a harder-eyed movement, shrill of voice, leaving its rubbish of rag and torn paper and orange peel cast upon sward and path.

"Yes, your grandson showed me a very fine specimen of a cuckoo's egg, as I was saying, Mr. Turney," went on Mr. Newman. "I fancy it had been laid in the robin's nest by mistake, for it had the purple shading of one usually found among the tit-larks, or tree pipits."

"I remember that m' Father once shot a cuckoo with an egg in its beak. He had it stuffed and set up" remarked Tom Turney. "He said at the time that it was flying to put it in another bird's nest."

"Ah, but you said, Mr. Newman, that the *kuckuck*, what you call googoo, *laid* its egg in the nest of another bird, did you not? Then how, would I ask you, why should Mr. Turney's respected Father's googoo be carrying the egg in the beak also to lay it at the same time?"

"That, my dear Sir," began Mr. Newman, in his throaty voice, turning to Herr Krebs, "is a most interesting controversy, and one that has engaged the speculations of many naturalists since Gilbert White of Selborne. Perhaps our little friend Phillip, who shows such a bent for field study, will be able to solve the problem one day, with his camera."

Another valetudinarian shuffled past, pulled by a bulldog. From under the seat came the steely growl of Thomas Turney's cat, followed by an uneasy or sneezy sniffle from Bogey the pug. They had recognised a well-known ugly landmark in the local animal world.

"What is your son's line of business, Mr. Turney?" said Mr. Bolton, somewhat diffidently.

"The latest is, or was, so far as we know, something in the import business, but perhaps he means the term to apply only to himself, ha-ha-ha!"

Tom Turney's laughter was from his belly, beneath the blue serge waistcoat stained with wine and cigar ash; the jacket almost purple, faded in the sun of summers upon the Hill.

Sometimes Phillip cycled to school; but most mornings he preferred to walk over the Hill, as there was more to see that way. He was always happy when he walked with Milton; he felt clearer, simpler, somehow, in Milton's company. They talked of the coming summer holidays: every day brought the enchanted prospect nearer and nearer. There was an almost breathless magic in the words *Summer Holidays!* Phillip saw them in his mind as sunlight for ever upon the grass and under the shade of familiar trees; kites dancing in the wind; baking spuds in the embers of his camp-fire in the Backfield; expeditions with Desmond to the Seven Fields; cycling with roach-tackle to the Fish Ponds of Reynard's Common; playing tennis with Mavis and her friends on the Hill. Perhaps, who knew, one day Milton and Helena, with his sister and her sister, might be playing there; perhaps they might invite him to join in with them—it was almost too much to be hoped for.

Phillip loved tennis. Mother said they might take up a tea-basket and have a picnic in the holidays, when they played. Aunt Theodora had sent them some racquets and balls, from her Somerset school which had closed down; also a box of croquet sticks and hoops; but they were no good in the garden, the lawn sloped too steeply. Anyway it was too small, unlike Cousin Percy's at Beau Brickhill. O, the summer holidays! They were going again to Hayling Island, he told Milton, and he was looking forward to taking some snaps of the life-boat house, the fishermen with their net, the west floating-pier where the naval steam-pinnaces came in, bringing officers to play golf, and the wonderful blue Channel waves crashing on the shingle shore by the life-saving cable, and big hauls of striped mackerel and green-boned garfish slapping on the brown pebbles.

If only Milton and his people were coming to Hayling, with the Rolls—for the two families went away to the seaside together, every summer. But they were going to the Isle of Wight—far across the sea from Hayling. Still, he could think of them there in the sunlight, gay laughter and merriment all the time. He could lie in bed at night, and think of the beautiful people, in the darkness of the nights over Hayling Island.

Bad news: they were not going to Hayling after all! Mother had left applying for apartments too long, and so they would not see the sea that year! The sea that was the same sea in which *she* would be swimming—he would not be able to speak, in secret, to the waves of the tide sweeping from the Isle of Wight, around the shingle shores of Hayling!

Phillip walked to school by himself for two days, after that news. Then his spirits rose again. Mother said if Aunt Liz would have them, they might go instead to Beau Brickhill. Still, there would be dear old Percy to be with, and singing duets at the piano at night, and games of billiards, bat-shooting in the twilight by the ivied stable walls; and the ponds full of roach and dace. Summer Holidays! If only the end of July would come quicker!

One Saturday morning, hastening home alone from school, Phillip was beckoned by Gran'pa, to the seat where he always sat with other old men. He wanted to pass on, pretending not to see or hear Gran'pa; but since it might mean a penny for an ice-cream in the refreshment shelter, he decided to go and see what he wanted. No such luck, however; all Gran'pa wanted was to tell him that his cousins would be coming home soon, from Africa, a thing which he knew already. Gran'pa, of course, *had* to ask about lessons, as he always did, telling him to make the most of his opportunity while he was young.

And, of course, the inevitable question, "Are they going to teach you Spanish at your school? The future of world commerce lies in South America." Phillip made his escape as Gran'pa turned to the other old men and said, "If only my boy Charley had taken it into his head to go to the Argentine, he would have shown better sense."

What would Gran'pa say if, one day, he answered that all he knew about Spanish at school so far was about Spanish Fly? That was a powder prepared from dried green-bottles, which if rubbed gently into the back of a girl's hand, as you pretended to stroke it, would make her hot. Phillip had heard this with some uneasiness, as he thought nowadays of girls only in the abstract; smiles, eyes, gleaming brushed hair, alluring wonder; except Helena Rolls, who was his Ideal.

At first the talk about Uncle Charley was of little interest to him; but as the days went on, and the Union Castle liner passed the White Man's Grave, and entered the Bay of Biscay, as recorded in *The Daily Telegraph* which Gran'pa read, Phillip began to form a picture of this new uncle as a sort of rolling stone, a mixture of Lieutenant Oakfall of the Kent Guides, (who had turned out to be not a real lieutenant at all, but a swanker like Mr. Prout) and a ne'er-do-well remittance man who lived on his wits, as in the stories he read in magazines. Would Uncle Charley arrive in a khaki suit, and Stetson hat, a revolver in his hip pocket? Phillip had these ideas from remarks he had overheard from time to time, in both houses. Father, cross as usual with Mother, had said that most of her people were either wasters or remittance men: and since Uncle Hugh was obviously meant as the waster, Uncle Charley must be the remittance man. He discussed it with his mother.

"Gran'pa said he stopped sending Uncle Charley money when he threw up his farming job in Manitoba, Mum. Was it a nice farm, with plenty of birds to watch in spring? And game to shoot in autumn? Were there any pheasants, as well as prairie hens of the kind you brought some eggs back with you? You know, the ones you gave me when I was too young, so that I broke them. And that whippoorwill's egg, too. What a pity, wasn't it? Why ever did you do it?"

This was a perennial regret from Phillip, which brought the same reply every time the question was asked, "Well you see, dear, a little boy asked and asked for them so many times that in the end I gave them to him, for the sake of peace and quiet."

"But you ought to have known I was too young!"

"I did, my son, I did!" said Hetty. "But you were you, a very very inquisitive and persistent little person!"

"But you knew very well I had taken Father's butterflies and smashed them up, and eggs are just as easily broken!"

"Ah well, it is done now, Phillip, so it is best forgotten, dear, like many other things that can no longer be helped. But always remember, my son, what the poem says—

Boys flying kites haul in their white winged birds
But you can't do that when you are flying words.
Thoughts unexpressed, sometimes fall back dead
But God Himself can't kill them when they're said."

Phillip had heard that too, many times from his mother.

"Tell me about Uncle Charley, Mum."

"Well, dear, all I can tell you is that he has had a very variegated life, but it was all very interesting, I am sure."

"I suppose he is a sort of ne'er-do-well, really?"

"No dear, of course he is not, and never has been! I won't have you even thinking such a thing! Wherever did you get such ideas from?"

"From Father. Also Uncle Hugh said Charley rode underneath a train all the way from Canada to San Francisco, as he had not the wherewithal for a ticket. Those trains have rods underneath, and he rode on them for hundreds and hundreds of miles."

"It is wrong of Uncle Hugh to give you such an impression, Phillip. I shall speak to him about it, the very next time I see him. For goodness gracious sake don't you repeat to Uncle Charley what you have just said! He would never forgive us!"

"But Gran'pa did kick him out of house and home, didn't he?"

"If he did, then it was a very long time ago, and all forgotten now, Phillip."

"Uncle Hugh said that if it had not been summer, Charley would have frozen to death, and been found, when the thaw came, a skeleton on the rods."

"It was Uncle Hugh's fun, Phillip. Canada is a new country, dear, and life is very hard for newcomers. Anyway, I am sure what Uncle Hugh said is very exaggerated."

"Uncle Hugh said that at San Francisco Charley signed on as a hand in a ship to Cape Town. Uncle Hugh told me how he met him out there, thin as a lath, building huts in the war for the Boer families taken from their farms in the veldt, and herded behind barbed wire. Later, when he got married, Uncle Charley and his wife spent their honeymoon eating Nestlé's milk out of tins, with one spoon, taking turns. They had a whole box of tins in their hotel bedroom, said Uncle Hugh."

"They were both very young, Phillip. Uncle Charley was a light-hearted boy, always. Oh, I am so longing to see him!" said Hetty, thinking of happy days.

"Mum, is it true that, when he became a farmer, diamonds were found under his land? Uncle Hugh said he sold the farm, and bought an import business, dealing largely in bikes. Uncle Hugh said that it took the rich niggers off their feet and put Charley on his. And what did Uncle Hugh mean when he said to Gramps, 'Your prodigious son is returning, sir'?"

Hetty looked at Phillip with astonishment mixed with apprehension. He was growing up fast, and it behoved them all to be more careful than ever about what was said in his presence. She was anxious about her brother's home-coming, remembering the terrible scenes that had occurred in the past between Papa and Charley. Mamma was anxious, too, though hopeful that the past would be forgotten, and forgiven, by all concerned.

Hetty dared not think about the scene just before Charley had left the house for good, after Papa had knocked Mamma down with his fist, and Charley had attacked Papa with his fists, and cut Papa's lips. The terrible swearing! Only the intervention of Jim, the coachman, had prevented what might have been a tragedy. In a way Charley took after Papa; he flew into the same terrible rages. But there, all that was over and done with, and best forgotten.

Phillip hoped that Uncle Charley would have, in addition to the revolver in his hip pocket, a pigskin bag, fitted with heavy brass locks, and filled with diamonds. Perhaps he would have lion skins, and a faithful black kaffir servant, who had been with him in many fights against Zulus. Phillip had already passed on these imaginative details, which had their origin in *King Solomon's Mines*, as facts in a letter to Desmond.

On the day Uncle Charley was expected, Phillip cycled home fast from school. Tommy, his new cousin, named after Gran'pa, was to sleep in his bedroom, as there was no room next door. That would be wonderful: they would be able to talk far into the night, in whispers!

Pushing the Swift up Hillside Road, he saw Mrs. Rolls talking to Mr. Pye at the top. At once he felt subdued. Was Mr. Pye saying anything about him? Mrs. Rolls had recently spoken to him for throwing his orange peel about on the Hill instead of putting it in one of the iron containers. He had picked it all up afterwards, but with a feeling that he had disgraced himself forever in her eyes.

This small, treble-voiced fifteen-year-old boy still dreamed of the unrealisable, the terrifying moment when he might find himself suddenly invited into the Rolls' house; and with accompanying pang knew he never would be. But oh, if Uncle Charley turned out to be *very* well-off, as high up as his Uncle Hilary Maddison who had once visited them in his motorcar, it might help his cause! Uncle Hilary, after that one occasion many years ago, had never come to see them again. Mother said he was a very busy man; and, of course, they were poor relations.

With some trepidation Phillip saw that Mr. Pye had raised his hat to Mrs. Rolls, and had started to walk down the road. It was too late to hurry on now, and get into his gateway before meeting Mr. Pye. With relief Phillip saw that there was something else to take Mr. Pye's attention: a telegraph boy on a red bicycle had turned the corner, and standing on the pedals, was exerting all his strength to ride up the road. He passed Phillip, grunting as he heaved at the handle-bars. He got off outside Gran'pa's house, just as Mr. Pye, a dark curved figure under grey Homburg hat, and swinging rolled umbrella, loomed with pale heavy face upon him.

Raising his cap, Phillip blurted out, to break the nervous constriction,

"That telegram is from my Uncle, who owns ever so many diamond mines in Kimberley."

"Oh really?" said Mr. Pye, with a short mirthless laugh, as he passed. Oh, *why* had he said that to Mr. Pye? He would be sure to find out it was not true, and tell Mrs. Rolls! As Mother often told him, he was his own worst enemy.

Uncle Hugh came out to meet the telegraph boy. Phillip heard the boy say that he had passed two cabs along Charlotte Road.

"One of'm's full of fevvers and spears, sir."

"That sounds like my long-lost brother," said Uncle Hugh. "Hey, lend me your jigger for a couple of minutes, boy. Here, take this in to the Old Man, Phillip."

Telegram in hand, Phillip watched him mounting the red bike from the kerb. After one or two swerves, Uncle Hugh went down the road. He waited in trepidation to see if Uncle Hugh would fall off at the corner; after all, Uncle was very groggy on his pins, and perhaps would not have the strength to back-pedal, since it was a fixed wheel. He watched him zigzag round the corner; held his breath as Uncle seemed to be about to crash into the kerb opposite; and with relief saw that he was not going to fall off. With head held well down, and back rising and falling, Uncle Hugh wobbled up the slight rise to St. Cyprian's church; and there with a crash he fell off.

"Nobody didn't ought to take my grid," complained the telegraph boy. "Tain't allowed, by rights."

"It won't hurt your old iron," retorted Phillip, contempt in his tone, at the smaller boy's whine. He was still feeling squeezed in by Mr. Pye.

"I'll get the sack," the telegraph boy whined, with unhappy face. To think of losing his job was to be in utter darkness. He could say or do nothing more. He waited, with the usual dull expressionless look of a poor child from an unhappy home.

Two cabs came in sight along Charlotte Road, beyond the church. Phillip ran in to tell his mother. She was already hastening to her bedroom window, calling, "Here they are at last! Mavis! Doris! They're coming, oh I am so happy!"

Phillip returned outside. The front windows of the house were open. Why was Mother always so excitable? Why could she not behave calmly, like Mrs. Rolls? Father was always saying she was too excitable.

The two cabs stopped by Uncle Hugh. Then the clopping of the horses' hoofs came over the grass again. Surely Mrs. Rolls would hear them? *Two* cabs! Then he heard Gran'pa's voice, from the balcony above, saying "Sarah, Sarah, come along do, here's Charley come already, he-he-he!" Gran'pa always laughed like that when he said anything.

Phillip stood against the privet hedge, not wanting to be seen. He preferred to be alone, to think his own thoughts. And then, to spoil it all, the others came out on the pavement! Why couldn't they wait until the cabs arrived? He moved apart from them. To the waiting telegraph boy he said, "My uncle has just come from South Africa."

"I fort so," replied the boy. "When I seed a blackamoor's face in the last keb."

"Good lord! Then he *has* got a Kaffir servant!"

Just as he had invented in the letter to Desmond!

A few moments later he saw Mrs. Bigge's head at her gate. Of course, she *would* have to pop out from under her red-and-white striped awning, which *dear* Josiah had put up to save the paint of his precious front door from blistering!

Ever since Phillip had shot holes in Mr. Bigge's tiny greenhouse with his father's air rifle, and Mr. Bigge had remained silent about the damage, he had been wary of the Bigges. During the years this attitude had developed into a scorn for the harmless old gentleman, an attitude Phillip did not have towards their next-door neighbours, the Groats, who had promptly complained when he had broken their windows, and made him pay for the damage. He did not like the Groats; but he did have respect for them.

Mrs. Bigge, however, had not allowed her feelings about her husband's spoiled plantarium to alter her attitude towards Phillip's mother, for whom she had a deep, instinctive sympathy.

"Hullo, Mrs. Emm! I expect you feel very happy, to see your long-lost brother again, eh, dear?"

"Yes, Mrs. Bigge, it is splendid, after all these years!"

Mrs. Bigge stood beside her gate-post, scarcely taller than its top, and ready to disappear at the right time.

Phillip decided to cross the road, in the hope that Mrs. Rolls or Helena were looking from their bedroom window. From his new position he took surreptitious glances at the top house, but saw no sign. Then, quizzing farther down the road, he detected a movement of the bedroom curtain of No. 9. There she was, Old Mother Groat, glass eye and all, spying out the land! Inquisitive old devil! He sent an imaginary clay-bullet whizzing in her direction—it had a bit of loose grass sticking out of it, whoosh, it whizzed through the air. He heard the imaginary bull's-eye. *Crack!* right in the middle of the pane, *tinkle tankle* of falling glass. That would settle *her* hash!

Who else was playing peeping Tom? Ah, there was old "Sailor" Jenkins, of No. 8, the swanker, white yachting cap on head, shielding his eyes from the sun, as he stood between his arch of privet trained over his gate, trying to look like the captain of a ship.

Mr. Jenkins was a tall, handsome man of about thirty; he had told Phillip, soon after coming to live in the road, that everyone mistook him for Lewis Waller, the matinee idol. At first Phillip had been greatly impressed by Mr. Jenkins. During the summer evenings, while trimming his hedge, which he did with almost mathematical exactitude, Mr. Jenkins whistled, with a flute-like whistle, musical comedy songs as he stood, wearing yachting cap and brass-buttoned blue reefer jacket, and white canvas shoes below his trousers, clipping here, peering there, sometimes hesitating before making a delicate snip. Phillip had admired the sailor, until one evening a very strange thing had happened.

Phillip, walking silently in rubber plimsolls, had gone down to speak with his new and admired grown-up friend; and there he had seen, to his utter surprise, an entirely different Mr. Jenkins. His face no longer resembled an actor's. Mr. Jenkins, who had not seen him, was swearing in a level cold deadly quiet voice at lowly Mrs. Jenkins, who was standing by an open window, crying, a handkerchief to her eyes. When Mr. Jenkins saw him, his face changed, and coming through his gate, he bent down to whisper something to him, while holding his arm at the elbow, as Mr. Prout had done when he was afraid. "Don't tell a soul about what you heard, will you?" Mr. Jenkins had whispered. "My wife and I don't get on! We don't see eye to eye. How could we? When I married her, she was only a back-street woman."

Phillip did not quite understand what "Sailor" Jenkins meant; but he was never quite the same romantic figure afterwards.

So *Whoosh!* a second imaginary clay-bullet whizzed through the air—*whopp!* and old Jenkins' pavement yachting hat was sent spinning off the black wavy-haired head. Who else was there who deserved the Order of the Clay Bullet?

Looking down the road, Phillip saw Mrs. Neville sitting in the window of her flat. He waved. She waved back. She was all right, she was allowed to look. He had already told her all about Uncle Charley's home-coming.

In Mrs. Neville's presence Phillip now talked freely, as he could not talk to his mother, and certainly never to his father. Mrs. Neville encouraged him to say anything he wanted to; she knew all about overbearing fathers and egotistical husbands, having suffered from, and left, both.

Chapter 21

ROLLING STONE

THE two cabs were now approaching the bottom of Hillside Road. The rear one, an open growler, had the luggage in it, and what appeared to be a bundle of feathery grasses standing up in the back. A man followed it on foot, obviously hoping for a tip for helping with the luggage.

As they came up the road, Phillip saw that there was a second bundle, which he recognised as assegais, in the last cab, and more than that: for several striped cow-hide shields, and a cluster of knobkerries, were tied on top of a pile of portmanteaux. Then the flat dull notes of a kaffir cow-bell began to sound from the growler behind. When the leading cab pulled to one side, he saw a boy sitting up in it, shaking the bell. But he had a white face. Where then was the Zulu?

As the vehicles came nearer a head was poked out of the first one. Phillip saw a brown face with gold spectacles, open mouth showing gold teeth. What was the laughter for?

The man, wearing a Panama, got out, took off his hat and waved it while he shouted, "Hullo Mamma! Bless you, you don't look a day older. Hullo, Papa! How are you, sir? Why, if it isn't Hetty! Bless you, my dear sister! How are you? These your three kids? Here's Flo, come on Flo, don't be shy, come out and face the worst!" Then he laughed long and loudly once more.

Phillip saw that Grannie, beside Gran'pa on the balcony, was trying to say something. "Where is Hugh? Did you meet him?"

"We gave him a lift, Mamma, he's in the cab with Flo. I'll give him a hand out. Come on, Hugh, old man, take my arm."

"What's the gent done wiv my grid?" whined the telegraph boy, to Phillip.

"How should I know? Do you think he pinched it?" muttered Phillip as he watched Uncle Hugh being helped out of the cab. He was followed by a lady and a girl with a big red bow on her black hair. They must be Aunt Flo and Petal.

Uncle Charley helped Uncle Hugh to the gate of Gran'pa's house, where Uncle Hugh rested.

"I'll be all right in a jiffy, Charley old man, you attend to the others, really, I'm quite all right, a little blown, that is all."

The out-of-work, who had followed the cabs from Waterloo, hovered only too eager to be of any help. Then, while greetings continued, he retired to a respectful distance.

"We weren't expecting you quite so soon, Charley!" called out Gran'pa, from the balcony.

"Didn't you get my telegram, sir?"

"We haven't received any telegram. When did you send it?"

"About ten minutes ago, from around the corner, sir!" shouted Uncle Charley. "I intended our arrival to be a surprise, you see."

"Oh," said Gran'pa, and laughed. Suddenly Phillip remembered that he had it in his pocket. He decided to keep quiet about it.

"Please, sir, where's my grid? And is there any——"

"Oh, was that your red bike, my son? It's standing against the railings along the road there. I thought it was the fire-engine coming along." Uncle Charley felt in his pocket, and pulled out half-a-crown. "Here you are, my lad. Don't get drunk on it."

The boy's face went white. Then, as colour returned, he said, "Please, sir, is there any reply?"

At the question Uncle Charley threw back his head and roared with laughter. Then he called up to Gran'pa, "This boy wants to know if you want to send any reply to my telegram notifying you of our arrival, sir. Ha ha ha!"

"He-he-he," laughed Thomas Turney, thinking that Charley was the same harum-scarum boy that had gone away. He checked his thoughts, telling himself that there must be no upsets this time. Even so, he could not help feeling a weight of doubt come upon him: if that was the way Charley did business, he might very well soon be faced with having him, and his family too, on his hands, as he already had Hugh, as well as Dorrie and her children, for the past ten years.

"Welcome home, m'boy, come in and have some tea! I expect you're all ready for some after your journey, eh? I'll come down, Charley, and meet all your family. Why bless my soul, what's that I see down there?" He pointed to the other cab, where a black face had appeared, only to disappear again immediately, among the trunks.

"That's Kimberley, sir. Come on, Kimberley, don't be shy.

He's been hiding ever since the ragamuffins in the Old Kent Road saw him. Come on out, Kimberley, no one here will hurt you, my son."

The black boy, with a wild glance at the out-of-work man, scrambled back among the luggage.

"Futsack, you!" cried Uncle Charley to the out-of-work.

The seedy fellow, as eager as he was hungry, at once retired out of sight behind the other cab, wondering if the toff's expression meant what it sounded like.

"I thought at first he had come over by mistake among the grasses, he-he-he," said Thomas Turney, pointing at the black boy, whose curly mop and scared eyes were visible over one of the big corded boxes.

Mrs. Bigge, of course, long before this, had popped out of sight behind her awning, and now was regarding the scene from behind her Nottingham lace curtains. So was Mrs. Groat from the upstairs of No. 9; while Mr. Jenkins in No. 8 peered through a parting in his hedge extending behind the wooden fence belonging to his neighbour. One of the Higher Lows was looking from the bedroom window in No. 7. One door down, in No. 6, Mrs. Todd was also watching. Below her house, the people were strangers, as far as Phillip was concerned. Across the road, in her upstairs flat, Mrs. Neville, helped by a pair of opera glasses, was enjoying herself at the open window.

Then Phillip saw Mr. Bolton turn the corner. He walked up the road with his usual slow pace, one gloved hand held behind him for balance, the other holding the lead of Bogey the pug.

Feeling important with all these spectators, Phillip went down to speak to his new cousin Tommy. Tommy was attempting to pull the black boy from his refuge among the luggage.

"Come on, skellum!" he said, to which the black boy replied, "Futsack!" Good lord, was that African swearing? Phillip helped Tommy to pull Kimberley over the pavement to where the others were standing.

"Kimberley's my part of the black man's burden!" cried Uncle Charley, with more loud laughter. "Come on, shake hands, my son, with your new Auntie Hettie!"

Grinning, hand over face, Kimberley wriggled behind Uncle Charley. From there he tugged himself free from Tommy's hold, and darted back among the luggage.

"Ha ha ha!" laughed Uncle Charley, throwing back his head. "Like a baboon back to the rocks! He'll settle down. Well, this is my wife Flo, Hetty old girl. Kiss each other, for God's sake, there's too much constraint about. This is Pet, short for Petal, my daughter."

Phillip thought that the new uncle was rather fun.

Hetty was smiling, a little strained. What did Charley mean when he said that the black boy—*could* it be? Oh, surely not! Kimberley was obviously so much younger than Petal—— At this point the telegraph boy, during a pause in the talking, asked again if there was any reply.

"Good God, you still here?" said Uncle Charley. "Are we coming or going?"

"Charley, I want you to meet Mr. Bolton," Gran'pa's voice called from the balcony. "I was telling him only this morning about your arrival, Charley. Mr. Bolton, here's m'boy Charley and his wife."

The introduction was a little premature. Mr. Bolton was still approaching the gathering, majestically it might appear, but in reality his slowness of gait was due to a permanently overloaded stomach and intestines. Mr. Bolton was no glutton; he ate moderately, in his own view, never more than a couple of pounds of meat a day, for luncheon and dinner. He believed in a good breakfast, of course, to start the day with—the usual bacon, eggs, sausages, and kidneys, with toast, butter, marmalade, and coffee; and porridge in winter. Thus fortified daily, at the age of sixty Mr. Bolton thought of himself as a dull old man, worthy of no woman's regard. He had given up; but seldom a day passed without yearning for womanly beauty and care to revisit his life.

Bogey the pug was likewise overfed and slow, but with the difference that, having no speech with which to conceal his thoughts, he held his tail in perpetual query, his nose being as keen as ever.

After many bows, handshakes, hat-liftings and dignified remarks, Mr. Bolton proceeded on up the gully to the constitutional airs of the Hill.

Halfway up the gully he passed Richard, coming down with his swinging stride, straw-yard held in hand; and lifting his hat once more, Mr. Bolton paused and remarked, "The wanderer has returned to the patriarchal bosom, I perceive, Mr. Maddison, and a fine afternoon for the occasion," to which the non-committal reply, "Ah, I expect they will all be happy now, Mr. Bolton," as Richard braced himself for the encounter, concealing under his aloof amiability feelings akin to those of Phillip when he saw Father approaching—the difference being that the boy always showed his feelings in his face. However, Phillip had learned that speech was given him to conceal his thoughts—at least, in the classroom, and at home.

"Well, I expect you will all have much to say to one another, so I must not keep you," remarked Richard, as soon as he could politely get away. With a bow he went into his own house, to try and reassemble himself out of a hollowness which was literal, since his stomach was empty except for gas.

He still took the quarter-pound Player's Navy Cut tobacco tin box, filled with marmalade sandwiches, for his luncheon every day. He was still saving for a rainy day. Like Mr. Bolton, fifteen years his senior, Richard had given up hope of love in his life. Confound all the Turneys! He wanted to change and have his tea, then to cycle into the country, to get away from them all. There he could lie on the earth, face held to the sun, and be alive for awhile. For what? Oh well, sufficient unto the day——

In the slight pause after Richard's departure, the wretched telegraph boy made another attempt to be heard.

"Please, sir——" he began, but his small voice was unheeded in the general unloading of luggage. A strained anxiety remained unobserved upon the insignificant face.

Someone else was feeling anxiety, too.

"I had better go in now, Papa, for Dickie will be wanting his tea," said Hetty. "Come on, Phillip, Mavis, Doris. Say goodbye to Tommy and Petal for the moment, dears. Well, Charley and Flo, you must be very tired after your long journey. Tommy is to sleep on the folding bed in Phillip's room, it is all arranged with Mamma. I'll come and see you as soon as Dickie has gone off for his ride," and so saying, Hetty turned away, to hurry into her house.

Richard heard what she said, since all the bedroom windows upstairs were open, including the balcony door. Could not a fellow have a little privacy? The departure of Mr. Turney from his section of the balcony enabled him quietly to adjust this thoughtlessness on Hetty's part, before he went downstairs again.

"I am so sorry not to have had everything ready for you, Dickie. You must be tired. Charley's arrival was a little unexpected."

"Oh," replied Richard. "I thought you had all decided this morning that he would be here about five o'clock. It is now a quarter after five." He confirmed the time of the hall clock with his watch.

"Yes, Dickie, but Papa was expecting them to come by train from Randiswell, but they came all the way instead by cab. We were expecting a telegram, too, but Charley decided to make his coming a surprise, I think. Then he changed his mind, apparently, and sent one from Wakenham station, on the way here. So you see, the telegram arrived at the same time as the cab. It was all a little unexpected."

"It must be the Irish blood coming out," remarked Richard.

"Yes," laughed Hetty, relieved by his tone. "Now you will be wanting your bath, dear. Phillip, run up and turn on the tap for your Father."

Phillip, eager to be of service, leapt up the stairs.

"Steady, boy, or you will pull out the banister rail!" called out Richard; and Phillip slowed instantly. "And don't forget to put in the plug first."

"No, Father."

"I'll soon have the kettle boiling, and your meal ready, dear. I expect you are hungry."

"Oh, don't put yourself out on my account," he replied. "Blood is thicker than water. Phillip! Only half bore, the cold tap, remember!"

"Yes, Father."

Pleased with the way Hetty had remembered his bath, and set about telling Phillip what to do, Richard said to her, "I have a jolly good mind to stop at the rifle range under the Seven Hills this evening, and enquire about the possibility of joining the club. The members fire a course of the new charger-loading service three-o-three, for the Bisley competitions, I am told. I always wanted to join such a club, you know, ever since Lord Roberts sponsored the idea about ten years ago. You may recall that I read out to you, from the *Trident*, the particulars of the Rifle Association, at the time."

"Yes, dear, I think I do, now you come to mention it. Mavis, put on the kettle, fill it from the tap nearest the wall, put it on the big ring, and light the toasting bar, too."

"This German challenge is no myth, you know! You ought to read what the *Trident* has to say about the subject today! Many of the younger fellows in the office are in the Territorials, but I'm too old for them, more's the pity. However, the Rifle Clubs are not to be sneezed at, should any trouble arise. What do you think?"

"I think it a splendid idea, Dickie," replied Hetty. What the poor man needed was a hobby that would take him among other men.

"Oh Mavis, fill a pan and put it over the toaster, for your Father's egg, there's a good girl."

"Well, I'll go and have my tub, Hetty."

Richard had recovered his equilibrium. He could hear by the hiss that the cold tap was not turned on enough: and having adjusted it, he went into his room to undress. From there he tip-toed into Hetty's room. There would be no breach of manners by taking a brief look, he thought. Down in the road the cabbies were being paid off. The black boy stood by a pile of luggage, looking as though he were afraid to leave it. Poor little fellow, thought Richard, what a shame to bring him away from his own people. The cab-men touched their tarred bowlers, apparently well-pleased with the tips they had received. Then mounting, they turned round the horses, and went away down the hill.

Richard was wondering about the presence of the runner—he well remembered the occasion when his blessed father-in-law had given a tip of a cigar-butt to a down-and-out who had carried his bag from Liverpool Street to London Bridge Station—when the prodigal son turned to the telegraph boy in a loud voice, and said, "Well, what are *you* waiting for? Aren't you satisfied with the tip I gave you?"

"Yes, sir, thank you, sir. Only is there any——"

"Now tell me, my son. What make is your bicycle? I sell hundreds every month where I come from."

"I don't know, sir, it ain't mine, sir. Please, sir, is there any reply?"

More laughter came up from the road below. Richard saw Charley pat the boy on the head.

"Look, my son, I've arrived, haven't I? I sent a telegram to announce my arrival, and the telegram got here half a minute or so before I did. Then how in the name of all that's holy should I want to reply to myself? Come on, answer me, my son!"

"I didn't know but what you might want to send a reply to someone else, sir. Please, sir, it was a prepaid answer."

More loud laughter. "Oh, we appear to you to be birds of rapid passage, do we? Well, it might easily be, my son! I like your grit and determination anyway, and sense of duty. If ever you find yourself in Cape Town, come and see me. Capricorn Importers Limited. Remember that word, Capricorn. Think of goats eating corn, my son. D'you like chocolate?"

The boy was given a large packet, and touching his cap, hurried off down the road.

H'm, not at all a bad sort of fellow, thought Richard, as leaving the window, he went to the bathroom, lest it be filling beyond his usual nine inches. He could not bear the idea of wasting water, or anything else. Besides, it was a householder's duty to conserve water in a drought.

During tea, animated by the idea of joining the Rifle Club, Richard said to Phillip, "Would you care to come for a ride with me tonight, old chap? We can go as far as the Seven Fields together, then you can come home by yourself, to do your homework. The exercise will do you good. I am going to watch the firing on the range there."

"No thank you Father."

"Oh, do go with your Father," said Hetty. "It would be such a nice ride for you."

"There's no need to persuade him, Hetty. A volunteer is worth a dozen press-men. Well, if you'll excuse me, I'll be off." He rose from the table.

"Go on, go when you're asked!" whispered Hetty to the boy, as soon as Richard was out of the room.

"The boy would much prefer to be with his own sort," called out Richard, as he lifted his Sunbeam from its place by the wall in the lavatory. "Well Hetty, don't expect me back much before dimmit-light. I want to make the most of the long evenings."

As soon as Father had left the house, Phillip went next door by the back way. He found Kimberley sitting at the kitchen table with the cook, and Winnie, the daily girl who went home to Randiswell at night. It was a surprise to hear Kimberley speak English like an ordinary boy, and not like in *Uncle Tom's Cabin.*

"What does 'futsack' mean?" Phillip asked him. "Is it a very rude expression?"

"It means 'Go away', baas," replied the black boy, solemnly.

"Like getting the sack, sort of, eh?"

"Yes, baas."

Phillip liked being called 'Baas'. He felt kindly towards Kimberley as he went into the front room.

"Hullo! hullo!" All the faces looked at him. "Come and sit beside me, Phillip," said Gran'pa. Tom Turney made a place beside his chair.

"Draw up the stool, that's right, m'boy, only don't let the cat hook your food off your plate." He carved some ham, and put it on Phillip's plate. "Have a glass of wine and water with it, it will put colour into your cheeks, m'boy."

Phillip had a helping of pickled pears as well. It was a party! Every moment he liked the newcomers more and more. They were all so merry and bright, particularly Uncle Charley, whose gold teeth were to be seen again and again as he laughed, telling Uncle Hugh about the voyage, and life in Cape Town since the war.

"By God, Charley," said Uncle Hugh, as he took the cigar offered him at the end of the meal. "By God, old man, I can't tell you how good it is to hear the laughter of Jove in the Benighted Swamp." He bit the end of the cigar with his teeth.

"Here, wait a moment m'boy," said Gran'pa. "Don't spoil a good cigar!"

But Uncle Hugh had already twisted off the end, before Gran'pa could unfasten the cutter from his watch-chain.

"Our respectable suburbanites must be thinking in their top flats in Charlotte Road that it was Stentor himself shaking the tiles off Mr. Antill's jerry-built roofs!" went on Uncle Hugh. "The churchwardens of St. Cyprian's too, must be damned glad that 'the tower is not yet built' for otherwise the bricks would have come tumbling about their ears."

Uncle Hugh lit the cigar, and sucked hard. The children laughed at his comical face as he took it from his mouth and stared at it.

"What cabbage family turned this offspring out to fend for itself, Charley?"

Phillip saw Grannie give a quick look in the direction of

Gran'pa. He remembered that Gran'pa had kicked Charley out, long ago.

Uncle Hugh took another pull; and then addressing Charley, with a serious, perturbed air, he said, "By God, brother, whence *did* you get this specimen of mummified matter? What old dorp produced it?"

Phillip thought this was very funny. He laughed. Cousin Tommy was laughing, too, and exchanging glances with Uncle Charley.

"You should not take the name of the Almighty in vain, dear," said Grannie, who, with lace cap on hair and shawl over shoulders was sitting at the other end of the table, sipping her gruel. "Think of the dear children. If Phillip repeats what he hears——"

The children were watching their uncle sucking at the black cigar.

"Here, use the spike," said Gran'pa, unfastening his gold cigar cutter from his watch-chain. "Pass it down, will ye?"

"No no, sir, do not let me contaminate Treyer and Freyburg's best with this dried Afrikaner biltong." Uncle Hugh coughed. "What in the name of all that's mysterious is the brand, Charley? The Black Death, or the Would-be-Widow's Friend? How did you acquire it, from some ju-ju rite, some voodoo how-do?" He rolled it in his fingers, near his ear. "Do I hear it hissing? Can it be that it is full of potential lightning, and the foul vapours of the witch Sycorax? Is it by-blow of some November night, the fifth to be exact? Is this the weed that turned the hair of Dingaan grey, and caused Allan Quatermain to prophesy an eclipse of the moon?"

Phillip thought that Uncle Hugh was awfully funny. He had stuck the cigar on a fork, and held it out over the table, far away from his nose. "Phew! I am back in the old picket lines with a vengeance!"

"Don't spoil a good cigar," repeated Gran'pa.

"Surely the language of Euphues, sir, is inapplicable to this specimen of Terminus Dessicatus Elephantibus! It should join those other relics of tropical travel on the walls of the Savage Club."

Then, as Uncle Hugh was pretending that the cigar on his fork was an airship, sailing through the sky with smoke behind it, it suddenly went off with a loud *bang!* In the air was the smell of a Chinese cracker. It was a wonderful joke! Uncle Charley laughed loudest of all. Gran'pa made little noises, like his usual he-he-he; but Phillip saw that Gran'ma only smiled. He saw that she was clutching the arms of her chair. Grannie did not look as though she had really enjoyed the joke. He remembered Mother saying that Grannie must be careful of her heart; and then he thought no more about it, but searched with cousin Tom for any smouldering pieces on the carpet. Oh, it was tremendous fun now that Uncle Charley had come home!

Uncle Charley was an awfully nice man. Later, Tommy told him that he had given the cab runner five shillings, as he had a wife and family. Phillip was glad, for two reasons. It showed that Uncle Charley was very rich; and the runner had obviously been, like Cranmer's people, very poor.

Chapter 22

THE WHIRLIGIG

AFTER what he considered to be a highly satisfactory visit to the Seven Fields rifle range people, Richard went on to the Fish Ponds, and beyond. Cycling along the ridge of the North Downs, he dismounted at a point where, looking to the north-north-west, he could see a cluster of glints in the blue misty horizon. It pleased him to think that the sun at that moment was making an obtuse angle between itself at one point, the distant Sydenham ridge at a second, and himself among the waving barley fields completing the triangle. It was a very wide angle, for the reflected glints, shimmering in the ascending heat, were visibly shifting and diminishing almost momentarily as the sun moved to the west.

The sun was swinging down towards the unseen ocean: even so, the great mass of its rolling body, every flame of its hydrogen fires brilliant upon the great curved extent, was such that it would take an appreciable time to pass any given point in the southern glass front of the Crystal Palace. What was the speed of light, ninety thousand odd miles per second? And what was the diameter, or rather half the circumference, of the sun? Oh dash it all, he had enough of figures during the day! There it was, rolling and flaming along, its power maintaining the life of the earth, and for a few moments he, the sun, and Paxton, the designer of the Crystal Palace, as well as those associated with him and indeed the entire project—glaziers, foundrymen (for the framework was iron) and even the window-cleaners (if they still cleaned the glass)—for a few moments he and the sun and the originators and begetters of the vast glass building were in conjunction.

It was an exalting thought, a comforting thought. All the life of the planet was balanced and in relation to itself, physical and otherwise. Why, his own Sunbeam bicycle illustrated that fact! The balls in their cones, which bore the hubs which held the spokes which secured the rims that held the tyres—the balls were like stars in a system, revolving round one another. The Sunbeam had been made at Wolverhampton, the earth had been made—where? In far blue space, in the infinite universe; and the earth was but a satellite of one of the smallest ageing stars, according to an article by H. G. Wells in *The Daily Trident*. The sun was a dwarf-yellow star; it was burning itself out; a few more trillion years, and the earth would be in darkness, frozen like the moon. And even as he stood there, near a disused windmill half of whose sails had rotted and fallen, Richard told himself that he was in process of observing part of the declining incandescence, as demonstrated in the rapid diminishment of the sun's rays upon the Crystal Palace.

He watched the last reflection fading away. Ah well, a few moments nearer death!

Deprived of that impersonal gleam, his thoughts wandered into the state of his personal dilemma; he thought of the increase in the number of the Turneys next door in terms of his own violated privacy, and sighed. If only he had seized his opportunity years ago, to escape to Australia! He should have taken his chance when Mr. Turney had insulted him, and ordered him out of the house. By now he might have been a fruit farmer, with his own copyhold—instead of a failure, an office hack in the City, unwanted by both wife and children in his own home.

Well, if Phillip was wise, he would emigrate when he left school.

The Crystal Palace was now a faint grey chrysalis in the hazy distance. Richard returned to the roadway, and took up his cycle. With one foot on the step, he pushed off with the other, mounted the saddle, found the pedals. He had never thrown a leg over the saddle, as other men did, including Mr. Mundy the vicar, now in his sixty-fifth year—twenty years the senior of Richard Maddison.

When Richard got home that evening he found a woeful Phillip, with tear-stained face, standing in his nightshirt in the kitchen—so unusual a sight (not the tears, but the nightshirt downstairs) that at once he asked what was the matter. On being told, he said "Oh!" and looked judicially at his son.

"Now you will know, old chap, what it feels like to have your things spoiled. One lives and learns by experience!"

What had happened was that Phillip, bubbling over with his new friendship with young Tommy Turney, had shown him all his treasures, including the wooden custard-powder box, inlaid with sawdust, on which lay the blown eggshells of linnet and tomtit, robin and hedge sparrow, wagtail, wren, jay, and, best of all, the cuckoo. The box was in the corner cupboard of his room, with his other toys and possessions.

"I say, you must meet my friend Desmond when he comes home from school, Tommy old boy! We'll have a wonderful time together! I'll take you in my woods, and we'll fish in the ponds on Reynard's Common! It will be wonderful! Look, I'll show you my eggs, if you promise not to touch them."

Phillip, rattling on nineteen to the dozen, as Hetty sometimes said, gave Tommy the history of each specimen; and Tommy listened, fascinated.

The boys were to have a bath before bed. Tommy, the junior, had his first; then it was Phillip's turn. When he returned to the bedroom, Tommy was apparently asleep in the wooden folding bed that lay beside his own. Phillip thought he would take another look at his birds' eggs, of which he knew every blotch, spot, hair-line, tint, speckle, and texture of shell—the cuckoo's egg, for example, being ever so much smaller than such a large bird would suggest; the shell was considerably thicker than any other egg of its size; the yoke had seemed more redly concentrated when he had blown it, over a basin of water, with a glass blow-pipe at the neat round hole drilled in the side.

Putting the wooden box on his counterpane, Phillip opened it. He stared. The eggs were gone.

He awakened Tommy. He accused Tommy of having taken them. Tommy's sheepish denials made Phillip sharper. In a tone of voice derived from his father, he demanded to know, where were his eggs? Pulling Tommy out of bed, he threatened to inform the police unless he "produced" the eggs. Then, looking under Tommy's pillow, he found them. Every one was crushed.

"Well," remarked Richard, a couple of hours later, from his armchair in the sitting room, "this will at least teach your best boy, Hetty, to appreciate what it feels like to have his things taken and spoiled by another! I had some butterflies once, you know; and some good chisels, and other tools. It seems to be a clear case of the whirligig of Time, doesn't it? The law of meum et tuum works both ways, as now he has found out, to his sorrow."

Richard spoke mildly; things were evened up a bit better now, he felt.

There was a lot of noise nowadays from next door, particularly in the morning. It started fairly early. Phillip recognised the voice of Uncle Charley singing behind the opposite bathroom window, down the glass of which steam ran in streams. From the adjoining bedroom Aunt Flo sang, too, in her high tremulant voice. She had been trained for the concert platform, said Mother, and marriage to Uncle Charley at the age of sixteen had interrupted a very promising career.

"A woman has to give up everything for her children, you see, dear, unless she can afford a retinue of servants." Hetty went on to explain that, less than a year after Aunt's marriage her little girl, Petal, had come along; and now Petal was to have singing lessons, in order to achieve what Aunt Flo had missed through marriage. Petal's voice added to the nest of singing birds, as Father called it at breakfast. Father said also that the starling on the chimney-pot—a new one had taken the place of the bird shot by Phillip—would henceforward be adding to its repertory the Bride of Lammermuir, La Traviata, Our Miss Gibbs, Floradora, Cherry Ripe and the Tune the Old Tom Cat Died of.

"Father used to sing a song in his tub once, Uncle Hugh. It was 'The Arab's Farewell to his Steed'. He always sang that as the bath-water was running in."

"Ah," said Uncle Hugh, "I expect that particular nag bolted as soon as the Old Man came to live next door, my son."

"Why, Uncle Hugh?"

"Perhaps the shock caused him to sing the song as the bath-water was running out, and so the nag went down the drain."

Phillip was puzzled by this reply; but Uncle Hugh would not explain. He never did explain anything; but looked tired when he was asked.

It was not always singing that came from next door in the

morning. The Charles Turneys had the bedroom next to Richard's; and one morning, quietly, he shut his window to keep out the loud and even strident noises of bickering, which his nervous nature found unbearable. At breakfast Hetty said they would settle down in time.

"Everything is new to them, Dickie. I think it best to pretend not to notice anything too much at first."

Did he connect her remark with "something nearer home"? she wondered. She had not intended any implication. Richard was silent.

After a couple of nights it was discovered that there was room for Tommy in Gran'pa's house, after all. So Tommy moved into the box room, nearly opposite Phillip's room. Kimberley, the black boy, continued to spend the night in the broom cupboard under Gran'pa's stairs.

Petal was in the room immediately opposite Phillip's. About this fact he had already made a discovery as fascinating as it was secret: if he went to bed without a light, and kept quiet, he could lie on the end of his bed and watch through a space of a couple of inches, under the sash of his open window, what happened when Petal came up to bed.

There were lace curtains over Petal's bedroom window, and venetian blinds; but for some reason the blinds stopped about a foot short when let down. Peering under his sash, Phillip could watch Petal, through the lace curtains, brushing her hair, as she sat on the bed in her camisole. Petal had long black hair. On hot nights she sat on a stool before the looking glass with only her vest on, so that he could see her shape above the waist. And one wonderful night she brushed her hair after taking off her vest, and he saw her breasts, pink, soft, and alluring—a sight that filled him with longing. Every night he kept vigil on his bed, to watch Petal brush her hair, to hear her singing softly her favourite song, "Now Sleeps the Crimson Petal", and if he were lucky, to see glimpses of her naked body.

Part of the excitement he felt was caused by knowing that it was what Father would call forbidden fruit. If Father caught him playing peeping Tom, he would be very angry, call him a dirty little beast, and probably thrash him, as he had once long ago, when he had asked Mavis to let him see her body under the front-room table. So Phillip listened carefully while he watched in the darkness, ready at a slippered tread on the stairs to turn round and dive under the sheets, and pretend to be asleep.

Petal by day was not Petal by night. By day she was ordinary; by night she was like a lovely dream, which he gazed upon and felt only holy thoughts, which were sad, too, for some reason. Petal by night was of a world which he would never, never be able to enter. Helena Rolls lived in that world, and so did the migrant birds, who had to make such perilous journeys, in which many died, and all for the sake of springtime in England.

Chapter 23

DOCTOR BRIGHTON

ONE morning, the last of the term, soon after Father had left for the office, Mother called up the stairs, asking Phillip to come down at once. He was fitting a padlock to his cupboard door; Tommy was in bed next door with a bilious attack; it served him jolly well right; but he might recover any moment, and creep over to see what he could pinch next. At breakfast Father, hearing about the proposed padlock, had said something about locking the stable door after the horse had been stolen; but Phillip was taking no more chances with that skellum Tommy.

"Come at once, Phillip! Gerry wants to see you, he says."

At the mention of his admired cousin, Phillip dashed along the passage and down the stairs. Gerry stood there.

"Don't breathe a word to anyone, young Phil, but Uncle Charley sent me to ask you if you'd like to come with me, Uncle Hugh and himself, for the day to Brighton? Just us four."

"But we don't break up until this afternoon! Oh, damn!"

"We broke up yesterday."

Phillip paused, irresolute. "Mum, will you advise me?"

"Well dear, you must decide for yourself. Do you do any work on the last day?"

"No, Mum. We've been weighed, and measured for the report, and all that."

"You'll probably get your remove next term, and there'll be a different roll-call, so no one will know," said Gerry. "Come on, chance your arm! I would. If they do remember, say you were bilious, after crabs, like Tommy. I'll write you an excuse."

"All right!"

The sky was blue, the sun shone, the cab waited round the corner. Uncle Hugh walked down the road with the aid of two sticks, a new straw boater on his head, watched by Mrs. Neville from her sitting-room window. She told Phillip, later on, that she found the fact of a cab waiting nearly opposite Hillside Road, but out of sight of the houses, decidedly intriguing. She had observed the arrival of Uncle Charley—with black piccaninny!—from her window seat, and had come to the conclusion, she said, that Uncle Charley was a decided character.

Mrs. Neville watched the two men, and the two boys, getting into the cab, before it went down the road. Later, she heard from Hern the grocer, calling for orders, that the cab had stopped outside his shop while Phillip had bought a pound of ginger snaps, with the news that he was going to Brighton for the day.

To Phillip, since there had been no imaginative wastage before action, and no tension, it did not seem like going to the seaside at all. Without any luggage, or even overcoats, they just got in a train without any fuss, and soon were rushing along past houses and so into the countryside.

The brothers were in jolly mood to be together again, recapturing the spirit of far away days, the old happy days when the family of five children, with Mamma, had set off every summer for a month with "Dr. Brighton." The Old Man had joined them for week-ends, and odd days and nights; but most of the time they had been with Mamma, so that they had had what they called a high old time. What fun, what excitement, at the annual setting-off, Charley home from boarding school and Dorrie from the convent near Brussels, smaller Hetty and Hugh from their dame school, and baby Jo in charge of Susan the nurse-maid!

In the next carriage, Gerry and Phillip began to sky-lark. They pulled down the blinds; and let them go again to roll up with a snap. They jumped on the cushioned seats; tried to get underneath them. The luggage racks seemed the very place in which to travel, so they clambered up, pretending they were monkeys at the Zoo. They hung down by their toes, scratching elaborately, and uttering screaks of mock antagonism. Finally they settled to read their comics, stretched out on the netting, Phillip reading the ha'penny pink *Cuts* and Gerry the coloured penny *Puck*. When the uncles looked in, they pretended to be asleep; the wonderful thing for Phillip was that he had not, for the slightest moment, felt the least bit sick.

The train rushed into a tunnel. For some reason there were no lights in the carriage. Promptly Gerry howled like a wolf in the smoky darkness, Phillip imitating the hound of the Baskervilles. If only he had some luminous paint to put on his face! The train thudded out into dirty daylight, clearing itself as the embankment dropped away. On it rushed, smoke-clear through the sunshine, past fields of grass and corn.

How quickly they were at Brighton!

"Well, here we are, Hugh," said Charley, outside the station. "Same old cab rank. I wonder if 'Shepherd's Warning' will be here still?"

Alas, the old familiar red-face on the box was not to be seen. An ordinary face, more concerned with securing a fare, with no joviality, opened a door for them.

During the drive to the Old Steine the brothers had an argument about the exact place in Kemp Town where they had stayed as children. Hugh declared that it was in the fourth square behind the sea-front hotels of Marine Parade; Charley was convinced that it was the fifth square. There was a church near one corner, said Hugh; Charley remembered the church well, but it was in the adjoining square. Finally they had a bet about it.

"The sea, Uncle Hugh, the sea!"

Phillip stood up in the cab, staring at the prospect of white-flecked waves beyond buildings and trees, a steamship on the horizon. He gave Uncle Hugh a wide smile, thinking that he had seen the sea at the same time as himself, and therefore must be feeling as he was. How could anyone possibly feel otherwise?

"Coo, what's that huge place?" he cried, as the cupolas and minarets of the Royal Pavilion came into sight. "Look, the roofs are like those huge onions Uncle Jim grows at Beau Brickhill. Is it the Aquarium, Uncle Hugh?"

"Well," replied Uncle Hugh, setting his boater a little on one side. "It was built to hold as good fish as ever came out of the sea, by one who was somewhat of a poor fish himself, but otherwise it is not what the Lord Mayor and Corporation would exactly describe as the Brighton Aquarium."

"No really, Uncle Hugh, is it the Aquarium?"

"In a word, my dear boy—No. The Aquarium is on the front, convenient to the sea which is constantly being pumped into the various tanks holding their finny denizens. Thus the good burghers of this village—I said burghers, not what you think I said, my boy—though what you think I said would be, I admit, a more apt description of many of the more corpulent of theatrical folk who regularly visit this excrescence upon old Brighthelmstone."

Phillip wondered why Uncle Hugh spoke like that, in a sort of sarcastic voice. Uncle Hugh looked quite ill.

The cab stopped under a tree in the square.

"What are we stopping for?" said Uncle Charley.

"We've got to stop somewhere," replied Uncle Hugh. "And this is as good a place as any." He tried to pull himself upright.

Hugh Turney had an overwhelming desire to walk to the old lodgings, as he had hundreds of times in his boyhood, up St. James Street. His face was pale, more angular; he was breathing more quickly: a ghost of himself, in search of his lost innocence.

"Much better drive, old man, I don't want you to exhaust yourself," suggested Charley, whereupon Hugh laughed a loud mocking laugh, imitating his brother's laugh.

This mock of himself made Charley angry. Like his father, he was a man of violent temper on occasion. Charley had had a quiet, gentle laugh before his father had turned him out of the house, with five pounds and a second-class passage from Liverpool to Montreal, nearly twenty years before. The laugh was part of a new boisterous personality he had built upon the unstable foundations of the old. Sometimes the old broke through, in what was called temper, but was more truly distemper.

Charley controlled his temper, telling himself that Hugh was not really himself. All the same, he could not resist the desire to explain why he had decided—it being his treat—they should drive to their old apartments in the cab, and not walk.

"We always drove there, first go off, you know, Hugh old man."

"I know, I know," came Hugh's voice from his downheld head. He was resting his brow on his hands clasping the top of his walking stick.

At the collapse of his brother, Charley yielded.

"Very well then, we'll walk, just as you wish. But I'll double the bet, as you're so damned sure of your own opinion. Make it an even ten bob that it was the fifth square up. Are you on?"

Hugh did not reply for a few moments; then he spoke in a quiet and bitter voice.

"Ten bob! That's about my total value, rags, bones, and all! Charley, old man, I couldn't get that from any hospital, if I tried to sell my worthless carcass now, to the bodysnatchers! I've tried, so I know. So damned well stop laughing like a jackass!"

"What's fretting you, my son?"

"Forget it, forget it I tell you! For God's sake stop being the heavy elder brother! What does it matter where we used to stay in the golden age? A hundred thousand tons of chalk have fallen from the cliffs since those days. Even our bones are in part chalk. A man's life is no more than a fly's—a walking maggot's."

"Cheer up, old man, while there's life, there's hope. And talking of flies, your fly-buttons are undone, my son."

Hugh glanced downwards. "Do not be anxious," he said. "A dead bird never falls from the nest."

Charley's loud laughter rang out again. He loved his young brother; he had cherished his memory of him during the years of exile—as he thought of them—abroad; and he had been deeply shocked to see what was left of little Hugh when, with at first amazement, he had realized that the flapping object on the small red bicycle, approaching the cab, and then collapsing, had been Hugh. Later, from the Old Man, he had learned that an early death, preceded by loss of all his faculties, was inevitable.

Charles Turney had gone, the very next day, to Cavendish Street, to see the specialist to whom Thomas Turney had originally taken his son: to be told that the newly-discovered salvarsan, six-o-six, was useless: the disease was in its tertiary stage, the nerve-centres were in process of rapid disintegration; nothing could be done. Poor little devil, and from his first go-off, at nineteen! At least the Old Man had done his best for Hugh! That was something in his favour.

"Hold your horse awhile, cabby!"

Hugh Turney's thoughts as he sat in the open cab were a somewhat complicated linkage of effect and cause: if the Old Man had not been so damned intolerant and critical of Mamma, Charley would not have needed to stand up for her, and so draw upon himself the ire of the Old Man. Charley had ability, he would have settled down with the Firm. Then the Old Man would have left himself, Hugh, alone. But the swine had kicked

Charley out: then he, taking Charley's place, had been put into the blasted business, to give the Old Man contentment in his desire for immortality. That compulsion had made him go against his own grain: he had done things he had never wanted to do; and now, in retrospect, it seemed to Hugh that in deliberately setting out to destroy himself, he had done so only because the Old Man had already started the destruction. He had followed the pattern, without knowing what he had been doing. He had destroyed himself, out of destroyed love of his Father! He had never cared for drinking; alcohol made him sick; and as for those awful tarts in the Alhambra, the Leicester Lounge, and the Empire Promenade, they had always revolted him. Yet he had been drunk night after night, and gone with those appalling females! And now he, in sudden revelation, knew the answer to the enigma! It was all linked up with the maniac power of fathers over their sons! If only he could live to write a novel upon that theme! The hidden malaise of modern society! But no respectable publisher would look at it, even though the *hoi polloi* were no longer outraged by the remote frenzies of Swinburne, or cared whether Hardy, innocent as a wind-torn oak upon the downs, was either rude or lewd, or both! G. K. Chesterton's 'village atheist brooding over the village idiot'—Thomas Hardy! The English had always lacked imagination, regarding trade as having made the best of all possible worlds, behind the ironclad strength of the British Navy assuring material wealth!

"Just a minute, Charley old man. I'll be all right. Just give me time."

Hugh wanted to return home at once, to shut himself in his garden room, and write, write, write . . . before the last darkness got him. Shaken by his emotions, he rested his head upon his hands supported by the stick.

The boys looked at each other. Gerry winked at Phillip. Charley raised a finger. He was now in tune with his brother.

The leaves rustled above the open cab, with the sea-breeze. Hugh looked up. He had seen his complete theme in a revelatory flash: scene upon scene like the cards flicking in one of the automatic machines on the pier when you put in your penny and turned the handle—half-glimpses of vanished childhood, doomed youth, mock heroics of the Boer War, himself trampled in the stony shallows of Modder River, as the Gordon Highlanders broke and ran, himself standing up when they had gone, to receive a bullet through the heart, fired by a Boer but impelled by the dark forces of the Money Lords . . . his body carried away, but gently, in the waters of the plain . . . "a hero to the ignoramuses at home." That would be the final sentence!

As a fact, Hugh Turney had never been under fire in the recent war, to his lasting regret. He had wanted to be killed; but it was that white man, Sidney Cakebread, who had died there. Did Gerry ever think of his father? O God, the wastage of life—dream, hope, and love! Hugh Turney looked at the boys' faces on the seat before him, and felt himself to be like Gray, who in the *Elegy* had produced, he thought, the best poem in the English language outside Shakespeare. Ah well, mustn't spoil their fun. 'Regardless of their doom, the little victims play.'

"Well, Charley, we may as well get out here, what?"

Nothing loath, the boys jumped out, and talked together of what they should do while Uncle Charley helped Uncle Hugh to the pavement.

"Gent not feeling well, sir?" asked the cabby, pocketing half a crown (the fare being a shilling) and thus able to extend a little sympathy.

"Malaria from the Boer War," said Charley.

The cabby made clucking noises of sympathy with tongue and teeth, before lifting the reins and preparing to turn round, already casting his eyes about for the next fare.

At the word *malaria* Gerry exchanged a glance with Phillip, and winked.

Hugh saw the wink. In sudden fury he cried to Gerry, "You young devil, you! Clear out of my sight, d'ye hear? I don't want you near me! You'll never be the man your Father was!"

Gerry looked with astonishment from one face to another.

"You two go and have a look at the sea," said Uncle Charley, a hand on each boy's shoulder, as he urged them to the kerb. "Uncle Hugh's a bit upset, coming back after all these years, you see. We'll meet on the promenade, down there by the sea, in half an hour. Don't be late, or you'll miss what I'm planning for you. Hugh'll be all right when you return. He's not feeling up to the mark, that's all."

"I say, Gerry, what *is* up with Uncle Hugh?" asked Phillip, as they stood on the promenade.

"Don't you know?"

"Only what Mother said. He got rheumatism when he lived in a damp room by himself in London, after he'd left the Firm, didn't he? Father never lets him come into our house, saying it's catching, or something awful. Is it? Look, that's a Rolls-Royce stopping! And crikey, a balloon! Look, over the sea!"

They stood by the railings. While they were staring at the balloon, some gentlemen got out of the motorcar, and came to the railings near them. Phillip could see at once that they were very high-up people.

"I bet it's started from the Crystal Palace," he said, wanting to show off his knowledge.

"Perhaps it's trying for the Gordon Bennett cup," said Gerry.

"Huh, the Gordon Bennett race is for motorcars, anyone knows that!" retorted Phillip, sharply, loud enough for the gentlemen beside them to hear.

"It's also for balloons, young Phil."

"What, motorcars and balloons racing together? You'll tell me next that the Derby's for horses and push-bikes."

One of the gentlemen gave him a glance. Immediately he felt abashed. The big red face under a fur collar continued to regard him for a few moments, before he spoke.

"Your friend is right," he said, with a faintly Irish voice. "The Gordon Bennett race for motorcars was abandoned two years ago. It was considered too dangerous for unclosed continental roads. The race is now the Grand Prix, on a closed circuit. You should read *The Daily Trident* and be sure that your knowledge is up-to-date in future, young man!"

Then he smiled so charmingly that Phillip forgot he was a very high-up person. He had on the longest overcoat he had ever seen, with a fur lining all the way down to his boots.

Before he could think, Phillip heard himself saying, "I do read *The Daily Trident*, sir, it's my favourite newspaper."

"Do you see other newspapers, then?"

"Yes, sir."

"Where?"

"In the Free Library, sir."

"What do you like about the *Trident*, particularly?"

Phillip did not know what to reply. He was overawed by the magnificence of the gentleman; and when the others turned to look at him, he felt himself going pale. Then he remembered what Father had said once.

"It's inspired by common sense, sir."

The gentleman in the fur collar laughed; the others smiled.

"I am highly complimented that one of your generation should appreciate what I am trying to do."

The gentleman held out his hand. Phillip held out his, expecting his bones to be hurt in a very manly handshake; but the gentleman bent down, and took his hand between his two hands, very gently, and said to him, "Don't let anyone drive that clear, direct look from your face, with too much schooling, will you? Young men who get Firsts at the universities are burned up, their minds overstocked and legalised. The future requires new minds, to face the new patterns of nature. Now I am extremely interested in having met you, and before we part, do tell me, why do you *really* read the *Trident*?"

"Because my Father has it, sir."

At this reply the others, as well as Gerry, laughed. Phillip wondered if he had given the wrong answer, and so made the gentleman feel disappointed. But the gentleman looked kindly as before, and said, "Do tell me your name."

"Phillip Maddison, sir."

"I will remember it. Mine is Castleton. Give my compliments to your Father, and thank him for his support. Is he in Fleet Street?"

"No, sir, he is in the Moon Fire Office."

"Oh yes, I know it, just a little younger than the Sun."

This was a joke Phillip could understand, and he laughed freely with the wonderfully nice gentleman.

"That balloon up there," the gentleman went on, in the same friendly voice, "belongs to the Comte de La Vaulx, who is attempting to break the world's record of one thousand, one hundred and ninety three miles made last October. I hope we shall meet again sometime. Au revoir!"

Both Phillip and Gerry raised their caps. Silent, side by side, prim with best behaviour and entirely overcome by the most friendly presence of the important personage, they stared out to sea until, hearing the Rolls-Royce blow its horn, and waiting for it to glide some way away, they dared to turn their heads and look upon the departing splendour.

"I suppose you know who that was?" asked a man, coming up to them. He had been standing by the railings, listening. "That was none other than the great Sir Wilfred Castleton who spoke to you, the millionaire owner of *The Daily Trident.* I've seen him about here before, he usually stays at the Royal York Hotel over there. Every celebrity in the world comes to Brighton, sooner or later, and stays there. Castleton took quite a fancy to you, I could see that. That's why he asked you your name. He never forgets a face or a fact. That's why he's got on. There now, don't you feel proud, to know who he was?"

As soon as they saw the uncles approaching, the boys ran to tell the exciting news. They sat on a seat. When Phillip had finished his story, Uncle Hugh said,

"Castleton and his Yellow Press! A catchpenny Empire of Money, Bluff and Blarney! I wouldn't touch his dam' Daily Liar with a barge pole."

Phillip was puzzled by Uncle Hugh's remark. He felt that it reflected, too, on Father and Mr. Rolls, who both took *The Daily Trident.* They were easily the best men in Hillside Road. Then Gerry whispered to him, "Tell him he couldn't use a barge pole if he tried."

Phillip did so, and Uncle Hugh replied, as he shrugged his thin shoulders, "Even you, Marshal Ney, whom I raised in my tent?"

Phillip did not know what this meant, but he could feel that Uncle Hugh was somewhat disappointed in him when he went on, "Yes, as you so kindly suggest, I am a wreck all right. I couldn't handle a Boy Sprout's broomstick, let alone a barge pole." Uncle Hugh looked yellow about the face, with his up-turned black moustache ends waxed to points.

"Now you two boys run away and play," said Uncle Charley. "Wait a moment. Here!" He felt in his pocket, and gave Gerry the return halves of their excursion tickets. "In case you get lost, we're going back on the six-twenty." Opening his sovereign purse, he gave Gerry a coin. "Buy yourselves some tuck with this. Now listen carefully to what I have to say. We'll meet you two by the West Pier, at the turnstile, at three o'clock. Remember that, both of you. West Pier, three p.m. sharp, and no excuses for being late. Have a good time, watch the traffic, keep your eyes skinned for road-hogs when you cross the road. Don't forget to visit the Aquarium, and the fish market down below the promenade. And for God's sake keep out of mischief! Remember I'm responsible to both your mammas, you young rips."

Uncle Hugh added, "Have a ride on Volk's electric railway

—that's a family institution—but don't try any tricks, like touching the live rail with wet sea-weed! I tried it once, remember, Charley? I thought my blasted arm was broken."

"Au revoir, Uncle Charley. Au revoir, Uncle Hugh."

On the way to the Aquarium, Gerry opened his palm, and showed Phillip—a half-sovereign. They hastened on with visions of sharks, electric eels, seals, porpoises, octopuses; and in the background ice-cream, ginger-pop, Brighton rock, and fried fish and chips for lunch, or failing that pease-pudding and bacon. Both sorts were tasty and cheap, said Gerry, and the advantages of saving on lunch meant more cash for other things. How about a sail in the Skylark, for instance?

Gerry quoted the old familiar rhyme.

Any more for the Skylark?
A shilling round the Bay
Any more for the Skylark?
If you don't come back, don't pay!

"Couldn't we buy some lines, and spin for mackerel as we sail, Gerry?"

"I don't know, ask me!"

"Oh, be serious for once!"

"Course we can! Only there isn't much time. Here's the Aquarium. Hi Cockalorum, isn't this a ripping day?"

There was nine-and-eight change from the half sovereign; and this pocketed, they entered a long underground gloomy hall of green plates of glass enclosing on each side misty sea-water in which languid shapes moved slowly, or rested on sand and rock behind bubbling streams of air. They passed dogfish, cuttlefish, rays, skates, wrasse, pollock, cod, turbot; paused to admire the delicate sea-horses, like rusty curls of iron-work moved by whirring propellers; then on to the crabs, lobsters, eels, octopuses—from window to window they went, saying that they would like to stab that ugly brute, smash the other's fearful face, shoot the shark between the cruel button eyes.

"I say, Gerry, let's go to a shooting gallery. I'd give anything to fire off a revolver!"

"There's one on the West Pier, where we're going this afternoon. Have you had enough? This way out. How about a ride on the electric railway? The tide's in, and swoosh! we may be drenched!"

"Ripping! Let's buy some fishing tackle, too, and fish off the groins."

"They're dangerous, and you can't swim yet. The waves sweep over them, and suck you under."

Phillip had tried to learn in the Randiswell Baths, which had white tiles, which often showed the dirt on the bottom, at least in the second class; but he had been too afraid of the water, and of being ducked by roughs. Now, with his new sense of freedom, he thought that if he made himself swim when in the water, he would be able to keep up all right; for he knew the strokes.

"There are two quays, sort of, over the sewers, with walls, we can fish from them. One is just by the West Pier. We'll have a go early afternoon."

The ride on Volk's electric railway was exciting. They sat in front, by the driver. The tide was in, and waves slapped against the wall of the esplanade, throwing up water, spume, and shingle. The glass windows were crusted with salt, where they were not being wetted anew. Blue flashes and trails of sparks came off the live-rail; they could smell ozone. They went all the way to Black Rock, then returned.

Seeing a man with a white barrow selling ices, they dashed away through the turnstiles to secure large vanilla cornets; and licking these appreciatively, decided to see what was interesting down below, where nets were spread to dry, and tarred fishing boats with brown sails drying were drawn up by windlass out of the rearing plunge of waves, beyond the snarl of brown shingle. This was the fish market. Passing through it, some boxes of fish laid on planks decided them to try their luck as soon as possible.

They went into the smaller streets across the promenade to seek a tackle shop. There they passed an oyster bar, and saw, through the wide glass window, the uncles sitting at a table, a bottle of wine between them. They hurried past, lest they be called in, and asked to account for the change so far.

"How about going to the Bioscope?" suggested Gerry. "Though we can see the flicks at home anytime. I'll tell you what, Ralph told me there's a place where you can see wax-works, absolutely lifelike, girls nearly naked, breathing and smiling and their eyes turn and look at you. It's here somewhere, run by a Frenchman."

"All right," said Phillip, feeling very daring.

A tackle shop, however, changed their thoughts. There were

rods, reels, paternosters with gimp wire and leads, baskets, folding canvas seats, and a whole cardboard of Redditch sample hooks, from tiny sneck bends to huge swivelled conger hooks six inches long. Phillip could hardly wait to buy some; but there were too many in boxes on the counter, too many kinds of line, in all colours, plaited, twisted, and woven, hemp, hunk, and cord, to choose from. In the end they bought two plain winders, already assembled with spreaders, gut, hooks, and leads. These cost sixpence each. Worms could be bought a penny the tin, from men down by the fish-market.

When they had bought the bait—purple-red, hairy lugworms with thin green tails—they wandered about the High Street, staring at motorcars and noting their makes and numbers; and feeling hungry, decided it was time to have dinner. They must not spend much time eating now, said Gerry, but save up for a big tea on the pier. Also fish came in to feed on the high tide, which was the best time to try and catch them. He bought a packet of Ogden's Tabs, to keep them going between bites, he said. With these in his pocket, hidden from any slop they might encounter, they sought a restaurant.

Finally they stopped by one which had all sorts of shell-fish in the window, which was curved, and had gold lettering on it. Behind the glass were lobsters, crabs, smoked salmon, with prawns and escallops, all among sea-weed. The lobsters were blue, and their claws tied with string. Some moved red feelers.

"They boil the feelers first, to prevent them knowing what's to come, I suppose," said Phillip. "Ugh, I don't think I'd like to eat any."

"The feelers are red when they come out of the sea," replied Gerry. "That's what most people don't know. Can you tell me what author made a famous blunder over the lobster?"

"Doctor Watson?" ventured Phillip.

"He was a detective, not an author! No, I am wrong! Sorry! Of course Watson told the Sherlock Holmes stories, so he was the author. No, it was Victor Hugo. Gran'pa told me. Victor Hugo wrote that the lobster was 'the cardinal of the sea'. A cardinal is a sort of Catholic bishop, and wears all red. Get the idea?"

Phillip was puzzled. "A lobster has no religion," he guessed.

"Go to the bottom of the class, young Phillip. The lobster is *blue* until it is boiled, so Victor Hugo was caught bending. You can always catch people over that fact. I caught our English master in the end-of-term general knowledge questions yesterday with it. So you owe me a tanner."

"But we didn't bet!"

"Oh, sorry. Have a fag instead."

Gerry took out his packet of Tabs and offered it to Phillip. Greatly daring, Phillip took one. Calmly Gerry offered him a light, before lighting his own; then opening the door, he walked into the restaurant.

Phillip hid his cigarette as he followed Gerry, overcome with awe of such a rich-looking place. There were men in evening dress serving people at the tables. Wine glasses were on the tables, with flowers. A fat dark man with greasy locks and buffalo-horn moustaches, and waving fat be-ringed hands, came bouncing towards them. Staring round-eyed at the winders in their hands, and the tin of lug-worms, he demanded what they wanted.

"Fried fish and chip potatoes, if you've got it," said Gerry, with a grin, puffing his cigarette.

"This is Fattorini! Into the next street, please you go, right away!"

With a flutter of be-ringed fingers the fat man led them to the door.

"Now you a-go to Sam Isaacs' for feesh an' cheeps, never to Fattorini!"

"Keep your hair on," said Gerry; but Phillip almost ran before the black-eyed figure. Then hearing Uncle Charley's laugh, he glanced over his shoulder to see him sitting at a table with Uncle Hugh, a bottle of wine between them, just as in the oyster bar.

"That's my uncle," said Gerry. At once the restaurant owner stopped.

"Many many many pardons, sir, please you-a come-a right-away with me," he exclaimed, turning without pause on his heel, a sparkling smile on his face. "Many thanks, please come this-way-a-rightaway!"

"It suits me rightaway this-a-way!" said Gerry, and dashing for the door, he and Phillip ran through, no longer able to keep back their laughter.

"Golly," said Gerry, "that was a close shave! Did you see Roly-poly's eyes pop out when he saw the lugworms? I thought he was going to explode! What a name, Fattorini! Just suits him!"

"Do you think they saw the fags?"

"No, they didn't spot us. They wouldn't split if they did. Here, this place is more our mark, young Phil."

They looked into a window with a big ham in a pink frill surrounded by tomatoes, beside another plate holding a baron of beef. There were oblongs of pressed beef in brown jelly, pies of pork and steak and kidney, cooked sausages of all shapes and sizes.

They entered, and bought two meat pies, a pound of tomatoes, four hard-boiled eggs, some cold sausages, and a packet of beef sandwiches. This, said Gerry, would keep them going until tea.

When the uncles met them by the West Pier, Gerry presented Uncle Charley with his catch—an ugly, toad-like fish with big mouth and blue-white belly, saying that it would do for his supper, if fried. Uncle's laughter rang out, as he exclaimed, "A sting ray!" Phillip's contribution was a handkerchief tied at the four corners containing an assortment of green crabs, and a small dab.

The turnstiles clicked; they were on the magic pier, the shingle roaring in surf far down below, waves rolling past the iron supports. There was too much on the pier itself to see, to think any more of the waves, however. They ran ahead of the grown-ups, passing the glass-panelled shelter down the middle of the pier, pausing to look at anglers with empty baskets and rods elevated on the railings, some with little bells on their tips to announce a dreamed-on catch of the season.

"Any luck?" asked Gerry, of a solitary fisherman. The man turned away; the question broke into his illusion of being alone in a world of sea and air, away from domesticity and civilisation.

The automatic machines were of every sort, far too many to try in one day, even with unlimited cash. Why were there so many, when so few people were on the pier? It was hard to think where to begin. You could try your strength on two brass handles, trying to make them meet, when your penny would be returned. Or there were football matches behind glass, little metal marionettes worked by levers. A goal on either side earned twopence for the lucky one. If no goal, the pennies dropped into the machine; the game was over, the marionettes rested, painted and still, their duty done—to the proprietor. There were horses to race; silver balls to be shot into penny-back holes; bags of sweets and pink-and-white sugared popcorn to be grabbed by miniature cranes, while clockwork ticked away the seconds allowed during the short penn'orth of time. Dark-eyed gipsies with fingers pointing to revolving coloured disks printed with fortunes, told your own fortune by nodding as the disk stopped. Others shot them out on little printed cards. Gerry's card said that he had a noble nature which would bring its own reward, but he must beware of a dark woman, whose wiles sought to entangle him, while a fortune awaited his endeavours. Phillip was generous, and inclined to accept others at their own valuation; a life of hazard and adventure lay before him, and romance in which fair hair and blue-eyes were indicated. Phillip was astounded: he put this ticket of fortune with some care in his pocket-book, thinking with elation of Helena Rolls. How *could* the gipsy have known? Or was it all just spoof? Either way it was the same thing!

They looked into the shooting gallery, and Phillip saw a small revolver on the counter. He hesitated; he needed a plan to nick it; and after asking how much the rifle shots cost—"Seven for thruppence"—his heart quailed; and saying he would come back later, left with Gerry.

The uncles sat on a seat near the end of the pier; Uncle Charley then asked Gerry for the change. Phillip wondered what he would say when he found out they had spent some of the money on winders, as Gerry pulled various coins from his pockets.

"Well, you haven't spent much," was all he said, as he examined the money in Gerry's palm. "Hugh, the younger generation doesn't know how to enjoy itself, I can see that. Keep those brown things," said Uncle Charley, as he picked out the silver from the outstretched palm, and put it in his pocket. "Too early for tea, you boys run away and play and come back in half an hour."

"He's decent, isn't he?" said Phillip. "He never minded about us buying the winders. D'you think he knew?"

"Yes, but he didn't say anything, being a sport, young Phillip. Let's go down the steps, under the pier. You can climb about all over the shop down there. Then we'll go back to the shooting gallery, shall us?"

"Carramba!" cried Phillip, scared at the thought of nicking the revolver. Dare he tell Gerry his plan? Supposing it failed, and he was copped!

They crept down slippery iron steps, past many green circular piles, to a lower sunless level where the most serious of the fishermen stood, some with many rods elevated before them. Not one seemed to have caught even a sting-ray, judging by the empty rush bags. "I bet they'll go home with some kippers, and swear they caught 'em!" said Gerry.

After climbing about in the underworld, pretending they were in a submarine, they got on deck again, and made for the shooting gallery. It was Phillip's idea that, while Gerry was occupying the attention of the attendant with a rifle, firing at the balls on jets of water, and the moving targets of ducks, rabbits, and old men's faces with clay pipes stuck in their mouths, he would nick the revolver on the counter, and hide it among the crabs in his handkerchief. If caught, he could say it had slipped down there without him knowing it. The very idea made him feel faintly sick.

They entered the gallery, and there the revolver was, on the counter as before.

"I'll have seven shots with the rifle," said Gerry, while Phillip pretended to be interested in the man dropping little copper cartridges into the magazine with a clicking noise. While he did so, Phillip thought of policemen, himself being led off; and his mouth filled with water. His hands were wet, too; and he imagined his finger-prints all over the revolver. He began to wish that the man had not left it there. Was it a trap, to tempt someone to steal it? He saw Mother's face, if he was caught. More water ran into his mouth. His hands smelt horribly fishy. *Crack crack crack*, went Gerry's rifle. He counted seven shots.

"What's up, young Phillip? You look green about the gills."

"Leave me alone," said Phillip, miserably. "I think I'm going to be sick. Oh damn."

"You'll feel better when you've shot your bundle."

Gerry took his arm, and led him to the rails. Phillip leaned over. Nothing happened.

"Put your finger in your throat, Phil, try that."

All that happened was retching. Then Gerry shoved the bait can under his nose.

"You sod!" moaned Phillip weakly, as water drowned his tongue. Then the worst happened. Past the row of fishermen below fell a mixture of chocolate, ice-cream, meat pie, hard-boiled egg, sausage, ginger biscuit, toffee, cocoanut, and American ice-cream soda.

"Hi, you up there! Look what you're about!"

"It's some ground-bait for you, old cock!" Gerry shouted back.

"Ugh!" said Phillip, shuddering. "I think it was that last pie. Oogh! I'd like some beef-tea, it always puts me right."

Returning to the uncles, Gerry said that Phillip had been poorly, and needed beef tea to settle his stomach.

Uncle Charley slipped another half-sovereign from the round metal purse on the end of his watch-chain, and said, "Go and have some tea, boys. We'll wait here."

In the tea-room, which they had to themselves, Gerry ordered a cup of Bovril, to be followed by a pot of tea for two, a plate of cakes, and two Neapolitan ices, the largest sizes, sixpennies.

"Coo, I say," said Phillip, never having had such a splendid ice before. The biggest he had had was a penny vanilla, served in thick glass holder, in the Refreshment Room on the Hill. This sixpenny Neapolitan was pink and yellow, about four inches long, two wide, and one and a half inches thick, half strawberry and half vanilla. It was smooth and cold with real cream and real strawberries; while the vanilla end was utterly different from the ices on the Hill, good as they were.

"I'd like a stone-ginger beer with it," he said, having recovered completely, with the aid of the Bovril. "Make it two," said Gerry to the girl.

"What, with tea as well? You'll be sick!"

"Oh no, we've both been vaccinated!"

The waitress brought the glasses, each with a straw in it. Gerry poured out the tea. "A good strong cup for you, just in case your tum-tum isn't yet in order, young Phillip. Have a doughnut, or a custard tart? What else is there on this plate? Not so bad. Marzipan sandwich in three colours. Real short-breads. How about that cocoanut macaroon? Eccles cakes, too. Jam puffs. How hypocritical is this cream puff? Some human rat may have been here already."

Gerry opened the sugar-powdered shape with his fork, found it intact, prodded, and tasted. "Yum Yum! Real cream! Bags I this one! You've got to take it easy for awhile, young Phil. Anyway, we can always order another plateful."

Phillip had an excellent appetite.

"Two more ices, please," said Gerry, after about five minutes. "Yes, like the last."

They had another plate, of greengage and raspberry tarts, custard tarts, mince pies—they sat at the table, enjoying themselves the more that Phillip's revolver-pinching plan had been abandoned. Phillip gave up after three Neapolitan ices; but Gerry seemed able to eat them without effort. At the end of the half-hour he asked for the bill.

"Let me pay it," said Phillip. "It's my turn, really."

Gerry gave him the half-sovereign. Phillip took the precious coin, so heavy in the palm of his hand, and stared at it, fascinated with the feel and presence of gold. Somehow it felt to be the only real and true thing in the world, like the sun itself. Ordinary acid could not dissolve gold, he had learned from the chemistry master at school. Gold was not a base metal like iron, copper, zinc, or lead. It was a precious metal; somehow it seemed to be part of the sun, which never set on the British Empire, lasting for ever. It was almost with a wrench that he gave the gold coin to the waitress smiling beside the table. He watched her taking it to the till, to get the change. Gerry took this; and having tipped the waitress with sixpence, they went back to Uncle Charley leaning on the rails of the pier, beside Uncle Hugh.

Uncle Charley looked at the change Gerry had given him. "Good God!" he cried, and then laughed loudly. "Where did you stow it all?" He showed his brother two shillings.

"Two bob change from half a sovereign, for two teas! How many sixpenny ices did you say? Ten? Talk about the fat boy of Peckham! Ha ha ha!"

It was time to leave the pier. As they went back Phillip and Gerry removed some of the little dull-looking electric light bulbs from the continuous chain under the glass shelter along the middle of the pier, and hid them in their pockets. They were old ones, with looped carbon filaments. The glass bulbs were dull with sea-salt, from storms.

They kept the bulbs hidden until they were on the Marine Parade above Madeira Drive, then threw them down behind passing motorcars, hoping that the chauffeurs would think the *pop* they made was a burst tyre. One automobile did stop. The driver, in a coat of hairy skins, looked up and shook his fist. The boys did a monkey dance above, to mock him, before running off to find the uncles waiting by a cab.

In the train going back to London, Uncle Charley discussed with Uncle Hugh the chance of finding suitable lodgings in the neighbourhood of the Hill, for the rest of the summer. Staying with the Old Man, Phillip heard him say, was a bit of a strain.

"What I'd like would be rooms in a farmhouse, but I'm about twenty years too late for that, I suppose."

"There's Joy Farm, Uncle Charley!" cried Phillip.

"Joy Farm? Can such a name exist in Wakenham?"

"I saw a notice on the gate-post in Randiswell Lane, saying 'Rooms to let'. Father used to live there before he married Mother, and he says they were respectable people. It was very clean in the cowhouse."

Uncle Charley roared with laughter. "Is that the part your respected parent lived in? Ha ha ha! Well, thanks for the tip, young feller."

Chapter 24

IN THE MIDST

Uncle Charley and Auntie Flo seemed pleased with Joy Farm. There was some sort of a garden, an orchard of apple and plum trees, and fields of cabbage surrounding the dingy Georgian yellow-brick house. No more corn-fields; no more rotation of crops; Joy Farm was a farm almost only in name. The land, said the farmer, had been sold over his head for building, and he was only hanging on until he could find another farm out in the country. He was glad to let his rooms.

On the following Sunday, when supposed to be going to St. Cyprian's church, Phillip went instead down past the cemetery, to Joy Farm. Once past the gates, he took Timmy Rat from under his jacket, and let him sit outside.

He hid Timmy Rat again before he went into the house, for a surprise. Through the window he saw his cousin Ralph Cakebread, whom he did not like. Ralph was no longer an apprentice in High Holborn, owing to his flat feet, Mother had said. Ralph was now hoping to go to sea, as an apprentice in the merchant service. At sea, Mother said, the flatness of Ralph's feet would not bother him so much, for he would not have to stand about a lot in one place. This information was slightly puzzling to Phillip, for decks of ships were more or less like floors, which were flat, and had made Ralph's feet flat by so much standing on them. Even if he moved from one spot to another on a ship's deck, it would still be flat under his feet. "Not through the Bay of Biscay, dear!" said Mother.

"Hullo," said Phillip, to Ralph, through the open window. "I hope your feet are a little better."

Thinking that this was meant for cheek, Ralph replied, in the sharp defensive manner of apprentices herded in garret dormitories, "You'd better ask them, I haven't seen them lately."

Phillip felt rebuffed, for he had meant the enquiry about Ralph's feet to be a kind one. Then a voice he recognised as Uncle Joseph's said, with a guffaw like a donkey's, "'A year ago I used Pears' Soap, since then I have used no other'," followed by his braying laugh. Uncle Joseph was Mother's youngest brother. Mother said he was a little different from the others, owing to having been dropped on his head as a baby, Uncle Joey, as he was called, usually made rather silly jokes about people's feet and things like that, except when ladies were present.

"Hullo, my son, come on in," said Uncle Charley, and Phillip went into the parlour, the white rat still hidden under his jacket. He saw Petal reading on the sofa, fingers plugged in ears; and Tommy was sticking stamps into his book, at the table.

Cousin Ralph had a new and very large pipe, which he was filling from Uncle Charley's crocodile skin pouch.

"What's this tobacco, Charley?" he asked, and on being told that it was John Cotton, he shouted, "Thank God I've got a large pipe, old man!" Then folding the pouch, he tossed it over the table to Uncle. "Got a light?" he asked next, in a new loud gruff voice, which sounded funny coming from his thin pale face with dark circles under the eyes, and high starched man's collar almost up to the lobes of his ears, which were unusually low-placed on his skull. He sat on the corner of the table, swinging his leg.

Staring down at Phillip, he cried, with exaggerated alarm, "God! Don't tell me I've got 'em again! Pink-eyed rats! I must take more water with it in future!" Jumping off the table, he went to Phillip and opened his jacket. Taking out Timmy Rat, he held it by the tail, while Timmy Rat twisted up, trying to catch his own tail and climb up it.

"Watch its eyes drop out!" said Ralph. "I bet it breaks its back first!"

"Don't torture my rat!" cried Phillip. "Give him to me, please."

Ralph ran round the room, holding the rat at arm's length and enjoying the fun.

"Timmy's not very strong, give him back to me," pleaded Phillip.

Ralph dodged him, and went to the open window, where sat the farm cat, an old grimalkin with wide tabby face and torn ears, obviously a fighter. Ralph approached it, as though he was going to give the rat to it.

"No!" screeched Phillip; then he ran at his cousin, and getting hold of the back of his collar, pulled Ralph over backwards. They fell together beside the table. The big curved pipe clattered over the oilcloth.

"You little toe-rag, I'll pay you out for that!" gasped Ralph, assuming the rage that had gone from Phillip, who now tried to be reasonable.

"Apologise!" cried Ralph.

"Shan't! You leave my rat alone!"

"Can't stand a joke, can you? Mother's little darling!" Ralph raised an arm to his ear, as though about to give Phillip a back-hander. Then, baring his teeth, he ran at Phillip.

"Don't get ratty, I say, I was only funning, Ralph!" said Phillip, diving under the table. Ralph pulled him out by a leg.

"Haw haw haw!" guffawed Uncle Joey, who had an innocent face with mild grey eyes, and a long upper-lip hidden by a thick drooping moustache. "Mind the smell of his feet don't knock you over, Ralph."

Joseph Turney's jokes about feet were never meant to be personal. Any feet would do for his sense of fun.

Phillip was now on his back. Holding up crossed fingers, he said, "Fainits! I cry Fainits!" Ralph still held his leg.

"If you can't take a joke, then take this!" said Ralph, twisting his leg. Raising himself on his hands, Phillip kicked himself free, and rolling over, got on his feet and darted round the table. Ralph grabbed him again by the jacket, and swung it sideways, trying to fling Phillip down. Then with a leap he landed on top of his much smaller cousin, and held him down.

"My ear, my ear!" yelled Phillip. "My head, oh my head! You swine!" as Ralph got his knees upon the bones of his arms, and started to grind the muscles. "Help, Tommy, help! Oh, you bloody——"

Tommy came to his aid. With a cry of "Skellum!" he tried to pull Ralph off. Failing to do this, he stepped back and took a swinging kick at him. Ralph dodged, caught a boot, gave a twist, and Tommy went down hard on the oilcloth.

Petal now came to the rescue. Putting down the *Life of Adelina Patti*, she darted up behind Ralph and nipped the short hairs of his neck between the fingers and thumbs of both hands, and pulled sideways. It was now Ralph's turn to yell. Uncle Charley threw back his head and roared with laughter.

Ralph got up, and glared about him, with the glare of the dormitory-hunted, and later on the hunter, showing his teeth. Petal took no notice of the glare, but stood her ground, and kicked him expertly on the shin. Ralph howled. She kicked him again. He retreated. She followed him round the table, while he tried to appear indifferent.

"You young bitch!" he hissed, as he backed away from her.

To Phillip, standing on the other side of the table and stroking Timmy Rat, it seemed an awful word. It was the first time he had heard it used for a girl or woman. It just showed how depraved Ralph's mind was. Mother had told him that Ralph had an unhealthy mind, and he must not take any notice of what he said, for he had run wild after his father had died of enteric in the Boer War, with Hubert his eldest brother away at boarding school, and only Aunt Dorrie to control him. It was strange that Uncle Charley did not seem to mind the word at all. Perhaps he had not heard it. Only the lowest of the low used words like that, about a woman. Cow was sometimes used, but it was not so bad as the other word.

"What is going on down there?" called Aunt Flo's voice from above. She was probably still in bed. Mother said that Aunt Flo's idea of a happy life was to lie warm in bed, a pot of tea beside her, a box of chocolates open on the counterpane, and a novelette in her hand.

Florence Turney, twelve years younger than her husband, had discovered the delights of reading since coming from the uncultured veldt, where the only book had been a Bible. Her favourite authors were Gertie de S. Wentworth James and Elinor Glyn; although it should be said that the older novelist was a little too serious for her taste. She liked, too, the works of Mrs. Florence M. Barclay, particularly *The Rosary*, a book generally said to be the favourite reading of the Tsar and Tsarina of Russia. Miss Gertie de S. Wentworth James most nearly expressed her own longings : the sevenpenny paper-backs were always somewhat guiltily concealed under counterpane or cushion whenever the children came into the room, for two reasons, the more obvious being the books' titles and lurid covers. The less obvious reason being that Flo was the daughter of a Calvinist Scots mother and a Dutch *voortrekker* father. Phillip had heard Uncle Hugh say to mother, "Through these latter-day romances many of the secret feelings of women approaching the change of life are exhaled;" and asking what this meant, was told that it was only the sort of things that Uncle Hugh was in the habit of saying; and he should take no notice.

"What's all the noise about?" Aunt Flo's voice called again, from upstairs.

"Only some horse-play among the lesser breeds," shouted her husband. "And Petal showing herself to be a chip off the old block."

He laughed again. Many times had his wife's feet, bare and shod, gone for his shins—the traditionally vulnerable spot on the body of a native "boy" in need of correction.

"Now futsack you two boys, Ralph and I want to talk business."

"Don't be late for lunch, Tommy," the voice of Aunt Flo called down.

"And don't you!" shouted Uncle Charley. "Remember that our good landlady visits her relations on Sunday afternoons."

"Petal and I will wash up, tell her. There's a cold chicken and salad in the safe, if you feel peckish. Are you coming back here for lunch, Phillip?"

"I can't, I didn't ask Father's permission before he went out on his bike, Aunty Flo. Thanks all the same. Oh, by the way, I forgot to tell you that Mother sent you her love, and hoped you would soon be better."

"Why did she say that, when I'm not ill, Phillip?"

"Oh, I think she thought you might be a bit ill in bed."

"But how does she know that I am in bed, Phillip?"

"Ha ha ha!" roared Uncle Charley. "Hetty obviously has the Turney second-sight, based on past experience!"

"You think you're very funny, don't you?" called down Aunt Flo. "Well, let me tell you this, you're not half so funny as you look, as you'll find out one of these days, my boy!" She sounded angry, as if a row were coming.

At this point Uncle Joey, the peace-maker as Uncle Hugh called him, attempted to calm things down by a story. It was about Crippen, who had been caught with Miss Le Neve on arrival in America by wireless telegraphy, the first murderer so to be caught. There were current innumerable stories on the subject of Dr. Crippen and the girl he had run away with after he had cut up his wife with a carving knife and hidden the sections in concrete, under a cellar of his London house. Phillip did not think much of the stories; he was secretly rather sorry for anyone, even a murderer, being caught, even if . . . he flinched from thinking further.

Uncle Joey, with several haw-haws, began his story.

"A feller went into a theatre late, and made a noise getting to his seat. He was knocked over by someone unlacing his tight boots, haw-haw! Getting up, he went on down the aisle to his row, near the front, on tip-toe. He went so slowly and quietly that the hero looked over the footlights and hissed, 'Who are you, Crippen?' 'No, I'm creepin',' the fellow explained. Haw-haw! Go on, Phillip, laugh!"

"I don't think it's funny, that's all," replied Phillip. "Come on, Tommy, let's go for a walk on the Hillies."

"Ee-aw, donkey boy!" cried Ralph. "Mind you don't grow up like your old man!"

"It's just like Ralph's cheek, apeing a man, to call Uncle Charley by his Christian name," remarked Phillip, as he and Tommy walked down the orchard path, through sooted trees gnarled with canker, which rose forlornly out of rank grass growing from acidulated yellow clay. All but twenty acres of the farm were now built upon; great boards advertised the weedy fields as Desirable Building Sites. Phillip, who had known these fields in former years, felt vaguely disturbed at the change. On the other side of the lane was the cemetery, looking whiter with marble tombstones every time he passed that way.

"Dad doesn't mind," said Tommy. "I call him Charley sometimes, so does Pet."

"Good lord, I wouldn't dare to do that to my Father," replied Phillip. "What was cousin Ralph talking about so earnestly with Uncle Charley?"

"He wants Dad to take up agencies for motorbikes, and give him a job when we return to South Africa."

"Motorbikes, how spiffing! Better'n push bikes, any old day!"

"That's what Dad said, when he sold the import business for

bikes. He says motorbikes will oust them in a few years. But Schleigermann stole a march on him, and got the agency for the best German and British motorbikes. Now Dad wants to get the Belgian agency, for F N's. Where're we going, on the Hill?"

People were coming out of church. Phillip looked at Tommy critically. He wore his weekday clothes. His black stockings were rolled down to his knees, his blue serge knickerbockers were untidy, and he wore only a blue jersey, with no coat. Obsessed with the Sunday idea of correctitude in connection with Helena Rolls, Phillip made an excuse to say goodbye to Tommy.

"I've just remembered I have to see somebody, Tommy." As a concession he added, "Will you take Timmy Rat home for me, and put him in his box? Latch the lid, won't you, for Gran'-pa's cat sometimes sneaks in, the brute. Well, au revoir, I'll see you soon," and with anxious heart he proceeded alone, upon his hopeless quest for beauty in one face in the Sunday parade.

The next morning the Rev. E. H. P. Mundy, M.A. came free-wheeling down the gully, front wheel shaky on the loose pebbles, one hand holding the brim of his black straw hat, a smile on his ruddy face. Slowing up at the green iron gates, he turned left, gave his handlebars a jerk at the kerbstone, and so continued his ride upon the pavement. There were, of course, rules against wheeled traffic on all pavements—the older people still spoke of them as sidewalks—but Mr. Mundy always declared that, as he had cycled there before they were made, he had an *a priori* right of way. Furthermore, why should he be delayed, in visiting his flock (most of them, he thought privately, were sheep, with a few honest goats here and there) by punctures? Was the work of the Almighty to be mocked by hissing air? Certainly not! So Mr. Mundy rode awheel on paving, flag-stone, cinder path and ballast walk, wherever the roads beside them were flinty. Policemen did not appear to see him.

Phillip saw Mr. Mundy leaving his bike outside the Rolls' house. He waited in his gateway, concealed by the privet hedge. He heard Mr. Mundy come out, Mrs. Rolls talking in her usual happy way, laughing as much as Mr. Mundy. Next Mr. Mundy entered the Pye gate, and ran up the hearth-stoned steps. From there he came to Phillip's house—that boy meanwhile having disappeared over the brick wall of the porch, to hide in Mr. Bigge's passage below. What was Mr. Mundy after?

When the jovial figure had gone, Phillip climbed back, and sought information from his mother. Mr. Mundy had come to ask her to help in the forthcoming Garden Party in the vicarage, It was to raise money for the Memorial Fund of the late King, in the fourth week of August.

"I told Mr. Mundy, dear, that unfortunately we were going to our country cousins in the latter half of August, but we would be back in time to take tickets."

"For me, too?" asked Phillip. When his mother said yes, if he liked, at once apprehensive excitement overcame him. The Rolls would be there!

Phillip knew vaguely that some people did not approve of Mr. Mundy, because he had married his secretary after his old wife's death. The new Mrs. Mundy did not come calling, like the old one, Mother had said. Mrs. Rolls, he understood, was among those who did not entirely approve of Mr. Mundy's marriage.

Desmond had gone away to Felixstowe for his holiday, so Phillip was alone again. Tommy was not much good for a friend. What could he do with himself, now that nesting for the year was over? The Backfield was rather dull, after the real country places. However, there were his spiders to visit. He had a number of them in the garden, his favourite being a strange black one, something like an ordinary garden spider, but much more secret and shy.

Sometimes in the day time the big brown white-spotted garden spiders sat or hung in the centre of their webs; but the black spider never left its hiding place by day. It crouched there unmoving, its rather dented-looking body close against its corner in the creosoted boards of the back fence. Only once at night had he seen it in the centre of its web; and when he gave it a fly he had been keeping in a wooden Beecham's Pill box, the spider dropped down at once on a line and vanished. It never seemed to feed; its web was never broken; and the gnats that got tangled there were never picked off, as the brown spiders sometimes did with their minute flies, stopping a few moments only to masticate them in their bull-horn jaws, turning them into liquid almost immediately, wings and all.

Phillip went into the kitchen, to catch flies. He was expert in this. One sweep of his right hand, and the fly, however swift, was held. It was a moment's work to remove it with his left finger and thumb. He could sweep up half a dozen flies, one after another, and get them all safely into the pill box. One by one they were jerked into the geometrical patterns, to hang in the threads dotted with gum, while he watched, fascinated.

Down ran the brown spider on its thick rope to the centre. There it waited a moment, while the spoke of the radial web nearest to the buzzing or struggling fly carried the vibrations to its legs. Down fell the spider, making a half outward turn as it hung with its forelegs, and with its hindlegs it pulled from its spinnerets thick skeins of white-blue silk; and turning the fly over and over, it bound it up like a mummy. Then came the intense moment. Peering with wide eyes, Phillip saw its bull-horn jaws open, its battery of eyes glinting tinily as the horns were thrust in, and a small gum-like drop would come out of the enwound fly. If it were a house-fly's head that was pierced, it would show bright red blood. Ooh! Phillip was not sure whether he really liked spiders, or not.

Then up went the spider. If it was hungry it would carry the bundle on its two hind legs, which were clawed. Up the rope it went, rapidly, then turning round in its silken arbour, it would adjust itself, get a firm hang with its back legs, then draw up the package, and open its pursey mouth to start rasping and sucking. Soon the fly would be shrunken and moist-black, as the spider turned it over and then over again, to try other tasty places, just as Uncle Charley did with his cigar as he smoked it—far too fast, said Gran'pa.

"Dammit it all, guv'nor," Uncle Charley had said, "Can't I smoke how I want to? By God, sir, I'm not a child any more to be brow-beaten." Then Grannie had said something about using God's name in vain before the children, and Uncle Charley had walked out of the room, laughing. After that they had moved to Joy Farm.

There was one spider which had had so many flies that it did not come down to any further ones put in its web. It was an old web, left with its gaps for several days. In addition to the house-flies, this particular spider had gorged itself on a butterfly, a grasshopper, several daddy-longlegs, and a bee; now it sulked in its arbour above its ruined web. He supposed it was making more silk for itself, while digesting its enormous catch; anyway, it was not interested in any more house-flies. So he tried with a grass, twisting it between finger and thumb, usually an unfailing attraction; still it did not move. He prodded it out of its eyrie, and as it dropped, on many strands almost as thick as sinew, he caught the sinew, and as the spider was climbing up, swung it lightly into another web.

Seeing its danger, the spider dropped again; once more he swung it on its line, and put it back in the web. A battle began, legs and horns inaudibly clashing: then both spiders dropped away at the same time. They were equally matched. Cowards, said Phillip, and holding one in each closed hand, while shaking them lest he get bitten, he bore them away to another kind of web in the virginian creeper which covered the fence between the Bigges and his own garden.

Here lived the Black Widow. Her web was like a carpet, with curled edges strengthened by many strands gummed to the stems of creeper above. At the fence end it narrowed into a tunnel, and down the tunnel stood the Black Widow, small of body but with long legs looking prickly with short savage hairs. The Black Widow could run at a great pace, forwards and back again. Her speciality was in dragging her prey into the tunnel, so rapidly and strongly that the tearing of threads could be heard, as they caught in the single stout claws at the end of each leg. This monster had eyes that glittered like a cluster of diamonds, her horned jaws were prolonged, she stood over the victim after biting it, until it died and then she took it back to the very end of the tunnel, where wings of flies and a clutter of legs and shell-like husks told of past feasts.

Phillip dropped one of the fat short-legged garden spiders in the web. The Black Widow rushed out, to be met by the fat brown garden spider on her back, with rather feebly open jaws.

Without pause, the Black Widow rushed back. Both cowards, thought Phillip, while relieved that the helpless fat spider had not been bitten. He allowed it to climb away, and set the second one on the creeper. He did not like any spiders who were fat and big; they were the females, and they ate their tiny, frail husbands.

What was wanted for the Black Widow was a wasp.

There were some in Gran'pa's house, in the glass trap standing on the kitchen sill. There was some beer in the lower rim of the trap; wasps flew to the open narrow top, attracted by the smell, crawled down inside the glass funnel, which widened at the bottom, and fell into the beer. There were hundreds of them sometimes in the trap, some swimming, others feebly kicking, nearly drowned; or acting as rafts to the newly-wet and struggling, above the beer-logged corpses on the bottom.

What was needed was a fresh one, to be trapped in a wine-glass, covered with a piece of cardboard, and taken to the web. That would be a proper fight, like Jack Johnson, the heavy-weight champion of the world, against a tiger. Wasp v. Black Widow. If the Widow funked again, he would put her in a garden-spider's web, where she would not be able to run away, but have to fight it out. It was very cruel, of course, and he knew he was mean to torture them like that; but spiders were cruel, and it was tit for tat.

Taking a wine-glass from Gran'pa's mahogany side-board, no one being about, Phillip got a wasp. He jerked it into the Widow's web. It buzzed angrily; the Widow rushed out to see what it was. The danger colours, as Father called them, black and yellow, made her rush back again. The wasp began to bite its way out of the web, and was crawling away, tearing threads as it did so, when the Widow ran out again, and seizing it, pulled it back by a wing towards the tunnel. Phillip felt an uneasy, fascinating, guilty feeling as he saw what he had done, for the wasp seemed not to have a chance: he knew that the Widow's poison would soon travel along the nerves of the wing. Should he smash them all up together? Then his feelings gave way to relief, as the wasp, bending backwards from its waist as thin as a bit of black cotton, stabbed the Black Widow in the thorax. Literally punctured, she seemed to shrink, while the wasp, already stricken, began to tremble, its movements to slacken. It was, at any rate, a satisfactory ending; and telling himself that in future he would not interfere in what Father called the Balance of Nature, Phillip went away. It was really unkind to hurt poor little insects, who were all afraid of one another. What a beastly little bully he was!

"Please God, forgive me," he thought, a little insincerely.

In this partly chastened mood he went indoors for his magazine, and a cushion, meaning to climb the elm and sit on his favourite branch, half way up, hidden by leaves, and read *The Field.*

It was a hot day, an open blue sky, and there was no better place to spend the morning. He had rigged up a string and pulley on the trunk, and by this means could haul up a basket containing a bottle of lemonade, a slice of cake, and anything else Mother gave him for his eleven o'clock lunch. It saved him getting down, and helped to preserve the pleasant feeling of being a tree-dweller.

Before opening his grimy-edged magazine—nevertheless much less finger-and-thumbed than in winter—he read again a letter he had received by post that morning from Cranmer. The letter was the more welcome, as Cranmer worked in the tanning yard belonging to the firm of which Mrs. Rolls' father, Mr. Gould, was one of the directors.

The letter asked how he was getting on, and if he was going to the seaside soon, and then told about Cranmer's work. He was a drayman's boy, and they had to get the skins from the shambles in Deptford, where bullocks were slaughtered for the market. Cranmer said he got some of the ears for stewing, as perks. Which was a bit of orl rite. Carramba, what a way to spell!

Cranmer was in the pink, he assured Phillip, as he hoped he was too. He longed to meet his old chum again. Wot-o the Bloodhounds. Cranmer spelt that word right.

Phillip examined the letter critically, each stroke of the pen, each shaky word. It was scrawled on a page torn from a penny exercise book. The paper smelt of leather. The ink, on what seemed to have been a very rusty nib, judging by the digs and splutters here and there, made Phillip think of a pond filled with old boots, dead cats, and decaying vegetation. It was a faint and watery mud-colour, with dried grit in some of the strokes. Phillip sniffed again. The ink smelt faintly of leather, or tanning—the same smell that came in the railway carriage on the way to London Bridge.

Phillip's fancy about the muddy pond had some basis in fact: the liquid had indeed come out of a hole, after being mixed, for some long period, with organic matter, to wit, dead flies and fag-ends which had found their way into the public ink-well in one of His Britannic Majesty's post offices in Bermondsey.

In a way, too, Phillip thought that the letter seemed like Mr. Gould himself, although he had never spoken to him; but he had seen him once outside Turret House: a man in a long grey-green coat, muffler round neck; big grey hat cleft on top, with a large upcurled brim bound with white-grey ribbon; a drooping grey moustache; leathery sort of yellow-grey face. Phillip had never been in a tan yard; but somehow Mr. Gould's appearance must be due to the fact that most of his life had been spent in yellow fog and the yellow-brown smell of the Bermondsey tan yards which came into the train to London Bridge. Apart from all that, Mr. Gould was a very important man, high-up, as he was the Churchwarden of St. Simon's church.

Phillip, reclining on a cushion in the elm, green leaves and specks of sunshine rustling and burnishing around him, felt himself to be very happy, in the very buoyancy of summer. He was reading about the golden eagle in Scotland when through the open french windows came the sound of a piano. Then he heard Petal's voice. She came to practise every morning. Some of her songs were lovely, particularly *Solvieg's Song*, which he had never heard before she sang it. Mavis and Doris sang things like *When you come down the Vale, Lad, there's music in the air, Little Grey Home in the West*, and other soppy songs like them. Petal's songs were rather sad, and faraway, yet somehow very clear.

Petal was singing *Now Sleeps the Crimson Petal*. The words of that song were absolutely beautiful. Phillip, after hearing Petal sing them for the first time, had sought them in his mother's book of Tennyson's poems, which had a scorched back.

> *Now slides the silent meteor on, and leaves*
> *A shining furrow, as thy thoughts in me!*

words which brought secret tears to his eyes, as he thought of the night-sky, and falling stars, which really were meteors, raining down in their last fire from ancient broken worlds. A meteor was silent, and it did *slide*. In winter, when they were to be seen most, the sky was blue-black, looking hard, a sort of blue-black ice in which little shining gems were stuck. He thought many things like that, but always he must keep his thoughts to himself, else others would scoff. When Mavis had returned from the Ursulines convent at Thildonck, where Mother had been as a girl, she had brought back a hammered silver sandal-wood box, shaped like a chapel, as a present for Mother. He had been surprised to learn she had made it; and then had told her about his nests that spring, and how sad they looked when the young birds had flown away, and the lanes and coverts were all empty. Mavis had said he was putting it on, then seeing a tear in his eye, she had pointed at it, as she always had done since he could remember, and laughed, making him furious with rage, and swearing that he would never again try and tell her anything.

Petal was different from Mavis. Although Petal was the same age, she was like someone grown up, yet decent, as grown-ups were not, as a rule. Mr. Newman was decent; so was Uncle Hugh, when he was not in a sneering mood. Petal played the piano almost as well as one of the records of Father's gramophone. She did not hit wrong notes and then laugh, like Mavis did, or Doris did—only Doris did not laugh, she merely went back and tried again, being a plodder on the piano, as Amelia Bigge next door, L.R.A.M., who taught her, said.

Doris on the piano is a plodder
Like a cow upon a meadow eating fodder.

Now folds the lily all her sweetness up,
And slips into the bosom of the lake.

It was true, too, for water-lilies in the Lake Woods belonging to the Dowager Countess did fold themselves up at evening, and slowly go down under water. The Lake Woods were enclosed in a high barb wire fence, with a tall locked iron gate at either end, set in the midst of the forest; but he and Desmond had crawled underneath the lowest strand, and explored the lakes. They had had to hide, when they saw the bailiff walking above the rhododendrons at the side. There were four lakes, the largest and deepest being at the top. On one bank of this was a decaying boathouse. The other three lakes lay below it, one feeding the other along little stone channels nearly covered with ferns and mosses. The lakes were very secret, Phillip had not mentioned them, even in code, in his diary.

So fold thyself, my dearest, thou, and slip
Into my bosom, and be lost—be lost—in me!

As Petal's voice ended Phillip swung down from the elm, using his hands only, branch under branch, to strengthen his muscles and to practise for any emergency when he was climbing trees. Then tip-toeing through the house, he crept into the front room, and stood still on the brown-and-yellow patterned carpet. Petal, her black hair tied with the red bow at her neck, and brushed straight down her back, was sitting quite still at the piano.

"Hullo," he said.

Petal looked round swiftly, and gave him a smile of her eyes, which were dark like her hair.

"I hoped you would come, I saw you up the tree," she said in a clear level voice. "Will you sing one of your songs, if I play the accompaniment, Phillip?"

The voice and the smile disturbed him. Though she was his cousin, she was also mysterious. He was a little awkward, being wary. He did not know that her feelings were making him feel as he did. Mother had said that girls grew up quicker in hot climates, that was why Petal, although three months younger than Mavis, looked much older.

"Oh, I can't sing, I'm no good at it. They wouldn't even have me in St. Mary's choir when I tried! I can't read music, either. I am a failure, you know."

"You have a natural ear, and your voice is very sweet, Phillip."

He shrugged his shoulders. "It's throaty. It's going to break, I think, any moment now."

"Are you sure? It's a pure treble. But perhaps you want it to break?"

"Well, sort of." He went pink, and lowered his gaze.

"Then you ought to sing while you can. Anyway, I like it as it is. Perhaps you don't practise enough?"

"Why should I? I tell you, my voice is no good. Please sing one of your green songs."

Petal laughed lightly. "My green songs? Oh, you mean *Grieg*."

Phillip frowned. Perceiving that she had embarrassed him, she said, "I think that a very good description, you know. They *are* green songs! Of course they are! Grieg loved the country, particularly the mountains, which are green on the slopes all the year. They are not parched, as in Cape Province. Music is coloured, you know. Don't you feel that some sounds are brown, others red, or blue, or green?"

"Why yes, do you feel like that, too? I thought I was silly, to think that!"

Sympathy lit their faces. A friendship was made.

"Will you practise singing, if I play for you every morning?"

"Well, I shan't be here much longer, you know. We are going away to Beau Brickhill the day after tomorrow. Do you know Polly and Percy?"

"No."

"Well, they are your cousins too. Why don't you come with us? They have a piano. I sing 'The Maiden of the Fleur-de-Lys', a duet, with Percy."

"Is Polly nice?"

"She's all right."

"Only all right?"

"I dunno. Why do you ask?"

"I thought you were supposed to be sweet on her."

"Me?"

"Yes. Do you kiss her?"

"No, of *course* not!"

Phillip became very shy. He felt drawn to Petal; and went away. It was a spidery feeling somehow.

Tommy arrived on his new bicycle. After inspection of this road racer, which had low, dropped handlebars, Phillip and he went for a ride. Phillip intended to go only so far as Fordesmill; but when they got there he saw some soldiers in khaki, sitting on horses which drew, among baggage waggons, some wheeled green field guns. He learned that it was a battery of the Royal Field Artillery from Woolwich, going by road to camp.

Free in the brilliant August sunshine, the boys followed beside the column for a while, then sped on ahead, lured by the thought of the reaper-and-binder in the harvest fields, of rabbits running out of the corn being cut and stooked. Away, away, into the everlasting summer day! Spokes faintly flashing as they hummed over tarred roads, seeking the white dust of new horizons!

The mirrored coolness and quiet of the Fish Ponds drew Phillip down to the sandy water edge. Here, under the burning blue heat of the sky, lay the unmoving wraiths of the pines, joined base to base with the actual trees rising upon the sloping banks. No sound came from their dark green crowns, except the thin high notes of the goldcrests seeking, with beaks scarcely thicker than pine-needles, the tiniest gossamer spiders who had drifted there with the drying of the morning dew.

"Tommy, look!"

Phillip pointed to the sight of hundreds of fish, with pale red fins, lying just under the surface at the far end, where white posts and rails guarded the sandy lane. And among the rudd were larger fish, floating brown-gold with scales as big as beech-leaves, basking in the sun, their back fins and curling tails glistening above the surface.

"Carp! The foxes of the water! And my God, there's the King Carp, the Fox of All!"

Among them lay a fish quite three feet in length. It was said to be one which no angler could catch, so cunning that it blew water from its mouth to wash bait off hooks, including green broad bean and small boiled potato. Never did float of quill or cork glide away gently, to slide under aslant and disappear, when the King Carp was feeding.

"They're all basking in the sun!"

Phillip remembered an article in *The Field*, which recommended a fine line to be cast among surface carp, a line fragile as horse-hair, lightly greased to float, to lie across water-lily leaves and dangle, just over one curled edge, a thin red worm well-scoured. Phillip knew where such worms were to be found in the Back-field, in the moss attached to tindery railway sleepers, which lay half-buried, an old track for carts to the ballast heap.

Afire with piscatorial ambition, the boys sped back the way they had come. Phillip's idea was to borrow Father's fly-rod, stored in the loft over the bathroom, and some of his tackle hidden in the japanned uniform trunk laid on the joists of that secret and forbidden place. Followed by Tommy, down the slope to Shooting Common he tore, past the Falcon Inn where was a tame magpie, the wind thrumming in his ears. Without pause they reached the market town, now noisy with horses and guns, and soldiers with bandoliers, puttees rolled the opposite way to those of the marching men, and spurs upon their heels. Onwards through the town, passing the yellow motorbuses, rivals to the red Thomas Tilling buses, with petrol-electric system. The new buses never broke down climbing the hill from Cutler's Pond, and could be beaten only by the hardest thrusting upon rat-trap pedals. There were other omnibuses as well, the Generals, which raced the others, often with steam shooting in geysers from their radiator caps. Sometimes by hanging on to the rail at the back it was possible to be towed on the flat, but you had to do it when the conductor was on top, collecting fares. It was tricky, too, for if the bus swerved suddenly, or ran too close to the raised grassy bank on the left of the road, you might easily come a cropper.

Phillip and Tommy stopped at the wooden shop below Cutler's

Pond, for ginger pop and broken biscuits. Phillip explained to Tommy, outside, that it was the dearest little shop in the world. It was part of a minute weather-boarded cot, standing on the edge of the Randisbourne brook, beside the road. Father liked the shop, too; he used to go there to see the dame, as he called her, before he was married, on his Starley Rover. There were jars of sweets on the counter, satin cushions or pralines, toffee-apples, Pontefract cakes of licorice, gelatine discs which quenched thirst, black aniseed balls which soon turned brown when sucked, and then white when you were half through—and in the very middle, when the ball was only so big as a Carter's Little Liver Pill, was a caraway seed, curved like a tiny wooden crescent moon. There were hundreds-and-thousands, millions of red, white, and blue dots that were as small as dust-shot used for snipe.

Did Tommy know how dust shot was made? He would never guess. Well, dust-shot was made by dropping a ladle of molten lead from a great height into a water tank. The lead broke into drops of different sizes as it fell, and when the tank was drained, pellets lay there. They were sifted, and the tiniest sold as dust shot, to scare birds in fruit orchards, and also for snipe, which zigzagged as they flew up, and "so would require a wide pattern of shot to encompass them." Father said there used to be snipe in the meadows beside the Randisbourne; but building was creeping up from London, and the snipe had all gone.

"Even in this old-world place, you see, a new red-brick building is going up. Let's see what the notice board says."

> The new and improved building of Messrs. Growley, Hopkins & Co.'s Entire will be opened to the Public in the Year of Coronation of His Most Gracious Britannic Majesty King George V.

"'New and improved' building! I like that! A gin palace, that's all it will be, Father said. Now Tommy, please don't laugh at the old woman in the shop, she is very very old, remember, and a friend of my Father's."

Phillip opened the door by the brass latch. Immediately a string, knotted many places where it had broken, was pulled down on a pulley hanging from the low ceiling, and a weight attached to the other end dropped on a brass shell-case from the Boer War, to give notice of a caller. As far back as he could remember the old woman had always been sitting behind the counter when he had opened the door, so the gong-like warning seemed a bit unnecessary.

"Good morning," said Phillip, raising his cap. "I hope you are in the best of health. I see they are building next door to you. A pity the old place is changing so. I expect they'll be cutting down all the trees next, which will be another pity. Two bottles of ginger pop, please, and a ha'poth of broken biscuits for two."

Tommy had a threepenny bit, which he called a tickey. Tommy was standing treat.

"Aye," said the old woman. "You med not see I no more soon, dear. 'Tis all comin' down hereabouts. They give I notice, 'tis the ground landlord a-doin' of it."

She had always worn the same flat and shapeless straw hat, over a face of brown wrinkled skin, with inflamed and dropped lower eyelids. Her hands were thin like claws, and although her voice croaked, she was always very kind to every child, calling them 'dear'. Father said her tiny cot probably stood beside the stream when highwaymen fled past after robbing people on Blackheath. It was of board, painted originally cream, and the pantiles of the sloping roof were grey and yellow with lichens.

They drank the ginger beer quickly, unable to make it last. The biscuits would last all the afternoon. Saying good-bye, they cycled on slowly home.

Phillip had not felt so serious as he had pretended about change; he had spoken like that to impress Tommy, an echo of his father. All the same, the idea remained; and on the way back, he was a little disturbed to see that it was actually true. The trees along the road *were* being cut down! Men with axes were cutting round the bases of some, while others were sawing with long whippy jagged two-handed saws. The boys watched the first elm falling. The road was going to be widened, drains were to be laid, electric trams were to run all the way to Cutler's Pond! Also, said the foreman to whom they spoke, a big new Tilling's Omnibus depot was to be built in one of the fields. And down by Fordesmill, a new theatre was being built, bigger than any other, to be called the Hippodrome.

Phillip said goodbye to Tommy at the junction of Randiswell Lane and Charlotte Road, and hurried up the hill to tell the news to his mother. As soon as he got home he saw at once that something serious had happened. Mavis and Doris, with Petal and Kimberley, were sitting very quietly together in the front room. Petal and Kimberley looked as though they had been crying.

"What's up? Where's Mother?"

"She's next door, Phillip, with Grannie. Something awful's happened."

"What? Don't sit there staring! Tell me!"

"Grannie's been taken ill. The doctor has just gone, and is coming back this afternoon."

"Good Lord. She promised me two shillings for my holiday money, only yesterday!"

"You would think only of yourself at a moment like this, wouldn't you?"

"Is she very ill, then?"

"Yes, she is. She's had a stroke, so there!"

"Well, there's no need to be nasty about it. I can't help it."

"Oh go away, go away, do! She may die, poor Grannie," wept Mavis.

Phillip was silenced. Slowly he realised what had happened. The others began to cry again. He wondered what to say. Their crying made him feel nothing. "I'm going to see for myself."

"But you mustn't, Phil, Mother said so, she asked me to tell you especially. Gran'pa is very very worried. Would you like your dinner now? It's laid in the sitting room."

"What is it? Oh, cold mutton again."

"The potatoes are in the pot, on the gas. Mrs. Feeney's here, having her lunch in the kitchen. She'll give you yours."

Mavis gave him a look, meaning that she wanted to speak to him outside. In the sitting room, behind the shut door, she told Phillip what had led up to the stroke. Aunt Flo had tried to kill herself. That was the beginning of it all.

"Kill herself? Good Lord! Whatever for?"

"Well, it started with a quarrel about Kimberley with Uncle Charley."

"But why? What has Kimberley got to do with it?"

"Don't you know? It's awful!"

"What's awful? Come on, tell me, quick!"

"I thought you knew! Uncle Charley is his father!"

"But how can he be, when Kimberley is black all over? He'd be a half-caste if he were."

"Well, you see, first sons always take after their mother. You do, you're a Turney, like Mum."

"I'm not a Turney! I'm a Maddison! Anyhow, Tommy is Uncle Charley's first son."

"Yes, and he takes after Aunt Flo's people, who are Dutch."

"That's why he stole my eggs, then. But look, Mavis, Kimberley doesn't take after either of them. I don't believe it, you're making it up!"

"I'm not, honestly. I heard Aunt Flo say so. It was after that she tried to commit suicide."

"It all seems double Dutch to me."

"Well, let me explain, and don't always interrupt. First there was a row between Aunt Flo and Uncle Charley in Gran'pa's house. It was over Kimberley. Have you got that? Aunt Flo said his mother was a black harlot. Then she ran out, crying. Before this, before the quarrel, she said to Mum that she wanted to get some spirits of salt to clean a straw hat with. Well, she went to Atkinson's the chemist, and returning over the Hill by herself, she suddenly screamed and tried to swallow the powder. Mr. Mundy saw her, and took her to Dr. Cave-Browne's house. He gave her an antidote, then used the stomach pump. Mr. Newman had already seen her on the Hill, and brought the news to Gran'pa and Uncle Charley. Now do you believe me?"

"Good Lord!"

"When Mr. Newman had gone," went on Mavis, "Uncle and Gran'pa had a frightful quarrel, after Uncle Charley had said to him, 'I see, my dear Father, that you still retain the habit of trying to suppress your children's opinions, regardless of their age.'

"Oh Phillip, it was terrible to hear them, shouting at one another. 'Get out of my sight, get out of my sight this instant, d'ye hear?' shouted Gran'pa. 'You've been nothing but a grief to me and your Mother all your life! And don't you dare to come back this time, d'ye hear what I'm saying? I disown you! You're no son of mine!' Gran'pa was terribly red in the face, all his veins swelled up. When Uncle Charley went, saying Gran'pa was a devil, Grannie cried a lot. Then, as Gran'pa was shouting at her she fell out of her chair. Isn't it awful, Phillip?"

Mavis looked tragically at Phillip, who remained calm.

"Don't you care, Phillip? There's a nurse with Grannie now, in her bedroom! She may die, oh, poor Gran, poor kind darling Gran!"

"I wonder what caused it all," remarked Phillip.

"I've just told you! Don't you understand?"

Phillip went to see Mrs. Feeney in the kitchen, where she was eating bread and cheese, her usual quart bottle of porter on the table beside her. It was the charwoman's whole day at their house.

"I shouldn't go in next door if I were you, Master Phil. I'll mash the potatoes for you, and bring them down. Now be a good boy, Master Phil, and do what your Mother asked of you. Keep away, there's enough people to worry her already. Be a good boy, and do as she asked, Master Phil."

"I'll be back in half a mo', really, Mrs. Feeney. I just want to tell Mother something."

He was not going to miss anything if he could help it. He went next door, and finding the kitchen empty, tiptoed to the hall, and listened.

There was the sound of voices upstairs. He went, silently in his plimsolls, to the half-open front room door, and peeped round. Gran'pa sat in a chair, staring straight ahead. There was a swelled vein beside his forehead. He could hear him breathing. Unobserved, Phillip withdrew his head.

Next, he crept down to Uncle Hugh's room. Uncle Hugh was sitting on his bed, supported by his hands flat on the counterpane, his head held down, staring at the carpet. He too was breathing harshly. Phillip tip-toed back.

After hesitation, he went softly up the stairs. He stood in the space of the open door of Gran'pa's room, the front one. Grannie was in the next room. Her door was half open. He hesitated, not liking to look round the door.

He went into Gran'pa's room, feeling the need for space and movement. There was an open roll-top desk there, full of useful things, like pocket diaries which the Firm sent to customers at Christmas, bundles of pencils and boxes of nibs with the firm's name stamped on them, indiarubbers, envelopes, all colours of blotting paper; there were Gran'pa's seals, in one small drawer, several watches in another, small spirit flasks, gold cuff-links and studs, and many other interesting nicknacks.

He recalled the time when he had stolen a number of these articles, and Father had found him with them, and caned him. Why had he stolen them, when he had not really wanted them? Was he really a throw-back? What was a throwback? A sort of Darwin monkey?

He decided he would not help himself to anything in the room this time. Like Tommy had, helping himself to his bird's eggs, the rotter. But if anyone found him there, they would be sure to suspect him. What ought he to do? Slip away over the balcony?

There were subdued voices in Grannie's room. What was happening? He moved to the door again. Then he heard a cry, and hid behind the door, pressing back against Gran'pa's bed. Mother ran out—he had never seen her run before—he saw her eyes were shut—her face puckered—her grey hair flying at the temples. She cried out in a low voice, "Oh Hugh, she is gone, she is gone!" and he thought she would fall as she went down the stairs.

Phillip was awed. Going to the other door, he looked round. Grannie's head lay sideways on the pillow, her mouth slightly open. The nurse was trying to lift her shoulders, as though she might otherwise fall sideways out of bed. She turned and saw him.

"Are you Mrs. Maddison's little boy?"

"Yes. Is Grannie dead?"

"Yes, dear, she was taken very suddenly, and so has been spared all pain, which is a mercy. I'll just lay her straight, and put pennies on her eyes, and then I'll leave her, dear. You ought to go to your Mother now. She will need you."

Phillip went slowly downstairs. Grannie was dead. It was a strange feeling, as though the house was now slightly altered, somehow. At the bottom of the stairs he stopped, and moved back against the wall, for Uncle Hugh was coming with his sticks up the passage. He struggled up the three stairs, his knees bent at the top, like the Black Widow's. Shaking a lot, slowly he pushed himself upright; then placing the sticks, one on either side again, he walked to the front room, his boots clopping on the carpet.

Phillip was now four steps up from the bottom of the staircase, sitting down on a stair, to keep hidden. He did not want Uncle to think he had been spying.

Uncle Hugh went into the front room. Phillip did not move.

Uncle Hugh stood just inside the doorway. With shaking hand he lifted up a stick and said, staring in Gran'pa's direction, in a harsh and trembling voice, "You killed my Mother!"

"Calm yourself, Hughie, sit down my boy," mumbled Gran'pa thickly. "This is no time to talk like that."

Uncle Hugh kept the stick pointing at Gran'pa. Uncle Hugh was breathing more harshly than before. His nostrils were wide open.

He said again, "You killed my Mother, with your brutal ways! You injured her head when you knocked her down, when you turned out Charley! She was never again the same woman afterwards!"

Gran'pa said nothing. Phillip could hear him breathing as harshly as Uncle Hugh.

Then Uncle Hugh fell sideways, with a clatter of sticks and boots on the floor. As he sprawled there, crying, Phillip turned and ran swiftly back to the kitchen, and then into his own house, where Mrs. Feeney was holding Mother in her arms. Mother was crying almost silently, and at the sight of her puckered face Phillip cried too, everything that he had always pretended to be, broken down, for the moment.

Part Four

WONDERFUL TO BE ALIVE

Chapter 25

SUMMER HEATS

HETTY thought it would be a good idea to repay some of the hospitality the children had received in the past by giving a little party to their friends in the country. Richard did not care about having parties in the house; besides, Grannie had not long been buried. It would be best to have the picnic away somewhere. Where should they go? To the Crystal Palace? To Reynard's Common, by train?

It was a hot summer, following the Coronation of King George V and Queen Mary. Later on, Hetty and the children were going to Whitstable in Kent, for a fortnight at the seaside. Meanwhile, where should they have the picnic? Mamma, she thought, would be the first to approve of such a thing, for the sake of the little ones, now that such a thing was made possible by the money Mamma had left her.

The publican of the Randiswell had a painted waggonette, and catered for parties, Mrs. Feeney told her. "The horses are quite safe, ma'am, and I should think unlikely to run away, being more than twenty years old."

In case there was any doubt, Mrs. Feeney added, the vicar of St. Mary's always hired the waggonette, for the Mothers' Meeting outing every year, as well as for the choir treat. Greenwich Park was a favourite place, she said. "Well, I mustn't stand here, mum, or I'll never get my work done!" and Mrs. Feeney hurried away with pail, swab, and lump of hearth-stone.

Hetty made enquiries, and learned that the waggonette, to hold twenty, would cost a sovereign to Greenwich Park and back. This sum, without Mamma's little legacy, would have been impossible, for of the seventy shillings a week Dickie gave her for housekeeping and all the clothes and incidental expenses of the children and herself, she seldom had been able to save more than a shilling a week—and what she had managed to save in any year had gone in pocket money and extras for the summer holiday.

Now, however, Mamma's money would enable her to be what she had always wanted to be—independent of Dickie, as regards money for the children's holidays. He was so very good, almost at times too good, in seldom spending anything on himself. Hetty cherished the idea of buying him a rifle of his own, which she could get, through the Firm, at trade price. The only thing that worried her was how could she find out what was the right kind of rifle? Could she approach the Secretary of the Rifle Club, and seek his advice? Would it be etiquette to ask him to keep her request as a confidence? For she must never for a moment put Dickie in a false light, among the other men. But supposing that part of the matter to be all right, and she bought the rifle, would Dickie perhaps feel hurt that she had gone to someone else for information? And in any case, would it, or could it, make him feel small that she, a woman, albeit his wife, had interfered in matters appertaining to a man's sphere?

One thing about the rifle Hetty was determined to observe: on no account would she mention the matter to Phillip. There had been enough trouble in the past with firearms, in his connection!

Meanwhile, that could wait. The picnic was the thing.

She outlined the proposed picnic to the little ones, as she still thought of them, after breakfast one morning.

"Now dears, the waggonette can take only twenty, so we must decide beforehand who of your friends, or our friends rather, you would like to invite. First, I think we must ask those who were so kind as to ask you all to their parties last Christmas, don't you? Very well then, first, I think we should ask the Pyes."

"Oh lord, not old Pye!" cried Phillip.

"No dear, of course not, naturally. But I think it only polite to ask Mrs. Pye and her two children, dear. After all, they did invite you twice to see their magic lantern, didn't they?"

"Yes, and the same slides on both occasions. *And* dried-up sandwiches, into the bargain." But, he thought, the Rolls girls weren't there the second time.

"You are mean to talk like that," said Mavis.

"Well, it's the truth. Old Pye is a fat fool."

"Hush, Phillip, that is not very kind of you. He cannot help being fat, you know."

"Then he should take cold tubs. Like Father does, to keep himself in shape."

"Just look who's talking. You never do, except in the hottest weather," rejoined Mavis. "But you are too skinny already, aren't you?"

"Fool!"

"Everyone's a fool except Phillip, according to him."

"Hush, children. If you are going to squabble, I shall not go on with the matter."

"Well then, tell Mavis to shut her ugly mug in future."

"Phillip! If only you could hear and see yourself sometimes!"

"I can, that's the trouble. I know very well I look horribly ugly."

Hetty could not help laughing. Phillip had a sense of humour which often redeemed his bickerings with his sister.

Mavis was prompt to detect favouritism.

"There, you encourage him, you see!"

"Oh dear, you two. It's six of one, and half a dozen of another. Now, who shall we ask? The Todds? I think we should. Very well, the Todds. How about the Jenkins?"

"Those kids! I haven't seen the pavement sailor for some time. Has he done a bunk?"

"No dear, of course not! Wherever do you get such ideas from? Mr. Jenkins is away in France, where he goes to buy silk for his firm. Anyway, he has been most kind to you children, so has Mrs. Jenkins. I think we should ask them."

"Mrs. 'Sailor's' going to have a baby, don't forget! Will the waggonette shake her up too much? Don't forget you'll be responsible if anything goes wrong."

"Well dear, it is kind of you to be so considerate. But I think it will be quite all right. Now Mavis, would you like to ask anyone in particular? Oh, by the way, Aunt Liz and Polly and Percy Pickering will be here then! They are coming for a few days, before we go to Whitstable, and then going on to Dovercourt. I forgot to tell you, I heard this morning by the eleven o'clock post."

"Oh good, good!"

The idea of Percy and Desmond with him immediately made the party desirable to Phillip. Thus encouraged, he wondered if he could ask Milton to come? And dare he ask Milton to suggest to the Rolls that they come too? He might ask Milton to sound them. He would seek Mother's advice first. But not before Mavis! She would be bound to laugh at him. He would ask Mother later, in private.

Looking intently at him, Mavis said, "Phillip's thinking about Helena! I always know when he is, by the look on his face!"

"I am not, you are a liar!"

"Hush children, hush! I did think of asking them, but perhaps we do not know them well enough, Mavis. Mrs. Rolls and I exchanged cards years ago, but she did not seem to want to follow it up. They have their own set of friends, you see. But do ask them dear, if you like".

Phillip's face was deathly pale. Hetty gave Mavis a glance, frowning and shaking her head slightly, to tell her to leave Phillip alone. She knew how Phillip felt, and always wanted to save him from unhappiness. At times he was desperately unhappy, in periods of black depression which seriously alarmed her. As for his devotion to Helena Rolls, it was like something fixed in his mind; nothing could change it. He was a strange little person, feeling things much more than ordinary children did, rather as Dickie did, and herself too, in their differing ways. Could he have inherited both their temperaments, and this account for his waywardness, and seeming contradiction at times? Oh, she hoped he was not going to turn out an unhappy man, like his father. Those black moods of despair alarmed her. And she had never forgotten how, when he had set the Backfield on fire years before, his face had looked when he had gone white and strained, and said, in a voice of sad despair, "Mother! Do you think I ought to commit suicide?"

No invitation was sent to Mrs. Rolls, and the Misses Rolls.

The day of the picnic was intensely hot. The girls wore white frocks and big floppy hats, with sash-like ribbons on them, matching the ribbons round their waists. The boys were bare-legged in shorts and shirts, with cricketing hats and plimsolls. Hetty wore a dove-grey skirt, with a flounced blouse fastened high up her neck with invisible bones, which made her hold her head, supporting a large straw hat bearing a fluffage of ostrich feathers Charley had given her, upright with a suggestion of dignity, which was enhanced by her white kid gloves and parasol, but denied immediately her smiling, sensitive lips were seen. She was often near to tears as she thought of Mamma, yet sustained by the belief that Mamma was glad that she did not show her grief. It was the children who mattered.

The Todds had gone to the sea, and the Jenkins; it was a small party after all. It began sedately; everyone on best behaviour.

Mrs. Neville, speaking in her clear voice, which somehow seemed to make her fat body unapparent, remarked upon the exceptional heat. "It is curious, but do you know, Mrs. Pickering, as soon as I heard that Sunstar had won the Derby last June, I knew we were in for a real scorcher this summer!"

"Then you think that all such things fit in together, Mrs. Neville? It certainly looks like it, I must say," replied Mrs. Pickering, determined to give the right answer to the rather grand manner of Mrs. Neville, and so show that, although she was from the country, she could hold her own with anybody of the town.

Aunt Liz's small person was dressed in a home-made print bodice and skirt from which the half-bustle, of the previous century's end, had been removed. Mrs. Neville had considered how to compliment Mrs. Pickering on that dress, but her mentally rehearsed remark appeared to be capable of being taken the wrong way. "How much more free and easy are the simple fashions of years ago than the present-day ones, which demand things like the hobble-skirt!" . . . so she fell back on the weather and topical subjects, as the brake turned with heavy trot into the High Street. Mrs. Neville tried another tack.

"I hear it is likely to be a vintage year for champagne, Mrs. Cakebread." Then she remembered that Phillip had told her that his Uncle Sidney, who had died in the war, had been in the wine trade. Oh dear!

To cover this dropped brick, she said, upon seeing a woman standing on the pavement, selling copies of *The Suffragette*, "Did you ever feel tempted to throw a brick through the window of the House of Commons, Mrs. Maddison? I must say I feel a good deal of sympathy with those who do! Fancy being forcibly fed in prison, through those horrible steel and rubber tubes! Did you read that food getting into the lungs caused one poor creature to develop septic pneumonia? They let her out in time, of course, not wanting her death at their door. Why, it was the same name as yourself, *no* relation of course!"

Seeing Hetty's face, Mrs. Neville's was filled with concern. "Oh dear, what have I been saying! I suppose that was the Aunt Phillip told me about, then! Oh, do forgive me, Mrs. Maddison, I had no idea! Very brave women they are, all of them! But what a pity they have to go about it the way they do, antagonising the public, still . . . Oh dear me, what am I talking for like this, *do* forgive me, dear, I am such a silly person, it is the excitement I suppose, this is my first real jaunt since I was a girl!"

"Yes, I think it is mine, too, Mrs. Neville!" said Hetty, with a smile, as Mrs. Neville wiped away a tear with a small lace-edged square of cambric from one of her large round grey eyes.

The tear did the trick; it made the women feel at one with each other; and after that the brake seemed to be rattling along on the cobbles between the electric tram-lines as though the old days of care-free girlhood had come again. Seeing their mothers' faces, the boys showed their peashooters openly, and small wrinkled seeds flew in all directions. Phillip had his catapult; the peas therefrom, half a dozen wrapped in thin lavatory paper, whizzed through the air to the puzzlement of straw-hatted butcher and fishmonger, already plagued by flies upon their near-tainted wares.

The picnic was a success, despite the close heat under the tall and spreading trees of the Park. Mist lay upon the leaden Thames below. The thermometer in the wall of the Observatory registered one hundred degrees Fahrenheit in the shade. Sparrows hopped for crumbs with gaping beaks. Ice melted in the lemonade too quickly, even so, the drink was too sweet. The picnic basket, delivered from a pastrycook in Tranquil Vale across the Heath, contained all sorts of delicious pies, rolls, cakes, and best of all, ice-creams flavoured with real raspberries.

In addition, Hetty had bought a box of various sweets, for the children. Some were old favourites of her own, from childhood days: the ones Mamma had given them all, Hughie and Charley, Dorrie and Joey, in faraway days. Among them were pink sugar mice, with string tails, pink sugar whistles, Cupid's Whispers—heart-shaped flat sugary things with mottoes like *Be Mine*, *I Love You*, *Always True*, printed on them in colours; sherbet bags, pralines or satin cushions, Pumfret cakes of Spanish licorice (good for the bowels) and other sweets not very interesting to Phillip. But to Hetty they were—Mamma.

Phillip was happy with his two lieutenants, Percy and Desmond, and did not make one sarcastic remark to the girls during the entire day, Hetty noticed with smiling happiness. If only Dickie, cooped up in a stifling office, could be with them! It must be, yes it was, eighteen years ago that she and Mamma, with Hughie driving the hired cob, had come all the way from Cross Aulton, to meet Dickie and Dora; and Dickie had proposed to her, over there, on that very seat near the tall, thick hawthorn trees, with the fallow deer grazing quietly beside them.

Poor Dickie—poor Hughie—poor Mamma—poor Dora. How Time altered people and places. There were no deer now—ah well, one must try and live for the children.

Mrs. Neville, resigned to the heat of the day and the tightness of her corsets, put out a hand, and touched Hetty on the wrist. A tear of sympathy stood in one of her own eyes. She knew, from the long intimate talks she had had with Phillip, more about the family than Hetty imagined. She said nothing; the tear, and the smile, said everything.

When the waggonette returned that evening, they heard the news that old Mr. Newman had died in the heat, just as he had reached the top of the gully. Hetty was very upset, but she did not show it. Mr. Newman was much older than Papa, of course; even so, it would be Papa's seventy-first birthday in the coming October. She could not imagine what life would be like without Papa. And Hughie. Hetty felt unhappy that she had not asked him to come, too; but there, it would not have been right, among the little children.

Change, change, everything was so different nowadays; the world seemed to be going wrong, and people with it. What *was* the cause of Phillip's dreadful depression, and his resultant awful behaviour at times?

"I shall never come away with you to the seaside again, my son! Never! Never!! Why, if one of my brothers had ever *dared* to speak to their Mother as you do, in the presence of their Father, he would, without any stretch of imagination whatsoever, have knocked them down!" said Hetty, in a voice which seemed to justify the righteousness of the punishment. "How dare you speak to your Mother like that? You are a bad, ungrateful boy!"

"Without any stretch of the imagination whatsoever," said Phillip, flipping a pebble into the black mud of the foreshore, "the Romans would never have invented the catapult."

Hetty tried not to smile. How like Hughie he was, at times. But no, she must not smile. Phillip's misbehaviour was a very serious business.

Nothing in the holiday at Whitstable seemed to have gone right. More than once Hetty had declared that it was the last time she would come away with Phillip again, without his father. They were sitting on the shingle, near a wooden groin, above a stretch of thick black oozy mud. Perhaps it was because there were no sands to play on that he found so many mischievous things to do. He was a very unkind little boy indeed to have stolen Doris's dolly: to have stood it up against the groin, and deliberately shot at it with his catapult.

A pebble shattering its face had shattered Doris's life. She sobbed in her mother's arms.

"I don't care," he said, with a peculiar smile on his face. *Why* did he do such things?

"You *are* so dreadfully unkind to Mother!" said Mavis. "She does everything for you, too."

"You don't seem like my son any more!" said Hetty.

"I'm not, I'm very glad to say." Again the skull-like grin on his face.

"I shall tell your Father when we get home."

"If I ever go home again, you mean."

With these words, Phillip got up, and walked away, in the direction of the docks, feeling dark despair jangling with a desire to destroy himself. Mummie, Mummie!

Hetty wished she had not listened to her brother Joey, but gone with Liz Pickering to Dovercourt instead. The trouble was, she had already engaged the rooms.

Everything was indeed wrong at Whitstable, for children. The apartments were in a side-street, near the red-bricked basin, or harbour. They faced north. The landlady looked as though she, too, had faced north all her life. Her expressionless face—her decamping husband had taken the natural expression off it—was like the food she served. It was not like being at the sea-side at all. Only at high tide was the black ooze hidden. Hetty reproached herself for ever having listened to Joey, who had sung the praises of the Thames estuary, particularly Whitstable and its suburb of Tankerton.

Joseph Turney, traveller for the Firm of Mallard, Carter & Turney Ltd., law stationers, printers, and lithographers, had had a big new order in the town, which had so surprised Mr. Hemming, the manager, that he had not believed that this fool of the family, as he regarded Joseph Turney, had not made a mistake. Mr. Hemming had shown scepticism on his face, thus antagonising the more the amiable and single-minded youngest son of the Chairman; and when the order for complete sets of ledgers, quires of blotting paper, a gallon bottle of Stephens Ink, reams of business headed writing paper, half a dozen bound copying-books, a press, a dozen gross of manilla envelopes with other quantities and qualities of the same, in best laid paper, had come in, Joey was triumphant. Whitstable shared in the triumph.

It was a very fine place, bracing and little known, declared Joey; the North Sea airs were health-giving; it was full of ozone, which was good for the hair. Apartments? He would find out. He did. And thither Hetty had gone for the annual fortnight at the seaside.

Phillip had bicycled all the way down, starting at six o'clock on his romantic journey. He was still a little apprehensive of possible malcontents waylaying him as he pedalled over wooded Shooter's Hill into the early morning sun, but body exercise soon reduced the doubts of the mind. He enjoyed himself greatly along straight Watling Street from Dartford to Strood, past heated cornfields to the valley of the Medway, over the water to Rochester by the low black wooden bridge—fishing boats and barges with brown sails beyond—up again to the heights of Chatham, and down the long stretch of road to Sittingbourne, while the sun climbed over his head and swung higher over the downs on his right, leaving the wide flat grey expanses of the distant sea on his left. Then a rest in the dusty wayside grasses munching mutton sandwiches as he watched finches dusting themselves in the chalky dust of the road, and listened to the dry bleats of sheep on the short pastures over the hedges. Onwards to Faversham!

At last (for he had studied the route on his map) he found himself turning off on the road to Whitstable, while distant guns boomed in the heat, and the wide flat sea drew nearer, with smoke-trails everywhere on the dull horizon. Father had cycled here in the past, and had told him of the lightships to be seen on a clear day from the higher ground before the turning; but Phillip had seen nothing in the haze; and now he was feeling the fierce beat of the sun through his cricketing hat, which he had promised to wear against sunstroke. The road shimmered in front, in the distance; the flint dust danced in the heat, as he pedalled on, in the grilling heat of August. At last, disappointed with everything, he got off the Swift, gritty all over, dust in his eyes from motorcars, and surveyed the port of Whitstable, with its smell of old fish and hot engine oil, and dirty streets. The "sands" were oozy black mud! What a hole! It was a swizz! It was not the real sea-side. It was not a proper holiday. It was muck. Mother was a fool for listening to Uncle Joey, with his donkey-laugh and walrus moustache, and silly stories about people's socks and feet.

Nothing went right. On the first morning Phillip cut his foot on a bit of broken glass in the black soft mud. Then a beach acquaintance took him out in a boat, to fish for flat-fish. The boat, a small one, bobbed up and down so much, and together with the smell of the old dried lugworms on the seats made him sick. Medicinal brandy, from a chemist's shop, made him feel better. Never again!

He went fishing, with lugworms and eel-hooks, in the red-bricked basin, or harbour. Slinging out his lead, the baited hooks on brass paternoster to follow, he got hooked in the hand, and by a big eel-hook, too, Hetty took him to a doctor, who worked it through the flesh, cut off the barb, and withdrew the sneck bend backwards. It was a beastly holiday, it was all Uncle Joey's fault, it had turned out just as Father had prophesied! But Mother had not listened to Father's advice. He had been to Whitstable, and knew what sort of a place it was! Instead, she had listened to Uncle Joey, the fool of the Turney family. Just fancy, after every bathe, you had to go home and have a bath, with *soap*, to take away the dirt of the so-called sea!

"Well, it's always best to be on the safe side, Phillip."

A woman told Hetty that the black mud was contaminated by sewage from London; and while she remained loyal to Joey, she did feel that, if this was true, Joey might have told her before she booked the rooms. Anyway, that did not excuse Phillip's behaviour in the very least.

"I hardly know what the world is coming to! Anyone would think your family were your deadly enemies, sometimes, to hear the way you speak, Phillip."

"You all are," he retorted, "only you don't know it." He felt himself twisted as the gut tied to the fish-hooks, as black as the mud of the shore, and hopeless as broken glass. Oh, why had they not gone to Hayling Island: then, across the sea, he could have thought of Helena Rolls in the clear blue waters around the wooded Isle of Wight, swimming in the waves with Milton, so happy together—he and Helena might have been brother and sister, even twins.

Hetty stared at the frowning face of her son. What had changed the dear little child he had been, years ago, before Mavis had come? Could her coming have put his nose out of joint? Or was he born selfish, like—like Dickie, in some of his moods? Why did Phillip go out of his way to do, and say, such needlessly hurtful things to himself, such unkind things to his sisters and mother? It was not his true nature, she knew; and yet—ah well, she had given up everything for her children, and so they expected everything from her. That was her fault. If you give all to others, they come to look down on you in the end.

"My son, if only you could see your face now! I think you would be shocked."

"Perhaps I wouldn't, you know," he cried, flinging himself away, and trudging off along the shingle.

"Don't pander to him, Mum."

He had been such a *dear* little child, so helpful, so eager to learn, so anxious to please Dickie, in the first years of his life, Hetty told herself, once more, as they went home by train the next day. There had been a tremendous thunderstorm on the afternoon of the last day ; Phillip had been out in it, returning soaked through, yet with colour in his cheeks. The storm had cleared the air for the time being; but more was to come, so it was decided that he should ride in the train, at least part of the way home, to Dartford. He had spent the last evening trying to mend Doris's doll with fish-glue, which was something in his favour. Of course she had never meant to tell Dickie; it would only upset things more; and he had been punished enough in his life already.

Ah well, she thought, her hope rising with her courage, seeing him happily reading *The Boy's Own Paper* in the seat opposite: perhaps it was, after all, but a phase, and he would grow out of it.

When they got home, Phillip saw at once that Father had put another bolt on the front door, and a second one on the back door. Soon afterwards he learned from next door that burglars had broken into Mr. Pye's house during that family's absence at the seaside; the burglars had lived quietly in the upstairs rooms for a fortnight, sleeping in the beds with their boots on. They had turned out all the cupboards and drawers, scattered the things about on the floors, and made messes in every room. Phillip was startled to hear of the messes they had made—even in Mr. Pye's bed, just before they had left, by way of the fence into the Backfield: but somehow, he felt, apart from the messes, it kind of served Old Pye right.

Chapter 26

WHITE CHRISTMAS

In the following winter there was a heavy fall of snow, making the Hill a place of joy for the young: while the old kept to their houses, before blazing coal fires. Phillip was cold, too, as he swotted in the kitchen at night, for the Oxford Local Examinations being held all that week at school. He wore his overcoat for warmth, despite the fire in the range.

On the last day of the exams, a Friday, Richard opened the trapdoor in the downstairs lavatory floor, and invited his son to follow him down the portable wooden steps into the foundations of the house. The way was lit by the jagged flame of a candle, which seemed vainly to be trying to give light against the cavernous blackness of the place.

Moving forward slowly, Phillip saw the 'cello, which had split its belly in the damp of years, standing against a brick support to the floor above. Voices mumbled beyond. He felt like a burglar, in a Sherlock Holmes story. Above was the Bank of England.

"Ah, here it is, Phillip," said Father. "You take it, my boy, and enjoy yourself on the Hill. The old runners are a bit rusty, but they will soon be bright, if I know anything about it! Exams do take it out of one, as I well remember, though I was only a bit of a boy at the time. Now go on the Hill and enjoy yourself, but be careful of the iron railings. We do not want an invalid on our hands this Christmas!"

This was Richard's way of showing his concern for his son. He had always been afraid, with both wife and children, of what he called sentimentality.

Phillip and Desmond travelled fast down the slope from the sheepfold, almost to the bottom where the big golden birch tree stood just inside the iron gates leading to Charlotte Road, east end. Scores of sledges were in movement. In the frosty air the cries of *Olley-olley-olley!* travelled over the pressed snow, echoing from the dull flats. Many and varied were the sportsmen and their vehicles. There were heroes on toboggans and sleighs—the real thing, not home-made—who slipped at a great rate down the incline, taking the bump a third of the way down in flying style, and rushing on to the bottom, hardly slowed before the gates; but steering upon the ice-laid path, shot through the narrow space, and gathering speed, hurtled on down Charlotte Road and round the corner—*Olley-olley-olley!* look out, get out of the way!—scrunch and slap and sway, laughter as precarious balance was maintained—then, triumph! The red and blue barber's pole, leaning out of Hawkins' shop, fifty yards short of the railway station, was the record run that year. The grand ones, of course, lived in Twistleton Road; Milton was one of their party.

At night the cries seemed to come fainter, in an arctic whiteness of dim stars and frosted street-lights, as black travelling objects moved upon all the slopes of the Hill. Father gave permission to go out again after supper. Oh, wonderful! Father liked Phillip's eldest cousin Hubert Cakebread, who now was with the Firm, and put Phillip in Bertie's charge, with Gerry. Boys, go to it, and enjoy yourselves, he said. What had come over Father?

Richard was reading the Sherlock Holmes' stories again. He had got the pale blue *Strand Magazines* from the drawer in Phillip's bedroom, and was back in the past, in the winter of 1894-5, when the moon turned blue, and the wild geese flew over the Hill from the Thames estuary, on their way south.

"Yes, it was a unique winter, the great freeze-up of 'ninety five, Hubert. With luck, we may see the Aurora Borealis again this year. It's cold enough. Well, you boys are only young once. But take care of yourselves!"

"Yes, sir, we will! Trust us!"

There was a ring of the front door bell. Desmond, wrapped in woollen muffler and helmet, gloved and gaitered, completed Phillip's happiness. If only the snow would hold over Christmas!

It thawed one day; then more snow fell, to cover the old tracks; and frost took the pink-streaked thermometer, hanging on the brick wall by the front door, to eight degrees below freezing. It was Christmas Eve.

A night of carols, heard near and far, of familiar echoing cries of the speeding crews, *Olley-olley-olley!* Hern the grocer—who was there with his girl-assistant, the tall dark young woman who called for orders every morning—told Phillip that the cries came from the Frenchmen who rode in the bicycle races round the Fordesmill track. *Allez-allez-allez!* they urged on their racing compatriots. Mr. Mundy, the vicar, gloved, gaitered, and muffled to the nose, to whom Phillip repeated this statement, suggested that it was perhaps older than that: it was the crier's *Oyez-oyez-oyez!* The Redskins of North America had the same cries. At this Hubert Cakebreak, who was invariably polite, as his Father had been, asked if *Oyez* should be pronounced *Oi!* as carters and others still cried to attract notice in the London streets.

"A very good point, that: I must send it to 'Notes and Queries'," said Mr. Mundy, and Phillip felt proud of Hubert's knowledge, proud that the splendid Milton had heard, too, what his cousin had said.

At nine o'clock the boys had promised to return; and Hubert insisted that time was time, and Uncle Dickie had been very decent in allowing him out, so home they ought to go. One last run down the road was suggested, all four up, from the top of the gully. Too dangerous, said Hubert, but they might try it from the sheep-fold. Four up! They were bound to come off at the bump! They did, amid much laughter; and now it really was time to go home.

Father was pleased that they were back, with five minutes grace, he said, looking at his watch. Mother was making cocoa for everyone in the kitchen. Aunt Dorrie was there, the place was crowded, with his sisters and cousins, and Desmond. Cake and cocoa, what more could anyone want?

Phillip took a plate and cup down to Father, in the armchair in the sitting room, reading *The Speckled Band*. He had hung the Japanese lanterns across the ceiling, and the girls had stuck holly all round the walls, and on the pictures. There was one piece of mistletoe, on the bracket of the gas lamp hanging from the ceiling, a very tiny bit, tied to the tap, of all things. How could anyone get under it to kiss, though of course no one would want to, in his house, thought Phillip. A daring thought came to him: under the table! Not with anyone else in the room, of course. And with only one person, Petal. But Petal had left immediately after Grannie's death, to live in Brighton. He often thought of Petal, and what had happened during the funeral in the summer. He, with Mavis, Doris, Kimberley, Tommy and Petal, had been left in the front room, to be quiet, when the carriages had left for the cemetery; they had gone down to see Gerry, at Aunt Dorrie's house in Charlotte Road. They had played hide and seek. They had gone into the attic, and Gerry had even climbed on the roof. It had been great fun. Then he and Petal had found themselves in the front room, sitting on chairs opposite to one another, having reached "home" while the others were still creeping about upstairs looking for them.

"My Father said that if Kimberley had been the son of a white father and a black mother he would have been coffee-coloured. Is it all a joke, really, I mean, about Kimberley being——"

"Well, hardly a joke," Petal had said. "Daddy admits he did it with our house-girl, but then you see a black boy might have been there first. They start very young, often at ten years old."

Thrilling words, made the more so by Petal speaking so coolly, as though she was talking about music. A thick brassy feeling gripped him. A picture of Jack Hart came to him, a sort of spider-feeling. Before he could think not to speak, Phillip said, looking across to Petal, who was sitting back in her chair, "Have you ever done it?"

Petal shook her head. She looked at him as he looked at her.

"I haven't, either. Shall we try, one day?"

Petal nodded. Phillip's throat felt dry. Then caution made him say, "You won't tell anyone I asked, will you?"

Petal shook her head. She looked very pretty, when her cheeks were faintly pink.

And that was the end of it.

Phillip stopped by the children's coat-rack outside the lavatory door, and thought of Petal's face, as she had sat in the chair, nodding.

It was Helena Rolls he really loved, all the same; though he never *could* think of her as he had of Petal. Helena was his ideal. Oh, if only Grannie had not died, then he would have gone to St. Simon's Garden Party, perhaps in fancy dress as a Zulu, with black face and arms, and sandalled feet, a top-knot of feathers in his hair, carrying cow-hide shield, knobkerry, assegai, bracelets, and cow-bell.

He looked at his face in the looking-glass between the knobs of the coat-hangers, illumined by his pocket torch. Oh, did he look like that? It was almost a ghost's face! With a sigh he turned away, to leap away from his thoughts, up the three steps and so to the merry throng in the kitchen.

Mother and Aunt Dorrie, who had been at the convent together, were talking about going to Midnight Mass in the Roman Catholic Church in the High Street. Mavis was going, too, and Hubert, to look after them. Why could he not go, as well? The Catholic service made him feel secretly like a bird must feel, very simple and clear. A wild bird's soul must be like a clear raindrop hanging on a thorn after a shower, with the world inside it, a little world of leaves and sky and curved horizon. He could think his own thoughts during the Roman Catholic service, especially during the beautiful monk-like chants. Please, could he go too? Oh, *must* he ask Father? Even on Christmas Eve? Father would say no. Other boys at school went to it, or to the Watch Night Service in St. Mary's, and the churches on the Heath. "Please ask Father, Mum."

"Very well, dear, but it must be for the very last time. You are old enough to ask for yourself now."

"Yes, don't funk it, young Phillip!" grinned Hubert. "Beard the lion in his den!"

"You can say that, but *your* Father was not like mine," retorted Phillip.

"Hush dear," said Hetty. Aunt Dorrie smiled at him, and put her hand on his head. Phillip liked Aunt Dorrie, she was very like Grannie. But why was there a tear in her eye? It dropped, while she was still smiling. Would a tear freeze in frost, like any other water? Yes, it would, of course, because even the sea froze when it was cold enough.

Several tears froze that night on the grave of Sarah Turney, in the cemetery that once had been the Great Field, now entirely grey-white and spectral under the glazing stars. The children, left in charge of Hubert, waited outside while their mothers went into the graveyard, after knocking at the door of the guardian in the house by the gates. Hetty and Dorrie, holding hands, prayed silently before the marble stone, with their Mother's name on it in letters of lead, with the text below, "Come unto Me".

The stars burned dully in the sky as the children waited, in the expectant night. While they stood there, Phillip saw a figure passing on the other side of the road, under the lamp-light. He recognised Cranmer. He crossed over to speak to him. Cranmer said he was going home for Christmas. Phillip told him about the sledge. Cranmer said he was learning boxing, in the Boys' Club, and Pat O'Keefe, the middle-weight champion, gave them lessons. Phillip determined to learn boxing, too. The boys parted, as they met, full of warm feeling for one another. So it had always been; they had never fallen out; Phillip had never tried to boss Cranmer, nor striven to get his own way. His way had been Cranmer's way also. Each made the other feel good. Even so, secretly Phillip looked down a little on Cranmer, as Cranmer looked up to Phillip. Mother had said once that she hoped Phillip would never say anything to hurt Cranmer's feelings, because he happened to come from a different station in life.

Phillip felt that Hubert was something like Cranmer, although kind of broader. Perhaps it was because Hubert always seemed happy and unruffled, whereas Cranmer's eyes looked sometimes as though they had been driven into his head. Most poor boys looked like that; but Cranmer's eyes came out again when he and Cranmer met. In a way, he had never had any friendship so good as Cranmer's. Desmond and Percy were nice to be with, but Cranmer was different.

"Well, Merry Christmas, Horace, and a Happy New Year."

"Fanks, Phil. Same to you, and many of'm. So long!"

"So long!"

During the Midnight Mass, and the haunting monk-like singing, and the ringing of the silver bell which reminded him of the note of the great titmouse in spring among the new leaves on the elm, a sort of light-of-the-sky sound, Phillip thought more about Cranmer, and Hubert, and Gerry, and why they were nice, and why some boys were not nice, like Ching, and even Jack Hart. Why had he never liked Mr. Prout? Was Gran'pa nice? He himself was not really nice. He had always been unkind to his sisters, and to Mother; sworn, told lies, stolen; been a coward, and never really gone straight. What else? He could not think of any other bad points. He prayed to God to make him a better boy.

Then other thoughts came into his head, taking away the clear, rather sad but lovely thoughts about the coming springtime, with new buds to the trees and windflowers coming through the skeleton leaves on the woodland floor, and the first timorous singing of the willow wren, until the nightingale seemed to give the smaller bird confidence. The nightingale was like the Queen of the coverts, not the King, but a sort of Princess. He thought of the Oxford Local exam, and the mess he had made of it. Simply awful! He had cooked at least one of the Geography answers, saying one of the *new* chief exports from Mexico was dried flies for feeding fish in aquariums. Phillip had imagined that, in a land where millions of flies buzzed, someone would think of catching and drying them, like currants, and exporting them for goldfish, and even trout farms. Perhaps the examiner would think this was a new industry he had not heard of himself, and pass it. As for Latin, not one question had been answerable. Euclid—hopeless. French—no good. And it was very nearly the end of his five-year scholarship! Would he have to leave school, after the spring term, and start work? Gran'pa had said something about him going into the Firm. How awful!

Overcome by the prospect, Phillip yawned. The snow and the exercise had made him sleepy. It would be so nice to be in bed, wiggling his toes like a fish's tail. The thought of Christmas presents made him perk up though he knew what most of them were.

All the snow echoed with church bells as they walked home; while from the lighted frowsty windows of the pubs came singing. Outside the Railway in Randiswell some children were waiting, holding hands, waiting for their parents inside to take them home. They looked very cold. It was very sad, said Mother, as they walked up Hillside Road, having said goodnight and Merry Christmas to the Cakebreads, but they must all look on the bright side.

Phillip fell behind, wanting to think his own thoughts, which were also sad, like the grey snow, and the loneliness of birds freezing on leafless branches, and children dreaming of Father Christmas outside the pub, and Grannie lying with her head on one side in the dark grave. He wished he had not always tried to get money out of her; but it was too late now.

Father, as soon as they got back, complained that Mother had kept the children up too late.

"Look at the boy's face, he looks as though he had seen a

ghost! He's had a week of exams, and gone up past his bedtime every night for the past fortnight. And all this emotional Roman Catholic business is bad for young people, in my opinion. Come now, my boy, off with your boots! Then straight up to bed. Hetty, Doris has been nearly hysterical in your absence—in the end I had to speak firmly to her. Please do not leave me alone in the house with her again."

Richard had read the last story of Sherlock Holmes, where he fell to death with Professor Moriarty in the Alps, with four interruptions from the disconsolate Doris; and reflecting in the armchair afterwards of the selfishness of his wife in leaving him alone with a wailing child on Christmas Eve, memories of his own childhood had drained him of energy.

Phillip went to bed without having kissed his Mother—he had deliberately avoided it—and without hanging up his stocking. Soon tears were running onto his pillow. Outside snow was falling, in the silence of a reborn world; and in the morning all was white, when he looked out. And there was a filled stocking, hanging on the bottom rail of his bed.

He had been asleep when Richard had crept down, to hang it there.

The traditional Christmas morning walk was to Cutler's Pond, and back, while Mother cooked the turkey at home. Phillip had never remembered Mother coming with them to the Pond, or on any other walk, except upon the Hill, which did not really count.

Gloved, overcoated, and correct, Phillip walked on the outside, while Mavis and Doris walked with Father. Gone were the elms beyond the extension of houses on either side of the road; there seemed no trees anywhere, only heaps of snow-covered bricks, scaffolding, and tarpaulins tied down upon piles of wooden planks and posts. Wooden blocks had replaced the old grey road, which was now wide with kerbstones along the sides, and iron-grilled drains at regular intervals. The great new red brick 'bus depot covered more than two acres, said Father, who told them again about the snipe and herons he had seen in the meadows beside the Randisbourne when first he had come to live in the district.

"Every other man seems to be smoking a new pipe," he said. "It does not need a Sherlock Holmes to deduce that this is Christmas morning."

Cutler's Pond was frozen over, and covered with stones and sticks flung on the ice. Some boys were venturing upon its black and white-bubbled surface near the bridge. Richard told them about boys in his young days who had fallen through the ice of a reservoir, and been unable to climb over the edge of the ice, as it had broken under their clutch; and all had been drowned.

"A warning to you, my boy, not to venture on any more thin ice!" laughed Richard. Phillip ignored Father's joke. He was thinking of the party in Gran'pa's that afternoon, and hoping that Father would not come, although he had been invited, and so spoil the fun.

He hoped, too, that Father would not grumble if the turkey was not cooked to his liking. Last Christmas Mother had cried, because he had found some small smuts on one of the plates. Father wore spectacles to find the smuts, but Mother had not got any, though her eyes were not so strong as they had been. She always tried to be cheerful, though Father was beastly to her.

All three children had one thing in common agreement: Father's beastliness to Mother. They were now imbued with resentment, dull as it was silent, towards Father; and this resentment at times rose in Phillip to active hatred. His world was entirely detached from that of his Father's, since affection, or love, had been denied in the forming early years. This had also happened with Doris, who had never, unlike Phillip as a small child, known her Father's affection. As for Mavis, she too was sealed off from her Father.

Standing by the pond with their Father in the bright exhilarating air of a white Christmas, each child was as a prisoner, its true self shut away in solitariness.

Cutler's Pond had a new brick high wall above it, raised to the new road level. There was a spiked iron railing above the brickwork. It looked rather beastly, said Father, but such things were deemed necessary in the cause of progress. Phillip understood that it was all due to that little Welshman, Lloyd George, who did not even know that pheasants did not eat mangold-wurzels, said Father.

Back home again, the girls went to help Mother bring in the dinner. The sprouts were a little watery, explained an anxious Hetty, owing to the frost. She did so hope the bird was cooked to his satisfaction. Phillip, who carried in the hot plates in a cloth, saw that they were clean. Father had the yellow-grey eye of a heron, peering down to inspect them. Phillip winked at his Mother. All was well.

The Christmas plateful had to be eaten with due regard to its rarity. A forkful of potato went into Phillip's mouth first, then a little bread-sauce. Then half a sprout, after inspection lest an old shrunken caterpillar be found in it. (Father had once found one in a sprout on his plate). Even spiders did not like caterpillars. Then a sip of water, to continue the dullness. More potato, while pretending there was no turkey. Then some sausage, and a bit of chestnut stuffing. Having mortified his taste, Phillip then put a slice of white breast on his fork, with potato in gravy, some more sausage, and some sprouts. This was the first real mouthful; and looking round at Mother with approval, he started to wolf his Christmas dinner.

Afterwards, into the front room, while Father had a sleep alone in the sitting room. On the front room table were plates of tangerines, raisins, peeled almonds, and Carlsbad plums; and a pile of old *Strands* on the wickerwork table to read.

Before a blazing fire, Phillip examined his presents carefully. There was a wooden model aeroplane, with steam-twisted propeller, driven by elastic. The wings were of thin varnished wood, and the bigger wing was at the back. He would keep it until the snow was gone, lest water warp the dihedral angle. *Flight* was now regularly studied in the Public Library, with *The Autocar*. Phillip knew all about nacelles, under-carriages, elevators, rudders, and skids. Players Cigarettes had a series on Aeroplanes, from Montgolfier to Santos-Dumont, Paulham, Bleriot, the Wright Brothers, Lilienthal, and the Curtis biplane. Balloons were now a thing of the past.

Good! they were going to have tea next door!

Gran'pa had a new housekeeper, called Miss Rooney, a small, sweet-faced, white-haired Irish woman who had been one of the hundreds replying to Mother's advertisement in the *Daily Telegraph*. Mother presided at tea next door, while Miss Rooney looked after everybody. Uncle Joey was staying there, with Aunt Ruth and cousin Arthur, and Arthur's two smaller sisters. Uncle Charley had sent a telegram of good wishes to all, from Brighton. Gran'pa looked cheerful, as always.

After tea the children played games, all over the house.

Phillip and Gerry became rowdy, and a wild chase took place. Cushions were hurled, until a vase crashed and the fun was stopped. Then they went into Uncle Hugh's room, and opening the stained glass window, shot peas at the opposite window, behind which Father was sitting. Phillip was a little anxious about this, although he had not shot any peas at the window. Seeing his face, Gerry said that perhaps they had better not do it any more.

"Uncle may think it was sparrows," he suggested.

They went back to the front room, where the table was being laid for supper. There was a ham, a cold turkey, mince pies, pressed beef, a pork pie, and many other things including cakes and jellies, and a huge dish of fruit, with grapes and nuts, bon-bons, everything. There was red wine, with water, for the boys, ginger and raisin wine for the girls, claret and port for the men. They ate in candle-light, with paper caps on their heads. The Christmas pudding came in flaming, and contained many bright silver shillings, with the new King's head on them. Where had Gran'pa got them from? He-he, said Gran'pa, that's a secret. He had a friend at court, said Mother. In the Mint, you mean, don't you, Aunt Hetty? asked Hubert. Hubert wore a new suit, with a man's high collar.

They drank to absent friends, including Ralph, who was at sea, and Charley and the others at Brighton. Phillip managed to swallow two glasses of port, unseen by Mother.

Snapdragon! Hubert went outside. Candles were put out. The room was lit only by firelight. He came in with the big dish, leaping with blue flames. Raisins were under the flames. You had to pick one out, and eat it while the blue flame played on your fingers and ran over your nails, but did not burn them if you blew quickly. Dare he do it?

"Wait a minute, boys, let our respected Patriarch speak his lines first!" cried Uncle Hugh.

Gran'pa began to sing, in his throaty voice, a song Phillip had not heard before.

" '*Here he comes with flaming bowl,*
Don't he mean to take his toll:
Snip! Snap! Dragon!'

"Now, everyone, all together next time when we come to Snip! Snap! Dragon!

" 'With due regard don't take too much,
Be not greedy in your clutch:
Snip! Snap! Dragon!

With his blue and lapping tongue,
Watch out or you'll be stung:
Snip! Snap! Dragon!

For he snaps at all that comes,
Snatching out his sugar plums:
Snip! Snap! Dragon!

'Tis Old Christmas makes him come
With his snorting fe-fi-fum!
Don't ye fear him, but be bold,
Out he goes, his flames are cold:
SNIP! SNAP! DRAGON!' "

followed by the laughter of all but Phillip. He was listening to the words.

The party ended disastrously for him. When the others had gone down into Uncle Hugh's room, for the clearing of the table, Phillip slipped back, and raising the empty snapdragon dish on high, drank the spirit lying in the gravely-bowl at one end. It tasted raw and nasty, rather like bullaces or wild plums at Beau Brickhill on the hedges, but he had swallowed an egg-cupful before he tasted it. It burned his inside. Half an hour later, after he had been very sick, and was shuddering with cold, he went home with Mother to be put to bed, clutching a hot-water bottle. He was sick again and again, all froth; but Richard said nothing, as he returned to his chair by the fire. He thought, however, of his Father's death from alcoholism, and wondered if Phillip, now at the age of adolescence, had inherited that fatal trait.

Chapter 27

A VISIT TO SPARHAWK STREET

THE great titmouse sang its gay bell-like notes about the nesting boxes Phillip had put up in his elm tree at the bottom of the garden; while the louder ringing of the muffin-man, wares on head in the tray covered with green baize cloth, gave some interest out of gas-lit school. On one Wednesday afternoon, when the ground was too hard for football, Hetty and her Papa took Phillip up to London to look round the premises of the Firm. The thought of finding Hubert there made the idea less unattractive than it would have been had the prospect been only of dull streets and houses, poor people working in the large rooms of the tall dreary building, and Mother and Gran'pa to talk to.

They went by tram, by way of Camberwell—"Father and I were married here, dear," whispered Hetty, while Gran'pa, muffled and wrapped in a thick dark long coat to his ankles, was talking to someone else on the seat beside him; and "Oh," replied Phillip laconically. They rode over the river by Westminster Bridge, then along the Embankment, past Cleopatra's Needle, to alight by Blackfriars Bridge, with its view over the river of tugs and barges, and a great effigy of Johnnie Walker about to stride over the rim of a tall factory chimney, apparently having drunk too much of his own whisky, said Gran'pa, he-he'ing at his joke.

Having crossed over Ludgate Circus, Phillip with Gran'pa and Mother went along Farringdon Street, to the steps up to High Holborn, and so to Sparhawk Street. Phillip thought of the old days of real trees and green fields, of sparrowhawks keeping down the pigeons. He would like to get a couple of young ones next year, tame them, and let them go early one morning in front of St. Paul's. With lots of hawks about, London might be a little more interesting, if he had to come and work in it. The sight of a hawk flying over would be a link with the past.

The offices of Mallard, Carter & Turney, Ltd., were in a tall brick building several stories high. The impression was of dinginess and many dirty glass windows, and flocks of sparrows in the road outside, on which drays and vans moved behind drivers with peaked caps, and small boys standing on the tail-boards, holding to ropes from the hooded roofs.

They entered by an iron-studded door, and there in front was a glass-partitioned office lit by two gas lights, not even mantles, but old jets, like Father had in the bathroom under the ring, to keep the little can of washing water warm for the morning. The ring at home was nearly worn out, by the fumes of all the years. Ever since he could remember, it had been there.

Phillip was introduced to a perky old gentleman with a bald head and fluffy bits of white hair as though stuck on its sides. This was the Secretary. Then to "Young Mr. Mallard, who is our Accountant," who had a cold clammy hand. Then to a fat man called Hemming, the General Manager, who smiled fatly and hurt his hand when shaking it.

"Pleased to meet you again. You don't remember me, do you? Now tell the truth and shame the devil. Do you remember me, eh?"

Phillip looked up at the fat smiling face, and thought that he did not like him. He did remember him chiefly because he had hurt his hand last time when he had shaken it. He did not know what to say, so he said nothing.

"Come come," said Mr. Hemming. "This will never do. If you come to join us one day, you must find your voice, you know. Customers don't like travellers who wait for them to speak first, otherwise they say to them 'Nothing this time'. Eh, Mr. Turney? Pleased to see you looking so well, sir."

While he had been speaking, Mr. Hemming was doing up some buttons on his waistcoat.

Gran'pa wanted to talk with Mr. Hemming, so Phillip and Mother went into the printing works, accompanied by "young Mr. Mallard". There were men in leather aprons and rolled shirt-sleeves, setting lead type with tweezers, picking out letters almost as fast as a woodpecker licked up ants on the ground with its long tongue. Further on, printing machines were moving backwards and forwards, while other men laid on sheets of paper, which they whisked away when the lever was raised and the inky roller passed over the type again. These were posters for a Sale by Auction, the foreman said, wiping his hands on his apron.

Upstairs they saw Hubert, and "young Mr. Mallard", who looked quite old and constantly stroked his chin, and hardly spoke at all, left them to return downstairs.

Soon afterwards Mother said she had to keep an appointment with the dentist, and would be back in an hour's time.

"Now be a good boy while I'm gone, and don't get into mischief," she whispered. "Look after him, Hubert."

"Oh rather, Aunt Hetty," said Hubert, laying his arm affectionately on Phillip's shoulder.

Hubert took him into the Lithography and Marbling Room.

The lithographic stones were yellow, and men were painting patterns and pictures on them, like making transfers, to be pressed on paper afterwards. But it was the Marbling which interested Phillip. There were many shallow troughs standing on three legs on the floor. The men liked the tripods, said Hubert, as they were steadier than four legs on the old uneven chestnut-slab floor. The liquid lying in the troughs was size, made of gum tragacanth dissolved in soft water; and upon this layer the paint, in various colours, was flipped and shaken, or straked and laid, according to the pattern that was wanted—they used five main patterns for the end-papers of the Firm's ledgers and account books, said Hubert. Some customers preferred Comb, other Snail, Peacock, Hair-veining, or Turkish.

One of the men showed how Comb was made. First he skimmed the size, to remove the film caused by evaporation. Then he took some brown paint on a small, soft-haired brush, and strewed it in a broad line upon the size. Next, some yellow paint with another brush, then blue, and finally vermilion. With the "master comb" he drew wavy lines through the paints, which stayed wavy when the comb had been lifted out.

"The colours don't run into one another, like they might if there wasn't no ox-gall mixed in wi' the paints," he explained. "The gall also helps the colours to marble, you see."

"What does marble mean?" asked Phillip.

"The paint spreads like, you see, an' 'olds the marble to isself like."

"It gives the paint a sort of coat, doesn't it, like gelatine?" Hubert enquired of the man, very politely, Phillip thought, although he was Gran'pa's grandson.

"That's it, sir, you've got it, you got my meaning all right."

"What's Snail like, Hubert?"

"Well, like snail shells, Phillip. You get that effect by tapping the side of the trough, don't you, and shaking drops on the size?" he asked the man, as though he did not know already.

"That's right, sir," smiled the man. "Then I makes the whirls with a goose-quill, see, like this."

He made some drops of all shapes and colours lie on the size, like moon and planets floating in space, then with the quill made them whirl about one another, but never in one another.

"The quill's the master, the colours follow it," said Hubert.

"And the ox-gall keeps them apart, like a sort of force of gravity," said Phillip. Hubert smiled at him.

"Jolly good simile, old man."

"But how do you get the colours off the size?" Phillip asked the man, imitating the manner of Hubert.

"I'll soon show you, sir."

The man got a length of paper, and held it before him.

"This sheet is wetted a day afore it's used, you see, and put wi' others in the screw press. Then, ten minutes afore it's used, my mate washes them sheets in alum water, to earth the pattern. I'll show you."

He laid the sheet in the Snail trough, pressed it down, gently and evenly.

"Now watch the tray carefully," he said. "An' you might see somefink strange."

Lifting up the sheet, the man said "Hey Presto!" and peering intently, Phillip saw only the liquid size, like barley water, lying in the trough. There was not even a speck of colour left.

"Where's it all gone?" he asked, pretending to be mystified. Of course, it was on the paper the man was holding in his hand.

"I forgot to put in the magic drops," said the man. "Look!" He turned over the paper. It was a blank. Phillip was now genuinely puzzled. It was a trick, of course, but how had he done it? Ah, he and Hubert had changed papers while he had been looking at the trough!

The pattern looked very shiny and bright on the paper. The man explained that now it would be dried, when it would be ready for glazing. That was done by the master marbler, on the table in the centre of the floor. He had been doing nothing else for over fifty years, Hubert explained, as they moved away, after thanking the man, who said, "It's quite all right," in a pleased voice.

The dry marbled sheets were smeared with a film of bees-wax, heated on a gas ring in a gummy iron pot, then polished with the swinging calendar. This calendar was a heavy block of white marble, with a polished under-surface, bolted to the end of an iron arm hanging from the beam in the ceiling. It swung down loosely, enabling the old man to use it like an iron, judging the weight to within a hundredth of an inch, said Hubert. The final gloss to the papers was given by an agate stone, which was kept in a wash-leather bag, to prevent dust and grit getting on it.

Upstairs were the binders, some of them girls, working at benches. Some were stitching the sheets with treadle machines, using fine white cord which Phillip thought would do for fishing, if it were dyed first. A man was cutting edges with a thing like a little guillotine. The girls kept glancing at him, some smiling, but Phillip pretended not to see them. They were probably bad, like those in the Randiswell Rec at night. Why else should they smile that sort of cunning smile?

Poor people were associated in Phillip's mind with bad people: white faces, many of them covered with pimples, some with scowling expressions, or blank looks, dull looks; all in shabby clothes. Poor people were quite different from ordinary people. Even Cranmer was really different, although he tried hard not to appear different. He thought that quite ordinary things were unusual, such as forks.

When Hubert spoke to one of the girls working at the bench, she giggled and looked round at the others, before giving Hubert a sort of scared look, and calling him "sir". Phillip had read in many magazine stories how women were inscrutable, mysterious, unpredictable (the dictionary gave this word a disappointing meaning when he looked it up, hoping to find in it a clue to Helena Rolls' nature). He kept well away from the benches, pretending to be preoccupied with some thought. But on leaving, he glanced back, and three girls waved at him as he went through the door. Greatly daring, Phillip waved back, then quickly retreated, his footfalls clanking down the fretwork iron stairs.

"Well," said Thomas Turney, "What d'you think of it all, eh?"

"Oh, it's all right, Gran'pa," replied Phillip; and wondered why Mr. Hemming laughed.

After tea in an A.B.C. shop Thomas Turney said to Phillip, "Your Mother tells me you met Sir Wilfred Castleton, proprietor of 'The Daily Trident'. Well, m'boy, his offices are only just across the street. We pass that way to the Embankment. You've got a bent for writing, how about calling on him, what d'you think? I've met 'im, he's a pleasant sort of man, he's Irish, like me mother. You'll be leavin' school in a year or so. It might lead to something, you never know. No time like the present—what d'you say?"

"No thanks, Gran'pa," replied Phillip immediately, in panic at the thought of having to leave the life he knew.

Chapter 28

JAUNT TO BELGIUM

"WELL done, m'boy!" exclaimed Gran'pa, when Phillip went in to tell him, casually, that he had passed the Oxford Local. He had got his remove, too, into the Upper Fifth. He had failed in History, Geography, Geometry, Trigonometry, and Latin; but was satisfactory in Algebra, Arithmetic, Divinity, Physics, and Chemistry.

"No Spanish? A pity, Spanish is the coming language, for trade in South America. Our future lies in the export trade, with our merchant navy. This intensifying competition with Germany will have to be diverted to the South Atlantic, where there are great potential markets for our manufactures. He-he-he." This last comment in pseudo laughter was caused by Phillip wandering out of the room.

"Phillip never listens to me," remarked Thomas Turney, turning to his housekeeper, Miss Rooney, who sat demurely, hands on lap, in one of the two upholstered chairs on either side of the fire-place. He himself sat in his usual wheel-backed yew chair, with the cane fire-and-draught guard on its back. His cat crouched, with shut eyes, on his cocked-up knee, cased in perennial blue serge. Thomas Turney now possessed more than two dozen such pairs of trousers, with their jackets and waistcoats, all bought at January sales during the last few years: thus he allayed one of his anxieties about the future.

Phillip went down to Uncle Hugh's room, to talk to Bob, Uncle's man. Uncle nowadays could walk only by clinging with one hand to the broad leather strap Bob wore round his jacket. Bob came from Mercy Terrace, down by the station, from a family of soldiers. There were four brothers, all of them with dark hair and dark, almost black eyes. It was a little scaring to go into Bob's house to see him, for when the brothers were at home they sat there so quiet, yet seeming ready at any time to break into frightful rages. They had joined the Army because they had not been able to get any work, Bob told Phillip. Two had worked in the docks, until the strike six months before, when they had taken the King's shilling.

The thing that disturbed Phillip, secretly, was the attitude of

Bob and his brothers towards the girls they met in the streets at night. They hunted them down, almost as though they were enemies. Bob told Phillip, with a sort of subdued angry satisfaction, what he and his pal did when they got off with a couple. He took a card out of his breast pocket, with a drawing, on one side, of a thing like a leg-of-mutton bone. On the other side was a heart.

"You show this to a girl, this side first, and say, 'This is the bone that breaks your heart,' then you turn the card over and say, 'And this is the heart what was broken.' Blime, me and Alf had some sport the other foggy night, outside the Mission! Two girls arst us what the card meant. They was pretendin', but us warn't! So we took 'em inside the Mission, and showed 'em. They didn't want to, then, but it was too late."

Bob was a sort of Jack Hart, Phillip thought. He grinned in the same rather frightening way. The station end of Randiswell beyond the Railway pub and the Mission, was rather a sinister place. That was where the Monks had lived. Phillip remembered how the father of Mona Monk, the servant Mother had had when he was little, had come up drunk one night and smashed in the front door. Father had knocked him out with his special constable's truncheon and blown his whistle for the police to come and take Monk away on a stretcher. Mona, although only fourteen, had had a baby afterwards. Gerry had told him that her own father had given it to her. How awful some people were!

Phillip's business with Bob in Uncle Hugh's room was over a silver cigarette box he had bought at a pawnshop. He wanted Bob to sell it back to the pawnbroker, and buy with the money a small plated derringer pistol lying in the window. With this he intended to shoot wild pigeons in the woods of Whitefoot Lane. Bob promised to sell the silver box, which was fairly heavy for its size, with flowers and ferns engraved on the lid, and buy the derringer, which was marked 1/6. Phillip had bought the box for that price, a month or so previously.

Bob was washing out Uncle Hugh's rubber thing, which was fixed to Uncle at night, to prevent him having accidents in bed. It was not very nice to look at, but Uncle had now lost control of his functions. Phillip was mildly sorry for Uncle Hugh, who soon would have to go away to a nursing home. He was failing fast, said Mother. Uncle Hugh was an awful warning, Mother often told him, never to do anything that he knew was wrong. "Ah, my son, I often say to myself that the saddest words in the language are, 'Too Late'."

Phillip "simply itched" to be the owner of the derringer. He had at least another year at school, now that he had passed the Oxford Local. Father had seen the Magister, and it had been agreed that he should stay an extra year at school after the five years of the scholarship period ran out in April, Father paying the fees. Father said that there were good prospects in the future for Actuaries in the Life Assurance companies, but he would have to buck up and improve the mathematical side of his studies, and get First Class Honours next time with distinctions, if he were to have any chance at all. Phillip had received this information with voiceless gloom. What he would like to be was an official in the Ministry of Agriculture and Fisheries, the sort who wrote the pamphlets about what birds were good for the farmer, and why.

This would entail a certain amount of examination upon the contents of various birds' crops, to see what they fed on. To get the specimens, they would have to be shot first. Phillip's idea of this work involved a motorcycle, the derringer pistol, and travelling about all over England. He could take a small tent, and camp out, cooking by a fire in the woods. He could take photographs of birds or their nests. Fishing, too, might be done, in order to find out what fish fed on. Then he never need go to work in London, inside the sort of office Father worked in, or the awful counting house of Mallard, Carter & Turney, Ltd.

Anyway, another year at school would put off the fateful time when he must grow up and become a slave like Father.

"Then, you'll do that for me, Bob?" Bob nodded.

"Phillip, m'boy," called out Gran'pa, as he came up from Uncle Hugh's room, gloating at the thought of the derringer, which took the same ammunition that Father fired in his .22 miniature rifle.

For a period, Phillip had dreamed of having the old rifle Mother had bought for Father, for a New Year's present, converted to take .22 ammunition, as Father did not want it. It was an old Martini-Henry rifle, practically a dummy, and used for drill only. Mother had bought it from Peter Wallace's father. Father had made a fuss, as usual, about the Martini-Henry, saying it was a white elephant, and why had she wasted her money, instead of consulting him first? Mother had in the end gone away to be by herself in the front room. When he had followed her there, she said, wiping her eyes. "I can never do anything to please your Father, Phillip. When the time comes for you to get married, I hope, if only for the sake of your little children, you will think always before you speak! I did not waste my money in buying it, anyway it was my own money, left me by Mamma, and——"

Here she had cried again; but was smiling soon, and telling Father that she was sorry she had made a mistake, and would he please buy the right kind at the Stores, and allow her to pay for it? Father had bought himself a .22 miniature rifle, but had insisted on paying for it himself. He had, however, consented to allow Mother to give him, for a present, the brown canvas bag in which it was carried.

"Mother has got only a very little money of her own, Phillip. I do not think that she should spend any of it on me. Anyway, your Mother knows that I do not want people to give me presents. I do not deserve them. I am well aware that I am a failure."

This admission had no effect on Phillip. Father had said that before; but had remained Father, as before.

When Phillip was in bed Richard, after greasing the Martini-Henry, and wrapping it in brown paper, took it down with him through the trap-door and stood it beside his violoncello, where, he said somewhat wryly to himself, it would stand on sentry go and see his time out. Which was not entirely prophetic, as the not-so-distant future was to reveal.

Presents to and from members of the Turney family were never unacceptable. Thomas Turney invited Hetty and Joey to accompany him on a visit to the Continent at Easter, and perhaps Phillip would like to come along too? It would help broaden the boy's outlook. Mavis did not come home from the convent for the Easter holidays, so it was proposed to visit her at Wespaeler. It would give Phillip a chance to practise his French, one of his shakiest subjects. What did Phillip say?

Phillip remained mute at first. It would mean missing Desmond, and hearing with him the first chiffchaff and willow wren in the coverts of Shooting Common. The carrion crow laid early, too. and there was a tawny owl's nest he had "suspected" in the Park of the Dowager Countess. He looked up dates in his *Schoolboy's Diary*. It would mean missing the first fortnight in April. The cuckoo arrived on April 15 in his preserves. The swallow on April 8. It would mean losing only a week or so. He decided to go.

"I think you ought to accept Gran'pa's invitation yourself, Phillip, and thank him at the same time, don't you? Otherwise he may think that you take everything for granted."

"Oh blow! You do it for me, Mum. I must do this trigonometry, if I am to be an actuary, you know."

Cousin Petal would be travelling with Mother and himself, as she was going to the convent. There might be a chance to have it out with her. Uncle Charley and Aunt Flo were going to New York. Tommy was to spend the holidays with Aunt Dorrie, before going to boarding school at Brighton College. Yes, Petal—

Soon after breaking up, Phillip and Petal, with Hetty, left Liverpool Street station for Harwich. They were crossing by the *Peter der Koeneck* to Ostend. Phillip was afraid that he would be sick, a dread confirmed by the smell of the engines before he went on board. Petal, on the other hand, said she loved the sea. Phillip tried to think that he did too; but not the oily engines. He disappeared into dark galleries below the deck, lit by yellow carbon-filament electric lamps, the filaments being shaped like the top half of a heart—a sight which, he thought wildly, was enough to make anyone sick, as it twisted the eyes. Hetty got a rug, and covered him on a bunk, a tin basin, talisman of safety, beside him. Oh, why had he come? Everything was so oily. Hetty decided a little unhappily that she had given him her weak stomach.

The ship pitched and rolled through the swell of the recent equinoctial gales. At last it was over, and a pale Phillip beside a pink-cheeked Petal crossed the gangway on to foreign soil. Once on shore, with a medicinal cognac inside him, Phillip began to notice how strange a place it was. The women wore black shawls and thick black skirts, and clopped past in wooden sabots. Horses looked very thin and uncared for. He was surprised to see a young woman straddling over a drain beside the pavement and behave just like a horse. After a momentary stare at the unexpected, Phillip looked the other way. A gendarme was standing quite near, too. Fancy doing that right in front of a policeman!

The Hotel Windsor, where their porter had led them, was a yellow-painted place. When they had tidied up in their rooms, and partaken of *café au lait* with *petit pain* with *beurre* and *confiture* in the *salle à manger* Phillip, exercising his French, said he felt *mieux*, and how about a *promenade?*

They went for a walk, and found themselves in a sort of circus or fair, where Hetty told them not to take out any money, in case they were robbed. So the five francs spending money, which Gran'pa had given Hetty for each of his grandchildren, remained in their purses. As they were leaving the fair-ground, Phillip saw something in a glass case which fascinated him. It was a girl, made of wax but absolutely life-like, with gleaming brown eyes and dark tresses over her shoulders and naked bosom, sitting back on her haunches; and as her head turned slowly from left to right in the glass case her mouth parted, she smiled with pearly teeth, and her bosom slowly rose and fell as she breathed. He fell in love with this dummy at first sight, and on return to the hotel, determined to see her again as soon as he could.

The opportunity occurred after a wonderful supper of *bifstek* and *pommes frits*, which beat any English chips to smithereens, he told his mother. And the French *moutarde*! And the salad they ate off a separate little plate! Why could they not have food like that at home?

"We would, dear, always, if Father could afford it."

After supper, Phillip slipped back to the fair. Naphtha flares were now alight, and great arcs of electric bulbs glowing like yellow pearls all over the place. Steam music was blaring, cymbals clashing, painted wooden horses flying. He found his inamorata again, and feasted his eyes on her, just as the hero did on the heroine in *Pearson's Magazine*.

In the garish light this figurante, for ever slowly turning, breathing, and flashing her eyes, began to look like Petal, as he had seen her without her clothes on, sitting on her bed and brushing her hair. A pang smote him. If he went back to the Hotel Windsor, it would not be like out here, but if he stayed out here, he would only feel lost and rather hopeless. And supposing someone demanded payment, what could he do? Feeling lonely, Phillip went back to the Windsor.

"You look tired, dear, I think we all ought to have an early night," said Hetty, seeing his face when he reappeared. When they went upstairs he gave a bare goodnight to his Mother, but no word for Petal, as he closed his door. He felt that a fine wire was pulling him away from Mother. The bed in his room had a horrible soft bag-like covering on top, shapeless and heavy. The whole room seemed dead, a part of the dirty cobbled streets, with little carts drawn by dogs, the scarecrow horses with raw sores on them, pulling the big heavy waggons. Men in dark shapeless coats and trousers with shapeless peaked caps, smoking acrid tobacco, spitting all the time, with big mufflers round their necks, and clopping wooden shoes.

He tried to open a window. The air in the room was stale. It looked as though it had never been opened. He could never sleep in a room unless the fresh air could come in. The window would not open. He sat on the bed, and took off his boots, in the light of his candles in heavy china sticks on the dressing table. Then in stockinged feet he went to the wash-hand-stand, and found the first friendly thing in the room, a brass can of hot-water wrapped in a clean white towel, like a turban. But there was no soap. Mother had the soap, in her bag. She had brought it from England, as the Belgian hotels, she said, did not provide soap. He *must* wash his hands before going to bed, he could never sleep unless his hands were clean and free.

Why hadn't Mother put some soap in his bag, one with a snap-fastener lent by Gran'pa? If she had known about no soap, she ought to have put some in.

But where was her room? It was next to his, but which way, up or down the corridor? Supposing he knocked on the wrong door? He dare not risk it. Why couldn't Mother be sensible?

While he was sitting on the bed, feeling cold, there came a tap on the door. He went to open it. Petal stood there, in her dressing gown.

He was relieved to see her. "Come in," he whispered, and shut the door behind her. "Isn't it a dismal old hole? Have you got any soap?"

"No, haven't you? That's what I came in for. It must be in Aunty Hetty's bag. Tell me, where did you go to after dinner, Phil?"

"Oh, just for a walk. My window doesn't open, does yours?"

"No. But it doesn't matter. We're only here for one night. Did you go back to the fair ground?"

"Yes."

"To see that mechanical girl in the glass case?"

"Yes I did, if you want to know. I wanted to see how it worked."

"Did you find out?"

"No, I can't speak French well enough."

"I could see she fascinated you."

"Poof, a dummy like that? What rot!"

"It was the attitude, wasn't it? Like this."

Petal seated herself on the bed, shook her hair loose, and squatted on her heels, her arms sideways, in the posture of the wax figure. Then she put on a smile, with parted lips, giving an imitation in candlelight which increased Phillip's rate of breathing before her.

"Do you think I'm a good actress, Phillip?"

He nodded. "Shall we do it now?" he managed to say.

It was Petal's turn to nod.

"Lie down then," he whispered. "Wait a mo', I'll chuck off this beastly eiderdown." Petal obeyed, like an obedient girl. Phillip lay upon her. He felt rather awkward. What was he supposed to do next?

"Is this right?" he asked.

"I don't think so."

He got off, and stood up. The feeling of fascination was gone. Petal got off the bed, and threw back her hair.

"Where's Aunt Hetty's room?"

"Next to mine, down the passage. I say, Petal."

"What?"

"Did you really come in for some soap?"

"Yes, of course. What else d'you think I came in for?"

"I don't know."

There was a tap on the door. Petal opened it.

"Petal, what are you doing here, dear?"

"I came in to try and borrow some soap, Aunt Hetty."

"Well dear, you should have come to me. I've just put some in your room. You'd better go back now, dear. We've got a long day before us tomorrow, and Phillip hasn't been very well. I've brought some for him, too. Don't catch a chill, Phillip. Come on, Petal, I am sure we are all very tired. Are you feeling all right now, Phillip?"

"Yes, Mum, quite all right. Goodnight. Goodnight Petal, see you tomorrow."

He yawned; and after washing his hands, for warmth got

into bed in his vest and shirt, to fall asleep thinking that he would have four days with Desmond on his return, before the new term beginning on the twentieth of April.

Coffee and rolls with *conserve* and *beurre* were very nice for breakfast; and in high expectation they drove to the *gâre* (Phillip played a game with himself, to see how many French words he could learn) in a *voiture* pulled by a *cheval sur le route de pierres*. The station was grimy like all London ones, but the trains quite different. This one, for Bruxelles, had an immense-wheeled engine, and a tinny little tooting horn which it obeyed in a vast cloud of steam. It was not much louder than Freddy Payne and his pewter bugle, in the scouting days of long ago.

The second class carriage was dark grey. A notice on a small white enamelled plate said *Niet rooken niet speuen*. Phillip fancied himself as a linguist as he explained to Mother and Petal that in this carriage people must neither smoke nor spit. On the other side of the carriage was a similar notice, which said *Défense de fumer et de crâcher*. He had learned a new word—*crâcher*. It somehow fitted the noise of a Belgian getting ready to expectorate.

"Ne crâchez vous, Mama! Niet speuen, Feuille de Fleur! Mum, why does it say it in two languages?"

"Some of the Belgians are of French extraction, or Walloon, dear, while the other half is Flemish, or Flamand. Oh, how it all comes back to me, my girlhood, I mean."

With a smile Hetty looked out of the window at the countryside, thinking of Dorrie and Mamma.

"Surely you didn't smoke and spit when you were at the convent?"

Hetty laughed. "Sometimes I can almost hear my brother Hugh in your tones, Phillip. You have the same sense of fun."

Poor Hughie! Hetty reflected, as she looked toward the window again, that he believed Papa would sooner or later want to get rid of him; and so of late he had been occupying himself with the idea of starting a stationery business by post. Laboriously Hughie was sending samples of brown paper, tarred on one side to make it water-proof, to some of his old customers, as he called them—the firms he had been visiting nearly twenty years before! It was pathetic, for of course those firms still dealt with Mallard, Carter & Turney. Hughie's mind often wandered back to that time, in what seemed to Hetty to be a desperate effort to make a fresh start in life, all over again. Too late, too late! The saddest words in the language.

"Look, Sonny, at the windmills. They pump up water from the dykes, for all this is very low-lying country."

The towers of Bruges came into view. Then they were on the way to Ghent, which the Flamands insisted on calling Gand. They were always quarrelling with the French section of the population, explained Hetty. Peace, peace! she thought, and saw Mamma's face smiling at her in space, a little sadly. In the cathedral of Bruges was a casket said to contain a drop of the blood of Christ, saved from the Cross. *Come unto Me . . . and I will give you rest.* Was Mamma watching over Hughie, and all of her children? Pray God that Phillip and Mavis and Doris would not have to go through what the older generation had had to suffer! Still, one must never give way to repining, one must keep one's spirits up, for the sake of the living.

Brussels of happy memory! The same big dogs drawing their little carts, with long loaves of bread in them, and urns of milk, and vegetables for market. And the *Pension Louise*, in the Avenue Louise, where she had stayed as a girl! Old Mme. Louise's daughter was now in charge, another Mme. Louise, just as friendly. Papa and Joey smiling, everyone pleased to see them! It was almost like being home again, for a moment.

Phillip had to share a room in the top of the house with his Uncle Joseph. There were two beds in the room, one very small, for a child really, the other large. Would he mind sharing with Uncle Joey? Phillip did not mind. Uncle Joey was not like an Uncle, really. He had no sternness in him. Phillip did not recognise pure kindness. He rather looked down on Uncle Joey for being childish. Phillip had heard Father saying, once, that he had been laughed at by Uncle Joey, something to do with the time when Father asked Gran'pa for Mother's hand in marriage. Fortunately he did not snore, and kept to his side of the bed, and made only one joke about feet, when he was washing his in a tiny little bowl shaped like a dolls' house bath; for there was no bathroom in the *Pension Louise*.

"These foreigners don't believe in soap and water, Phillip, haw-haw! When they do, the women wash inside a linen shroud, afraid of their own bodies! Haw-haw-haw!"

Phillip, entering into the joke, pretended to be trying to get into the little bath.

It was lovely, new kind of food, and nice to change into Etons for dinner at night. Gran'pa made a mistake the first night, by helping himself, after the soup, to most of the omelette for their table, which held six people. Gran'pa took a plateful, then had to put most of it back on the dish, else it would not have gone round. He-he-he, laughed Gran'pa, saying he had thought it was the main dish. The *garcon*, bending down, said in English that stewed pigeons and pears, the *spécialité de la maison*, was to follow. Phillip thought that when he had the derringer pistol, he would ask Mother to cook the pigeons he shot, with stewed pears.

The next day they went to Antwerp, called Anvers. Here they separated, agreeing to meet for *dejeuner* at The Golden Lion. Hetty, with Petal and Phillip, went on by train to Wespaeler, to fetch Mavis from the convent, for a day in the City.

There was a wood outside the convent, and as they went through the gates, Phillip saw a notice board on a tree, *Het ist verboden in het bosch tee gaan.* It was easy to translate that: It is forbidden in this wood to go. A long-tailed titmouse flitting by to perch on a hedge gave him an idea that there was a nest there.

Saying that he wanted to go to the lavatory, and would follow her to the convent—a grey building of turrets and high roof—he returned to enter the forbidden wood. It was full of small birds, pigeons, and pheasants. With a thrilling feeling, he went exploring.

The ashpoles were tall, among oaks and other trees. A jay screamed. It was just like England. But what was the hut doing at the top of one tree, made of brushwood around a platform? A flimsy sort of ladder, with cross pieces of stick nailed to the trunk, led up to it. It was very high to climb, especially on that wonky-looking ladder. Perhaps it was a robbers' look-out. What a story he would tell Desmond and Mrs. Neville when he got back! He had discovered a brigand's lair!

After wandering in the wood for some minutes, while all the time he was conscious of Mother's anxiety, Phillip went back the way he had come. He was keeping the nest of the bottle-bird, as Percy called it, to the end.

The leaves of the hedge were small and new. The nest, shaped like a little wooden barrel or ploughman's bottle before the days of glass among labourers, was visible at once. It was the first he had seen, other than those already pulled out by village boys at Beau Brickhill. Greatly excited, while the little smoke-hued birds twitted overhead, he put a finger in the hole at the side, feeling the interior to be warm with many layers of feathers, and at the bottom, some eggs. Trembling, he withdrew the finger, and inserted two, bringing out with extreme care an egg, scarcely bigger than a pea, between the tips.

It was white, scarcely freckled. Was it an old hen, who had lost power to colour an egg? Why were eggs, anyway, decorated with spots and blotches? If, as was said, for protective coloration only, then why the many many patterns? Were the coloured feathers of the birds for protective coloration? Why did women wear pretty dresses? For the same reason that eggs were decorated, and birds' feathers, of course! For beauty!

The nest was beautiful, made of moss and fibre and horsehair, and covered outside with thousands of pieces of green-grey lichen, off apple-trees and oaks and ashes, tacked together by spider-webs. A thousand journeys to a farm-yard must have been undertaken to line the nest with its warm wads of feathers. How *could* some village boys pull out such a nest, when the birds were so very very small, and unable to defend their home?

The bottle-bird laid up to sixteen eggs, so she would not miss one; and wrapping it carefully in his handkerchief, Phillip climbed the hedge of the bosch in which it was verboden tee gaan, and hurried to the entrance of the convent d'Ursulines.

Seeing no bell pull, he opened the church-like door and crept inside. A nun came forward, her hands clasped.

"Ah," she said softly, looking down at him. "You must be Hetty's boy. Your Mother is upstairs, if you will come with me."

Cap in hand, Phillip went beside her up some stone steps, an in-church expression on his face. He passed a room with an open door in which many girls in dark uniforms like Mavis' were sitting. They all had white starched collars like boy's collars, and white cuffs over their wrists, as he saw in a swift glance.

They went into a room of white walls, on one of which was an altar with Virgin and Child. Before it a candle burned, newly lighted. Mother was standing there, with a very old nun with a silver chain and rosary hanging before her, on her robes. She had an old sweet face.

"Ah," she said, in the same sort of soft voice, "here is your son, my child," to Mother, and as she said it, Phillip felt that the old nun really did look on her as a child.

Mother was smiling. She said, "Oh yes, here he is! This is my little boy, Mère Ambroisine."

The Mother Superior looked at him, and took his hand between her own soft, pink, wrinkled hands. Then another nun, with a larger kind of headdress, came forward, and he was introduced to her. She was shorter than the Mother Superior, with a fatter face, and a more jolly expression.

"I knew your Mamma when she was a very little girl," she whispered, smiling and bobbing her starched white head-dress.

"Are you all right, Phillip?" asked Mother, in a very soft voice.

"Yes, thank you, Mamma," replied Phillip, as softly, feeling that he was part of his song *In the Cathedral*, in a calm holy feeling, red sunset streaming . . . a choir-boy's surplice over him, white and clean. Mère Ambroisine looked at him steadily, a smile on her lips. Phillip looked up at Mère Ambroisine, feeling that she was a wonderful person, rather like Grannie, but Grannie was always back, somewhere, while Mère Ambroisine was forward. He felt himself to be rain-drop clear.

"Your son is a good boy, my child," said Mère Ambroisine, gently, smiling at Mother. "He will be a good man. I can see it in his face. He has your look, my child."

"Oh yes, he is a very good boy, really," said Mother, with a faraway little laugh. Phillip felt good as he looked up at the Mother Superior and smiled, feeling that when he had not been good, it was not really himself. Then Mavis came in, and hugged Mummie. Phillip saw that she had tears in her eyes.

Mavis was very nearly like her mother in temperament; but less unselfish, less broad in her complete submission to life. Mavis lived in a world of dreams; all her love flowed to her mother, and to her home. She saw her home as a lovely place; in her mind she went for walks on the Hill, which was ever in sunlight, birds singing in the trees and bushes, the grass green; her Father was the warm, safe Dads he had been before he had said to her, "I do not love you"; but she trembled whenever she thought of that time, and a heaviness filled her, until her mind turned away to Mother; and her love, tremulous and desperate, flowed again to the place of her home. So she prayed much at the convent, and dreamed of her house, always in sunshine; and hoped that always her mother would be happy as she worked religious texts with silken threads upon perforated white cardboard—always for Mummie.

Phillip thought that the convent was huge, with a church, and many large rooms and *salles à manger*. More rooms they passed had girls in them, all in black with white collars outside their uniforms, black bows at the throat, and white cuffs. Phillip kept his eyes on the ground, or anywhere but at the faces, to show how good and polite he was.

Mavis came back with them to Anvers. There was half an hour before *déjeuner*, and Gran'pa suggested they should take a walk and see the prison.

"The outside, only, of course, he-he-he!" Joseph added his haw-haw laugh. His eyes were always bright and kind, but oh, what a fool he was!

Suddenly Phillip decided to run away. When they were not looking, he went round a corner, and walked on straight down the street. The feeling drew him on, to hurt himself and Mother. He wanted to be alone, to feel as he had felt when in the wood, and when Mère Ambroisine was touching his head. He wanted to be alone with the sad but happy feeling. He crossed the road, and the rails of steam-trams, and went on towards a broad river he saw a long way in front of him. When he got there he saw it was a muddy colour, like the Thames at Greenwich. Steamships were moored along its docks, and tugs with high big bows were pressing against the tide, parting the waters and leaving creamy wakes behind them. Seagulls flew crying, seeming smaller than those at Hayling Island. They had black caps, and pink legs, and screamed more shrilly than herring gulls.

He walked down by the Scheldt, and came to a large covered shed, with open sides, extending for two hundred yards at least beside the quay. Old women were brushing something with long-handled brooms, in front. When he got nearer he saw that they were brushing the hides of bullocks, to which the tails and part of the leg-skin were still attached. There were stacks and stacks of hides. He did not connect these hides with the Geography he learnt at school, since there was no connection in his mind between the classroom and his life outside.

In the next shed were many motorcycles in rows, fixed inside wooden crates. They were painted dark green, and the letters F.N. on their tanks instantly made him think of Uncle Charley. A label tacked to one crate had written on the card, Capricorn Importers, Ltd., Cape Town, Sud Afrique. That was Uncle Charley's company! He wanted to rush up to a group of men in peaked caps and tell them the staggering news. They were going to his Uncle! His other Uncle, and their father Mr. Turney, was at that moment at the Golden Lion!

The great news made him run back the way he had come. He missed a turning, and thought he was lost. Fear struck into him. Never to see Mother again! He had only pretended to want to be lost before; now it was real. In his mind he saw Mother's face, and her sad smile. When she had lost anything, she always prayed to Saint Anthony. Phillip now prayed, asking to be shown the way to the *Lion d'Or*. There it was in front of him, but on the wrong side of the road he had imagined it to be.

He promised not to go for a walk by himself again, Mother saying that he was Gran'pa's guest, and had kept the meal waiting. She said he would have to go without his soup; but Gran'pa said there was no need for that, the lunch was *prix fixé*, and he might as well have what would have to be paid for anyway, he-he-he. Then Phillip told them about the motorbikes, feeling that his news in a way made up for his lateness.

"I only hope Charley has got customers for them, and isn't only speculating," said Gran'pa. "And why does he choose this moment to go to New York, for a holiday? He should be attending to his business in South Africa."

Uncle Joey said, "I suggest that we reserve judgment until we learn the facts, sir, and until then give Charley the benefit of the doubt."

Mother said, with a smile at Petal, "Oh, I am sure Charley knows what he is doing, Papa."

At this Gran'pa said, as he poured out some red wine for himself, his napkin tucked into the top of his waistcoat, "Well then, you are surer than I am, Hetty my girl, he-he-he."

Petal and Mavis went back with them to Brussels. The next day they all went to watch the ice-skating from a gallery above a large rectangular rink, the place brilliant with electric light. Two string bands played in turn, one at either end of the gallery. Girls in white dresses waltzed below. Phillip recognised one of the tunes from the old Polyphone records in the front room at home. It was the Skaters' Waltz. They were very graceful, said Mother, and how she would like to skate again. Had *she* ever skated? asked Phillip, much surprised.

"Of course I have, Phillip. Everyone learned to skate when I was a girl, and what fun it was, too. Ah well, when you have a little family, you see, you have no time for such things."

"Did Father skate, too?"

"Yes, dear, but not with me. You see, I did not know him then."

"I shouldn't think so, either," he muttered, with a shrug.

"Hush, dear," she whispered, glancing at Gran'pa, sitting with Uncle Joey at the next table. "Do listen to the music, Phillip, isn't it lovely?"

He thought it was; so was the *confiserie*. Much nicer than cakes in England; full of cream, and other luscious things, too. The *patisserie* shops were simply crammed with wonderful cakes. You went into one, took a fork and plate, helped yourself, and paid at the desk, then ate them standing up. One thing good about Gran'pa was that he provided plenty of pocket money. Good old Gramps, whatever Father said about him being a Turney! But then Gran'pa had a lot of money, compared with poor old Father, who entered up every ha'penny he spent in his diary at night, before locking it up again in his desk.

There were electric theatres, too, where films—Petal called them fillums—were shown, the same sort to be seen at home. Only some of the kinemas here—as the Magister of his school said they should be called from the Greek word—were named *High Life*, pronounced Hee Leef. They went to one, and saw the Mack Sennett Bathing Belles, and a French film in which men were constantly popping in and out of bedrooms, firing guns, falling into water-tubs, and turning hoses on frightfully funny gendarmes. One man fell off the Eiffel Tower, and splashed into the Seine; and then seeing a police launch approaching, fell all the way up again to the top of the tower. Could they have wound him up, all the way back, on an invisible wire? It was screamingly funny, and Phillip laughed all the louder to hide the fact that in the darkness his hand was resting on Petal's warm knee. He glowed all over with the warmth of her wonderful knee.

He walked back to the Avenue Louise arm in arm with her, Mavis on his other arm; and Hetty walking arm-in-arm with Papa and Joey behind said she was so glad to see him, Phillip, coming out of himself, that was what he needed, to see the wider world. It was just like old times. Dear Papa, no one could have a better father! Then, in loyalty to Dickie, she thought that he, too, needed at times to be taken out of his cramped surroundings. Dear Dickie, so concerned for the good of his little family.

Phillip was sorry to be going back, sorry to have to say good-bye to Mavis, who had been quite different from what she was at home. He felt glad to have such a nice sister. He was almost proud of her, and Petal too. Uncle Joey was quite nice when you came to know him. School in five days! Ah, but the English spring was there, waiting for him! Also, he would be seeing Desmond.

Phillip had had no thought of Helena Rolls during his visit abroad.

It was a rough crossing. He was sick; and Mother was sick as well. Gran'pa said at Dover that there must have been a head-wind in the Atlantic, and Charley and Flo had probably had a shaking aboard the new White Star liner anyway, as it was out for the Blue Riband.

In the train, feeling better, Phillip took out the pillbox (Mother never travelled without her little liver pills) in which, nestled in cotton-wool, lay the Belgian long-tailed tit's egg. No one else at school in the holidays would have got such a rare specimen!

At Victoria, when they got out of the train, a newsboy was shouting something as he ran along the platform. Many people were buying papers. Feeling the pill-box in his pocket, Phillip thought that the egg would be a memento of the holiday all his life.

"Hi, boy!" cried Gran'pa beside him, "A paper!" Then Gran'pa said, "Good God, Hetty! Joey! Charley! My boy!—my boy! !

Phillip looked at the newsbill, and saw, in big red letters, the words

TITANIC

SUNK

It was a sad journey home. When they got back, a wireless telegram awaited Thomas Turney. Charley and Flo had missed the White Star boat at Southampton, and had travelled on a Canadian Pacific boat.

"He-he!" Gran'pa wheezed in laughter. "Charley, I always said, would be late for his own funeral!"

Chapter 29

GHOSTS

THE derringer pistol remained for months in the pawnshop window. Bob, Uncle Hugh's man, said he had lost the silver cigarette box. Phillip knew that he had really stolen it, but said nothing, as he knew Bob would deny it; anyway Bob knew he would never dare to complain, as Bob knew too much about him. Bob was a rotter, and he would have nothing more to do with him. Bob was leaving Gran'pa's service, anyway, as Uncle Hugh was now so weak that he could not walk, even while hanging to the leather strap round Bob's waist. He was going into a nursing home, said Mother, after Christmas.

Then there was a very nice little varnished greenheart rod in the pawnshop window, price one-and-six. Phillip bought it with some of his Christmas present money, with one or two glances of regret at the little silver-plated derringer. There was a pair of boots on the counter, as he examined the rod; and after buying it, he asked, idly, how much the boots were. One-and-sixpence, said Mr. Sprunt.

When he heard that he was invited to visit his cousin Willie at Rookhurst, Phillip wondered how he should dress for the visit. He thought of the boots; they had patent leather toe-caps, and buttons; perhaps if he wore them with his best suit, and a bowler hat, it would be correct? Obsessed with the idea of correcting his inferior social status by the wearing of such boots at a country house—life in which he had read of in monthly fiction magazines—Phillip went with his mother to the shop, under the three gilt balls, and bought them. Father's stories of his old home, and the life there, had suddenly made Phillip feel afraid of the forthcoming visit.

He returned from Rookhurst with enthusiastic accounts of Willie and Uncle John, and the wonderful life in the West Country—and incidentally a present of a small saloon gun firing No. 2 cartridges and bulleted-breech-caps.

This Richard confiscated. It was a lethal weapon, he declared, and a suburb was no place for such a thing. His brother John should have known better than to give him it. However, he did not want to appear censorious, so would Phillip agree to let him have it, for safe-keeping, until such time as his future was decided?

This future to Phillip now loomed like the opaque barrier closing in upon his life. The opaque barrier had always been with him, since he could remember. Sometimes it had appeared in dreams, hopelessly sad dreams in which he was always unable to move away from some final, and most fearful, catastrophe. Only once had a dream been inexpressibly sweet, in the golden light of the sun and glowing blue sky that somehow were also the hair and eyes of a smiling Helena Rolls: but on awakening, down came the opaque barrier upon the heart, like a dead and heavy weight. Nothing could be done about it: the barrier was part of life, which was sad the moment you allowed yourself to realise things. Mother sometimes said that she did not think people were meant to be happy in this life. Yes, the opaque barrier was always there. *Why* was it? What you wanted to do, and what life made you do—the barrier was always in between. Tears, despair, fear, hopelessness—all were of the barrier.

This barrier, this hopelessness, this dim awareness of events controlling life, was now greyly near. It was involved with the idea of leaving home, and England, for ever; more particularly in Father's suggestion that he consider seriously emigration to Australia, to work on Uncle Hilary's farm in New South Wales, possibly with cousin Willie. Uncle Hilary was prepared to help, said Richard; he would arrange passage for both boys, and pay their fees at the Agricultural College, Sydney. Thus an open-air life, which Phillip and Willie both wanted, was possible. Well, let Phillip think it over.

Phillip had already talked it over with Cousin Willie. Both boys had, as their Fathers would have said, shied away from the idea. They both agreed that there was no place like England. The alternative was an office in London, perhaps in the Moon. Still, they would have Saturday afternoons off, and Sundays, for watching birds, a passion the cousins shared.

Richard had tried to be reasonable with Phillip over the saloon gun, which for scaring birds in orchards was fairly harmless, he said, when used with the blue-and-white chequered cartridges, and No. 7 shot, only. Each cartridge in the packet had been lovingly examined by Phillip; the blue squares of the case so blue, the white so white. Each was an inch long, and a quarter of an inch wide: enough for checking blackbirds at the currants or plums, said Richard, but the trouble, old chap, was those bulleted breech caps. The little copper cases fired a small lead ball, which might be lethal, if one struck a man at short range, particularly in the head.

Phillip said nothing, but looked dull.

"Why don't you work *with* me, instead of always *against* me?" cried Richard in exasperation. Then he used the word he had tried to avoid—*confiscate*; and seeing Phillip's face, the old irritation arose in him.

"No, not while I remain master in my own home, shall I permit a mere bit of a boy to have such a weapon!"

Richard knew about Phillip's latest catapult, made with powerful circular elastic, from which were fired lead balls made in a bullet-mould he had bought in a shop in Maidstone, whither he had cycled one day, alone. Phillip was an expert with this weapon, and had killed several wood-pigeons with it. The lead bullets had been made on the gas-stove, from lead heated in a tin held by pincers, and poured molten into the mould, which was then plunged in cold water. The balls had a range of over three hundred yards, and Richard had had a complaint from Mrs. Groat, ever anxious for her one remaining eye; but so far he had said nothing. The saloon gun was the last straw.

Now that he was soon to leave school, which he had hitherto said he hated, Phillip began to feel dismay at the thought of seeing no more the familiar faces in his world of classroom and fives-court, football field, and cricket pavilion at Colt Park, as the school playing fields were called. Colt Park was ten acres enclosed within trees, and yellow brick walls of Georgian residential houses. It lay back from the Dover road. Phillip had been as undistinguished an athlete as he was a scholar, showing no particular bent for anything, as regards the curriculum; unless it were literary piracy. There was the occasion when, asked to contribute to the school magazine, he had turned in a poem, presumably his own, entitled *To a Skylark*, beginning

Bird of the wilderness, blithesome and cumberless

which had been accepted by the three editors in the Sixth Form until the senior English Master pointed out that it was by James Hogg, "the Ettrick shepherd lad". To this master Phillip was "no ordinary potato", a boy of considerable intelligence which almost invariably was misapplied. He might find his place, the English Master once declared, in a circus; this was after he had appeared, one day at school luncheon, with a white rat on his shoulder. After this successful exhibition, Phillip had brought to the playing field at various times a pair of tame jackdaws called Jack and Jill, which disorganised an inter-house cricket match by flying down to perch on their foster-parent's head while he was fielding at cover point, and crying raucously to be fed. Then he had a tame jay called Jerry, which could not be kept out of the pavilion where doughnuts and cheese-cakes were sold; on another occasion he had turned up with a young brown owl, its baby-fluff still dreamy upon soft tawny feathers. This creature, pursued by sparrows, had flown off among the adjoining chimney pots and presumably taken thereafter to the wilds of Lee and the wide, flat extent of cabbage fields stretching to Eltham and beyond.

Richard had permitted these birds in the garden at home, and even in the house. Indeed, they had come into the bedrooms soon after sunrise, ejaculating, screaming, and in the case of the owl, chissicking for food. The jay had been the most inquisitive: morning after morning, soon after sunrise, Phillip had awakened to feel the bird perching on his head, industriously searching through his hair. Richard did not mind the occasional droppings about the house; the birds reminded him of his own boyhood, and, in particular, of his Father, for whom now he had much imaginative sympathy. Although nothing could condone the fact that his Father had failed in his duty to his Mother, yet, looking back, Richard saw that he had had some provocation—his Mother had not really been able to share his Father's life.

The term *no ordinary potato* was used in good-natured tolerance by the Senior English Master of what originally had been "The Free Grammar School of Queen Elizabeth in the Borough". Under the Elizabethan Letters Patent a body of governors had been appointed, but the establishment of the school faltered for want of funds; endowments were lacking, despite occasional gifts, such as that of a local resident who by his Will dated 7

December 1574 bequeathed, *Item 1 doe give towards the ereccon of the free scoole twenty shillings*, and another who gave the church-wardens of the parish *towards theire chargs in the perfectinge their assurances for the contynewaunce and maynteynaunce of theire free schoole there the somme of fyve poundes.*

Religious quarrels and persecutions made it a period of fear, submission, and uncertainty, until the Founder devoted life, and fortune, to the establishment of *all the best orders and exercises in use at the Free Schooles at Westminster, Paul's and Merchant Taylors' School, and in the Public Free School at Eaton.*

In such details Phillip had not the slightest interest, although Hetty, having bought a *History of the Borough*, had tried to share with him her own enthusiasm for the past, which had been kindled in her by listening to Mr. Mundy, when he came to sup with Papa.

Hetty had also met Mr. Graham, the author of the *History*, a most charming and elderly gentleman who had himself been at the school nearly forty years before. He was a bachelor, and devoted his life, apart from his work in the War Office in Whitehall, which had been recognised with the award of the M.V.O., between Antiquarianism and the furtherance of the social life of the school, particularly of the boys in their sports, games and pastimes.

Mr. Graham was usually to be seen on Saturday afternoons at Colt Park. In his high crowned black felt hat, always carrying an umbrella and wearing a cloak, with camera ever ready to snap groups upon the cricket or football fields, cross-country runs, or in the tented lines during the summer camp at Bisley, the tall, gentle figure of the distinguished Old Boy, with his flowing grey moustaches, was to be seen among the boys. Mr. Graham was the embodiment of tolerance and kindliness without exception, of devotion to the living material of his Alma Mater. Within his own home as a child he had been nurtured in love, from both his parents in balance. He was the selfless patron of the gentle Victorian age and ideal. There was seldom a Saturday afternoon when Mr. Graham did not leave Colt Park without three or four boys accompanying him, sure of hot buttered crumpets with poached eggs, pastries, buns, doughnuts, and seed-cake in the tea-shop opposite the tram-stop at Lee Green.

Phillip was often one of the invited, since he usually managed to be about as the welcome figure, gently prodding turf with the ferrule of his unrolled umbrella, lingered near the pavilion after football on Saturday afternoon in winter. Another boy, often invited, was Milton, now of the first eleven in both cricket and football.

History flowed through the life of this amiable patron, history was a living spirit to this bystander who never, by word or deed, strove to communicate his thoughts and beliefs directly. He was the good shepherd, whose dog never barks; whose eyes are as the shepherd's eyes, alive with the light of natural intelligence, which works with the flock by endowed thought, and knows direction of duty by a glance, a lift of the hand, a murmur: an animal which has never felt the strokes of pain without which lesser men deem such natures, and human life too, to be incorrigible. Life to this Friend of the School was for the purpose of high endeavour, to be lived for beauty, truth, and modesty in achievement.

Mr. Graham was of a generation which was soon to vanish from the Borough, even with the last traces of the county of Kent. In his earlier years he was by no means unique; he was a Christian gentleman, whose bearing had in some part been modulated by the possession of a private income. Mr. Graham had confided his interest in Phillip to Hetty: he thought that the boy showed signs of a talent for literature. It was his hope that one day the School would produce a boy whose work would do for it what the author of *Tom Brown's Schooldays* had done for Rugby.

From Mr. Graham's *History of the Borough* Hetty had learned many interesting things about the past. She shared with her father a love of history and literature, limited as the scope was. They had read and discussed *Pepys's Diary*, *The Letters of Jane Welsh Carlyle*, some of the novels of Thomas Hardy; and, from early years, there had been the readings, after supper, from the duodecimo set of Shakespeare's plays and sonnets.

Hetty wondered how Phillip, with his inability to learn Latin, would have fared at his school in the reign of Elizabeth, when the scholars in the upper forms had to speak to one another, and to the ushers, in Latin only. From Mr. Graham's book she learned that the school hours then were from seven o'clock in the spring and summer, and an hour later in the winter, to four o'clock in the afternoon, with an hour and a half for dinner and play. There were Praepostors appointed weekly to report misdemeanours both in and out of school, and neither masters nor boys were allowed to wear *long curl'd, frizzled, powdered or ruffin-like hair, but shall cut their Hair and wear it in such sort and manner that both the beauty of their Foreheads may be seen.* They were not to *use any clamorous cries nor casting stones nor fighting, nor use any rude or uncivil word or cries, nor to be whitlers or gravers of names in about the windows or other places.* They were not to indulge in *unlawful or hurtful pastimes as footballe, dice or cards or any game for money, nor to swim or wash in the river without leave.*

Boys, she thought, were very much the same in those days, as now. The Elizabethan scholars were allowed *shooting with long bows, stool-ball, running, wrestling, leaping, and other inoffensive exercises.* As for holidays, there were three weeks at Christmas, and a fortnight at Easter and Whitsuntide, with Shrove Monday and Tuesday.

Elbows on the plush table-cover, Hetty looked up from the book. "You ought to read this, dear, I am sure you would find it most interesting, how arithmetic was taught at your school, all that while ago—think of it, more than three hundred years!"

"Oh Mother, why must you talk about that mouldy book! Can't you see I'm busy? Anyhow, we have enough of that sort of muck at school. What's the good of it all? Anyway, I bet I've failed in my matriculation. The results will be out any day now. Oh lor'. Well, if you *must*, show me."

Under protest, he glanced at the book.

"Just read that piece, dear, and see how the scholar replied to his master in those days. *I* think it is rather funny!"

"Oh, very well."

Phillip gabbled, in mock of the Magister, as the Headmaster was called.

" 'Foure men gette a bootye or prise in tyme of warre'—why the bloke can't even spell!—'The prise is in valewe of mony 8190 £, and bicause the men be not of like degree'—that's me and Cranmer, after pinching the impedimenta of the Fordesmill Troop under old Purley-Prout—'therfore their shares may not be equall, but the chieffest person will haue of the bootye the third parte, and the tenth part ouer: the second will haue a quarter and the tenth part ouer'—half a mo'!"

Phillip decided to read it like a parson. He parted his black hair in the middle, and pressed each side on his head, like a jackdaw's wings. Then he folded a sheet of paper, for a "dog-collar," and continued in a droning voice,

" 'The second will haue a quarter and the tenthe parte ouer; the third will haue the syxt part: and so there is left for the fourth man a very small portion, but such is his lot (whether he be pleased or wroth)—'—and I bet he was using 'clamorous cries', Henrietta!—to continue, my dear friends—'he must be content with one XX part of the pray—' yea, verily, I bet afterwards he drank all of the XXX barrel as well, dear brethren —'Now I demaunde of you, what shall euery manne haue to his share?' " He flung down the book.

"Jumping Jehosophat, what a *frightful* sum!"

Doris was laughing so much that she almost fell from her chair. Thus encouraged, Phillip picked up the book again, and continued in a high, falsetto voice,

"*Scholar.* 'You must be fayne to answere to your owne question, Magister, els it is not lyke to be answered at this tyme'. Strike me pink, it must have been a bit of Merry England in those days, if boys could really give answers like that! 'I don't know; ask me', that's what 'Scholar' says, in effect! Fancy answering like that to Flib! Phew! ! Ten cuts with the cane, while studying the pattern of his study carpet!"

Flib was the nickname of the Magister, from his initials.

"There's another page, dear," said Hetty, "which tells how the Founder of your School was put in prison, for standing up for the Earl of Essex, after he had been beheaded. It is very, very sad, but then that is life. Do read it to us, won't you?"

" 'Standing up for the Earl of Essex after he had been beheaded'! Mother, I ask you! Surely the poor devil would be lying down, after losing his boko? You call that history! Seriously, Mum, do you know where my jar of preserving compound is? I want to skin that plover I found dead on the Seven Fields yesterday tonight—whatever are you laughing at?"

Hetty laughed till the tears came. Weakly she pointed a finger at Phillip. "Plover—found dead yesterday tonight——" she managed to say.

When Phillip was interested in a subject he would work, if he set his mind to it. During the recent examinations he had found the Arithmetic paper easy, despite preceding mental strain and flurry.

The ironic thing about his paper was that he was sharply suspect by the Magister for the very excellence of an unexpected performance, in connection with a disturbing letter received from the University people, which drew the Magister's attention to the paper of another boy who had, said the letter, presumably sat next to Maddison, since his surname also began with the letter M.

Before the scene that followed one January morning in the Magister's study, it is necessary first to describe the scholastic achievements of the Headmaster of Phillip's school.

He was, racially speaking, of Viking stock. Phillip, like Hetty, was a Celt. The Magister felt keen delight in problems of mathematics, which in the higher regions, as he thought of them, approached the poetry of universal truth. Mankind, in his belief, was finally perfectible; but only by transmuting the brute forces of the material universe into truths of the Spirit which ruled the cosmos mathematically. Beethoven, and Goethe, in this way of thinking, had expressed the same truths in music and poetry which were explicit in thought demonstrated by pure *mathematikos*.

The Magister was a Master of Arts and Bachelor of Science of London University. He had a twin brother, who resembled him in every particular. Between them in their University Arts course they had obtained the first and second places in the honours' list for English History, Language, and Literature; their M.A. degrees were obtained by examination in Logic, Philosophy and Economics; and again they took first and second places in their year.

The Magister had in addition taken a research course in Psychology for Ph.D. at Freiburg, under Professor Munsterberg, who had later gone to Harvard University, but did not qualify for the degree by residence. Before coming to his present post, he had been headmaster of a northern school which numbered amongst it *alumni* Laurence Sterne and Sir Robert Peel. Like his twin brother—who had gone to Colham Grammar School in the West Country—the Magister was also Fellow of the Royal Geographical Society, a Fellow of the Royal Historical Society, and a Member of the British Psychological Society.

He had come to the school when it had been enlarged, just after the Great Winter of 1895, when Phillip had been born. The school's number had been under one hundred; in scarcely more than a dozen years, it had increased to just short of three hundred. That was at the beginning of what was called the Renaissance of National Education. Under the Board established in 1901, the "Age of the Secondary School" had begun.

Because of ambition, because of his restless energy which was devoted to the mental well-being of nearly three hundred boys, the Magister was, intellectually speaking, the antithesis of Mr. Graham, the bachelor Old Boy with the unrolled umbrella, gentle smile, and soft voice.

And while the Second Master, the Housemasters, and the form masters of Heath School also strove, instilled, corrected, and punished, yet they were impersonal, and by that very impersonality were, paradoxically, human personalities. The Magister was personal in his aspiration, exhortation, and occasional anger—until the ultimate occasion of caning, when it became a ritual of catharsis, for the good of the caned alone. He loomed, big and terrifying, just and righteous, ever keen and dynamic, over the acquiescent and often evasive spirits of the youths who were submissive to his mental power, to his exhortatory will.

The Magister's ideal was, in effect, to put an old head on young shoulders.

The Magister expected his pupils to have an adult sense of honour, a perspective of maturity beyond the torments and desires of the growing flesh.

The Magister was always in tension for duty, duty, Duty towards a new Golden Age beyond the cup of Socratic hemlock.

The Magister was a Victorian

One morning, Milton, sitting near the head of the form in the back row of the classroom, threw a note, twisted up, when the Magister's back was turned, to Phillip sitting in the front row. Covertly opening the screw of paper, Phillip read the pencilled sentence, and was immediately puzzled.

Don't say we spoke to each other during the Arith. Exam.
Tear this up.

Phillip looked across to Milton. Milton put his finger to his lips, and pointed to the Magister who was drawing a formula in chalk upon the blackboard. Whatever did Milton mean?

Slowly he tore the note into little pieces, then having chewed them, rubbed them into pellets between finger and thumb, and hid them in the turn-ups of his trousers.

At eleven o'clock, when there was a five-minute break, the Magister asked Milton and Maddison to follow him into his Study. Seating himself at his bureau before the standing boys, he took up a letter from his desk: then fixing his pale-blue eyes upon Phillip, he said that in the Arithmetic paper of the Oxford Senior Examination Milton had got the correct answers to some of the problems, but with incorrect working-out. Maddison's paper on the contrary, had the correct answers and the correct working-out. They had sat next to one another. The question was, had there been any communication of results between them, during or after the examination?

"I have already spoken to Milton, Maddison. Now I have called you to stand before me, to hear what you have to say."

Phillip was amazed. He could not understand it. Had Milton cribbed from him? Milton? It was impossible!

He could not face the Magister's keen eyes. His voice was knotted in his throat.

"Come, Maddison, I am waiting!"

The Magister's eyes were on Phillip's face. A closed face, he was thinking: a secretive face: an evasive face: an untruthful face: a little face: a face of vague ruminations: a face of weak moral fibre: a face without character.

"Come sir, I am waiting!" The voice had a ring of impatience.

Phillip swallowed, and then managed to stammer, "I—I—d-don't know, sir."

"Did you speak to Milton at any time before your papers were collected?"

Phillip had his eyes fixed on the Magister's desk. Drip, drip went the sweat under his armpits.

"Milton, be so good as to repeat what you told me," the Magister said, in a softer voice.

Milton, with a slightly breathless smile upon his blue-eyed open face, said, as though he had rehearsed the words,

"If you please, sir, just before the papers were collected, I saw in an instant by mental calculation, that some of my answers were incorrect. I had already made my mental calculations, sir, viva voce to myself, so I quickly wrote down the answers I had worked out in my head. I can work better in my head than on paper, sir, for some reason."

"Yes, Milton, that is reasonable, to a point. Often I find that an abstruse problem will resolve itself suddenly, in my nightly walks upon the Heath. But it does not explain the duplication of your answers with those of Maddison's paper. Pray continue, Milton."

Looking the Magister straight in the eye, Milton said with a sort of jerky ease, "Well, sir, I just wrote them down, just before the time limit."

"And you did not speak to Maddison?"

"No, sir!"

"Did Maddison speak to you?"

Milton made no reply.

"Come, Milton, I am waiting," said the Magister softly.

"I don't remember, sir."

The keen eyes turned to Phillip.

"Well, Maddison?"

Phillip saw, in a kind of remote terror, as he had felt on a dozen or more occasions during the past years, the pink smooth cheeks, the large white moustache, the shiny domed brow, the severe glance immediately before him; and beyond, the mahogany cupboard where the canes were kept. He felt himself to be an icicle dripping away. He could not think; but vaguely he could see fragmentary rushing pictures of himself sitting up in his desk when his Arithmetic paper was finished. How could Milton have copied his answers? Milton's desk had been quite four feet away. Had his own paper been covered with blotting paper? He could not remember. He was sure he had never spoken to Milton. And yet, had he? With horror, he imagined himself talking to him under the big gas-ring in the centre of Hall. Milton would not tell a lie—Milton was not like himself.

"Come, Maddison, I am busy! Your reply, sir!"

"I don't know, sir."

The Magister shifted in his chair. "Your usual reply, sir! Again and again when you have been before me, you have not known anything! You are a corrupting influence, sir! Life without honour can be no higher than that of the beasts of the field! I shall have to consider your removal from the school, unless you can remember!"

I like the beasts of the field, thought Phillip wildly, as in a dream, or a nightmare, he heard his voice stammering, "If you please, sir, M-Milton asked me not to tell that we spoke to each other, before we c-c-came in here, sir."

"Well, Maddison?"

Phillip swallowed the lump that had risen into his throat, and managed to say, "Please don't blame Milton, sir, it was my fault, I think."

"In what way was it your fault, Maddison?"

Phillip tried to answer; but what could he say? All he could say was, "I don't know, sir. Except that Milton wanted to shield me, sir."

The Magister removed his gold-wire glasses. His face lost its keenness, he looked more like Mr. Graham without them, Phillip thought, remotely. The Magister seemed to be thinking. Phillip watched for some hopeful sign, as the Magister polished the lenses. Then putting them on again, the Magister looked at Phillip. He said softly,

"Are you not wanting also to shield Milton, Maddison?"

"No sir," said Phillip, feeling that now he was lost indeed.

"Then why did you tell me what Milton asked you?"

"Please sir, Milton was too far from my desk, to overlook my paper, sir. So I may have told him after all, sir."

The Magister smiled at him. Very softly he said, "You do not remember, Maddison, speaking to Milton?"

"No, Sir!"

"And you, Milton, what do you say?"

"I don't remember either, sir."

"You may go, Milton. Now, Maddison," said the Magister, when they were alone. "There is one explanation which cannot be ruled out. There are cases on record of mental phenomena, under shock, instantly manifesting themselves in material conditions. In the periodical *Nature*, recently, there was the case of a woman startled by an adder: the back of her hand ever afterwards bore the pattern of its back upon her skin. The medical and scientific journals have reported scores of similar occurrences. 'Knowledge is the consciousness of ignorance'. You are soon to leave the school, Maddison. I would help you, if you would let me. But nothing is truly possible between men without candour, or truth. Do you agree?"

"Yes sir," said Phillip, unable to disappoint the Magister.

"Then tell me, Maddison, did you give your answers to Milton?"

Abandoning himself to tears, Phillip said, "Yes, sir. I think I did, sir."

"I am glad that the element of honour has not, as I had thought, altogether remained undiscovered in your life so far, Maddison. Do you agree that you should be punished? Even our Founder, finding himself at fault, made confession to the great Burleigh, and having purged himself of *hubris*, thereafter saw how he might live a full and useful life. Soli Deo Honor et Gloria, Maddison."

The Magister always quoted the school motto before caning a boy. He turned to the portrait of the Founder, who with the ruff around his neck looked to be deliberately self-narrowed to a small scope, the natural imagination limited by experience. The unknown painter had painted what he had seen in the face of his sitter: the expression of a man subdued.

Three hundred and fourteen years previously, the Founder had made a wild speech in the Common Room at Christ Church, following the arrest and execution of his hero, the Earl of Essex, on a charge of treason.

The Founder's father had been a poor boy, who from Christ's Hospital went to the University of Oxford with a grant *of viii^{d} weklie untill he maie have a Skollershippe and also such bokes as he had writtn for*. He took his degree as Bachelor of Arts, proceeding four years later to Master of Arts; and so to a Vicarage, whence he became one of the Canons of Canterbury. In due course the son attended the King's School there, before going up to his father's college of Christ Church. It was there that he, the future Founder, in the testimony of a witness,

> "did publickly in the hall before a great parte of that house make a very offensiue declamation and hearing immediately that it was disleeked as a matter most scandalous, he goeth to his chamber and teareth his written copie and then burneth the peeces."

The scandalous behaviour by the undergraduate of Christ Church was reported to "the Lord High Treasurer of England, Sir Robert Cicil". In the actual words of the indictment,

> "He sate vp almost all night and transcribed a declamation far different (as it seemeth) from the former."

Statements of witnesses to the original, or seditious speech followed.

"His Theame was *Pejor morte est modus mortis*. His beginning was very passionate. He fell into commendations of a greate generall of the warres lately dead, whom hee called *Veri Dux*. Hee commended in this generall his infancy, younge yeeres, mans age, extolling all most highly; his embracing of learned men and warriours. His going foorth in two voiages, when all did folow him without any paye. Hee did call his souldiours not *milites*, but *commilitones mei*. Hee was *pater patriae*. Hee named the journey to Cales (as Cades) his owne forwardnesse there, and felicitye, and how men looked on him returning *tanquam in Solem orientem*. He beggered himselfe to maintaine his souldiours. After his coming home hee was *pessime erraticus quia cum esset Imperator, imperata non fecerit*. His vertue whiche drewe upon him envy of greate personages was the cause of his overthrow. One he called *Pestem Reipublicae, hominem ex faece oriundum, errore populi dignitatem consecutum*."

"How the executioner had three strokes at his heade: that his very enemies could not chuse but weepe, when they saw his heade cut of: yet that it was not lawfull for his wife and sister to bewail him. These things he lamented with *O lachrymae, lachrymae, ubi estis?*"

So the young "Scholler of Christ Church" found himself in Newgate Prison, where he wept more of the "tears of things", and wrote a long epistle addressed to Sir Robert Cicil, beginning,

"Icarus whilst he thought to behold ye sunne in his brightnes, suddainely his winges melted and he gaue a name to the vnknowne sea: much like to Icarus (right Honorable) whilst I too too vndiscreetly ventured to flye with ye winges of my contemplation aboue ye cloudes, and there to viewe ye Planetts. And among ye rest ye late Earle of Essex . . . most humbly now I beseech you that you will pardon this offence, making me rather a patterne of your mercy then of your iustice. Take pity I beseech your honour on ye miseries wch I haue indured: my armes haue bene pinnioned wth cordes for an example: my bodie hath bene humbled wth manie boltes: my hart hath been plowed vp wth sorrow, and ye furrowes thereof ouerwhelmed wth sheaues. In ye meane time my prayers shall ascend vp vnto Almighty God, desiring him of his mercy, that ye sacrifice of my lippes maye be acceptable in your sight like a sweetsmelling sauour: and that ye Lord will increase his guiftes aboundantly, wch he hathe allready bestowed vppon your honour. Newgate ye 21 May 1601.

When he left the study, after being caned, Phillip was ashamed of his tears, his throat seemed to be hollow and long; and, feeling gold and black dust in his being, he returned to the classroom, and waited there until the boys filed in from the interval, his head bowed over the text of the next lesson, Book Six of Virgil's *Aeneid*, where Aeneas descends into hell.

However, he reflected with some satisfaction, he had been allowed to keep his full marks for Arithmetic, with a Distinction, and had come out top of the Upper School in that subject. The Magister had told him that, until the Lists were published, he was placed on his honour not to reveal the results. He would keep the secret, too!

Secretly exulting in his trust, Phillip marvelled how he, one of the lowest boys in the form, had beaten Milton and all the others at the top, in arithmetic. *Could* Milton have looked over his shoulder and copied the answers? For he was sure he had done no more than smile at Milton, when he had laid down his pen. No matter: he was top in Arithmetic!

But Milton—a cheat? No, he was sure Milton would never be that: as he, Phillip, had been all his life. So he must have told Milton the answers; though he was sure he had not. Anyway, he had been beaten for it, that was a good thing! He had saved Milton, by confessing; so he was not altogether selfish!

By the end of the day Phillip felt happy about the incident. Milton had come to thank him; and had called him a stout fellow. Phillip began to like school, now that he would soon be leaving; and alas, no longer would he be able to cycle out in the coming spring to his preserves to see the woodpeckers, the warblers, the nightingales, the pigeons, the flycatchers; or the glistening brown dorsal fins of carp basking in the Fish Ponds.

And because he had protected Milton, he felt a glow of hope through the opaque barrier of life. He wished he had played more football with the chaps.

Life seemed keener, especially as cousin Willie might be

coming to work in London. With Desmond they could be like the Three Musketeers, all for one and one for all! He must wangle his way out of going to Australia somehow.

Oh, why did one have to grow up?

That night when Richard came home, he told Phillip that his Uncle Hilary was back from Australia, and was ready to discuss arrangements with him about going to the Agricultural College in Sydney. Uncle Hilary was in town for a few days, staying at his club, and had invited Phillip to luncheon. Now would Phillip write to his Uncle and thank him for what he had already done, and say that he would write again in the immediate future, and propose a day when he would be able to come and see him.

Phillip felt most unhappy, but thanked Father, who thereupon wrote to the Magister stating the circumstances and asking permission for his son to be away from school for a day, in the near future. Phillip posted both letters, to catch the 9.30 p.m. collection. He also wrote to Willie, saying he did not want to go to Australia after all.

The next morning Phillip was surprised that the Magister was so pleasant to him, as he gave the required permission.

"Labor omnia vincit, Maddison," he said kindly; while Phillip hastily agreed, although he did not know what it meant.

The Australian net seemed to be drawing tighter. How could he get out of it? Perhaps it would not be so bad, after all. He imagined himself galloping after cattle, cracking a stockwhip under a pitiless sun, while kangaroos loped away and the duck-billed platypus laid its eggs in sand, and suckled its young. Farewell, Fish Ponds! Goodbye to the bluebell woods of Whitefoot Lane, and Shooting Common! Adieu, ye cool green beechen glades where the woodpecker cried its laughing cry in spring! Instead, there would be the Laughing Jackass, long thin leaning trunks of eucalyptus trees, and rabbits, rabbits, rabbits, falling to both ball and shot of his No. 2 saloon gun.

In two minds, once more, Phillip faced his future with uncertainty.

Phillip put on his best suit, a dark grey one, and a borrowed bowler hat, stuffed with folds of paper to make it fit, belonging to cousin Bertie, to meet Uncle Hilary in London. He went by train to Charing Cross, where the traffic outside the station alarmed him, it was so fast and thick with taxicabs. He had been there once before, but at night, when Father had taken him to the only London theatre he had visited, to see *The Blue Bird*, by Maeterlinck. On that occasion Father had pointed out where Grandfather Maddison had been killed under the wheel of a heavy dray.

Phillip crossed again at this place. After staring at the fountains in Trafalgar Square, Nelson on top of his column, and the hundreds of pigeons, he asked a policeman the way to Pall Mall and the Voyagers Club. He wore his gloves, and carried his eighteenpenny umbrella, bought sale-price from Murrage's, on his arm. It had a cotton top, but would keep out rain. He swung it, rolled tight, on his hand by the handle, as he had observed a gentleman in a top hat swinging his umbrella.

With the help of two more policemen, Phillip found his way to the dark portals of the Voyagers Club. There was an awesome figure standing outside, in a top hat with a cockade and a gold band on it, and a uniform with many gold buttons. To Phillip's surprise, the figure saluted him as he hesitated by the revolving glass and mahogany door, of a kind not seen before.

"Up from the country, sir?" he said, his medals clinking as he leaned forward to push the door.

"Yes," said Phillip, after hesitation. It was true in a way, as he had come up from Rookhurst only three weeks before.

"I am supposed to meet my uncle, Mr. Hilary Maddison, here at twelve o'clock," he said hurriedly, lest the other ask more questions; for perhaps he knew Uncle.

"Mr. Maddison's just gone in," said the other, with a smile, and a bow, as he pushed the revolving door. Phillip got through somehow.

Inside was a sort of office, where other men in uniform stood. There were several small boys in uniform, as well. All wore white gloves. One of the men came forward, and to him Phillip repeated that he had come to see Mr. Maddison.

"You would like to leave your hat and umbrella, sir?"

The man beckoned, and a page ran forward.

"Take this gentleman to the cloakroom."

To Phillip he said, "If you come back here, sir, I will send another page with you to Mr. Maddison."

Phillip followed the page. After putting his bowler and umbrella on a hook, but his gloves in his pocket in case someone took them, he found himself being guided into what he thought must be a sort of public lavatory. By now he was uneasy, wondering if he would have to tip all these people, or be found out as poor. He had only his return half ticket, and fourpence.

Fortunately the page boy left at once. Then Phillip saw a man in a white coat, who moved to turn on the taps in one of the basins, saying, "Hot and cold mixed, sir?" as he laid a towel, and two ivory-backed brushes before the looking-glass over the particular basin. Dreading by now the thought of his poverty, Phillip stammered, "Oh, I have just washed, thank you." He wanted to go to the lavatory rather badly (oh, why hadn't he gone at Charing Cross station?) but the thought that the lock in the door might require sixpence in such a grand place, instead of the usual penny in the slot, made him hesitate. And hesitating, he was lost. He stood in a horror of growing indecision.

He was wondering what to do, when the man in the white coat said to an old man in a morning coat, who had just come in, "Mornin', m'lord!" Thereupon Phillip slipped out, before it could be discovered that he had gone into the wrong place.

He was additionally apprehensive about meeting Uncle Hilary, since he remembered how once, when he was very small and staying at Epsom with Aunt Victoria, Uncle had held him between his legs, in white duck trousers, and he had been unable to escape. That was the chief memory of Uncle Hilary, although since then of course there had been the motor ride in the Panhard et Lavassour out to the Fish Ponds. When Uncle had seen him being sick! Oh, why had he come?

But it was too late now. Told to follow another page, Phillip went into a big room full of leather sofas and armchairs, dark green like Father's "Sportsman" armchair. Old men were standing about and talking, glasses in their hands. Others were sitting down and reading newspapers, or magazines. It was rather like in the Free Library, only these men were all very clean, and fatter, with red faces, and wore expensive clothes. Could these be globe-trotters, travellers from all over the world?

"Your guest, Mr. Phillip Maddison, sir!"

"How do you do, Phillip?"

"Quite well, thank you, Uncle Hilary."

And could this be Uncle Hilary, whom he remembered as a big man with fair hair and bright blue eyes, and a long thin nose? Why, Uncle was almost an old man, rather fat, his nose was much bigger, and his face was on a lower level than his own. He held out a hand.

Uncle Hilary said breezily. "My word, you have grown since I last saw you! You must be nearly as tall as your Father, aren't you? How is he? How's your Mother? And your sisters? Come, let's sit down over here, and tell me all about yourself."

Hilary Maddison was disappointed in his nephew. As he told his wife, in his Hampshire home the next day, young Phillip was much too much wrapped up in himself, with not the slightest idea of how he wanted to earn his living, if indeed he wanted to earn it at all. He had no idea of conversation. He never spoke unless asked a question, and then his replies were as likely as not to be monosyllabic.

"I suppose it's his life in that suburb, but even so, Bee, after making all due allowances for his upbringing, I must agree with m'sister Viccy that he hasn't got the right stuff in 'im. Dick says he has a taste for low companions—goes about with a guttersnipe livin' in a slum. Dick forbade the friendship, such as it was, but it made no difference. No, he's a throw-back. Even so, one would have thought that he would have had something to say on his own behalf, considering one was taking the trouble to give him a start in life. Not a bit of it! He 'didn't really know' if he wanted to learn farming. What would he like to do, then? No answer! Had he any idea of any sort of a career? It was the same at table. What would he like to eat? 'He didn't mind'. Well then, had he any favourite dish? 'Oh no.'"

"I expect the poor dear was shy," said Beatrice. "Perhaps the sight of knives and forks positively frightened him. I know, when I first saw a fish knife, it scared me terribly. I didn't know which way up the thing went. I expect Phil was shy."

"Shy!" exclaimed Hilary. "That's only an excuse for lack of good manners."

"Not always," said Beatrice.

"What else, then?"

"Nervousness, due to unfamiliar surroundings."

"Damn it all, Bee, we all have to overcome that, sometime or other. But the point is, he made no effort to help me. I was only too willing to do anything I could. I told him so. It made no difference. He's gauche, and rather stupid, I consider."

"There is another possible reason, of course."

"I wish you would tell me what it is, then!"

"Boredom," said Beatrice.

"Boredom? A young fellow like that, a schoolboy still, invited to luncheon at the Voyagers? Why, half the mother country and Empire is run by the members! A boy of that age ought to be taking an interest in things beyond himself. Well, he's thrown away a damned good chance, as far as I am concerned."

"Who runs the other half, darling? The National Liberal Club?"

Hilary ignored this. He was thinking that, if Phillip was a typical specimen of the coming generation, then it was a poor look-out for the country.

"Anyway, talking about running, my precious nephew was apparently so eager to leave my company, that when I saw him off down Pall Mall, he took to his heels as soon as he thought I had turned back into the Club."

"Perhaps you kept him too long, and he had an appointment elsewhere, darling."

"Why do you invariably object to my assumptions, whatever the subject, my dear Bee? I had already offered to take Phillip to a matinee, but the idea seemed to fill him with positive fear. He must get back, he stuttered. Not a word of thanks! Only that he must get back and feed his white rat. What can you make of a youth like that?"

"I am sure, from what I remember of Phillip when he was a very little boy, that he would be very, very fond of his white rat."

Hilary ignored this remark as a typically feminine bit of contrariness. "It's just sheer bad manners, if you ask me. It comes from lack of a decent education. It's part of the spirit of the times. Young people don't want to work! They're out for pleasure, first and last. That's why we're being beaten in overseas trade by Germany. They make cheaper goods, because they work harder. It's different in the colonies; there a man has to work or starve, and if he does hard graft, as they call it, he gets on. It's here in England, with that damned Lloyd George's ideas, and women wanting the vote—as though the woman's place in the home isn't important enough—it's here in England that the rot starts!"

"Poor little Phillip and his white rat," murmured Beatrice. "What a lot he has to answer for."

Which conversation, or talk at cross-purposes, went to show, perhaps, that all was not well with the Hilary Maddisons.

Hilary was not the only middle-aged man who was irritated by a young face, or a young generation, which seemed without character: a face which was callow, covered in places with soft hairs, with lips that tended to droop at the corners and were infirm, with a tendency to looseness, and with eyes that too often looked beyond the immediate scene, that were filled with a melancholy to which was added indecision, and evasiveness in the presence of elders and betters.

"Why do you not do what I tell you?" cried Richard, a few evenings after receiving a letter from his brother hinting at the unpropitious visit to the Voyagers Club. "I distinctly told you to write the date of the month *before* the month, and not after it! I have my reasons for this, you know. In writing the date, it is best to separate the two sets of figures; but you have written January, then added the date and the year! No, do not scratch it out! Take another piece of writing paper, and start afresh. First appearances, both by letter and in person, are most important!"

Phillip copied out the letter again. It was to the General Manager of the Moon Fire Office, begging to apply for the position of junior clerk, age and educational qualifications being as stated. The fair copy, after being passed by Richard, was put in an envelope, stamped with a penny stamp, and taken down to the post-box opposite Peter Wallace's house in Charlotte Road, in time to catch the half-past nine post.

Having heard the fatal, slightly metallic flip of the letter in the box, Phillip ran to the flat of Mrs. Neville, to acquaint her with the latest news. She had already heard about the visit to the Voyagers, and had only just prevented tears as she realised Phillip's predicament—which he told as a joke—due to having what he thought to be not enough cash in his pocket for tips. She had heard, too, about the Arithmetic paper: further cause for perturbation within her ample bosom. What tragedies there were in life, all the more pitiable because so often young people could not express their thoughts, and dared not say what they really felt!

"I must hop back now, Mrs. Neville, if you don't mind. Father is going to try to teach me Chess, while Mother goes in to play bezique next door. Gran'pa's a bit lonely, now that Uncle Hugh is in the nursing home in Tranquil Vale."

Mrs. Neville gazed fondly at Phillip.

"I think it is very good of you to think of your Mother like that, dear. She must have a lot on her mind just now. How is your uncle, do you know?"

"I think he's still in a coma, Mrs. Neville. He won't last long now. The last thing he said was whispered to Mother—that he wanted to be burned, on the South Downs at night, and his ashes scattered to the winds. I think I know how he feels. I'll push the door after I've closed it, to make sure it is shut. Good night, Mrs. Neville.

"Good night, dear."

As he went down the stairs, Mrs. Neville wiped her eyes with one of the little squares of lawn that she made for herself, called handkerchiefs.

When Phillip appeared at breakfast the next morning, he saw at once that Mother had been crying. Doris was sitting silently over her Quaker Oats. Father was saying, "Nonsense, nonsense! It's pure hysteria on your part, Hetty. It's an illusion, and nothing you can say will alter my opinion!"

"What's the matter now," muttered Phillip.

"Oh, your Mother has been having one of her fancies, Phillip, that's all."

"It is true, Phillip," said Mother, in a strained voice, turning to him with a despairing face. "I know my brother is dead, I know that Uncle Hugh died this morning!"

She got up and went into the scullery, and closed the door gently behind her. Phillip helped himself to porridge, hating Father for his attitude to Mother.

"Phillip," came Mother's voice, faintly from behind the scullery door. Phillip looked at Father.

"She is hysterical," said Father in a sort of appealing, exasperated voice, which made Phillip think of the old tennis rackets in the downstairs lavatory, most of their strings broken and curly. "Your Mother had a dream, that is all, and now she insists that what she dreamed is bound to have happened! I tell her, as I have always told her, that she needlessly upsets herself when she gives way to her precious fads and fancies, and other people with them. Better go to your Mother, if she needs you. Perhaps what you say will reassure her. My words do not, of that I am certain!"

And having finished his haddock, Richard swallowed the rest of his tea, wiped his moustache with his table napkin, rolled it up and put it in its ring, and went upstairs to clean his teeth with precipitated chalk, toothbrush, and a rubber band for the interstices, before leaving for his train. He had the only good teeth in the family.

"What's up, Mum?" asked Phillip, when his Mother returned, smiling.

"I saw my Mother, dear," said Hetty, trying not to speak weakly, "as clearly as I see you children now. She was standing by my bed, when I woke up at half past six this morning. She was quite close to me. Mamma said, quite distinctly, 'I have come to fetch Hughie,' and then she smiled, and she slowly went away. I was sitting up in bed, Phillip, I saw her as clearly as I have ever seen anyone in my life. You do believe me, don't you, Sonny?"

"Do you think that Uncle Hugh is dead?" asked Phillip.

"Yes, dear, Iam as sure of that as I am sure of anything in my life," smiled Hetty. Then her face puckered, and she tried not to cry, as she said in a small strangled voice, "When I told your Father, he scoffed at me, and said that it was a delusion, and probably came from—no no, it does not matter, we shall see, we shall see," and she dried her eyes and smiled again. "It was exactly half past six, for I looked at the clock. I *knew* that my brother had passed on at that very moment. Mamma would never deceive her children, never!"

Richard looked round the kitchen door. Hetty turned her face away, not wanting to annoy him further. Phillip bent down to tie up the laces of his boots, thinking that Father's face had the same sort of look in it sometimes as the Magister's, but never so keen and clear and full. Nobody at school hated the Magister: he was too iceberg-towering for that, he was beyond hate. Father's forehead was not broad, like the Magister's, though both their eyes were the same colour. Father's eyes never really blazed, in an icy sort of way, a Northern Lights way, like the Magister's.

"Well, I may be late tonight, Hetty old girl. There are a lot of second-notice renewal premiums coming in now. So expect me when you see me, and not before."

With this mild joke, a sort of quarter-hearted attempt at amelioration, the bowler-hatted head was withdrawn.

The front door closed gently on its oiled multiple latches.

"Hur. Now we can breathe!" exclaimed Phillip.

At twenty minutes to nine Phillip left for school, whistling *I wouldn't leave my Little Wooden Hut for You*, which Petal, who with her brother Tommy lived with Aunt Dorrie during the holidays, had taught him to sing. Petal and Mavis and Maude, Aunt Dorrie's daughter, were all at the Convent together.

At fifteen minutes to the hour Doris left, for the Grey Ladies School.

At fourteen minutes to nine Hetty went in to see Papa, who was sitting at the breakfast table, staring straight in front of him. On the table-cloth beside him was a telegram, saying that Hugh Turney had died in the nursing home in Tranquil Vale at half past six that morning.

Chapter 30

BAGMEN'S OUTING

The General Manager of the Moon Fire Office replied to Phillip's letter, asking him to present himself at noon on Monday of the following week, and to confirm if the appointment was convenient. Phillip did so, under Richard's eye.

"You will have to get yourself some decent clothes to go up in. Today, I saw some black vicuna jackets in the sale at the Stores. You will want a pair of striped trousers, too; and while you are there, you might choose yourself a raincoat. Dark grey, or black, will be suitable."

"When shall I go, Father? I am playing footer on Wednesday afternoon."

"Then you had better go up on Saturday afternoon. Now I wonder if you can be trusted to get the right things?"

"Phillip can perhaps get them on approval, Dickie."

"When his appointment is next Monday? To hear you talk, no one would imagine that the boy's entire future is at stake!"

"I meant, Dickie, that there is time now to order the clothes on approval. They would be here in a matter of two days, and I could ask Carter Paterson to call the next day for anything that had to go back."

"You should know by now that articles in Sales are not sent on approval."

Richard looked at *The Daily Trident*, where there was an interesting article about the hazards of Polar exploration, with references to Peary, Amundsen, Scott, and Shackleton. But how could he read with such sloppy people in the room? With a sigh he looked up again.

"If I had been you, Phillip, I would have taken the opportunity to go to Sydney, when you had the chance! I had the same chance once, let me tell you, and I had to turn it down, as others were involved. However, that is past and done with." He looked at his paper again, found it impossible to read; and said, regarding Hetty, "If Phillip is sensible, he will go up on Wednesday. Let him choose for himself, he is old enough now. I will write down his requirements, then he can put the items down to my account, and bring them home here. Then we can all see the transformation of your best boy for ourselves, on Wednesday night."

"Then I shan't be playing football?" asked Phillip, disappointment in his voice.

Richard tossed the paper on to the table, and stood up. He had started the article half-way through tea, but owing to the feeling in the room he had never got beyond the third paragraph. Now, wagging a forefinger at Phillip, he said with scarcely suppressed exasperation, "You *are* a contrary cuss, aren't you! All these years you have been dodging games whenever you could, and now that you are on the point of leaving school, suddenly you find a game of football to be of paramount importance! Well, there is an old saying in the West Country, 'It be a lazy hoss what sweats to see the saddle'."

Hetty laughed. Her laugh broke the tension. Richard sat down, and took up the paper once more.

"Zzct! Gee up! Gee up!" said Phillip, pretending he was a horse.

"I'll see that he goes up on Wednesday, dear. I have something I want to do in London, so we can go together, can't we, Phillip?"

She nodded at him, plainly urging him to reply, to let Dickie see that he had some interest in what was being done for him. Phillip pretended to be eating grass off the tablecloth. Holding up the paper before him, Richard appeared to be oblivious of what was going on. Thus encouraged, Hetty remarked, "Well, I think at least you might say thank you to your Father, Phillip."

"Yes, of course, thank you very much, Father. Of course I will pay you back."

"H'm, I still think you will live to regret that you did not go to Australia."

Tea proceeded in silence, until Doris whispered something to her mother.

"Speak out, girl!" said Richard. "Anyone would think this house was a—well, whatever a whispering house is called."

Doris was still a reserved, at times a subdued, girl, despite her attendance at the College of Grey Ladies on the Heath. Thomas Turney had offered to pay the fees, as he paid, or had paid, for the education of some of his other grandchildren—Mavis and Maude at the Convent, Hubert at Dulwich as a boarder, Gerald and Ralph at day schools.

He had supported, in addition, his invalid son Hugh, and his widowed daughter Dorothy.

Since going to the convent, Petal had changed, thought Phillip, whenever he saw her during holidays from Thildonck. She had become withdrawn, reflective, cool. She and Tommy lived with Aunt Dorrie when they were home from school.

Mrs. Neville knew a great deal about the family and its doings from Phillip. He loved talking to her, and spent quite a lot of his time there. And to the flat he went when, returning with his mother on the following Wednesday, brown-paper parcel under arm, they came to the bottom of Hillside Road.

"I won't be long, Mum. Mrs. Neville is rather interested in how I get on, you see."

"Very well, dear, I am glad you have someone in whom you can confide. But don't be too long, will you? I think Gran'pa would like to see you. Your Father is also interested in you, you know."

Phillip had a second tea with Mrs. Neville. She said he looked extremely nice in his grown-up suit. Talking to her, he lost for the moment his apprehension of the interview on the coming Monday.

The black vicuna jacket, of smooth and soft and durable cloth, went with his dark hair and deep blue eyes, thought Mrs.

Neville. He had bought two new shirts, white with stiff starched cuffs, a ready-made bow-tie, and three standup winged collars. There was a black vest with the jacket, and the trousers had the new fashionable turn-ups at the bottom, he explained.

"Now, dear, I expect your Mother will be expecting you," said Mrs. Neville, after tea. "It was so kind of you to come in to see me. Come again, any time you feel like it. But I don't need to tell you that, do I?"

Phillip went home, while the feeling of apprehension grew again.

"H'm," said Richard. "'Now I see you stand before me, all this while you were disguised'," as he misquoted an old saying once applied to him by his own father.

The interview on the Monday took place in what to Phillip was an atmosphere of unreality, before the General Manager, a dark bearded man sitting at a big mahogany desk at the end of a large soft-carpeted room and two men standing beside him. One of these was the Secretary, a clean-shaven man who wore pince-nez spectacles on a fine gold chain slung over one ear. Neither smiled, but spoke in level, impersonal voices. Thus had new applicants been interviewed since time immemorial. The posts of general manager and secretary were filled, by custom, by members of the staff, long proven in steadiness and orthodoxy.

The third man had a pleasant expression on his face. He looked at Phillip with a look rather like that of Mr. Graham, the Old Boy who took snapshots on the school playing field. He had the same kind of eyes and moustache. After the bearded and clean-shaved men had spoken to Phillip, and read a letter which with sudden horror he recognised as having the coat-of-arms and the school address on the top, the letter was passed to this third man, who read it. Then they spoke together for a few moments, and the man with the moustache nodded, before looking at Phillip and smiling.

"This is Mr. Howlett, of our Wine Vault Lane Branch, who will shortly have a vacancy in his office——" began the bearded man, in a slow mumbling voice.

"Thank you, sir," said Phillip, on his best behaviour.

"I haven't finished yet," went on the General Manager, looking at Phillip's red silk handkerchief—given him by Gran'pa

—in his breast pocket. "I was about to say that Mr. Howlett is prepared to take you on probation, next Ladyday, at our usual commencing salary of forty pounds a year. Ladyday is the twenty-fifth of March. Will that be agreeable to you?"

"Oh yes, thank you, Sir!" exclaimed Phillip, much relieved at the thought of the two months ahead of him. The sand-martin and the chiff-chaff would arrive before then. He had been dreading that he might be told straight away to sit at a desk and do work of which he knew he would be entirely incapable.

This feeling was partly due to Richard's account to him of the good prospects available for actuaries, who had to work out statistics from masses of figures connected with the occupational risks, prospects of life, age-limits, records and analyses of hazards and diseases of hundreds of thousands of policy holders. True, Richard had been talking of Life Assurance, which the Moon Fire Office did not touch; and Phillip, with only half an eye and quarter of an ear on Father, had been reading about the nesting and fishing habits of the Osprey or Fish Hawk in *The Field* open on the table before him, at the time; so there existed some slight confusion in Phillip's mind, and considerable apprehension about his ability in actuarial affairs. His relief was therefore great, and his expression of gratitude entirely genuine, as he thought of not having to start before Ladyday.

"You will receive by post a letter confirming this arrangement, then," said the General Manager. "Good day to you."

"Good day to you, sir."

Phillip bowed, as Father had told him to do, and hastily left the room. He went along the corridor and ran down the wide carpeted stairs. At the bottom an old man in a frock coat and silk hat and white spats was being helped up the stairs, by a younger man most anxious to aid him. The old man had an immense face, with several chins, and an eyeglass stuck in one eye. He glared at Phillip, as he puffed and panted. Was this someone coming in to be insured? If so, it looked rather late in the day.

At the bottom of the stairs Phillip saw again the big mahogany swing doors he had passed on his way up. Would Father be working in there? He did not want to see Father. He was about to leave, when he saw through the glass of the doors the man who had smiled, approaching him. It was Mr. Howlett. Mr. Howlett raised his hand. It was too late to run away.

Howlett! What a queer name. He looked something like an owl, too.

"You disappeared before I could catch you, Maddison," said Mr. Howlett, in a soft voice. "I came down through the mezzanine room, to tell your Father, who is just round the corner. Which way did you come down?"

"By the staircase over there, sir."

"Ha, that was the Directors' Staircase, Maddison. Did you pass anyone?"

"Yes, sir, a very old gentleman."

"Good lord!" ejaculated Mr. Howlett, "that must have been Mr. Henry Chaplin, the Chairman. The staff use the stairs this way," and he pointed the way he had come.

"Yes, sir, I'll see to it in future."

"I was going to ask you if you would care to have lunch with me. I don't know if your Father wants you to go with him, but if not, I should be quite happy if you would come with me. We have a luncheon club at the top of the building, but that is only for the staff—so we'll go to a little place I know."

"Thank you, sir."

Phillip hoped it was not the Voyagers' Club, for he did not particularly want to meet Uncle Hilary just then.

Richard got down from his stool, and came forward smiling.

"Well, Phillip, Mr. Howlett, my colleague, has told me the good news, and it only remains for me to congratulate you."

Richard held out his hand, and Phillip shook it. His back felt very warm, for behind him was a huge rotund iron stove, in which a blazing coal fire burned. So they had fires in an office! It might not be too dusty after all.

Many other men were taking glances at them. A uniformed messenger smiled as he passed. Phillip began to feel that it was quite a nice place. From what Father had often said of City life, he had imagined it to be almost as grim as a prison, or at least as bad as school. This place wasn't half bad! He would be what Mother called one of the men in the moon!

Richard took him aside before he left, and said, "Do not forget to thank Mr. Howlett for his hospitality after luncheon, will you, old chap? Such little courtesies make all the difference in life."

"Yes, Father."

"Well, I must not keep you. Au revoir!" Father waved, and turned away.

Mr. Howlett seemed to Phillip to be ever so nice. They went to lunch in a chop house near the Bank of England. They sat among men wearing bowler hats before heavy wood tables, with high wooden partitions between each table. Most of the men read newspapers propped on cruets while eating, others played dominoes and drank coffee amidst clouds of pipe smoke. Mr. Howlett asked Phillip all about himself, and was told about the woodpeckers of Knollyswood Park, the rare willow tit in the alder over the brook Darenth, the peewits and other birds upon the Squire's land at Shooting Common. Mr. Howlett looked rather amused, Phillip thought, but the main thing about him was that he was all right.

It was quite different from lunch in the Voyagers Club with Uncle Hilary, where cigars, and not pipes, were smoked afterwards. Phillip preferred this chop house; it was exciting to be in the City, and to feel himself almost to be a City man. Mr. Howlett having removed his bowler, Phillip had done the same. Now, as they put them on again—Mr. Howlett having given the old shuffling waiter four coppers, Phillip noticed—Mr. Howlett said, "Well, Maddison, I shall look forward to seeing you at the office at a quarter to ten on Ladyday."

"Yes, Mr. Howlett! And thank you very much for your hospitality. Goodbye, sir!"

"Enjoy yourself in the meanwhile," said Mr. Howlett, puffing his pipe, outside the chop house.

"Yes, sir," replied Phillip, raising his bowler; and turning away, he went along the pavement, simmering with exaltation, revolving his rolled umbrella.

Phillip determined to enjoy himself, as Mr. Howlett had suggested, during the next two months. He was safe until the sand-martin returned, and the chiff-chaff.

He sat among other nondescripts like himself in the Commercial Class, a group of boys who were supposed to be learning, for their advantage in after-life, the practice of Pitman's Shorthand, Book-keeping, Bills of Lading and Discount, and commercial French and German. One of the junior masters set them tasks every morning, and again in the afternoon; after that, they were left to work by themselves. The senior boy was in charge. They all took turns to dictate passages to be taken down in shorthand, and business letters in the two languages, in the intervals of conversation upon personal matters.

Phillip did not take shorthand. It was too late, unless he were prepared, said the Magister, to carry on his lessons, either by postal tuition or evening classes elsewhere, when he had left school. Phillip said he did not think he was prepared; so he took only Book-keeping and Commercial Languages.

"No Spanish?" asked Gran'pa.

"No," said Phillip.

"A pity," said Gran'pa. "Spanish will be——"

"I know," said Phillip.

"What do you know, m'boy?"

"That I will see you at Pompeii, Gran'pa."

"He-he-he," chuckled Thomas Turney. "Don't you mean Philippi?"

But Phillip had gone. He was on his way to tell Mrs. Neville his news about the Bagmen, as the Commercial Class was called.

The only other class privileged to work by themselves were the prefects of the Upper Sixth, some of whom were preparing for University entrance exams. There was no connection between these aloof and lordly ones and the Bagmen except that they, too, possessed a nickname. Someone had heard one of the prefects, coming out of the Upper Sixth room, humming an operatic aria. Ever since they had been known as the Belle Cantos, shortened to the Belles, sometimes the Swells, or the Swelling Belles. They had a glorious future; whereas the Bagmen, a term out of Dickens, were considered to be little more than embryo pedlars, door-to-door salesmen, cheap-jacks at fairs, or tic-tac men for bookies. One of the Swells was Milton, who was preparing for the Little Go, for Cambridge.

The Bagmen were well-content. They had formed themselves into the Bagmen's Mutual Improvement and Protection Society, an unofficial intimate club. Timmy Rat was an honorary member, who entered the Club premises usually concealed under his owner's coat. Another member was not so honorary; this was Jerry the jay, who being accustomed to having its freedom about the rooftops and gardens of Hillside Road, and moreover having a voice more penetrating than any Sunday afternoon speaker by the Socialist Oak on the Hill, had to be left outside. The Magister heard the querulous screeches from the roof of the school, near the bell turret, and went into the playground and to his surprise a bird with light blue eyes, raised crest, and wings with blue-white bars flew down and perched on his gowned shoulder. Quite unperturbed, and realising that it was an escaped tame bird, the Magister stroked its poll, bore it to the porter's lodge, suggested a meal of beef scraps and peas with which to speed the visitor on his way, and returned to what to him was the universal poetry of Higher Mathematics.

The visitor, however, so liked the peas, and the white suet, that he stayed up by the turret and slept off his meal, to return for more at midday, when Phillip on his bicycle took him home.

The remarkable thing was that Jerry, who sometimes flew up to the elms on the Hill, must have recognised the distant trees to the north-east as those partly hiding the bell-turret of the school; and sloping thither on his short wings, made for slipping from tree to tree in woodland, by easy stages he returned; and during the afternoon his screeches of pleasure were once more heard up by the roof-ridge and the lead-covered bell turret. There he lived, more or less, accompanied by Jack and Jill the daws, whom Phillip had brought to school, thinking this a good chance to get rid of them.

There were wild daws on the Heath, and jays in the Crown Woods of Shooter's Hill. The birds wandered; they were reported in Greenwich Park; they were known to enter the windows of various houses in Tranquil Vale during sunny days; they were seen being chased out of a rookery by rooks which were claiming their old spring homes again. They were strong of wing; and one day they were seen no more.

The sand-martin returned, and the chiff-chaff.

On the last Friday morning, Phillip suggested a farewell outing for his special friends among the Bagmen, the following day. Nobody cared about the Bagmen on a Saturday morning. One of their number was a pale, quiet boy named Cundall, whom Phillip had taken once or twice into his preserves. Cundall was going into a bank. Another boy was Greenall, nicknamed Snouter, since his Christian names were Percy Ivor. A third was Lawrence Pett, the youngest of three brothers who came of a Thames barge-building family at Greenwich.

Phillip had taken Lawrence Pett one May day during the previous year, and shown him his nests, in hedges and trees around Knollyswood Park, in the area of the camps of the rival troops of Boy Scout days.

There had been coal titmouse, spotted flycatcher, bullfinch, chaffinch, blue-tit, wren, blackcap warbler, corncrake, gold-crest, turtle dove and woodpigeon, among others. Returning two evenings later, alone, Phillip had found that nearly every nest was empty. The following day he had accused Pett of betraying a friendship. Pett, a boy with bright curly hair and light blue eyes, looked so unhappy that Phillip was sorry he had spoken so severely to him. He did not know that Pett, who had thought nothing of birds before Phillip had taken him out, had been so imaginatively stirred by what Phillip had told and shown him, that he could not rest until he had returned with a friend; and between them they had shared the contents of the nests.

Lawrence Pett had looked at Phillip with such dejected humility in his face when Phillip accused him of treachery, saying that he was very sorry, that Phillip held out his hand.

Now, at the Bagmen's Outing, Lawrence Pett accompanied Phillip, Cundall, Snouter, and two others of the Commercial Class. Milton came by special invitation, from the Swells. They met at the Clock Tower, and took the tram to Whitefoot Lane, and walked up to the woods. There were more footpaths in these woods now; as game preserves they had been abandoned; red rows of houses from the north had come very near. In one strip of wood a rusty old bath was found, lying by itself. How had it come there? Phillip looked at it with sinking heart. In some way he could not express to himself, the bath, which had a hole in its bottom, was the final mark of doom upon the woods, and upon his own boyhood.

An old faded notice-board, hanging askew a tree, said *Trespassers will be prosecuted.*

They crossed the lane to the woods on the other side, which were less trodden. One of the Bagmen was a pale, almost muddy-faced boy named Pype, who was something of a naturalist. A flock of thrush-like birds flew out of the treetops, clucking and making rachety noises; these were fieldfares, explained Pype. They had come from Norway, and soon would be returning across the North Sea for the nesting season.

Farther down the narrow strip of woodland was a lightning-blasted tree, fairly narrow, and branchless to its broken top, where a coronet of dead bark was silhouetted against the sky. Pype swarmed up, gripping with his knees, and was about to put a hand over the rim when a large brown bird flew off. A tawny owl! Phillip had never found a nest with eggs, before. Pype held up a nearly round white egg. There were two others, he said. He descended, something else in cap held between teeth.

"Look," he said. "You can see what the tawny feeds on, by the broken pellets it disgorges."

There were several mice skulls and thigh bones, a sparrow's leg with the horn of toes dissolved away, innumerable minor bones of mice, rib and knee, knuckle and foot, together with dark blue gleaming shards or wing-cases of beetles.

Phillip held the egg in his hand. A hundred dreams of twilit nights, of stars and wind in darkness passing, passing, arose from the oval white egg. He decided to put it back. He looked at Pett. "I swear I don't want it, Phillip."

"There aren't many owls about, you know. And they do good."

Egg in cap, he swarmed up the tree, and put the egg with the other two. Among the litter and frass was an acorn which had sprouted there. Phillip brought it down, and planted it in leaf-mould on the ground. Goodbye, little tree, he whispered to it, before rising again.

At the end of the wood—a narrow strip which extended along the northern boundary of the Seven Fields until it joined the main road just beyond Cutler's Pond—they walked silently, in file, for they were now near Perry's mill, and might be seen. This tall boarded building, half covered with ivy, stood beyond the pond at the bend of the road, by the water-cress beds. The cedar tree, with its massive brown trunk covered with its dark strata of branches, which looked as though no wind would ever shake them, lay over most of the pond. The water was as clear as glass. Fish glided away under its surface. They were the last of the Randisbourne trout, for the brook was now polluted below Cutler's Pond. Even the stickle-bats, minute fishy urchins armed with spines, had not been able to survive the tar and creosote acids from the drains of the new road. The black county of London was steadily invading the green county of Kent.

It began to rain. They sheltered under the cypress, and when an omnibus came, grey mud squelching out from its solid rubber tyres, they decided to take it to the market town. It was full inside; but who cared about rain? They rode on top, under the tarpaulins fixed to the seats, and with occasional songs in the intervals of ragging and jokes, arrived at the market place.

Cundall now took charge; this was his country; the Elmstead woods were his preserves. They were divided by a railway; houses were creeping on them, too. The woods were of hazel-nut in rows among standard oaks. Celandines and primroses were out on the brown leaf-floor; bluebell plants were rising.

Pheasants were still preserved in the woods, for here were gibbets on which several domestic cats hung tail down, with more hedgehogs than Phillip had ever seen in his preserves. Perhaps, said Pype, the low, rather damp ground caused more slugs to be about; hedgehogs ate slugs for their main diet.

Phillip was not sure about the honesty of Pype. Recently the Dowager Countess had written him a brief note, declaring that as so many nests had been robbed in the past season, all permits would be withdrawn. *All* permits? Who else was there, besides himself and Desmond? This had been a shock to Phillip, since he had never robbed any nest, taking only one egg of each new species he had found. He had spotted Ching following him one day; Ching and Pype were rather thick. Had Pype written for a permit? Challenged, Pype admitted it. Pett had told Pype about his permit. As Mother always told him: he was his own enemy.

After his dismissal by the Dowager Countess, Phillip had gone to his preserves farther afield. The best of them was a large estate about five miles beyond Reynard's Common. Of rolling arable and pasture under the downs, among great beeches, Squerryes had, running through the park, a series of trout ponds. Above them, on the grassy slope, were rabbit warrens enclosed with wire-netting fences. Little doors were fixed in the fence, exits for feeding at night.

The keeper here had explained that, on the night before a shoot, when the rabbits had left the warren, the doors in the wire fence were dropped at the pull of a string. The rabbits, being unable to get to their burrows, lay out rough, and provided good sport, being driven rather in the manner of hares, towards the guns.

Phillip and Desmond had come upon the young squire of this estate, a schoolboy in a grey suit and grey felt hat, shooting with his friends, their keepers and loaders in attendance. In fantasy

Phillip had imagined himself performing some heroic act, such as climbing up the side of the mansion in flames, a cord, attached to a rope, round his waist. He saved the young squire's life; and was forthwith invited to shoot rabbits with him and his friends.

"This is my great friend, the Birdman of Britain (*vide Daily Trident*, 1920) who not only discovered a rare Willow Tit on my estate, but also saved my life. He has an eye like a hawk, and is a considerable Mathematician, having come top of his school in Arithmetic, despite great odds."

With the saloon gun firing bulleted breech-caps in this variation of *The Prince and the Pauper*, Phillip knocked over coney after coney, each ball striking in the head and killing instantaneously.

In reality Phillip, in silence with Desmond beside him, had hurried past the line of young shooters. From behind a great old beech tree in the park, half its trunk gaping where a limb had fallen, they had watched the splendid and rich young men firing at rabbits.

A dead barn owl hung half out of the hole in the beech trunk, where it had been chucked when the keeper had shot it during the past winter. A shame! For the white owl took only mice; but keepers were ignorant men, explained Phillip, to Desmond. Behind the trunk they had watched while one of the under-keepers flung up a bottle, for the shooters to take pot-shots at it. Again and again the bottle was missed after being flung up; no one had hit it. Later in the afternoon, when the party had gone, the keeper explained that he had rammed a cork into the bottle, to make an air-cushion within. This caused the shot to rebound off the glass.

"My young gents had a sweepstake, a bob a head, and when no one won it, they gi'ed me the money," he said, with a grin.

Phillip thought that he and Desmond must give him some money, too, just to show him they were not exactly ordinary boys. A packet of twenty Goldflake was eventually decided upon.

He would take care that neither Pype nor Pett heard of his other preserves. So Pype knew all about hedgehogs, did he?

"How about baking some in clay?" he said, pointing to the rows of hedgehogs hanging before them. "Pretty toothsome dishes, I can tell you!"

"Ooh, you horrible cannibal!" said Cundall.

"You may be a hedgehog in disguise, but I'm not," replied

Phillip, cutting the string of what looked to be a recent addition to the gibbet. "Let's make a fire, and roast this one. Come on, Pype."

"Honestly, do you mean to say you're going to eat that thing?" asked Milton.

"What's wrong with hedge-pig?" retorted Phillip, casually. "Their flesh is rather like chicken. I've had many a good tuck-in of hedge-pig."

Phillip imagined himself to be Bill Nye, the crowstarver he had met at Rookhurst. "They have a good flavour, from slugs, as Pype says. After all, chickens eat slugs. Let's have one each. Where shall we make the fire?"

"I'll bet you a tanner you don't eat one," said Pett.

"Taken!" cried Phillip. Ha-ha, he had fallen into his trap!

They collected sticks. Someone found a fire-pail, full of pick-holes, outside a hut of sleepers beside the railway line, and carried it up. Soon smoke was arising, flames licked round the sticks. To dry their clothes, more fire was needed. Bigger branches were laid on top of the bucket; acrid smoke poured forth; stick-ends began to bubble and steam. They stood around, watching the fire grow, glad of its warmth, while Phillip toasted the hedgehog on a green stick.

He was bound to win the bet: for Pype had bet him sixpence that he would not eat it. Well, he would not! The tanner was won! The prickles were beginning to glow when there was a cry of *Cave!* from Cundall, dragging a six-foot branch. He dropped it, and following his glance, they saw a man hurrying down the path between the hazel-nut stoles. He did not look like a keeper; but he shouted, he waved a stick. A burly great brute of a farmer!

"Hop it, chaps! Follow me into the tunnel!" cried Cundall.

In great excitement they ran and slithered down the path to the wire fence bordering the railway. Slipping through the strands, they hopped along the railway sleepers. The man shouted. Before them lay a blackened tunnel.

"Forward," cried Cundall. "Into the Tunnel of Death, rode the Six Bagmen!"

Phillip followed with some apprehension into darkness.

"Keep into the left," cried the booming echoing voice of Cundall somewhere in front.

Phillip stumbled on, in complete blackness. Looking back, he saw the shiny oval opening, and thought that a fly taken into a spider's tunnel must see the last of its life rather like that. He bumped into someone. The others had stopped. Water drips splashed from the unseen roof above.

"He may go to the other end, to wait for us. How about trying to race him. If a train comes, press against the wall. Then it won't hit you, unless some idiot chucks out a bottle. He's always chasing chaps out of his wood."

"Who is he, Vic?"

"Old Blanchflower the builder. He's bought the mansion and the wood, and fancies himself as a sportsman, don't-cher-know. If he tells the police, and they guard the other end, we may have to wait for a goods train going this way, and shin over the side of a truck. I did that once, and found myself in Nine Elms Yard, beside the Gas Light and Coke Company. It's a fact! When I got out, a bloke with a red flag waved it at me. The traffic stopped, and I walked past as though I owned the bloody works!"

"You bloody liar!" remarked Pett, in admiration.

"S' fact," said Cundall. "What's more, I didn't have to walk back. I hopped into a truck loaded with coke, one of many, all labelled for Chislehurst; and within an hour I was back in this very tunnel, though going the other way this time. I got off, and bifurcate me if I didn't see, at each end, when the smoke had cleared, a copper on guard at the station! So I had to do the whole journey over again, when the trucks returned empty."

"What happened?" asked Milton.

"Yes, tell us," urged Phillip.

What had started as rot was now interesting, as Cundall's dry sort of matter-of-fact stories always were.

"Well, I found myself back at Nine Elms yards. I was about to slip away, as before, but there the same bloke was, with the same red flag. 'What's the gaime, mate?" he asked. 'I'm trying to trace a lost truck,' I said. 'What's in it?' he asked, suspiciously. 'Coal,' I replied. Fortunately just then I spotted a truck, filled with coal, and by luck it was labelled for Chislehurst. It was coupled to a lot of other trucks filled with coke. 'Ah, there it is!' I said. 'Loaded with coal, you see. That's the one I've been trying to trace. You see, my good fellow, people in Chislehurst only burn coke, all of them being members of the Smoke Abatement Society. Thank you very much for helping me find it. I must follow it and report it to London Bridge. I will commend you for good service in the matter.' And so saying, I climbed up among the lumps, while he held up his red flag to stop the traffic, as before. So back I came here again, through the tunnel, and so to the station."

"You are a fool!" said Pype, admiringly. "Do you think we believe that?"

Pype was a scholarship boy; and being small as well he had assumed an aggressive sort of manner.

"Belief is entirely a matter of faith," replied Cundall. "And faith is a personal matter since the Reformation. Well, for my efforts I was made an honorary member of the Chislehurst Branch of the Smoke Abatement Society. The truck of coal went back to Nine Elms, where they discovered it to be anthracite, no good for gas, so back it came to Chislehurst. Forgetting to inform the stationmaster what it was, he returned it. And ever since then, for two years and more, the truck has been going up and down the line, nobody's baybee. You see," concluded Cundall blandly, "there just aren't any slow-burning stoves in Chislehurst. Coke, as you know, needs something of a draught. Hullo, hullo, I hear a familiar rumble. Listen! Back comes the old truck of anthracite!"

The rail, on which Phillip was standing, appeared to be alive; it was stirring under his foot as though squirming, without actually moving. "Seriously, it's the Hastings-Tonbridge express," said Cundall. "We'll be all right if we keep pressed against the wall. Turn your faces to the wall and shut your eyes against bottles and smuts. I've done it lots of times."

Phillip was frightened. Supposing someone opened a door in the tunnel? The wall was very near to the rail.

Turning his head, he watched the distant white oval as the noise approached: the white space dimmed out as the tunnel roared and then thundered with an increasing pink glow. The engine rushed upon him so fast in its haze of deepening red above a gold blur along the walls that without being able to think he flung himself at the foot of the wall, in terror lest his legs be lying too close to the rails. Water splashed in his face unheeded. Were his legs lying aslant the rails, black thought asked him. He had forgotten his companions as he pressed his eyes hard shut upon his hands and waited for the obliterating blow. It swished and increased upon him, with a great screeching of steam with the overbearing sound of a whistle dropping in pitch as though pressure of steam had blown the brass dome off the boiler. He knew he was safe, but pressed hard away from the battering rush of wheels. It was gone.

He got on hands and knees, and then upright, trying to pull himself up by the wall. Soon they were all laughing, Phillip among them. It had been grand fun.

They voted to continue through the tunnel, now that its terrors were known, and overcome. At the other end they climbed the cutting and came upon a golf course. From some bushes they watched several people driving off from a green, one of them a tall old gentleman with big beaky nose, a very thin body and a red jacket. He wore a very small, tight-fitting cap, and knickerbockers with spats half-way up his calves.

"That figure," said Cundall, "is the ghost of the Duke of Wellington."

He told them that recently some Suffragettes had appeared on the course, one of them blowing a bugle, while others bore banners and gave away leaflets. The old bloke, said Cundall, had gone on playing as though they were not there; and when one had seized his club, saying, "Mr. Asquith, I believe?" the ghost of the Duke had raised his cap, and replied, "If you believe that, you will believe anything, mar'm," whereat he vanished.

"I don't think that's funny," declared Pype.

"A sense of humour depends on the digestive juices," said Cundall. "A dose of Epsom salts can work wonders. Try it, my boy."

Phillip thought of Aunt Dora, and hoped that no one knew that it was his aunt who had been to prison, and out again, many times, on the Cat and Mouse Act. Uncle Hilary had told him that she was now in hospital, as some of the forcible feeding had gone into her lungs.

Where were they going? No one seemed to know. It didn't really matter. They were having fine sport, just by being together. What matter that their trousers and jackets were still wet? The March wind would dry them. Forward the Bagmen!

"How about going to the first house at the Hippo?"

"What time does it start?"

"Ten to six. We could have tea first."

"I haven't got much money."

"Nor've I."

"We'll have to hunger-strike, that's all."

"It's only tuppence up in the gods."

"Tuppence? I'm broke."

"I'll stand treat to you all," said Milton. "I'm rather flush just now."

"You owe me a tanner, Pett, for not eating the hedgehog."

"But you didn't eat it!"

"Exactly! You said, 'I bet you *don't* eat it'—well, I didn't!"

Pett handed over a sixpence.

"No, really, I was only joking, Pett. I didn't mean it, honestly."

"No, you won the bet, Phillip. Take it, be a good boy."

"Well, thanks," said Phillip.

They crossed the Seven Fields, and came to the woods south of Whitefoot Lane. Phillip determined to treat them all to a glass of stone ginger beer in the little cottage just back from the lane. They went to the door. There was a bit of paper in the window, saying *Minerals*. The old woman invited them into a small front room, which had a cuckoo clock on the wall. She was very respectful, and brought the six bottles and glasses on a tray. She kept looking at Phillip, and when he paid her, she asked him if he had been there before, saying that his face was familiar. He remembered that Father had said something about having stayed there; but his face was quite different from Father's, so the resemblance could not be the cause. Phillip hoped none of the chaps would mention his surname, in case she knew Father by name, and said something about him which the chaps would hear.

He never knew that his father had often gone to visit the woman and had shown her his photograph.

It was a pleasantly tired body of Bagmen which, after a feed of peas-pudding and bacon in a cook-shop, crossed the tram-lines to the Hippodrome shortly after half past five that Saturday evening. The new moon and evening star, looking, Phillip thought, like a silver ring set with a big white diamond, hung in the clear duck-egg green of the sky. Milton paid a shilling for their entry into the gallery. It was the first time Phillip had been to the Hippodrome, which had been built about eighteen months before.

It was a wonderful experience, all the tiers of dark red seats below, the huge safety curtain, the boxes for rich people beside the stage, the orchestra filing in from under it shortly before the lights went down. Cundall said they were in for something, as the star was Marie Lloyd. This name meant something rather wicked and fearsome to Phillip, from what he had heard. Marie Lloyd was the hottest of the hot stuff.

Pett, who knew his way about the world, said that the dud turns always came on first. Phillip thought they were pretty good, all the same. A man who could ride a bike with only one wheel, and that the front one, wasn't to be sneezed at. He was followed by two dancers, a man and a woman, who also sang together in the sizzling white beam from a box in the middle of the gallery. Sometimes the light clicked, and changed colour.

Three jugglers followed. They threw a sort of Indian clubs for one another to catch, flip flip flip, quick as that, sideways and from behind their backs, between their legs, six always in the air at once.

The next turn was awaited with some excitement. A footman with powdered wig and golden livery came on, and put a board with a name on it by the gold pillar of the wings. Gertie Gitana!

A storm of clapping and whistling greeted the slight figure of a dark girl, dressed in a pink frock with a short skirt, appearing from the wings. Her dark hair, tied with two pink bows on her head, was brushed down her back. She looked like Petal. She wore pink stockings and shoes with pink bows. She bowed to the applause before lifting her head again, and, as the violins and cellos stilled all sounds, began to sing words which immediately found all hearts. She hadn't any gold, to leave when she grew old . . . the sad, haunting voice arose into the darkened auditorium.

I'll leave the sunshine to the flowers
I'll leave the songbirds to the trees,
And to the old folks I'll leave the memory
Of a baby about their knees.
I'll leave the stars to the night-time
And the quiet hills to the breeze,
To those in love, I'll leave the moon above,
When I leave the world behind, when I leave the world behind.

Phillip's heart ached with longing for the singer to stand there always, so that he could feel his heart going out to her while the Bagmen sat beside him, for ever and for ever. Soon the wonderful afternoon would be but a memory, with all the sunshine, and the birds, and the new moon sinking with the white star in the western sky. He held down his face, to hide the moisture in his eyes, glad of the storm of whistles and clapping which greeted Gertie Gitana's bowing. Then he was clapping and clapping and clapping for her return, and she came back again, and once more the song arose into the hushed gallery, with its rows of silent white faces.

Phillip did not want to hear the funny fat man in a bowler hat who followed, singing Yorkshire songs. The audience liked him, but Phillip did not think so much of him as of Gertie Gitana. Who was he? George Formby the Lancashire Lad, said Pett. Phillip thought that it was not bad to have guessed that he came from near Lancashire, which was almost part of Yorkshire, or vice versa.

The Poluski Brothers followed, two men in lavender suits and felt hats, who did cross-talk. Phillip could not really understand the jokes. He was glad when the next turn came on, G. H. Elliott the Chocolate Coloured Coon, who danced very gracefully and sang as he danced *I used to sigh for the silvery moon.* His voice went up and up, from baritone to contralto and then to treble, like a sort of whistling bird he was, gay like a green woodpecker in the beech glades of Knollyswood Park. Had Pype robbed the nests there? Had Milton cribbed? Oh, no matter; they were his pals. He would meet them again at the Old Boys' Meetings and *Soirees.* And there were his preserves, the Squire's by Shooting Common, and the new places in the valley of the Darenth. There would be Saturday afternoons from the Moon! It would only be like a sort of school over again! It was simply wonderful to be alive!

Phillip had not yet given any thought to the money he would receive: a fledgling still in the nest.

After the interval, the Lunatic Bakers. Tall men, obviously on stilts under their long white trousers, and tiny little dwarfs, tottered and tumbled, threw flour about and lumps of dough, assembled in pyramids only to quarrel voicelessly, shake and wobble and collapse, spring up again with expressionless floury faces and fall into ovens and out again into flour barrels, kicking legs, pulling off one another's trousers (women *shrieking* with laughter, why? for they had pants on underneath, surely women knew men wore long woollen pants as well as trousers?) and bounding about all over the place. Phillip was so interested that he did not laugh.

After the Lunatic Bakers, Harry Tate and his motorcar. That was screamingly funny, the man in the loud check cap and big twitching moustache. Why won't the car go, Papa! After a lot of funny arguments with the chauffeur, the boy in the back in a top hat discovered the reason. The wheels were not round! Not round? They looked round enough. Ah, but they were not *going* round! It was terribly funny. Then the schoolboy tried to prove that the reason was that while the circumference of ordinary wheels was $3\pi r$, his Father's wheels were $4\pi r$! They had one-third more circumference than ordinary wheels! A mathematical joke! Fancy telling that to the Magister, phew!

Then with a sudden hollow bumpy feeling Phillip realised that he had left school . . .

At last, Marie Lloyd. The audience seemed to be going mad as the bewigged footman with the notice board came on. He felt frightfully excited. Then he saw a woman with what looked to be a big-corseted waist, a big hat with ostrich feathers in it, and a parasol. As she sang she looked sideways at the audience, her big teeth protruding. Sometimes she paused, and sniffed in a knowing way as she made suggestive remarks and pretended to wipe her nose on the back of her hand. *A little of what you fancy does you good!* He knew what that meant, and by the way she said it, it was rather like the women in the Rec. Then suddenly the rays of light from the arc-lamp in the box made her eyes glitter Cambridge-blue. They were like a turquoise: he saw only the sky-blue glint, which seemed somehow to make her more than a woman who was rather like a principal boy wearing fancy clothes instead of tights.

He stared, fascinated, a little frightened. After that blue eye-glint he was held to her every movement on the stage, as she sang in a rather hoarse voice, her big feather hat nodding, her parasol held out with its point on the stage as she stopped, showed her teeth sideways, wiped away a sniff with her hand, said to him (how had she seen him?) *Every little movement has a meaning of its own!* As she said it, there came the sudden and startling blue glitter of her eyes; and although she was ever so far away and below, Phillip was rather thrilled.

When he got home at nearly half past nine, Phillip took off

his muddy boots, put on slippers, and went down into the sitting-room. Father did not even ask him where he had been, or why he was late. He just turned his head in the armchair, from reading *The Daily Trident*, and said, "Hullo, old chap, had a good time?"

"Yes thank you, Father. Some friends and I have been walking over the Seven Fields, and on the way home we went to the Hippodrome to see Harry Tate."

Father did not say anything further. Phillip sat down behind Father's chair, his usual place. He could hear Mother in the kitchen making sop for his supper. There was his book, given him the day before, lying on the table, near Father's elbow. It was the history of the School, by Mr. Graham. Every boy on leaving was given a copy.

Phillip thought, a little unsteadily, that never again would he sit among the Bagmen. Taking the book, he opened it at random. Head on hands, he read the first verse of the School song, which he knew by heart, from the six times he had sung it with the massed choir on Founder's Day, before all the parents (though Father had never come) in Hall.

Who'll sing us a song of the sports of the year
And the tales that around each cling?
Who'll sing in praise of the tented field,
And the glories that cricket and footer yield,
Or the trophies the swimmers bring?
Let each man tell his story well, and the chorus shall go with a swing!

Here's to the tented field, swimming, footer, and cricket!
Here's to the rifle and camp, the butts, the goal, and the wicket!
Here's to our teamsmen all, my lads, and the friendship nought can sever!
Here's to the good old school, my lads, may it flourish for ever and ever!

Phillip turned back to the early pages, to the recantation of the Founder, lying in Newgate Prison, over three hundred years before.

"Surely I shal be able to saye nothing, but hang down my heade like a bullrush for verry greife of heart, yea trembling and confounded before your honour. My sacrifice must be a contrite and a broken hart. I confesse I thought to prayse the vertues of ye Earle (whose flesh is now clothed with wormes, and dust of ye earth) and darkely to poynt at his death vnder ye historie of Cicero, but not to greive at ye sentence of his condemnation, proposed by our most iust and wise prince: for God knowes who searchest ye verry veynes and intralls of men, that I was neuer yet disloyall unto her Maiestie, eyther in thought, worde or deed. Yea it is and hath bene my morning incense and my euvening sacrifice vnto Almighty God, that he would preserve her Maiestie as ye apple of his eye, and that he would wound ye head of her enimies, and ye heary scalpe of euery one who doeth intend to shorten ye dayes of his annoynted Gloriana."

What a dry book, Phillip thought; all unreal like the rest of history, which belonged to another kind of world altogether, when men were very cruel, and there were traitors, and people were being tortured, tried, beheaded, and killed in rebellions or wars, all the time. It was quite a different world now; all that was a thing of the past; men knew so much better nowadays.

He closed the book and put it away, before Mother could come in and, seeing it, talk about the old times which, for some strange reason, she could not see were uninteresting, like fossils.

Then resting his head on his hands once more, Phillip thought of his last goodbye to the Bagmen outside the Hippo. Never would they be all together again. It was over, his boyhood was over. He sat as one transfixed.

In the green russian-leather armchair Richard held the newspaper before him. He was not reading it. Quietly he laid it on his lap, and closed his eyes. Phillip's mention of the Seven Fields had brought pictures of the past before what he called the camera obscura of his mind. Only a little while ago, it seemed, he and Hetty were arriving at the keeper's cottage, for their brief honeymoon; and the woodcock had pitched beside them as they lay in Knollyswood Park, on the dry skeleton leaves of the year's end. He thought of Phillip's arrival, and the little chap suddenly smiling at him, as he nursed him at night through his illness—ah! he liked his Daddy then, why, the little chap had always wanted him to hold him by the hand, in his cot, for a minute or two, before he settled to sleep.

His eyes still closed, Richard drew in a deep breath, then released his thoughts in a long sigh, inaudibly, before taking up his newspaper again and reading about the empty houses the suffragettes were burning down, the windows they were smashing, the bombs they were leaving in public buildings, the acid poured into pillar boxes. Theodora—his own sister! What had come over the world? That a gentlewoman could so far forget all her upbringing, and sense of decorum, and associate herself with such dastardly behaviour? And that was the Theodora who, mark you, had criticised him for doing his duty in punishing Phillip for bad behaviour in the past. It was all of a piece! There was something very rotten in the State of Denmark!

Well, now the boy was off his hands. And with the workaday balance of his mind adjusted again, Richard poured himself his nightly cup of hot water, half an hour before his bed-time.

"I expect you feel ready for bed, after your long walk, Phillip. Don't forget to clean your teeth."

"No, Father. Good night."

"Good night, old man."

Hetty came into the room, carrying her work-basket. She took out her darning needle, wool, and leopard-spotted large cowrie shell, which went inside the sock she darned—one of the presents of her brother Charley from Africa.

Richard looked up and smiled.

"Well," he said, with a sudden air of ease. "How about a game of chess, old girl?"

October 1952 - *August* 1953
Devon.